Strange Fire

A Mike Jacobs Environmental Legal Thriller
Mike Jacobs Book 3

Joel Burcat

Publisher Page
an imprint of Headline Books
Terra Alta, WV

Strange Fire

by Joel Burcat

To order additional copies of this book or for book publishing information, or to contact the author:

Headline Books
P.O. Box 52
Terra Alta, WV 26764
www.HeadlineBooks.com

Tel: 304-789-3001
Email: mybook@headlinebooks.com

Publisher Page is an imprint of Headline Books

Chapter 1 won Second Place in the Pennwriters Annual Writing Contest 2020 (Novel Beginnings category)

ISBN 13: 9781951556808

Library of Congress Control Number: 2021952579

PRINTED IN THE UNITED STATES OF AMERICA

For my mentors:
Roger Adelman, Esq., Carl A. Belin, Jr., Esq.,
Richard O. Brooks, Esq., PhD, Donald A. Brown, Esq.,
John P. Krill, Jr., Esq., Robert Larkin, PhD,
Steven J. Picco, Esq., and Irwin Richman, PhD

"Nadab and Abihu, the sons of Aaron, took their censers, put fire in them, and added incense; and they offered strange fire before the Lord, contrary to His command. The Lord sent out fire which devoured them, and they died before the Lord."

—*Leviticus, ch. 10, v. 1-2*

"The chant is 'drill, baby, drill.' And that's what we hear all across this country in our rallies because people are so hungry for those domestic sources of energy to be tapped into."

—Sarah Palin, at the vice-presidential debate
with Joe Biden (October 2, 2008)

Mr. Conaway: (02:14:40): "Fracking is a controversial issue within our nation. If we did away with fracking, the United States would not be in a position today to dominate the oil production within the world and would play into strengthening [Russian President Vladimir] Putin's hands with respect to the oil—"

Fiona Hill: (02:14:52): "That's correct. And actually I'd like to point out that in November 2011, I actually sat next to Vladimir Putin at a conference in which he made precisely that point. It was the first time that he had actually done so to a group of American journalists and experts who were brought to something called the Valdai Discussion Club. So he started in 2011 making it very clear that he saw American fracking as a great threat to Russian interests. We were all struck by how much he stressed this issue and it's since . . . that particular juncture, that Putin has made a big deal of this."

—Testimony of Dr. Fiona Hill, former Deputy Assistant to the President and Senior Director for European and Russian Affairs on the National Security Council, Transcript, House Intelligence Committee, First Impeachment Hearing, Day 5 (Nov. 21, 2019)

1

A hunting we will go . . .

Bones Benson fumbled the Remington Magnum rifle that his boss, Norby Lafleur, heaved to him like a drill sergeant. "We're going hunting."

"When? Now?" Bones looked out the window of their office, located in a work trailer at the Campbell drill pad. At 4:50 a.m., it was still dark, and sunrise wasn't until 6:41 a.m. on this cold April morning in Bradford County, Pennsylvania.

Norby didn't respond. Instead, he placed a box of ammo, 7mm rounds, on the worktable. Bones loaded the rifle and shoved a handful of bullets into his pocket. He wondered what his boss was up to. Generally, Norby never explained himself. He just gave orders.

Norby's Weatherby hunting rifle was already loaded and slung over his shoulder, muzzle pointed down. He looked out the small window, past the glare of the LED security lights, and into the darkness.

Bones glanced at the Remington. "Boss, what are we hunting? It's a little late for deer, maybe a little early, and last I checked, there were no elk out here. This is some heavy-duty firepower."

Norby stared him quiet. He pushed past Bones and clanged down the work trailer's three metal steps. The black and gold letters, glinting in the bluish security light, read *YUKON O & G OPS*. Bones had to jog to keep up with him.

Bones noticed the cacophony of birdsongs as he struggled

to keep up with Norby. They crossed the drill pad and headed straight for the three steel production trees located dead center on the pad. The trees controlled the flow of natural gas out of the already-drilled gas wells and connected them to a nearby pipeline. Norby took a small flashlight out of his pocket and flashed it on the steel upper master valve.

"See, over here, these are the pockmarks from that sumbitch's shots."

Over the previous weeks, Norby had used a black felt-tip marker to circle the divots in the steel. He'd written dates next to the dings—3/30, 4/1, 4/2. In all, a half-dozen pockmarks in the steel.

"Looky here." Norby played the light on a shining divot that did not have a circle drawn around it. The gouge looked fresh. "And here." Another fresh divot, no circle. "He did this early this morning before we got here. Middle of the night, like the others."

Norby looked at his assistant. "Corsica. He's out there."

He turned his flashlight to the perimeter of the pad. Norby narrowed his eyes. "I aim to put him down like the dog he is once and for all."

Bones nodded. "Maybe this is a job for law enforcement? I mean, if he's shooting at our production facilities, well, maybe it'd be better to let them handle this?"

Norby glared at him and shook his head. "Did you forget already? That night when we killed him? I thought Texas boys were supposed to be smart, but you're a Dr. Pepper short of a six-pack. No law enforcement for this deal. We handle it ourselves."

Bones was about to say Norby had been the one who cracked Corsica over the head with that big Maglite. Twice. All Bones had done was help bury the body. The look on Norby's face told him to keep his mouth shut.

Norby, with his lean physique and high and tight hair, had grown up on a hog farm in Forrest, Louisiana, outside of Baton Rouge, and didn't care at all for the geography, geology, hydrology, climate, workers, locals, or regulators in Pennsylvania or anywhere else in the Northeast. As far as he was concerned, there was too much up and down, not enough flat, too many streams, too much cold weather, and, most importantly, not nearly enough trained local workers. He disliked all of it, but this job was a means to an end as long as no one screwed it up for him.

The men had to walk back to the entrance gate since the pad was encircled by a new chain-link fence, passing the two white pickups emblazoned with the *Yukon Oil and Gas Co.* logo parked inside the gate. They continued up the trail.

Most of the thousands of drill pads in Pennsylvania are not fenced. For this site, however, Norby had recently ordered a chain-link fence topped with barbed wire, which now enclosed the five-acre drill pad. He'd increased the security patrols from once a week to twice a day.

They left the relative safety of the drill pad. Bones noticed that the bird songs had stopped. The woods were silent; the wind blew through him. He was chilled to the bone.

Was it the wind that chilled him?

Or something else?

Like Corsica.

In the indigo darkness, the men hustled on a well-worn trail to the top of the hill overlooking the glaring lights of the drill pad about two hundred yards away. A small clearing provided a clear shot for a marksman. When they reached it, the older man didn't take an extra breath. Bones was panting.

"I think he was lying on the ground up here when he took those shots," Norby said. "Steadied his rifle on these rocks. I have no idea what kind of rifle he's using; he policed his brass. Probably a deer rifle, a .223 or .243, with some kind of scope, but he's a pretty good shot."

In the dim early morning light, Norby held up his Weatherby and sighted through his Zeiss scope on the production tree in the middle of the brightly lit pad. Like a golfer lining up his putt, he pretended to pull the trigger.

"You really think it's him? Corsica? I mean, when we buried him, we thought the guy was dead. If he didn't die a few hours after he crawled outta that grave, he had to survive out here all winter. No food, no medicine. Other than the missing person report the police emailed back in February, we never heard squat about him. I figure one way or another he's long gone."

"It's got to be him. Never heard back from the cops or Corsica. Trust me, this ain't the local kids and their .22's taking potshots at our pad. Not some goddamn monkey-wrench idiot. He's out here. Playin' with us. Bastard was an Army Ranger. Knows how to live off the land. Survival. That kind of shit." He ran his free hand through his military-style haircut and looked into the woods. "Follow me."

Bones hesitated to continue along the trail. "Considering all of that, maybe we should get another couple of men—guys we trust. You know, Texas, Louisiana guys. Develop a plan. Circle him, then drop him. I mean, he hit them production trees at two hundred yards, and if it was Corsica, he's not gonna be happy to see us. I ain't sure this is such a great idea . . ."

Norby flinched at Bones with the butt of his rifle. Came close to hitting him. The younger man's father had been a mean drunk. Beat Bones, his ma, and sisters. At least weekly. More often than that, too. Bones' arm flew up to protect his head. It would never have occurred to him to hit back. Norby didn't have to utter another word.

The men hiked along the ridge in the semi-darkness. Then they headed down a deer trail into the woods. Bones slid the last few feet down the ridge and stopped himself from falling only by grabbing a sapling. Norby didn't slow until they were about a half-mile from the pad.

Deep in the woods.

Alone.

Bones hoped.

Dawn penetrated the leafless trees and cast an eerie gray light on the early spring woods. The sight lines were fairly clear this time of year. In another month, vegetation would choke off any clear views.

Or clear shots.

Norby held his index finger to his lips then squatted behind a pile of lichen-covered rocks. He reached into an inside pocket of his parka and pulled out a compact spotting scope. He focused on a spot in the woods, then handed the scope to Bones.

Bones sat on the cold ground, smelling the damp, dead leaves and sphagnum moss, and steadied the scope on a rock. He stared through the eyepiece for about a minute. "Looks like a run-down huntin' cabin. No electric. I'm guessing a hand pump for water inside or out back. Beat-up outhouse. Overgrown Jeep trail coming up to it. No truck or car."

Norby nodded. "One of our local guys, a water truck driver, told me about this place a couple of weeks ago. I had him show it to me, and I've been watching it for weeks. No one's huntin' this time of year. But I've seen some activity at the cabin."

"Activity? Did you see him?"

"No. I've seen nobody—just changes. Like one day, the shutter's down, and another day it's up. Maybe the outhouse door is slightly open. Nothing major. No trucks, Jeeps. No lights or smoke from the woodstove. More subtle-like. Whoever's using it is being careful."

"Maybe it ain't him. Maybe the owner. Kids. Maybe a squatter?"

"Maybe."

Bones knew better.

It was Corsica.

Holed up.

Not hiding. Awaiting his opportunity.

The men shivered behind the rocks, shifting their bodies and sitting or stooping on the ground in the cold and damp woods while they watched.

Their high-powered hunting rifles were balanced on the rocks, pointed toward the cabin.

Two against one.

Corsica, if he was there, was outnumbered and outgunned.

A dead man.

Twice.

The sky turned from indigo to blue to orange to light blue as the sun rose. The cabin was as quiet as a tomb. They didn't see a chipmunk or hear a bird chirp.

It was quiet.

Real quiet.

Too quiet.

The minutes slowly ticked by as the hunters stalked their prey. They looked through the scope every few minutes. An hour passed, and Bones began to recognize a feeling. What was it? The hair on his neck bristled all at once. The woods were silent, but something had changed.

They were being watched.

A shiver ran through his body. Different from the shivers from the cold April air.

He looked at Norby. They exchanged a glance. Norby must've felt it too. Norby took the Weatherby, placed his finger on the trigger, and slowly swiveled his body, studying the woods around them. He aimed his rifle at the shadows in the woods as he turned.

Bones jerked his head back toward the pad and raised his eyebrows.

They stared at each other. Expressionless. Finally, Norby patted Bones on the shoulder and whispered, "Okay, let's get the hell out of here."

They stretched and quietly made their way back along the narrow path toward the pad. Both men were careful not to step on twigs or make any noise as they made their silent retreat.

They hadn't gotten more than one hundred feet up the trail when Bones, who was in the lead, walked into the fishing line. It hadn't been there an hour ago. The nearly transparent, nylon monofilament hit him at about chest height and brought a pile of leaves, human excrement, and twigs crashing down on the men. A groundhog fell out of the tree. It was bloody and dead. More fishing line held it up at eye level, and its forepaws were stretched out by the line as if it awaited an embrace. The animal had been decapitated, blood still oozing from the crater where its head had been. The remains of the creature swung back and forth in front of them. This was a fresh kill.

Bones shrieked and jumped back. He crashed into Norby and lost control of the Remington. He accidentally pulled the trigger on his way down. The 7mm bullet sounded like an explosion in the cold air of the quiet woods. It ricocheted off some trees. The two men flattened themselves on the trail and covered their heads to avoid getting hit by the ricochet. Bones made himself as small as possible.

"Crap, he's here." Bones laid on the trail, his face in the leaves and the stinking shit, and he turned his head in twitchy movements. He grabbed for his rifle, but his hands shook too much to operate the bolt. He expected Corsica's bullets to come at any moment. Picking them off.

After a few seconds, Norby stood up to his full height and pivoted around, searching. He held his rifle to his shoulder and aimed at ghosts behind the trees.

"Jesus, Norby, you're making yourself a target. Get down."

Norby laughed. "If that boy wanted us dead, he would've kilt us an hour ago. Sumbitch's just playin' with us. Let's get the hell outta here."

The men gathered themselves and circled wide around the dead animal swinging in the breeze. They double-timed it back to the safety of the fence and the pad.

The whole way back, Bones felt like—no, he *knew*—they were being tracked. He wondered if Corsica's bullet would enter the back of his head or maybe his guts. The head shot would be quick. He'd be dead before he hit the ground.

A shot to the guts would mean a long, painful death.

Like having your skull fractured.

Being buried in a hastily dug grave.

Left for dead under an impoundment.

Alive.

2

January, Four Months Earlier
"Cross"-examination

Mike Jacobs, Assistant Counsel with the Pennsylvania Department of Environmental Protection, commonly known as the DEP, stood and cleared his throat. He'd prepared for this cross-examination for days. He wrote out lines of questions, spent hours thinking and drafting notes covering two legal pads, and rehearsed some of the phrases he wanted to say just so. Then he boiled it all down to single-word bullets on three pages of a fresh legal pad. He knew other lawyers who winged cross-examinations. He was not one of those. Mike took chances, but he wasn't reckless. Especially not with a critical expert witness.

Mike looked through his papers and pretended to need a little time. He held up a finger toward Judge Calvin of the Environmental Hearing Board, EHB, as though one or two more seconds would be enough. The judge nodded assent. Mike was doing precisely the same thing a catcher does when he walks to the pitcher's mound to talk with the pitcher: He was trying to get a hot batter off his game with a brief delay. If Mike really wanted to ruffle the witness, he might ask for a three-minute break to review his notes.

Mike's ears rang with the admonition his boss, Roger Alden, the regional counsel, gave him five minutes earlier outside the hearing room. "Don't try to win your case on cross. Keep it limited to discrediting the expert's testimony."

Mike, twenty-nine years old and a seasoned fourth-year lawyer, knew all of this, but he could feel Roger's eyes boring into his head from the back of the hearing room. The temptation was there.

John J. James, PE, the expert witness, had hawk-like features, a sharp nose, black eyes, black hair, and tanned skin. He wore a dark grey business suit that clung to his marathoner's frame, a white shirt, and a bright red necktie. He was the CEO of Lancaster, Livingston, James Engineering, Inc., and he looked like his lawyer picked him from central casting under *ideal expert witnesses.* James sat in the witness chair, feigning a relaxed expression, but his arms and legs were crossed, which said otherwise. In front of him was a narrow shelf holding four three-ring binders containing eight inches of numbered exhibits.

Still pretending to look at his papers, Mike sniffed and noticed again the new carpet smell. The EHB's new courtroom was a huge step up from the shabby multi-purpose room in which the board had sat for dozens of years. It was laid out like a real courtroom, with an elevated judge's bench, a table for the law clerk—officially called an assistant counsel by almost no one—witness stand, tables for the department and the opponent, and a bar behind which a small public gallery was located. The tables, bar, and chairs were all constructed of the same light oak. The seat cushions were a handsome royal blue. Everything was procured in accordance with strict Pennsylvania Department of General Services regulations. Of course, it was just a coincidence that the governor was friends with the senator from York County who was best friends with the successful contractor.

Mike glanced at his opposing counsel's table. Jacob Berliner, one of the most respected lawyers at Finkel & Updike, Washington, D.C.'s leading corporate litigation firm, was scrutinizing him. In the legal world and corporate boardrooms, Finkel & Updike was universally referred to as "FU." If they could have gotten away with it, their two thousand-dollar suits would have sported patches proudly embroidered with *FU,* just like the sponsor logos that race car drivers and soccer players wear. The letters defined the firm.

Berliner, who was exactly twice Mike's age, had a face as smooth as a pineapple, with thin curly grey hair that was more kink than curl. His worsted wool, chalk-pinstriped blue suit was amply cut to cover his corpulent frame and to ensure he could keep his coat buttoned while he sat. His coat was buttoned now, of course. He crossed his arms. Berliner knew exactly what Mike was up to. He stuck an elbow into the side of his associate. Under the policy of the EHB, only one lawyer per side could examine a particular witness and object, and this witness belonged to Berliner's associate, Darius Moore.

Darius Moore rose to his full height, nearly six feet. "Your honor, could you ask my distinguished colleague either to begin his cross or to waive examining this witness?" Darius Moore had risen through the ranks like a rocket, and word was he would become a partner at FU more quickly than any of his predecessors.

Darius Moore was exactly Mike's age, and both had attended Vermont Law School. As they say, the two of them had some history. Darius Moore was lanky with a tennis player's body. He wore his hair closely cropped, and, unlike Berliner, he didn't have an ounce of fat on him. He'd been a tennis star at his alma mater, the University of Pennsylvania, where he graduated magna cum laude. Darius Moore was the smartest kid in their class at Vermont Law, probably the brightest man Mike knew, editor-in-chief of the law review, and arrogant beyond measure. He also happened to be African American, the son of one of a handful of Black female federal appeals court judges and a surgeon. Darius Moore had attended Vermont for the same reason Mike did: He wanted to be an environmental lawyer. But while Mike spent his spare time in the Environmental Law Society and hiking in the woods to clear his head, Darius Moore took a deep dive into corporate and constitutional law and joined the Federalist Society. Mike struggled to get B's and C's in his classes while Darius Moore easily aced every class.

The two young men agreed on one thing—they hated each other. This was the first time Mike and Darius Moore were on opposite sides in a trial.

On the other side of Berliner was his client, H. Hans Ziegler, the CEO of U.S. Dynamics, a defense contractor and Adams County's largest employer and taxpayer. He had the look of a squat bobble-head doll with an expression that alternated between bored and pissed.

Ziegler was outraged by what he thought was DEP harassment over a trivial infraction. Less than one thousand fish—mostly minnows—had been killed when his company accidentally released untreated wastewater into Conewago Creek. His fury extended beyond DEP to the governor for not bailing him out despite the hour-long meeting at the Capitol arranged by U.S. Dynamics' lobbyist. He was particularly peeved since he and his C-suite executives had each contributed five thousand dollars directly to the governor's most recent campaign and ten thousand dollars each to Pennsylvanians for Good Government, a soft-money political outfit that ran negative ads against the governor's political opponents.

At the mandatory pre-trial settlement conference, Ziegler made it clear his company "would rather pay Finkel & Updike ten million dollars in legal fees than pay a civil penalty to DEP of one point five million." Mike took that as a challenge and suspected no one at FU objected.

"Mr. Jacobs?" asked the judge.

"My apologies, Your Honor. Mr. Moore's examination of his expert witness was quite long and skillful. Let me see if I can keep up."

The courtroom was full. About half a dozen DEP lawyers had stopped in to watch both Darius Moore's examination and Mike's cross-examination of the star expert witness. Junior associates and paralegals from FU and various employees from U.S. Dynamics and DEP took up most of the remaining seats. Muffled laughter from all corners of the courtroom reached the judge's annoyed ears. He responded with light taps of his gavel.

Roger Alden and DEP's new chief counsel, Kate Gerard, watched from the last row. U.S. Dynamics deserved to be penalized, but Alden and Gerard would be reporting back directly to the governor on Mike's performance and the outcome of the proceedings.

Mike glanced at Darius Moore, who glared back at him. Berliner gave him the slightest wink.

"Well, are you ready to proceed?" The judge looked down on the litigants from his high bench.

Mike nodded. He approached the witness. As he buttoned his navy-blue jacket, he noticed it was just the slightest bit tight. He smoothed his red-and-blue rep tie against his best white shirt and ran a hand through his longish dark brown hair. Mike straightened himself, walked to a position in front of the judge, and slowly raised his head to look directly into the witness's eyes. This hearing had a jury of one, the judge; nevertheless, Mike choreographed every move to increase the tension in the courtroom.

"Good afternoon, Mr. James. How are you today?"

"Fine, thank you. Let's get on with it."

I'm already under Johnny's skin. Good. "You are CEO of Lancaster, Livingston, James Engineering?"

"That's correct."

"According to your bio, you've been CEO now for nine years, right?"

"Yes."

"If I read your LinkedIn profile correctly, you're fifty-four years old and have been CEO of your firm since you were forty-five. Is that right?"

"Yes. I'm not sure why any of this matters, but that's correct."

"As CEO, is it correct to say you are responsible for the overall management of your firm?"

"That's right."

"You set policy for LL&J?"

"Yes, the board of directors and I do that."

"You are responsible for the profitability of the company?"

"Yes, ultimately."

"You participate in selecting and opening new offices?"

"Correct."

"Are you involved in business development and other marketing activities for your company?"

"Yes, if that matters here."

"Would it be fair to say that your primary responsibilities are the administration of the company, maintaining its profitability, and marketing the company?"

"Yes, that's fair to say." James swiveled toward the judge, looked at him, and said, "other responsibilities, too."

"Would it also be fair to say you do not draft permit applications or compliance plans?"

"I might review an occasional application or compliance plan, but I'm not involved in the actual drafting of these documents at this point in my career."

Not for a long time, Johnny.

"Do you ever spend more than ten or twenty minutes reviewing these types of documents?"

"Honestly? I'm way too busy for that anymore. Maybe five minutes and then just a few times a year."

"Thank you for your candor," Mike said, suppressing a smile.

Darius Moore bolted to his feet. "Your Honor, really?"

Mike nodded. "Apologies, Your Honor, I really did appreciate his honesty. I'll try not to let that happen again."

There was some laughter from the DEP attorneys in the back of the courtroom, and the judge tapped his gavel, frowning. Berliner pressed his lips together.

"Prior to that, you were vice president of environmental engineering for six years, beginning when you were thirty-nine. Correct?"

"That's all in my bio. It's correct."

"Prior to that, you were the regional vice president for environmental engineering for the eastern half of the United States for nine years, from the time you were thirty years old. Right?"

James made eye contact with Darius Moore, nodded ever so slightly, and paused.

Darius Moore jumped to his feet. "Your Honor, all of this history is contained in Mr. James' bio, and we're prepared to stipulate to it. It's a waste of the board's time going through all this background."

Ziegler's head bounced up and down.

The judge looked at Mike and raised his eyebrows.

"Your Honor, first of all, I don't appreciate Mr. James looking to his lawyer for help during my cross-examination, and secondly, the purpose of these questions will become completely clear after I've asked several more. I'd ask for an admonition from the board to Mr. James that he is not to look at his counsel for assistance in answering questions."

Darius Moore, who was still on his feet, said, "I object to Mr. Jacobs' characterization. That's outrageous."

"I'd say it was outrageous. I saw it too," said the judge. "Mr. James, do not look at your attorney for assistance during the examination. Mr. Moore is fully capable of objecting if the need arises. The defendant's objection is overruled."

"Mr. James, I asked you whether you had been the regional vice president of environmental engineering for the eastern half of the United States from the time you were thirty years old. Is it correct to say you've been primarily involved in the administration of your company since the time you were regional vice president, in other words, the last twenty-four years?"

James nodded, looked at a spot on the ceiling, then said, "Yes, that's basically correct."

"By the way, you never worked at DEP, did you?"

James chuckled. "No, my first job after I graduated from Bucknell University was at LLJ. I've always worked there."

"Would it also be fair to say the only time you were involved in the actual engineering aspects of a project was from the time you joined your company, over thirty years ago, until you became the regional vice president twenty-four years ago?"

Mike caught James's eyes drifting toward Darius Moore and moved to stand between the men.

"That's about right. I wouldn't say that I haven't done any engineering over the past twenty-four years, but my primary responsibilities have been marketing, management, and administration."

Okay, dude, you've done no engineering for most of the time I've been alive. Time to move on.

"Your firm, Lancaster, Livingston, and James, exactly how many employees do you have?"

James relaxed and sat back. "Well, Mr. Jacobs, the number changes on a daily basis. As of last Friday, we employed 26,472 people."

"That makes you one of the largest engineering firms in the United States, correct?"

"There are larger. AECOM, Fluor, WSP-Parsons, and a handful of others, but we're one of the largest in the US."

"According to your website, as of last night, you had sixty-four offices in the United States, five in Canada, five in Europe and Great Britain, and one in Saudi Arabia. Is that correct, or has it changed since you last checked?"

"Well, I haven't checked our website in a couple of weeks, but that's correct, we haven't added an office since last month." James smiled at the judge.

This time, the muffled laughter came from the entire courtroom.

"As CEO, you're at the top of the pyramid of all of the 26,000-plus employees and seventy-five offices. Right?"

"That's right. That's what the title implies."

"U.S. Dynamics is a client of your firm?"

"Yes."

"How long has U.S. Dynamics been a client of LLJ?"

"If you go all the way back, one of the predecessors of U.S. Dynamics was Philadelphia Aircraft Products. We began representing them in 1917. So, that long."

"According to your annual report, currently they account for over thirty-five million dollars in revenue. Is that correct?"

"Well, that's total revenue. Profit is a lot less."

"They're one of LLJ's top ten clients?"

"Number three, to be exact."

That's a big-assed client, Johnny. Mike kept a straight face.

"Mr. James, I sent out a statewide email and checked with my colleagues across DEP, and no one says they recall you ever being directly involved in a matter with the department in the last twenty-four years. Is it correct to say you've not been directly involved in a DEP matter in twenty-four years?"

"Well, not exactly correct. I mean, I'm involved behind the scenes."

Yeah, way behind the scenes, Johnny-Boy.

"But never directly in a matter with the department, right?"

"That's correct."

The thing about an expert witness is that the expert is, well, an *expert*. In environmental cases, this means he or she probably has an advanced degree in geology, biology, engineering, or the like. Mike, or any other competent environmental lawyer, had to study up and know the area of the witness's expertise at least as well as the expert, ideally even better. That was the only way you could deal with evasive answers or complicated, technical responses. James was a Professional Engineer, a PE. He'd spent years studying and then practicing engineering, even though he'd spent many more years acting as an administrator of a company. Mike had a Bachelor of Science degree in geography. At bottom, the most important thing for him to do was to sound confident.

"When Mr. Moore asked for your opinion regarding the size of the civil penalty proposed by DEP against U.S. Dynamics . . ." at this point Mike turned and looked directly at the judge, "One-point-five million dollars, a fraction of the amount of profit generated by the company on a single day, you didn't calculate that yourself, did you?"

"Well, no."

Darius Moore was on his feet. "Your Honor, I object. Move to strike. Mr. Jacobs knows full well an expert witness can base his report and testimony on anything that's brought to his attention, including reports and calculations prepared by others. We supplied all of that to the department during discovery."

"I'm not disputing that, Your Honor," Mike said sharply. "The point I'm making is even though Mr. James is CEO of one of the largest engineering firms in the country, he has virtually no basis, as an expert or otherwise, to dispute the civil penalty calculation made by the department. Other people at his firm may have calculated the numbers he has offered into evidence, but this witness, as he sits here today, this man who is responsible for the administration and profitability of one of the ten largest engineering firms in the country, this man who is a manager and marketer, this man who is offering his opinion on behalf of a thirty-five-million-dollar-a-year client, has no facts or information at his disposal to support his opinion that the department's penalty calculation is unreasonable. He's really not qualified to render an opinion. If nothing else, his opinion has little weight in this case."

The judge sat forward. "Objection overruled. I'd like to hear this."

Without missing a beat, Mike asked, "Mr. James, do you know who José Martinez is?"

James looked up at the ceiling and tried to make eye contact with Darius Moore, but Mike moved and blocked the direct line of sight. "That name is not familiar to me."

Game . . .

"Does the name Steve Simon mean anything to you?"

James thought again, then said, "No, not at this time."

Set . . .

"How about Ronnie Nguyen?"

"That name sounds familiar, but I can't place him."

"Would it surprise you to know that Mr. Martinez, Mr. Simon, and *Ms.* Nguyen are all former employees of the department?"

"If you say so. Those names really don't mean anything to me."

"Do you have any idea where José Martinez, Steve Simon, and Ronnie Nguyen currently work?"

"No, but I'm guessing you're about to tell me."

"Since you don't know them, do you value the opinions of the former DEP employees Martinez, Simon, and Nguyen?"

"How can I value them? I don't even know who they are."

Match. Mike suppressed a smile.

Mike stepped back to his counsel's table. He had no co-counsel or paralegal, so he had to pull a paper out of a file on his own. He tossed a copy of an exhibit to Darius Moore, who fumbled it in the air for a moment before it settled on the table.

"Mr. James, I'd like you to turn to binder one, American Dynamics' exhibit number fourteen."

Berliner's junior associates and paralegals pawed through the exhibits and hammered on laptops to bring up the exhibit. The junior DEP lawyers angled their heads for a better view. Mike snatched an extra copy of the exhibit and gently settled it in front of the judge.

"Do you remember Mr. Moore asking you questions about this document yesterday afternoon? I believe your exact testimony was that this was one of the key documents you relied upon in formulating your opinion that the department's proposed penalty was over one hundred times too high, and the penalty for polluting the waters of the Commonwealth should be no greater than ten-thousand dollars. Do you recall testifying that you relied on this document?"

James quickly scanned the exhibit, an email, and attached four-page memorandum:

MEMORANDUM

TO: John J. James, PE, CEO

FROM: José Martinez, Ronnie Nguyen, Steve Simon,
Harrisburg Office, Lancaster, Livingston,
James Engineering, Inc.

SUBJECT: LL&J's recalculation of DEP's proposed civil
penalty for American Dynamics

"Oh, crap." James scrubbed his face with a hand and pinched his eyes together. "Sorry, judge. Can I ask for a recess? A continuance, whatever?"

"He can't do that, judge," Mike barked. "We're right in the middle of my cross-examination."

"But I can," said Darius Moore. "Judge, I beg the board's indulgence. Mr. James understandably has been confused by Mr. Jacobs' unartful line of questioning. May we have a five-minute recess so I can confer with my expert?"

"I strongly object, judge, I'm in the middle of cross-examination, and this witness has just admitted that the very memorandum on which he relied yesterday for his opinion that the penalty amount was over one hundred times too high is from people he does not know, whose opinions he does not value. I'm not about to allow Mr. Moore to confer with his witness in the middle of my cross so he can figure out how he can worm out of this."

"Judge!"

"Sit down Mr. Moore. I followed Mr. Jacobs' rather *adept* line of questioning from start to finish. It's clear as a bell. Your request for a recess is denied. If you want to rehabilitate your witness, you can do that during your re-direct after his cross-examination. Mr. Jacobs, you may continue."

"So you do recall testifying from this yesterday?"

"Yes, but if I can explain—"

"No, you cannot explain at this time, just limit your responses to answering my questions."

Darius Moore pushed his chair back and stood. Then he sat down. Mike was elated. Darius Moore had reached the point where he realized another objection would only help Mike, and the judge wasn't doing Darius Moore any favors.

Mike nodded. "Just a few more questions for you, Mr. James. Your company, Lancaster, Livingston, James Engineering, when was it founded?"

James looked confused and shrugged. "Elmore Lancaster was a consulting engineer in Philadelphia and had a solo engineering firm in 1876. He hired Harlan Livingston in 1890. In 1905 my great-grandfather, Lincoln Douglas James, married Mr. Lancaster's niece, Mary Higgins, and became a partner in the firm. So, the firm has been around for over 140 years."

"Are there any Lancasters or Livingstons still involved with the company?"

"Regrettably, no. Mr. Lancaster never had any children of his own, and Mr. Livingston's descendants went into other professions."

"Your firm is now publicly traded?"

"Yes."

Mike held up two thick documents. "I see from your company's annual report and 10-K report with the SEC that you and the James family are the largest shareholders. Between you and the other members of your family, you control fifty-one percent of the company's voting stock. Correct?"

"Yes, but I fail to see how this is relevant."

Mike could hear Darius Moore's chair scraping on the floor as he stood. "I object, Your Honor; I also fail to see how this is relevant."

Mike was about to respond when the judge waved his hands. "You may be right, Mr. Moore, but I'm curious to see where Mr. Jacobs is going with this. If it's irrelevant, I'll ignore it. Overruled."

"I have just a few more questions anyway, Your Honor."

The judge nodded.

"Since the James family is the fifty-one percent voting shareholder of your company, doesn't your family get to select the CEO and other officers?"

"Well, technically, the board does that."

"And over one-half of the board is made up of you, your sister, cousins, and other relatives. Correct?"

"That's right, but—"

"Mr. James, you're the CEO of Lancaster, Livingston, and James Engineering solely because your family insisted you be made CEO and stay on as CEO despite the wishes of the other forty-nine percent of the shareholders. Correct?"

"I wouldn't say that."

Mike removed a newspaper article from a file folder and handed it to Darius Moore and the judge. Then he handed a copy to James.

"Mr. James, this is Commonwealth's exhibit 65, a copy of an article from the *Wall Street Journal,* last year. It's titled, 'Proxy Fight Fails—John James Reappointed as CEO of LL&J Engineering Over Objection of Minority Shareholders.' Are you familiar with this article?"

James crumbled the article in his hand and said quietly, "fake news."

"So, you *are* familiar with this article?"

"Yes, but I disagree with it."

Mike held up another file folder. "Mr. James, this is Commonwealth's exhibit 66, a notarized affidavit from the Senior Vice President of Acquisitions at Markowitz Rudd & Company, the leading investment banking firm in New York. In it, he says that forty-nine percent of the shareholders wanted you out, and it was only because you and your family voted to keep you in that you remained CEO. Is that fake news too?"

***

When the hearing was over and the lawyers cleaned up their papers, James ran from the courtroom as quickly as possible. A decision would not be issued for several months, but Mike was confident. A gaggle of young DEP lawyers surrounded Mike, slapping him on the back and chatting loudly. They cleared a path when the chief counsel, Kate Gerard, and Roger Alden approached.

"Good job today, Mike," said Gerard, shaking his hand.

"Thanks. All in a day's work."

She quickly turned and left the room. Roger paused long enough to wiggle his eyebrows up and down.

"Nice going, bud. We'll talk later." He lightly punched him on the shoulder.

Several of the DEP lawyers volunteered to help get Mike's papers back to his office. As the room cleared out, Berliner and Darius Moore were among the last to go.

"Good work today, Mike," said Berliner shaking his hand warmly. "Mr. Ziegler wants to have a conference call tomorrow, you, me, Darius, and Hans to discuss a potential settlement."

"I'm happy to talk, but not if we're talking about a crappy settlement at one percent of our proposed civil penalty."

"No, this will be more realistic, especially in light of the hearing."

They shook hands again, and Berliner patted Mike on the shoulder as he turned to leave. Darius Moore approached Mike and quickly shook his hand. "You did adequately today," Darius Moore said through gritted teeth. "I guess even a blind pig can find a truffle from time to time."

Mike smiled. "Looking forward to our next get-together, Darius. I can hardly wait."

"Yeah, right." Darius Moore eyed him with contempt as Berliner called him from the hallway.

Mike forced a smile and watched as Darius Moore stalked out of the courtroom. The moment he cleared the door, Mike took a deep breath and allowed his shoulders to slump.

3

January

Bonjour, Mon Ami

Norby Lafleur hated having anything out of order or beyond his control. Nothing enraged him more than things not happening according to plan. *His* plan. He was enraged a lot. He was enraged now.

"Look at this bullshit," he said to his number two, Bones Benson. He read through the email again, his veins popping. He had received it just five minutes earlier, directly from Blade Harris, Yukon's VP of US operations in Houston. "That cocksucker is caving in to those politically correct bastards who are trying to take over the company."

Bones nodded but kept his mouth shut while his boss ranted.

Norby was Yukon's director of operations for the northeastern United States. Among other things, he was responsible for constructing impoundments and pits for the storage of fresh water and flowback water in the Marcellus Region of Pennsylvania, Ohio, and West Virginia. His office was a drafty work trailer at the Paxton drill pad in Bradford County, Pennsylvania, hardly what he thought he deserved. In his military-oriented mind, Norby was a full-bird colonel. The next promotion would be to Regional Vice-President for Operations, with an office in Houston and membership in the San Jacinto River Club, Texas's most prestigious hunting and fishing club.

He was tired of working out of the Army's Quonset huts in Iraq and Kuwait. And Yukon's trailer offices in Bradford County. And North Dakota. And Oklahoma. And wherever the hell else it was, they sent him. He was ready to settle into an office in the HQ on Louisiana Street in downtown Houston. And buy a sprawling house in The Woodlands. And take the money and all the privileges accompanying the big promotion. He'd finally be a brigadier general in Yukon's chain of command. He was ready, sure as shit.

"I'm telling you, Bones, it's bad enough dealing with some of the idiots who work for me and their constant ability to screw things up. I shouldn't have to deal with idiots in Houston who haven't been out in the field in decades. Don't get me started on those New York cocksuckers who bought forty-nine percent of the company last year and don't have a clue about the industry."

Bones nodded.

"Listen to this bullshit from Blade: '*The company continues to get bad press since we have allegedly failed to hire local talent to work at our drill sites. After consultation with management in Houston, the decision has been made to begin immediately hiring contractors from or based in the states we operate in.*' Blah, blah, blah. '*The following positions and tasks will be filled by such individuals: geologists, laborers, truck drivers, pit and impoundment contractors.*' Blah, blah, blah."

While Norby read, Bones looked around the prefab office. He looked out the grimy window at the snow, sleet, and rain that pelted the trailer.

Norby handed Bones a printed copy of the email. "Of course, we failed to hire local talent. We're in this to turn a profit, not be a bunch of goddamn social workers." He looked at Bones. "What do you think of that?"

Bones read the email. "Well, Norby, at the very least, we should have complete control over our men. We've done okay with the boys from Louisiana and Texas and Oklahoma. Those men have years of experience working on a drill site and can handle the crappy weather, the 24/7 work schedule, the unexpected bull crap. We hire a bunch of untested local boys, and who knows what might happen?"

"Exactly. Now here's some career advice for you: We can't come right out and challenge Blade on this. This here Cajun spent eight years in the Army. Rose from an E-1 to first sergeant in the minimum amount of time. One thing I learned was it's a bad career move to question an officer about his orders, and Blade is the closest thing to a general around here."

"So, what do we do?"

Norby stared for a moment at the football resting on the worktable, a pristine ornament cradled on a white stand with *LSU-2007* printed in gold. It was the only decoration in the trailer. "If we hire local boys and they screw up, you know Blade won't be around to take the blame. It'll be on me. *Merde*."

Bones nodded.

"Man, I don't like this. It's a lose-lose situation for me. If I don't follow Blade's orders, I'll be canned. If I do and the bastard screws up, I'll be up shit creek. Goddammit."

"What are you going to do, Norby?"

"We got us a geologist and truck drivers, but we still haven't begun buildin' that freshwater pit." He took a deep breath, "First thing, like Blade told us, is we call that impoundment contractor we used in Colorado and North Dakota and give him the bad news. Then hire the local talent. That'll keep Blade happy for now. One thing, we've got to stay on top of the new bastard like stink on shit."

Norby reached into the battered steel file cabinet next to his desk and pulled out the thick file of promotional materials from all the contractors in Pennsylvania who were begging for work with Yukon. Like a card dealer in Vegas, he shuffled through the color glossy brochures until he found two from contractors claiming to be able to build an impervious freshwater pit.

"Here's one." Norby began reading it. "From Pittsburgh. Not too shabby. They say they have experience. Built dozens of pits . . . Interesting. They did twenty EPA-approved hazardous waste impoundments, too . . . Worked in the industry . . . They have some serious qualifications . . . Wait. Looky here." He put his thumb next to some words and held it up for Bones to see. "MWBE Company. *Merde*. That's a minority and women-owned business. I hate having to hire someone because he's from here. I sure as hell ain't hiring some colored- and bitch-owned business." He laughed.

Norby tossed the brochure into his waste can. He opened the second brochure. It featured a picture of a decent-sized impoundment that appeared to be made from high-quality construction materials, although he couldn't tell from the picture how large it really was. Nothing in the brochure even stated the photo was of an impoundment constructed by the company. It could have been a stock photo. They claimed to have twenty-five years of experience, but the text was vague on details.

"PITS, Inc." Norby flipped through the brochure. "It looks professional enough. . . from Horsham, Pennsylvania," he pronounced it *Whorse-ham*. "And looky here. The president of PITS is Christopher Corsica. Corsica, that's an island. Part of France, I'm pretty sure. Shoot, I don't recall. Close enough. Cajun and Corsican both are French. I think. Corsica could be a French name, and someday I'll ask the guy if he *parlez-vous* any French. Probably only knows the same French cuss words I do." He chuckled. "The owner, Corsica, was Army, a Ranger. That seals the deal for me."

He handed the brochure to Bones, who studied it. "I'm not so sure about these guys, Norby. I mean, they don't have much experience. I'm not sure they ever built a pit. Says nothing about building hazardous waste impoundments. And look at this. In tiny print, it says PITS is a subsidiary of Corsica Roofing Company, a *roofing* company. Does it matter? I mean, that's not anywhere near the kind of experience we need."

Norby thought for a moment. "There are many odd things in this industry, my friend. A lot of oil and gas contractors we work with started out as general construction boys. All that matters is if they can build a pit to hold water. I mean, honestly, anyone with half a brain could do that."

Bones nodded.

"I'm going to send an email to *Monsieur* Corsica, my *campagnard* from *Whorse-ham, P- A-*, and invite him in for an interview. What could possibly go wrong?"

4

Git'er Done

Chris Corsica sat in his decrepit RV combination field office and motel room, the rain pounding on the roof, with his number two, Hector Torres, who sat on a tiny bench that folded out of the wall. The side door hung open. Corsica stared at his blue lawn chair, soaked and bedraggled in a pool of mud. A black and gold U.S. Army Ranger flag, one grommet missing, saturated with rainwater, drooped from a pole on the side of the camper.

Thirty-four-degree damp February air blew into the camper, chilling Corsica through his grey hooded sweatshirt and well-worn windbreaker, a cracked and faded Corsica Roofing Company logo stamped on each one. He tugged down his old Corsica Roofing ball cap, its brim tattered and folded into three sections. It provided little warmth. He needed to leave the door open to survey the mud-filled, half-finished excavation for Yukon's freshwater impoundment and to air out the shit smell that permeated the camper.

Corsica had banned everyone from using the camper's mini-toilet after it became apparent it couldn't handle the loads of beer and pizza-fueled diarrhea regularly deposited into its small tank. He had made the junior-most member of his crew, his nephew, clean out the tank and bathroom, but the stench had permanently soaked into the walls of the camper. Everyone, including Corsica, now either took a whiz in the woods or a dump in Yukon's porta-potties.

Frigid torrential rains fell for the third day in a row. A nor'easter had stalled over Bradford County, and the rain alternately poured down in buckets and as sheets of sleet. Corsica took a sip of cold, over-cooked coffee from a filthy Corsica Roofing mug. The spreadsheet on the micro kitchen table that served as his desk detailed his company's failing finances. He wasn't sure if it was the rain, the coffee, or the numbers that gave him heartburn, but he shoved the morning's fifth Tums into his mouth and chewed it to bits in seconds.

At six-foot-two, with a gut hanging over his belt, he had to fold himself into the cracked captain's chair next to his desk. Corsica looked at his watch. It was a little after 8 a.m.

"If we can't get out there to excavate soon, we're going to be totally fucked," Corsica muttered.

Torres, almost a foot shorter than his boss, wore a Corsica Roofing sweatshirt. Corsica was a difficult man to work for, but he'd been good to Torres and his family. Since Corsica was a former Army Ranger, he hired vets whenever he could, and Torres had served in the Marines. He never complained.

"I'm pretty sure we can push the mud around, boss, even in this rain," Torres said while looking out the door. "The small dozer we have might get stuck, but that D-8 you rented can do the job."

"That bastard is costing me seven grand a week just to sit there. It's bad enough I'm paying a crew to sit in a motel and jerk off all day, but I'm also paying for all of this equipment that's just sitting in the rain. I've already maxed out the loan. I'm so fucked."

Torres stood and looked out the door. He lit a cigarette and blew the smoke outside. "It looks like it's getting lighter to the south, boss. Maybe the storm is going to blow over soon."

Corsica played with his cell phone and shook his head. "Can't hardly get any reception out here. Last time I got that weather dot com, it said we're going to get rain and then showers for the next ten hours. What the hell is the difference between rain and showers? It's all friggin' wet."

Torres leaned outside, his cigarette dangling from his mouth, and extended his open palm into the rain. "Hey boss, honest to God, I think it's letting up."

Corsica's cell phone lit up and blasted an old car horn *aah-ooo-gah*. The screen said *NORBY LAFLEUR*.

"Phone doesn't work when I want it to out here. When I want some peace and quiet, I get this."

He let the phone honk three times, then answered. "Norby, what's happening, buddy?" He smiled broadly and sounded like a man who'd just won the lottery.

"Y'all done yet building my impoundment?" Lafleur barked. To Corsica, the voice sounded like a French country music singer with marbles in his mouth.

Silence.

"I have sixty water tankers lined up in Sayre to begin filling that pit, and we're waiting on you bastards." Lafleur's voice had none of Corsica's enthusiasm, and it was obvious from his tone that his face was a long way from a smile.

"Norby, I told you we hit rock and had to blast. I didn't want to put the pit here because I could see the rock ledge sticking out of the ground, but that Bones guy ordered us to do it anyway. Now it's too wet, and you know I can't excavate in this weather. The DEP permit specifically says we can't excavate in wet weather. Shit, I'd do it in a New York minute, but the permit doesn't allow it. Not only that, but we'd probably just be rearranging the mud and getting nowhere."

There was a long pause. Then Lafleur swore in French, or Cajun, or Creole, or whatever mongrel language the bastard spoke. "Looky here, boy, you were supposed to have the goddamn pit completed over a week ago. That was excavation, leveling, rock and sand base, and two layers of impervious liner material to hold water. I don't want to hear excuses. If y'all'd been on time, you'd've beat the storm. Not only that, with all this fuckin' rain, God himself would have helped fill the goddamn impoundment. Without the pit, I don't have water for fracking. Without the water for fracking, I can't frack. If I can't frack, I don't get paid. And if I don't get paid, *y'all* don't get paid. Am I making myself clear?"

"Yes, sir. I'll do everything humanly possible to finish excavating and get the job done. We'll work through the night, 24/7, to get it done."

"Not good enough, Corsica. I don't want *humanly* possible. I want the job done no matter what. Finish up in three days, or you're off the job."

The line went dead.

Corsica laid his cell phone on the table and stood up. *Finish up in three days or you're off the job.*

Torres eyed him.

"Get the guys. We're starting up in an hour. I want them all here. I don't know how but we gotta excavate in the friggin' rain and lay down the gravel and sand base."

"Sure, boss. What about the liner? I mean, when we went to the training in Dallas, they said we shouldn't do it in the rain."

"It never rains in Texas. What do those assholes know? I've put roofs on thousands of houses—half of them in the rain. If you can seal a rubber roof in the rain, you can do a pit liner. It's only going to hold water, for Christ's sake, anyway. Now get going and get those guys moving."

Torres jogged through the pelting rain and mud to his beat-up Toyota pickup. Corsica looked at the half-dug impoundment and the rain. Torres was wrong; it was coming down harder. He shook his head, reached for his pocket flask, and sucked down the remaining drops of Jack Daniels he had carefully funneled into it at 5 a.m. He flipped up his hood and stepped into the rain to fire up the big dozer.

Corsica's boots sunk into four inches of mud.

"I'm so fucked."

5

I Hate When That Happens

The rains would not let up. A nor'easter would ride over Bradford County, dump two or three inches of rain over two days, ease up, and then the next storm would move in and dump even more rain. The temperature hovered in the thirties, sometimes dropping into the high twenties. Mostly it would rain, but big, fat snowflakes would also fall and melt when they grazed the sodden ground. What wasn't a pond was mud, and mud and water were everywhere.

Drilling continued ceaselessly at Yukon's Campbell pad. The roughnecks wearily climbed the derrick in the frigid rain, and the paper-pushers, geologists, cake-eaters, and other workers who could hide in their warm work-trailers never ventured out. A borehole had been drilled to its full length, over one mile vertically and nearly two miles horizontally, and the drill rig had been moved to accommodate the completions team so the well could be hydraulically fractured. A reinforced floor had been installed on the drill pad to hold the additional equipment. Five million gallons of fresh water had been trucked to the impoundment, and it had been used to frack the well. The pumps and a pipeline had been set up to pump the contaminated flowback water into an army of frac tanks that would collect up to five million gallons. The only trouble was that the frac tanks weren't there.

Norby chewed on Pepto-Bismol and Gas-X tablets like a cow chews her cud. After midnight he'd lost track of time as he banged furiously on his keyboard in the small modular office a dozen miles from the Campbell pad, desperately trying to work his way out of this nightmare. From time to time, he scrolled through his satellite phone and shouted commands at exhausted underlings. The hours raced by.

"Where the hell are my frac tanks, Bones? They're supposed to have been set up yesterday. What the hell is going on?"

The storm nearly drowned out Bones. His voice crackled as winter lightning interrupted the transmission. "Norby, that little bridge crossing that no-name crick five miles down on Campbelltown Road got undermined by rainwater yesterday. The state troopers wouldn't let us on it during the storm, and then the bastard washed out. All of your tanks are lined up on the wrong side of the crick."

"Can you turn 'em around?" Lafleur shouted. "There's got to be another route to get them up to the pad. I need them there, like yesterday."

"Sorry, Norby, it's a narrow road. I already tried to turn 'em, and they got stuck in the mud on the shoulder. It's a hot mess."

Lafleur paused and gathered his thoughts. "Can we get in a temporary bridge? I've done that before. In Kuwait." *Kew-wait.* "Shoot, I did it there in the Army; I can do it here."

"I thought of that too. It'll be at least two, maybe three days or more to get in a temporary bridge. That's assuming the State Police allow it. They don't get how important this is and have been perfect pricks about it."

Lafleur muttered, *"connards."* He paused briefly. "Can you get me different frac tanks? Bring them in from the other end of Campbelltown Road. I don't care what it costs."

"If you can find 'em, sure," Bones replied. "The ones here stuck next to the crick were the last ones available in P-A-. Every other frac tank in P-A-, Ohio, and West Virginia, and I mean literally every one, is in use somewhere else. Other than those, the closest ones are all down south. It'll take at least forty-eight hours to find enough tanks, drive 'em up here, get 'em on the pad and tied together so they can be used. I can do it, but that's what it's going to take."

"*Merde. Merde-merde-merde-merde.*" Lafleur knew Bones was right, but he hammered on his keyboard and, five minutes later, finally found frac tanks that were the right dimensions and were immediately available.

They were in Tulsa.

Oklahoma.

"*Merde.*"

While he searched for a solution to this nearly insurmountable problem, Norby thought back on an incident just a few months earlier when he made the mistake of allowing his men to come off the drilling rig during a nearby lightning storm. Generally, the rigs ran 24/7, Christmas, Easter, blizzards, you name it, *except* when there was lightning nearby. He ordered his men off the derrick, and they missed a drilling milestone by two hours, waiting for the storm to pass. Blade's exact words to him over the satellite phone, etched in his medulla oblongata, were, "You stupid Cajun asshole, if you ever fall behind again, you're through. I'll kick your lazy ass back to the fuckin' swamp myself." Lafleur desperately wanted that promotion to Houston and was not going to let that happen again.

"*Merde, merde, merde.*"

"What about that water pit, Norby?" Bones asked, his voice crackling. "I mean, it's right there and empty. All it's got to do is hold the flowback water for two, maybe three days. When we get those tanks up from Tulsa, we can pump the flowback out of the freshwater pit, clean 'er up, and she's as good as new."

Bones' suggestion had occurred to Norby earlier in the day. He kept rejecting the idea because he just didn't trust Corsica and that crappy pit he'd built in the storm. Norby had inspected the job after it was completed, and had they not been desperate to move forward, he would've told that incompetent Pennsylvania sumbitch asshole shit-eating *bâtard* to pull it apart and start over. He had a gut feeling that the impoundment wasn't tight. Lafleur was prepared to lose some freshwater out of the pit, that was a manageable loss, and they could fix it when things dried out, but if he lost contaminated fracking water, the DEP would be up in his ass.

He had no choice.

"Bones, I'm going to order those tanks from Tulsa. Stay down there with the State Police and see if you can un-fuck that situation with the bridge. Do whatever it takes."

Lafleur clicked off, then clicked the number for the tank-rental company in Tulsa. Yukon was a good customer, and he had no doubts when the sales rep told him the tanks would be on the move within sixty minutes. Even so, if everything went right, it would still take over twenty hours of continuous driving, with two drivers in each cab switching off, for the convoy of empty frac tanks to travel the 1,200 miles from Tulsa to Bradford County, and another twelve to twenty-four hours for a team of expert installers from Texas to hook up the tanks.

A minimum of thirty-two hours.

If everything went right.

Nothing had gone right.

Lafleur scrolled through his contacts and dialed Corsica. The phone rang four times before a sleepy voice answered.

"Corsica, I need you to get your men right now and have them realign and reverse the pumps at the pit you dug. My guys'll work with you."

"Shit, Norby, it's what, 3 a.m.? What do you mean reverse the pumps? You mean pump the frack water out of the gas well into the pit? All the water that went into the well is contaminated now. The pit I built for you is a *freshwater* pit. It's not designed—"

"Look, boy, quit arguing with me and just do it."

"No, pal, you can't put frack water into the pit. It's a freshwater pit."

"Hey asshole, we've got no choice. I'll be there in ten minutes." He hung up on Corsica.

Norby's truck skidded the last fifteen feet in the mud to stop next to Corsica's crappy RV. A light on the side of the camper barely lit the steps. The Cajun grabbed a heavy industrial-sized Maglite as he leaped from the pickup into the blackness. The light played against the side of the RV; he noticed the soaked

Army Ranger flag dangling from one grommet in the rain. He took the stairs into the RV in one step. No one was there. He turned around at the door and, in a flash of winter lightning, he saw Corsica standing at the edge of the pit.

Norby jogged and came up behind Corsica.

"Your men on the way?" He yelled, waving the Maglite in the driving rain.

"No way. I didn't call them." Corsica drunkenly waved around an empty Jack Daniels bottle as he spoke.

Norby felt his face flush and his blood pressure rise. "We need to reverse them pumps. The frac tanks are forty-eight hours out. That frack water has to go somewhere, and it has to happen now."

"Yeah? That's not my problem, buddy. You're the expert on getting things from A to B. It's not my fault you didn't get your fuckin' frac tanks where they were supposed to be. I built you a freshwater pit; it's not designed to handle frack water. I'm not gonna participate in this. Not me or my men."

"You Yankee cocksucker. Do you think you'll ever get another job out here? All the boys who work in the industry, every company, they know me, known me for twenty years. Shit, I've worked with ninety percent of them. Not a single one'll hire you. Not just Yukon, I mean none of them. You can go back to Philly and clean gutters. That's all that'll be left for you, you damn Yankee."

"You redneck Cajun asshole. You wanna blackball me? Go ahead. I'll be back up here with some of my buddies from the city, and we'll light you up. We aren't gonna take this bullshit." Corsica waved the bottle at Norby and began to stagger away.

Since the time Norby had become an NCO in the Army, all the way through that moment, no subordinate had been so insolent, so stubborn, so stupid as to say *no* to him. Norby felt as though his being had split into two parts, an angry earthbound man and a winged avenging angel that looked down from above as his arm reared back and smashed the Maglite into the insolent Yankee sumbitch's skull with a sickening *crack*. He recalled as a boy chopping wood on the farm the sound of a log splitting. Every now and again, if you hit the log just right, it split perfectly in two with a loud crack.

That noise.

He hovered above the scene, watching as he hammered the man again, in slow motion, a second blow, this one in the face. Blood. Tissue. Teeth. He watched as they all flew out of Corsica's head.

The man went down.

Hard.

Face first, into a pool of mud.

He didn't move.

Dead.

Corsica never saw it coming. His back was to Norby, and his reflexes had been dulled by half a bottle of whiskey.

Norby blinked himself back to reality and looked around. He didn't see any angel.

He saw the devil.

6

Where, Oh Where Has My Little Dog Gone?

Hector Torres was shocked. Chris's RV was gone. It had been at the little campsite next to the impoundment barely twelve hours earlier. He looked away, then looked back, hoping it would magically reappear. It didn't.

He parked his truck next to where the RV had been and called Chris. It went to voice mail. It had gone to voice mail all morning. He'd expected a call from Chris at 6 a.m. to tell him to get the men together to start building the second freshwater impoundment but was shocked at what he found. Or didn't find.

There were tire tracks in the mud. Several sets of them. He had no doubt the RV had driven off. The tracks were so fresh he assumed Chris must have left recently. The place smelled of mud, dead leaves, rotting barbeque, and something else. Some of Chris's stuff was on the ground, his lawn chair and hibachi grill, a yellow chock he used to secure his wheels, and other odds and ends.

He walked the fifty feet from the campsite to the impoundment and was surprised to see it was being filled, the water spilling into the pond from the same hoses they'd used to pump water out of the pond to the fracking operation just a few days earlier. He knew the specs they'd been given were for a freshwater pit. If the water entering the pit was flowback water, the pit wasn't designed to handle it.

Torres sat in his old pickup and lit a cigarette, watching the pit slowly fill. He had a bad feeling about this. Chris could be a difficult man to work for, but he'd never run off a job. That just wasn't his style. Chris drank too much. Yelled from time to time. But he was intensely loyal, and he'd never run away.

Never.

That wasn't like him.

A half-hour later, Torres was at the Paxton pad. He tapped politely on the modular office's door just below the black and gold glued-on letters that read *YUKON O & G OPS*. While he hadn't been there before, he knew this was the office of Norby Lafleur, the big boss. Torres's stomach grumbled loudly. He'd never been introduced to Lafleur, and Chris had never said a nice word about him. The only time he'd encountered Lafleur was when the man inspected the impoundment. He had nothing good to say to the men, and he threatened Chris for his sloppy work.

Torres was certain he'd heard voices coming from inside. He tapped again and wondered whether this was the kind of office you walked right into, like a doctor's office, or whether you waited for someone to let you in. He shifted his weight on the small metal step and blew on his calloused hands. The mist dissipated in the freezing drizzle. He was about to risk entry when the door opened from inside.

"Yeah? What do you want?" Torres recognized Bones, skinny as a razor's edge. He'd met Bones several times at the impoundment. He was always snooping around, ordering them to do some additional work that wasn't in the specs or undo something they'd been ordered to do. The man didn't know his ass from a hole in the wall.

"Excuse me, sir, is Mr. Lafleur here?"

"He's busy."

Although Bones was partially blocking the door, Torres could see Lafleur sitting behind a small metal desk watching them.

"Mr. Lafleur," Torres said, angling his head to talk past Bones, "could I have just a minute, sir, please?"

Bones shifted to block Torres's view, and Torres moved his head to see around Bones' narrow frame.

"Let him in. I can give the boy maybe twenty seconds," Lafleur said in his Louisiana drawl. Torres was forty years old. "I've got a convoy of frac tanks ten hours out."

Torres slipped past Bones into the small office. He glanced around smelling the heavy scent of Pine-Sol, like someone was covering over a foul stench and over-cooked coffee from an ancient Mr. Coffee machine in the corner. Lafleur had a small desk with a laptop, a battered metal filing cabinet, shelves with three-ring binders and stand-up files, and a small card table. The only decoration was a football resting on a stand.

"What is it? I'm very busy right now," Lafleur said.

"I'm sorry to bother you, sir. Have you seen Chris? Chris Corsica? I haven't seen him since about nine o'clock last night. I was just up at the pit, and his RV is gone. I've called his cell, but it goes straight to voice mail."

Lafleur said nothing. He glanced at Bones and then said, "Sorry partner, I haven't been to the Campbell pad today. That's ten miles from here. You say his RV is gone? I can't help you there."

"The thing is, we have a contract with you to build another impoundment, and we're supposed to begin as soon as the rain lets up. We were hoping to start today. There's no way he would've just taken off without telling me. We have a crew of three guys over at the All-American Motel waiting to get to work. It doesn't make any sense."

Lafleur nodded. "I hear you. I did speak with Corsica last night. You guys did a for-shit job on the first impoundment. I don't need any more of that kind of work. Also, it turns out we're not going to need a new impoundment, so I canceled the contract. Maybe he just took off since you didn't have any more work up here."

Torres looked from Lafleur to Bones and then down to his hands. His stomach flipped. "You canceled the contract?" he asked softly, swallowing back vomit. "Chris rented the D-8 dozer for a full two weeks, cash in advance. That's $14,000. We were going to build you two impoundments. We have other expenses. Four guys, hotel, food, fuel, crushed stone." He paused. "I'm an investor in this business. Ten thousand dollars." His voice drifted off.

"I can't help you there, partner. Take a look at your contract. Yukon can cancel it at any time if our needs change. Our needs changed."

Torres looked at the floor and said nothing for a long moment. "He wouldn't have just taken off. We would have to make arrangements with the rental company to come and pick up their dozer. Then there's cleanup and whatever. He would've called me and the men before he took off."

Lafleur looked at his watch and made conspicuous eye contact with Bones. He lifted his chin in the direction of the door. "I'm real busy right now. Nothing I could say will help you. I have no idea where your guy went. We're done here."

Bones opened the door wide. Didn't offer his hand.

"You know what, Mr. Lafleur? You can't do this to us," Torres said, his voice rising. "We put it all on the line for you, for Yukon. You can't just flip us off like that."

"Get out of my office, boy." Norby rose to his feet. His face was red. "I'm a busy man. I've got work to do. Clear the rest of your shit off my pad by this afternoon, or I'll have it hauled to the dump. Now git."

Bones pushed his body up against Torres. He was sorely tempted to punch the Texan in the face. He could take that skinny shit out with one punch. Instead, he backed away from the office. As he left, he glanced over his shoulder in time to see Bones begin speaking quietly and quickly with Lafleur. Then the door closed.

***

Later that morning, Norby walked around the embankment at the pit. He watched the water as it pumped in. The whole thing was muddy, and the berm was covered with crushed stone #1, as required by the contract. He studied the impervious black membrane liner they had installed in the pit. As he walked away, he noticed something in the mud on the berm.

It was a Corsica Roofing Company ball cap, old, muddy, the brim folded into three sections the way some people do. Just the way Corsica wore it.

Something was smeared across the side.

Sticky.

He smashed the substance between his thumb and forefinger.

He smelled it.

Blood.

Norby looked around to see if anyone was watching. He was about to toss the cap into the woods when a thought occurred to him. He found an old McDonald's bag in his truck, shoved the hat inside, and rolled it closed. He'd toss the bag into a dumpster in town.

Now all he wanted to do was get out of there.

7

I Last Saw Him by The Bulldozer Playing and Running Around

Hector Torres had unwillingly visited police departments on several occasions. As a teenager, he frequently came in through the back door in handcuffs. After the Marines finally straightened him out, he didn't visit again until his son became a teenager. Between father and son, he'd seen his share of police stations. He'd never seen one he liked.

The Washington Township Police Department building was brand-new. It lacked the stink of caked-on filth, piss, and sweat found in the lockups he was accustomed to. Some of the township's furniture may have been recycled, but most looked like it was right out of the box.

Torres approached a counter and noticed an old white woman sitting behind a desk. No one else seemed to be in the building. She looked at him, made a face, shook her head, and went back to sorting her papers for a full five minutes.

Torres shifted uncomfortably and cleared his throat. He knew she'd seen him. He was accustomed to insults, but this was over the top—racist crap.

Finally, the woman put down the papers and approached the counter.

"Can I help you?"

"I'd like to report a missing person," Torres said, watching her eyes.

"Is this a relative?" She looked him over, her expression turning into a frown.

Torres was short, about five-foot-five, and he found himself looking up to this woman who squinted at him through tortoise-shell eyeglasses.

"No." He realized that what he was about to say sounded foolish. "It's my boss."

"Your boss? Your boss is a missing person?" She raised her eyebrows, and her mouth curled into a slight smile.

"Yes, I haven't seen him since last night, and his RV is missing."

"Are you reporting a missing RV, too?" she asked. The woman finally smiled full-on. It wasn't pleasant.

Torres shifted uncomfortably.

"I've got this, Mildred." A uniformed officer walked up behind the woman and patted her on the shoulder.

"Cliff, this uh. . . gentleman is reporting a missing boss and a missing RV. Maybe you can help him?" Her voice sounded mirthful.

The officer smiled and turned to Torres. "I'm Chief West. Your boss and your RV are missing?"

"No. I mean, yes. My boss is missing, and so is *his* RV." Torres stood almost a foot shorter than the chief.

"Let's start at the beginning. What's your name?"

"Hector Torres."

The chief wrote a note on a legal pad. "Torres?" He angled his head. "Are you an American citizen?"

Torres paused. *What the hell?* In his forty years, he'd never been asked that question. Not once. "Excuse me? What did you say?"

"I think you heard me. Are you a citizen of the United States?" The chief spoke slowly and loudly, the way some Americans do when they think they're helpful to someone who doesn't speak English.

Torres narrowed his eyes and raised his chin. He tensed his body, the way he used to do, nearly thirty years ago, a moment before he threw down and started a fight. "Yeah. I was born in Camden. That's in New Jersey. USA." He refrained from saying *asshole*, although his tone clearly conveyed that sentiment.

"Okay, *Mr.* Torres, have you ever lived outside the U.S.?"

Torres smirked at him, nearly laughed. "Spent my whole life here except for two years in Afghanistan."

"Excuse me?" The chief's voice rose. "Afghanistan?" The chief shifted his hand to his belt, near his service weapon, and turned his body slightly sideways, protectively.

Torres held back a smile. "Yes sir, 1st Division, 1st Battalion, 4th Marines. Two tours."

Surprisingly, the chief blinked, then held out his hand. "Me too. Coast Guard, served on the Mighty Mo, the Cutter Mohawk. Thank you for your service."

Torres was startled but shook it. "You were a Coastie?" He smiled, nearly laughed, at the chief. "Thanks for *your* service."

"Okay, let's get back to business," West said, looking at his paper. "Address?"

"Levittown."

"The whole city or do you have a residence?" His demeanor had warmed, and this time when he smiled, it was friendly.

"5299 Crabtree Drive, Levittown."

"Okay, Mr. Torres, who did you say was missing?"

"My boss, Chris Corsica. We're here doing a job for Yukon. I last saw him in his RV, our mobile office, at around nine last night. I was there at seven this morning, and he's gone, so's the RV."

"Where's he from?"

"Philly area. Horsham, P-A-."

West looked up from his notes. "Maybe he went to the grocery store? Maybe somewhere else to get supplies? I mean, it's only a little after eleven."

"Officer—"

"Chief."

"I'm sorry, chief, it's not like him. We've gone on supply runs, and we always take my truck. Maybe one of the other guys' trucks. The RV is a pain in the ass to drive on these hills and dirt roads, and I really doubt he would've driven away from the worksite just to pick up some groceries."

"Is he married? Did you call his wife?"

"Divorced. Since his youngest kid turned eighteen and the child support ran out, they barely talk anymore. I didn't call her to ask, but I'd be surprised if he checked in."

West had stopped writing. "What about another woman? A girlfriend? Maybe a prostitute? You say the RV was parked at a job site. Maybe he drove off into the woods for a little privacy?"

"I don't think he has a girlfriend back home right now. Last I saw the boss, he was about halfway into a bottle of Jack Daniels. I doubt he was able to drive anywhere last night. He was pretty lit up. I doubt he could have done anything else if you get what I mean."

The two men exchanged raised eyebrows and nodded.

"Are you sure the RV is missing? Did you look around the job site to see if he moved it? Maybe it was in the way of something, a derrick or some of that crap?" West asked.

"I looked. All over. Yukon only has about seven acres up there, and mostly it's on the side of a hill in a farm field. It's pretty open. I walked around and didn't see any RV. I drove around to a bunch of other places we'd been to. Bars, pizza shops, other job sites. Nothing. If he were going to move to another place, another drilling pad, that would be miles away, and he would've called me on my cell. It's not like him, chief. I've known the guy for ten years, and he wouldn't just disappear. Besides, aren't *you* supposed to be heading out to look for him?"

"Well, Mr. Torres, I'll tell you what. We have a lot of people up here who are from out of town. Now I admit that most of them are from Texas, down south, and the like. But we have quite a few workers from Pennsylvania. They come and go pretty quick. Unless you have evidence of foul play, all we know right now is that we don't know where he is, not that he's missing."

Torres nodded slowly.

"I'll tell you what, I'll hold these papers. You say you last saw Mr. Corsica at about 9 p.m. last night? If he's not back by tomorrow morning, come back in here, and we'll complete the paperwork."

Torres nodded.

"I hate to say this," said the chief, "but I've seen this happen too many times in the past few years. Men are here away from home, their wives, girlfriends. They're lonely, bored, whatever, and have a few dollars in their pockets from all the drilling work. Ladies, and I use the term loosely, go onto job sites when the bars close and, drunk or not, provide a variety of, uh, personal services for the guys who are stuck out there. He's probably parked off in the woods somewhere with some whore nursing a nasty hangover and praying he doesn't have AIDS. Stop back tomorrow, and we'll take it from there. Okay?"

The chief smiled warmly as he held up the papers in his left hand and held out his right.

Torres shook his hand and walked from the counter. At the door, he turned and said, "This police station. I've seen a few, and they're all old and beat to hell. This one looks brand-new. What's the deal?"

"Gas money," said the chief, still smiling. "For the last few years, the Township's been getting almost a million dollars a year in impact-fee money from the gas companies. After the supervisors built themselves a palatial new township building and a new rec hall for the residents, they built me a new police station. There's also a new fire hall down the street. Nice, huh?"

"So, the drilling industry paid for your new station?"

"The local cheapskates sure as heck didn't."

Torres gritted his teeth and nodded, not so much at the chief as at the new police station. As the door closed behind him, he glanced back in time to see the chief tossing the papers into a banker's box.

8

June

Those Who Were Seen Dancing Were Thought to Be Insane by Those Who Could Not Hear the Music (Friedrich Nietzsche)

Teresa Bruno-Campbell hurried through the house, getting ready to take her ten-year-old daughter Isabella to her ballet lesson. She scurried around the kitchen, cooking dinner for the family, pausing briefly to shop on the kitchen laptop, and picking up her kids' stuff. Her son, six-year-old Lucas, seemed to have a different pair of sneakers for every sport. All of them were muddy, and he'd tracked dirt across the new kitchen floor. She mopped as she texted back and forth with her husband, Jared.

I thought you were going to be back here by 3?

Sorry babe got really busy. 6 if I'm lucky. Maybe 7

I'm making pasta with meat sauce. I'm using the frozen fresh kind you like from D'Angelo's in Annadale. Not sure how long the kids will want to wait to eat

Maybe feed them at 5. We can eat later. Can you open a bottle of Tignanello at 6 if I'm not home by then? Sorry babe

Yep

She called again for her daughter. "Isabella? Come on. We have to get going."

Nothing. The story of her life.

Teresa stirred the meat sauce and inhaled the intense aroma of Italian sausage, onion, garlic, basil, and oregano. She poked at a lump of sausage that wasn't covered by the sauce, put the heavy lid on top of the pot, and turned the heat down to low. She checked her emails and deleted most, saving for later the ads for shoes and lingerie.

Teresa checked one more time to see if her husband had anything further to say.

Nothing.

Teresa glanced around the kitchen and saw it was more or less in order, then headed to the den, regretting again that the old house didn't have the large open floor plan she wanted. Her daughter was on the wide leather couch, wearing earbuds and watching TV. Teresa pointed the remote control at the television, turned it off, and removed the earbuds from her daughter's ears.

"Didn't you hear me? You're going to be late for your ballet lesson."

"I don't want to go. My stomach hurts."

Teresa felt Isabella's head. It was cool. She looked at her face. Maybe it was pale, but nothing out of the ordinary.

"Sweetie, you love ballet. I think once you get there, you'll feel better."

Teresa patted her daughter on the back, and she slowly slid off the couch. Isabella was already wearing her pink ballet outfit and black ballet shoes. Teresa gave Lucas a push. He stumbled to the car, barely looking up from his iPhone.

Teresa started down Campbelltown Road in her BMW X6 SUV. She glanced at her odometer: 4276.5 miles. She reached the location of the first drill pad, the closest one to her house, at 4277.8 miles. The driller was Yukon Oil and Gas, but the land belonged to her husband's family. The drill site was only 1.3 miles from her house, and she remembered the racket it made over spring break. Although Jared's family owned seven hundred acres, Yukon insisted they drill within a particular target zone. Jared's lawyer, a lamebrain hick shyster from Williamsport, was able to add an addendum to the lease agreement requiring any drill pad be no closer than one mile from the house and that no drilling take place under the house. She understood that somehow the drillers could drill horizontally and wondered if they'd drilled under her home despite the restriction. Who would know?

A hill separated the house from the work site, but when Yukon was drilling, she could still hear the rumble and clanking through the night and see their bright lights on the horizon. The noise kept her up all night, partly from the commotion but partly from the worry. Teresa was no environmentalist, but she harbored some anxiety about what the drilling might be doing to her family.

Jared said considering the one-million-dollar bonus payment from Yukon for the natural gas rights and the significant royalties they anticipated once the boreholes were fracked and tied into the pipelines, it was a small price to pay for the windfall. Of course, he lived and worked in Manhattan during the week and only had to put up with the inconvenience on weekends.

Teresa heard Yukon was going to drill more wells, but she didn't know when they would begin. She and the kids would suffer through it all summer, not Jared.

As far as Teresa was concerned, this was yet another reason to sell this dump out in the middle of nowhere and get a house in Long Beach, New Jersey, where all of her New York friends had beach houses. She hated the country, and now that she was done renovating Jared's family's dilapidated house, she had little to do. She regretted pouring so much of the bonus money into rehabbing the old place: nearly a quarter-million on upgrades, enlarging and modernizing the kitchen; and another hundred thousand on redecorating and new furniture. The money could have been a nice down payment on the beach house, but Jared insisted, and she went along with him since the money came from his family's land. This time.

Her daughter saw her dance friends and scampered off. Lucas strolled behind, his face glued to his phone.

As she walked to the entrance, Teresa mused again about finding a physical trainer to come to the house. Maybe he'd be her boy toy, or was it a toyboy? She decided she didn't want a boy; she wanted a man. A handyman. She smiled as she imagined telling Jared she'd found a handyman to "take care of a few things around the house." She found herself fantasizing about this more and more often, especially at night when she was in their big bed alone.

All she needed was a little arrangement to keep her occupied while Jared was at work in the city, Monday through Friday and sometimes Saturdays.

While her kids were in camp or at one of their many lessons or team sports.

Nothing serious, just a little fun.

A younger man, definitely.

More pumped than Jared, which ought to be easy enough to find.

She'd have to keep it from him, of course, but she knew she was capable of doing that. Finding a guy in Bradford County with all of his teeth would be a challenge. Still . . .

She sauntered into the studio and admired herself in the wall of mirrors at the ballet barre. She was glad she hadn't let herself get fat like so many of the other moms had. She could pass for twenty-eight or twenty-nine, at least ten years younger than her forty-two years. She took a sideways glance. The boob job and tummy tuck were good investments.

She couldn't help but smile at herself.

A little extra-curricular activity with the right guy, no strings, no attachments. That would be good for everyone.

It would make her happy, hopefully, less cranky, and Jared would be none the wiser.

All fun.

Win-win.

The idea pleased her.

The lesson was one hour, not enough time to run home or do anything other than sit with the other moms, all of whom were from Bradford County, and listen to them complain about their dreary lives.

"Hi, Teresa. Quick question, how far is the nearest frack site from your house?"

The inquisitor, Roberta Something, was a woman in her late thirties, easily 180 pounds, and worked nights as a nurse at the local hospital. She probably thought the blousy scrubs she wore disguised her chubby body.

"Funny you should ask, I just measured. They haven't drilled since the spring, but the frack site is 1.3 miles from the house."

"Yeah, but that doesn't mean the frackers don't have any frack holes crisscrossing under your house," said Caitlin Martin. "We wouldn't allow any fracking under our house." Caitlin and her husband owned a dump of a house and maybe five acres. Teresa couldn't imagine that any drilling company would have any interest whatsoever in the Martins' property. "It's been proven by scientists at Duke and Cornell that fracking causes myalgia, listlessness, birth defects, even cancer."

"Then why would they allow it?" asked Roberta. "I mean, if it's as bad as you say, then wouldn't the government just shut it down? I mean, EPA, DEP, they wouldn't allow fracking if it was as open-and-shut bad as you say."

Caitlin stared at her. "I can hardly believe my ears. Don't you know that all of them are in bed together? EPA, DEP, the frackers. It's them against us."

"I don't believe it," replied Roberta. "That's just a giant conspiracy theory. The next thing you know, you'll be saying Obama wasn't born in the United States or the FDA is hiding the cure for cancer."

They stared at each other for several seconds.

"Well, in fact, my son's been sick now for months, and the doctors can't figure it out. Also, the dog died mysteriously. We found him out back. Dead."

"Seriously? I'm sorry about your son, but there could be a thousand reasons. Maybe you need to take him to Geisinger or Hershey, you know, a big medical center, instead of the local quacks. Most of the local doctors aren't even trained in the United States anymore. It could be something simple like a vitamin deficiency."

Caitlin said nothing for a moment, then said, "Well, what about our dog?"

Roberta smirked. "You need to check with your neighbors about your dog. A lot of farmers around here use poison to control mice and rats. The poor thing could've gotten into some of that."

Teresa took advantage of a pause in the debate and said, "Caitlin, do you really think it's possible to get some illness from the fracking?"

"Absolutely," Caitlin said immediately.

"I doubt it," Roberta interjected. "I read a lot online, and there's a lot of BS about fracking chemicals."

Caitlin said, "I don't know what you read, but everything *I* read online says all of that stuff is bad for you. That's why we don't allow any fracking on our property." She held up a plastic workout bottle full of water. "Also, we only drink bottled water."

"I'll admit some people truly seem to be hurting because fracking has ruined their water and their peace and quiet," Roberta said. "I have no doubt it's ruined some water wells. But I think most of the complainers are just that, complainers."

Caitlin shook her head. "You think I'm a complainer? You just haven't talked with the right people. There really are a lot of people who've been hurt by fracking. The fracking poison gets into your water supply. It can kill your livestock, and then you drink it too. What then? Our children drink the water and breathe the chemicals they spew into the air. We've all seen how it's changed Campbelltown."

The women were silent for a moment.

"We had our water tested not too long ago, and it was pretty good," Teresa said. "There was a little of this and that in our water, but it was just the salesman trying to sell us a crapload of filters, so I told him to go to hell. I went online and bought one of those filter thingies you put on the end of your faucet. Also, we only drink Fiji Water."

"Well, better safe than sorry," Caitlin said in a singsong voice, holding up her water bottle again.

At that moment, there was the commotion of ten-year-old girls, the lesson was over, and the women talked loudly as they gathered up their things.

"Mom, can I go over to Emma's house? We want to hang out," Isabella said. Emma and Isabella had their arms locked together. Teresa thought it was just a short while ago they wanted to get together to "play."

"Only if it's okay with her mom."

"It is. Emma already checked."

On her way back home, Teresa stopped on Campbelltown Road as close to the drill pad as possible. A large sign next to the access road read *Yukon Oil and Gas—Campbell Pad.*

The site was quiet now, but she remembered the sound of workers and the racket from the drill rig. She rolled down the window and sniffed the air. She didn't notice any odors from the drilling, although she wasn't certain what that might smell like. Right now, the air was filled with the putrid stench of rotting cow shit and hay, smells she could live without.

Still, she wondered.

Teresa parked her BMW next to the mailbox at the end of her walk. When she and Jared first moved into the house, she found it quaint that their mail was delivered to a box along the road. In a moment of country gentility, she was inspired to order from Amazon a rural mailbox shaped like a BMW. She liked the look. However, the first time she had to get the mail outside in the pouring rain, rather than have the mailman push it through a door slot like in the city, she decided it was a pain in the ass. Molly Something-or-other, the postmaster, refused her angry demands to get service anywhere other than roadside, unless Ms. Bruno-Campbell wanted to come to the post office every day and pick it up.

She had a stack of mail, mostly junk and several advertising circulars. In addition, Jared subscribed to the weekly Bradford County Tribune, which was stuffed into an adjoining newspaper box. She thought it was crap, and he got it mainly for nostalgic reasons. Neither of them cared much for the local news. Any news they needed, like Jared's laundry list of investment and technical publications, they could get online.

She quickly glanced through the mail, setting the bills aside for her husband. She did enough around the house and long ago decided he would do most of the bills. She noticed her Amazon credit card statement and shoved that into her purse. She despised Walmart and the crappy little stores in the area. Amazon Prime was her lifeline. Rather than have to explain to Jared all of her charges and deliveries, which she timed to arrive when he was in the city, it was much simpler just to pay it herself from her house account, without Jared's questions or commentary.

Teresa maintained a small checking account in her own name and tried to maintain a balance of about $10,000. Just for presents for Jared and the kids, if he ever found out about it. The trick was replenishing the account. She took the small checks that came in the mail, ones Jared wouldn't notice, like small dividends from some of their investments and refund checks. Still, she knew it would be nice to have her own money to beef up her account, just in case. She hadn't yet thought through *just in case of what?*

A letter from DEP caught her eye. She ripped it open and read the short note from the inspector who had been out to her property a month earlier. The letter may as well have been written in Greek. She understood almost none of it. One sentence did catch her attention:

> *Based on the sample results and other information obtained to date, the Department has determined that the Water Supply was not adversely affected by oil and gas activities, including but not limited to the drilling, alteration, or operation of oil or gas wells.*

It was signed by the chubby girl who came to the house to do the testing, Melissa Shelton, a geologist for DEP. Teresa pulled out the second page. It was covered with numbers that appeared to represent test results. They meant nothing to her. She noted, however, that a number of the test results were bolded. She assumed they were significant.

Teresa looked again at the letter and focused on the statement that her water well was not affected by the nearby drilling. She immediately dialed the geologist's number and left a reasonably calm message. Then she dialed Caitlin.

"The girls are having so much fun. I hope you aren't calling to pick up Isabella already," Caitlin said.

"No, I'd like to pick her up an hour or two before dinner, though, so I can get her washed up. I did have a question for you. You remember how you said you were researching fracking and what it could do to our water?"

"Researching? It's more like an obsession," she said as she laughed. "I read everything I can get my hands on."

"Everything?"

"Well, I don't read anything sponsored by the industry. You know, their geologists and scientists are just like those so-called scientists who work for the tobacco industry. They're completely discredited, as far as I'm concerned. All of their information is corrupt, entirely tilted in their favor. You know, they can find the exact same chemical that's in the fracking fluid in your well water and claim it came from natural sources. They publish papers all the time, but you can't believe a word they say."

"What about colleges, you know, professors doing research?"

"Ha," Caitlin cackled loudly, "I don't read anything from any university that gets grants from the industry. So, Penn State, Pitt, Colorado, any college in Texas or Oklahoma, are out. The industry gives them millions of dollars for research. Did you know one of the biggest frackers gave Penn State over one hundred million dollars to start an ice hockey team? One hundred million dollars! Do you think that money doesn't come with strings attached?" Caitlin was speaking quickly now and didn't await an answer. "Of course there are strings. They don't just hand out stacks of hundred-dollar bills without expecting positive results. A quid pro quo. Those universities have prostituted themselves. I read all about it in an article online, and I believe it. They're just not trustworthy."

"Wow, really?" asked Teresa. "I'd think big universities, like the ones you mentioned, would have, like, people looking over their shoulders. Standards. Peer review or something. That kind of thing."

"And who do you think pays for the people looking over the shoulder of the scientists at Penn State and the others?" she said in her singsongy voice. "Hundreds of millions of dollars are at stake. Those schools aren't going to kill the golden goose. I read online that some professors are so fed up they left those schools." Caitlin paused long enough to take a breath, "I mean, I'm sure there are some good ones at those places, but how would you know? Who could you trust?"

"Well, someone has to be doing research that's not with the industry," Teresa said. "I get that the industry has millions of dollars to throw at research, and I suppose I agree with you that you just can't trust it. But who's doing the research we trust?"

"Fortunately, there are some colleges and a lot of independent scientists out there who are not bought and paid for by the industry. I trust them." Caitlin said. "They're independent. Some work for colleges, but only the good ones who don't rely on blood money from the oil and gas industry. Some work for organizations, like the NRDC, Sierra Club."

"Okay, I get that, but who pays *them?*"

"The vast majority of their money comes from people who give, you know, ten-dollar contributions."

"Ten dollars? Really? When that company tested my water last year, it cost us $2,500. You'd need, what, 250 contributors at ten dollars to test one water well."

"Okay, maybe twenty dollars, but lots and lots of people giving ten, twenty dollars can really add up. Also, actors and rock stars, even some billionaires, give pretty generously to those organizations. Millions of dollars."

"Well, who's watching over their shoulders?" Teresa asked. "I don't want to be difficult, but how do those researchers get paid? I mean, even a scientist working on the good side has to eat and have a roof over his head."

There was a long pause, then Caitlin said, "People do pay them. It's just a fraction of what they would get paid if they worked for the industry. They're true believers. We should be glad some scientists are willing to work like that. Peer review occurs, but it's less important because they wouldn't make stuff up. We—I—trust them."

"What about DEP, EPA? I mean, don't they have to do the right thing? Be even-handed at least. Do you trust DEP?"

"Ugh. They're the worst of all," Caitlin said. "At least the universities put out press releases boasting when some fracker gives them money. I mean, DEP relies on money from the frackers to get by. If there's no fracking, there's no money. That's not just me saying it; it's a fact, the law. Also, DEP is infested with people who are just waiting to go through the revolving door and work for the industry. It's like you scratch my back, I'll scratch yours, that kind of thing. I know at least one family who has fracking chemicals in their well, and DEP says they have to prove it. *Fracking chemicals.* I mean, how did they get there unless the drillers allowed it to leach into the ground? You can't trust the government, that's for sure."

"So what happens to the people with chemicals in their water?"

"It means they can't use their water," Caitlin said. "Not for anything except maybe flushing toilets."

"How can they say the chemicals didn't come from fracking?" Teresa asked.

"That's what the frackers say, the water always was bad, their water well wasn't properly drilled or cased, the water well was never cleaned out."

"And?"

"I'll admit that maybe in some cases that's what happened. But you can't explain every bad well by saying the chemicals occurred naturally. Not when the water goes bad a day or two after the fracking."

"What would happen if they prove someone's water was contaminated? Do the frackers fix it? Pay for your water?"

"I guess both, Caitlin said. "I suppose DEP or the court could order them to fix it. I've heard of some big settlements where the frackers had to pay damages to the homeowners—"

"Damages? How much?" Teresa asked.

"I don't know. Thousands, millions of dollars. It's all kept secret. You know, NDAs, non-disclosure agreements."

"Millions? Really?" Teresa said.

"Something like that. Why don't you come over here an hour early next time, and we can have a cup of herbal tea made with bottled water and go through those results you got from DEP together. The results may be okay; it's also possible the frackers caused problems with your water. It'll be easier if I can see the spreadsheet from DEP. We can go online and see what it says about those chemicals. Also, if your water has been fracked, I can get you in touch with people who can help. I really wouldn't want you or your family using that water."

***

The temperature was warm, and Teresa kept the windows down as they drove back from Caitlin and Emma's house. Isabella chirped away in her booster seat, impressed with a video game she played with Emma that afternoon. Lucas was still playing a game on his iPhone. Although Isabella was ten years old, she was so small she still had to sit in a child's booster seat. While Jared was willing to let her sit on the regular car seat, Teresa wouldn't hear of it. Although the car was new, the booster was bound into the seat so tightly that it was just about glued to the leather.

As the car approached the fracking site on Campbelltown Road, Teresa instinctively rolled up the windows. She took a deep breath just before they reached the pad and didn't expel it until they were almost home.

9

A System Designed by Geniuses to be Carried Out by Idiots, Part I (Herman Wouk)

Professor Wilbur McCrory was the head of the Geology Department at Penn State University. Despite that, he insisted to the Dean of the College of Earth and Mineral Sciences that he be permitted to teach an introductory course every year and have his choice of classrooms. He chose the most deteriorated, most unattractive classroom in the oldest, least renovated building, the venerable Mineral Products and Industries Building.

He liked teaching Environmental Geology 101. The course required some science background, high school chemistry was enough, but a deep knowledge of geology was not required. That would come later as the baby geology students made their way through Penn State's rigorous curriculum.

He enjoyed teaching the course because he had a mix of what he liked to call "quirky students." Some were deeply interested in geology. Others had heard he was a good lecturer. Still others were in it for a fairly easy B. Several were preparing themselves for a career in industry; others would never come close to working for any industry. Some were passionate environmentalists with a deep concern for the environment but still lacking scientific knowledge to back up their convictions. Of course, there were football players and other student-athletes, particularly if the class was given at the right time of day, after the morning workouts and before afternoon practice.

Many things had changed since the professor had obtained his Ph.D. from Penn State in the 1970s. When he was a young geology student, in this very classroom, there were rarely any women students, "co-eds," a term he never heard anymore. Today, almost half the students were women; although, since they were all as young as his grandchildren, he tended to think of them as "girls" (but he never uttered *that* word).

The students dressed in a chaotic array of fashions, from pajama bottoms and revealing tank tops to shorts and flip-flops in the snow to preppy. The professor modeled his own dress after one of *his* favorite professors, and when in the classroom, as opposed to a geology field trip, he dressed in a fine Saville Row three-piece suit and bow tie. Professor McCrory was a cup of tea in a world of lattes.

When he was a student, the only computers were in the computer lab, massive IBM 360s, which required stacks of punch cards or reels of magnetic tape. Today, almost every student had a laptop, each with more computing power than a room full of 360s. He looked out at the faces of his students, most with only eyes peering above glowing laptop monitors.

He loved teaching this course more than some of the upper-level seminars because this one kept him on his toes. It exposed him to the most relevant thinking of the kids, and it was fun to teach. At the end of each class, the professor felt he had learned something new.

"Ladies and gentlemen, we are going to continue our discussion of horizontal drilling for oil and gas," said Professor McCrory. About forty of the fifty students were present. He expected this since class began at 8:30 a.m. on Mondays. The geology nerds sat in the front row, the football players lounged in the back with the other athletes, and everyone else, many propped up on their elbows nursing from Starbucks cups, sat in the middle.

"Unlike so-called conventional drilling, after the borehole and lateral are drilled, the formation has to be hydraulically fractured to free the natural gas or oil found in the tight rock formation. It's a little like pumping air into a tire. The air inflates the tire. Unlike your tire, however, hydraulic fracturing is supposed to cause the target formation to fracture into a multitude of cracks to release the oil and gas that's trapped inside of it. If you put too much air into your tire, you'd achieve a similar result." He showed a short video clip demonstrating the process.

Tyler Duffy, a sophomore from Philadelphia, limply raised his hand. "Yo, professor, why don't you call it *fracking* like the rest of the world?" Tyler slouched in his chair, his loose basketball shorts giving way to hairy legs sprawled wide apart.

"In fact, Mr. Duffy, historically, the industry always shortened the term *hydraulic fracturing* to *frac*. He wrote *FRAC* in large, precise block letters on a whiteboard. "The process generally is referred to as *completion of the well* or *stimulation of the well* by the industry. This is a geology class, so I prefer to use the technical terms."

"Okay, but I thought it had a K in it," said Duffy. "Like frack, fracking, frack you."

Some of the students laughed.

McCrory listened to Duffy, then wrote *FRACK* in large letters beneath *FRAC*. "Opponents of drilling referred to the process as *frack* because high school English teachers would not tolerate the letter c being used in its hard pronunciation at the end of a word unless it was followed by a 'k.' More importantly, Mr. Duffy, *frack* looks and sounds like the F-word. In a puerile way, it's funnier to say, *we don't want your fracking well*, rather than *we don't want your hydraulically fractured well.* Also, *frack you* fits better on a hand-made poster at an anti-drilling rally than, *we strongly disagree with your approach to drilling that involves the injection of 99.5% water and sand and ½% chemicals into boreholes*. If anyone here is fortunate enough to work for the industry, you will *not* use the letter K; however, the rest of you probably will use it."

The classroom awoke with peals of laughter; even Duffy laughed. Three students Googled the word "puerile," although one got stuck looking up "pure aisle" and never found it. Most of the others remembered the word from the SATs or AP English classes.

"I thought the whole thing from start to finish was called fracking, not just the hydraulic fracturing part," said Duffy. He straightened himself in the chair and crossed his legs. A flip-flop dangled at the end of his foot.

"The industry refers to the process by its component parts, such as exploration, site preparation, drilling, and completions, while opponents refer to the whole thing as *fracking*. Since this is a science class, let's address it from a technical perspective. A team of specialists is employed by the drilling company to conduct completions. That is to say, they inject the hydraulic fracturing fluid into the borehole. That fluid contains ninety to ninety-nine percent fresh water. Only one-half percent is chemicals. The rest is sand, which the industry calls *proppant*." The professor displayed another PowerPoint slide.

One of the front-row students, a woman named Li Ying, raised her hand. "Yes, Ms. Li?"

"Sir, excuse me, but what exactly is the makeup of the completions fluid?" she asked in her typically formal way.

"Well, Ms. Li, the companies that specialize in fracking jealously guard the formula the way Coca-Cola guards the formula for Coke or Burger King guards the formula for its secret sauce." More laughter, muffled this time.

He advanced to the next slide. "This is a rather typical list of eighty or so chemicals found in completions fluid. Some of this is fairly common stuff, like methanol, ethylene glycol aka anti-freeze, sodium hypochlorite aka liquid bleach. Some chemicals are proprietary. By the way, the fact that some of this stuff is common doesn't mean you'd want to ingest it. I surely wouldn't, but for the most part, it's fairly common stuff."

Duffy leaned forward and scraped his chair on the old linoleum floor. "Wait a minute. I thought the chemicals used in fracking were a secret?"

"Not a secret at all, not for several years anyway. For quite a while, many companies have disclosed the fluid's content. More recently, state and federal regulators require most of the information to be posted online, and, with few exceptions, most of the chemicals can be found with a simple Google search. Just look up FracFocus dot org." With his precise engineering-style printing, he wrote it out on the whiteboard. "Each completions company has its own secret formula, really just percentages of each chemical from this list, that is remarkably similar to the others. By the way, everyone in the industry has a really good idea of what's in their competitors' fluid. There are a small handful of proprietary chemicals that are kept confidential as trade secrets, but since employees move from one company to the next on a regular basis, nothing stays a secret for very long."

Duffy didn't bother raising his hand again but leaned his chair back on two legs and clasped his hands behind his head. "Professor, all of that fluid, whatever you want to call the process, has to go somewhere. Where does it go? I mean, what concerns me and a lot of other people who oppose fracking is that it has to go somewhere. Either it stays in the ground or gets into groundwater, where it can get into drinking water. Isn't that right?"

"Good question, Mr. Duffy. Once stimulation of the minerals has been completed, about twenty-five to ninety percent of the fracking fluid returns to the surface as flowback. Keep in mind that, in Pennsylvania, the fluid is forced about a mile or more underground—5,280 feet down—which is where the fracking takes place. You may recall from one of our first classes that potable groundwater is no deeper than five hundred to one thousand feet underground. Undrinkable connate water is below that. The likelihood is very tiny indeed that the flowback water will get into drinking water."

An African-American woman in the front row, one of the budding geologists, raised her hand.

"Ms. Jackson?"

"Professor, picking up on what Tyler asked, what's in the flowback fluid that comes back to the surface? Isn't it even more contaminated and dangerous than what went down during the completions process?"

"Good questions. In addition to the chemicals intentionally added to the mixture, the flowback fluid, as it is called, also picks up substances found naturally underground. This *produced water* or *flowback water*," he wrote these terms out on the whiteboard, "contains minerals it picked up underground, such as chloride, sodium, barium, strontium, bromine, and lithium." He wrote on the white board: Cl, Ba, Sr, Br, and Li. "It can also contain a small amount of radiation, which is naturally occurring beneath the surface. The radiation is known as *NORM*, which sounds like the friendly guy who runs the corner garage or the bartender at your corner tavern. The jury is still out on whether this is toxic, but it comes back in such minuscule amounts I don't believe it is. For the most part, the scientists who have researched this agree with me."

"Okay, I hear you, Professor," said Duffy, half-rising in his chair, "but it seems to me that it's too dangerous to play with this stuff. The flowback or completions water, fracking water, has all these chemicals, including radiation, and it's coming to the surface where it can come into contact with humans and animals. It's just too dangerous."

"The whole point is to prevent it from coming into contact with humans and animals," the professor answered serenely.

"But where does it go?" Duffy pressed, leaning forward now, his elbows on the desk.

"Today, much of it goes into frac tanks, that's *F-R-A-C-* tanks, no K, or Baker tanks as they're sometimes called." He wrote again on the whiteboard. "From there, it's shipped off for recycling or disposal. In some states, some of it still goes into pits where it can be re-used or stored until it's disposed. At one time, the industry did not re-use this water because it was too contaminated, they said, to be used in the completions process. But because it was difficult and expensive to dispose of this water, and government agencies urged them to recycle it, and, oh yes, because it was less expensive, drilling companies started re-using this water in the completion process. They don't all do it, but more and more of them are."

The professor looked at Duffy, who was shaking his head. "Professor, I trust you. You seem like a decent guy. I just don't trust the fracking companies. Many have awful reputations, and there's a lot of information out there," he pointed at his laptop, "that just says the process is too dangerous. Too many people have been hurt. Then there's the whole issue of methane which is a dangerous greenhouse gas. We should stop it."

"I hear you, Mr. Duffy. We'll have to agree to disagree." Then he surveyed the room to make sure he wasn't losing anyone. Many of the students were typing furiously.

"Wait a minute, Professor, you said some of the flowback goes into open-air pits. Right?" Jackson asked.

"You are correct, Ms. Jackson. Some of it does. The engineers and professors in Austin, Tulsa, Norman, Golden, Tomball, and other locations have thoroughly researched the subject and have ordained standards for the construction of flowback water impoundments. These include a subbase of four inches of clay covered by a crushed rock and sand subsurface base. They decided this was the best way to keep the produced water inside the impoundment and prevent it from leaking. Government regulators have largely agreed with them. The standards for these impoundments require a sealed double-liner system and monitoring probes strategically placed in the subbase under the liner to detect leakage. These impoundments should also include a network of monitoring wells surrounding the pit to detect the presence of contaminated water should any of it leak out. The fact of the matter is many states have banned storing the stuff in pits just to be sure."

Duffy didn't let up, "But, Professor, the science is still being determined. It seems so dangerous. Also, those people with the contaminated wells, the sick children and animals . . ."

"I appreciate your passion, Mr. Duffy, but I have to disagree with you. The process has been used in its current form for over eighty years, a million wells have been stimulated using this method of hydraulic fracturing, and the instances of injury are anecdotal at best."

"It's not just me, Professor," replied Duffy. "What about New York? Maryland? Vermont? They all banned fracking."

"Well, I'd be more sympathetic to the politicians in those states if they also banned the *import* of oil and gas that had been fracked, as you like to say. As it is, they are benefitting from the low cost of gas and oil coming from unconventional formations, but they bear none of the cost of the drilling. I think those bans were entirely political, not based on science at all. One other thing, who here can tell me if there are any recoverable gas formations in the great state of Vermont? Ms. Jackson?"

She was taken by surprise as she had not raised her hand. "Umm, none? I don't recall seeing any gas deposits in Vermont on the maps we studied."

"You are correct. They have no skin in the game. It's easy to ban hydraulic fracturing of natural gas formations when you don't have any unconventional gas. They may as well ban polar bear hunting, and perhaps they will."

The class laughed at that. Then there was silence, except for the clicking of laptop keys.

The Professor looked at the clock. His time was almost up. "One more thought, class. Herman Wouk wrote a book when I was a young man called *The Caine Mutiny*. Have any of you read it?"

No one responded.

"Did any of you see the movie?"

Two hands went halfway up.

"Regardless, Wouk described the Navy the same way some might describe the drilling industry, '*A system designed by geniuses to be carried out by idiots.*'"

About half of the heads, mostly hidden behind their laptop monitors, nodded. Some typed.

"Okay, class, read ahead in your textbook, chapter twelve. I hope to see more of you on Wednesday morning."

Back in his office, the professor entered his password on his computer, *4.543BillionYears!* An email popped up from someone he had never met before, a lawyer named Darius Moore from a firm called Finkel & Updike.

Professor McCrory-- This Firm represents Yukon Oil and Gas Co. We have a case that is heating up in Bradford County, Pennsylvania, dealing with allegations of contamination from natural gas drilling. DEP has verbally told us there was no contamination and Yukon's in-house geology section agrees with that. We support them in their determination. I'd like to talk with you about possibly retaining you as our expert. The people on the other side are named Teresa and Jared Campbell. If you are interested and do not have any conflicts, kindly respond, and I will set up a conference call to give you the details. We can discuss your expert fees during the call.
Thank you.
--Darius Moore, Esq.
Senior Associate
Finkel & Updike

The Professor looked at the email and thought for maybe ten seconds. Then he replied:

Mr. Moore, you have piqued my interest. When can we talk?
Will McCrory

10

Opportunity Knocks

After taking fourteen pages of notes, Winifred Hedges hung up the phone and laid her pen next to her legal pad. She opened and closed her hand and swiveled her weary wrist. The potential client, Teresa Bruno-Campbell, had started out polite and friendly, then became shrill and offensive, and finally, by the end of the call, she was sobbing. At one point, her potential client used the words "fuckers" and "assholes," words that never slipped out of Winnie's mouth, in nearly every sentence. Winnie wasn't sure if she should be sympathetic, empathetic, or just plain disgusted.

Winnie stood up, and her creaky wooden desk chair slowly regained its upright position. Her old metal desk was large but covered with stacks of paper, geodes, fossils, and a heavy bronze trophy attached to a walnut base, *Pennsylvania Environmental Advocate of the Year ~ 2015*. Behind her desk was a large green and white banner she had swiped after some event and tacked to the wall, *Pennsylvania's Advocates for the Environment.*

Winnie held her hands over her head and flexed her slim frame from side to side, her floral sleeveless dress rising and falling with each stretch. She checked herself in the mirror and patted her shoulder-length blonde hair. Her face was still youthful enough, but she noticed lines creeping in and laughed at the thought of the Botox some of her friends at the gym discussed.

Winnie went down the short hallway and tapped on a half-open door. Cynthia Voigt, the Advocates' executive director, smiled from behind her laptop and beckoned her in. Cynthia's office was as neatly kept as Winnie's was messy. She wore white slacks and a mint green and white striped sleeveless top, slimmer than Winnie, with narrower hips and a smaller bust. Her blonde hair was cut short and framed her ice-blue eyes; her blazer draped over her chair. Rachel McAdams or a young Audrey Hepburn came to Winnie's mind. Classy. Winnie admired her friend's good looks. Who wouldn't?

On Cynthia's desk was a large seventeen-inch laptop, a single pad of paper, and two meticulously maintained bonsai trees. Both were Pennsylvania mountain laurels. One, she told everyone, was twenty-five years old and the other merely six. The rest of her office was just as fastidiously kept.

A spreadsheet blinked on Cynthia's screen. She held the organization together and stretched the truth when needed. For financial support, they relied on two pro-environment foundations, three large private contributors, and hundreds of small ones, plus a foundation run by her parents who lived on Youngs Ford Road in Gladwyne, Pennsylvania. The tiny budget limited the effectiveness of the organization and the ability to attract anyone to work there other than recent college or law school graduates and volunteers. Virtually all of the professional staff other than Cynthia and Winnie moved on after a year or two when other environmental non-governmental organizations made better offers. As a result, they were always talked about as the "minor leagues" of ENGOs.

"Cyn, do you know how we're always looking for a great case in the Marcellus region? I think I have one."

Cynthia sat back in her plush desk chair. "Okay, you've got my attention."

Winnie crossed her legs on the brightly colored loveseat across from Cynthia's desk. "This family, the Campbells, they're one of the original families in Bradford County. They leased their land to Yukon Oil & Gas out of Texas. Yukon put in a drill pad and began drilling the property for gas. The woman, client, whatever, Teresa Bruno-Campbell, says all of this is a little over one mile from their home and their water well. Teresa said they drilled three or four wells last winter and put in a reservoir. She claims her water, it's well water, was always excellent before the drilling. Now her water has started smelling and turned brown."

"Sounds pretty open and shut to me. Isn't this just a contaminated water-well case? We have pretty limited resources and need to deploy them carefully. What does DEP say?"

"That's the thing," said Winnie. "DEP sent them a letter last week saying the contamination in her well doesn't come from drilling. The department's position is that other sources may be contaminating the well."

"So, if we took this case, both DEP and Yukon would be the enemy? I guess this would give us a chance to fight with both the turncoats at the department and the evil frackers," she said without malice or humor. She was simply stating facts. She looked at her manicured nails. "That's a pretty good case, but I have a feeling it would be expensive to litigate. Wouldn't you need an expert witness?"

"Yes, at least a geologist and preferably a former industry engineer, too. There's a geologist in Texas, Ruby Sunshine, and before you ask, that's her legal name. She used to be Ruby Solomon, but she changed it in grad school. Anyway, a number of other environmental groups have used her. She has a Ph.D. and hates the industry. I've checked around with lawyers at other environmental NGOs, and she's pretty solid. Still, she's all over YouTube and Twitter trashing the industry, and I hear from some of the lawyers that she's been roughed up in court during cross-examinations because of her bias."

Cynthia nodded and made a note on her pad.

"Also, there's this engineer in Colorado who spent thirty years working for several oil companies, all defunct, and then worked as a consultant to the industry. About six years ago, he went rogue and now testifies against them all over the country."

"Billy? William Benedict? I heard him talk at the conference last year in Banff. He's good. Knowledgeable. Smart."

"Yeah, well, Billy Benedict, or Benedict Arnold as he's now known in the industry, costs about $300 an hour to testify." Winnie made a face and shook her head. "I just don't know how we're going to afford this and, the more I think about it, I'm not sure this is the big fracking case we've been looking for to make a splash in Pennsylvania. Maybe we should leave this for some private lawyer or other ENGO. There are plenty now who want to jump on the Marcellus litigation bandwagon."

"Well, I'm concerned about the finances, too." Cynthia pointed at the spreadsheet. "We have a half-dozen paid employees in our organization right now. Of those, only two are lawyers. I suspect you'd need more to handle your existing work and take on the new case."

"We really have just one and a half lawyers. Justina and me, and technically she's only part-time until she passes the bar exam." Winnie paused and looked out the window at the back of the building across the alley. "This is ridiculous. I ought to know better; we can't afford this."

The women looked at each other in silence.

Cynthia pushed her laptop to the side and leaned forward on her elbows. "Do you remember that international climate-change conference I went to in Banff?"

Winnie thought about the controversy surrounding Cynthia's expensive trip to the famous resort in Alberta, Canada. She justified it to the Board of Directors as necessary for making new contacts and rubbing shoulders with potential high-roller contributors. As expected, even with help from her wealthy family, the airfare, room, and board for three nights at the Lake Louise Resort, among other expenses, took a big chunk out of their small budget. The farthest Winnie had traveled for a conference was Pittsburgh. Even then, she drove herself and stayed with friends.

"The one with all the actors and former politicians?" Winnie smiled and raised her narrow eyebrows. "Champagne cocktails in the bathing suit-optional hot tub overlooking the Rockies?"

Cynthia rolled her eyes. "Yes, and millionaires and billionaires with a passion for fighting climate change. I connected with several high-rollers. There was this guy, I told you about him, someone there who may be able to help us. He offered significant financial assistance, but only if we lined up the right case. One that has the chance of stopping the industry in Pennsylvania. A big victory in this case would really set back DEP and make them slow down, maybe even stop, those drilling permits they're giving away like candy at Halloween."

"The Russian guy? Yeah, Cyn, but to do this case right we'd have to fly in those experts and pay a ton of money for depositions, testing, and exhibits. The experts alone would cost more than we've paid for any other case. Because of the other work that I do, we'd need to hire another full-time lawyer to take over my cases, and I'd want someone with real experience—ideally, a former DEP lawyer. The whole thing, including the new lawyer, would cost us maybe two, $250,000. We struggle to pay our expenses every year on a $750,000 budget. Let's say your buddy Boris gives us $100,000. That would be a fantastic gift. We still couldn't afford litigation that's going to cost us $250,000." Winnie laughed her soft laugh. "Here I am talking *you* out of this."

"It's *Vladimir Zhirkov*. I'm CEO and chief fundraiser," Cynthia said. "You're General Counsel. Let me see if I can pull this off. If I do, you owe me a Macallan at Rubicon."

"I don't know, honey." Winnie only called Cynthia "honey" when she strongly disagreed with her. "It's a lot of money, a bigger contribution than anyone has ever given us before, and it'll come with strings. Don't forget the strings. We'd owe your buddy Vlad, and I have no idea what he'd want in return."

Winnie smiled at her friend with faux sweetness.

"Let me worry about the details," Cynthia said. "One thing's for certain: I can't go back to my mom and dad for another contribution. If we get the money from Vlad, fine. I can deal with the strings. If I don't get the money, we don't take the case."

When she returned to her office, Winnie went online and looked up Ruby Sunshine's YouTube performances before local ENGOs and citizen groups. The audiences were all friendly, and Sunshine played to the groups without any discernable filter, as though no one was recording her presentation. The local organizations to whom she spoke had posted the presentations for the world to see, not because they wanted to discredit her, but because they were so delighted with her anti-industry diatribe.

The environmentalist in her wanted to raise a fist and say, "Right on!" The litigator in her cringed and shook her head.

She wasn't sure about this case. She trusted Cynthia, but a part of her hoped she wouldn't be successful with the mysterious Russian.

11

More Dollars than Sense

Cynthia looked around her neat but cramped Harrisburg office with its ugly view of the backs of houses converted into offices and apartments. Wires from utility poles to the neighboring buildings and to the building which housed the third-floor office of the Advocates seemed haphazardly strung, making dozens of polygons in the sky. The wires met in a rat's nest of connection boxes on either side of the alley that faced her office. On a good day, the alley reminded her of Charles Demuth's painting, *My Egypt*, but it wasn't exactly a scenic view.

How had she and Winnie's dream of starting an environmental advocacy group faltered? Ten years earlier, three hours into cocktails at Stock's, the two best friends were inspired to write a business plan on a cocktail napkin about an organization they would run. It would exist to advocate for people suffering from environmental harm caused by callous corporations and DEP. Three scotches into their planning, they called it Advocates for Pennsylvania's Environment, until they realized the acronym was *APE*. She and Winnie laughed so hard they had to hold each other up so they wouldn't fall off their barstools. They rearranged the words and laughed and toasted their idea into the night. She recalled several innocent celebratory drunken kisses at the bar, followed by several not-so-innocent ones pressed hard against each other on Second Street. Once and done.

A few weeks later, Cynthia left her safe job working on the staff of a liberal state senator from Philly, and Winnie left her job working in the chief counsel's office at DEP. They rented a tiny one-room office they shared on the second floor of the same building they currently occupied. Now she spent almost all of her time schmoozing contributors, tinkering with the budget, and trying to keep the Advocates afloat. The sizable money they expected never came. When things got bad, her parents' foundation kept them going. They never got the epic cases they wanted.

Still, there was one call she knew she could make. Someone who potentially could make this happen. The Russian whom she met at the Banff conference who had promised the stars but who seemed more than a little smarmy. Vladimir Zhirkov's business card had only his name, cell phone number, and Gmail address.

No title.

No street address.

No company affiliation.

He'd told her a company name which she didn't catch, then he laughed and said he owned many companies, both domestic and offshore, so it really didn't matter. She flipped the card over in her hand. In a vaguely European hand, it said, Call me, 24-7. *I am ready to help you.*

Vlad, unlike several of the other men at the conference, had been a perfect gentleman. No excessive hello or goodbye kisses or hugs, no hands accidentally grazing her butt, in fact, no kisses or hugs at all. She never caught him looking her over, not even when they were getting into the large hot tub together—both wearing bathing suits, unlike some of the others—and not after they'd both had several drinks at the bar. Vlad was an attractive man, very fit for his forties, she guessed, with some interesting tattoos on his body and arms. He wore no wedding band and never discussed a wife or kids. Cynthia thought of herself as attractive—and she was—for late thirties, so she wondered if maybe he was gay, which, of course, didn't matter. He'd lavished a lot of attention on her but also on several others from the Pennsylvania delegation now that she thought about it. Maybe he was just as he appeared, a rich Russian gentleman with a pro-environment agenda. It wasn't personal; it was business.

Vlad told Cynthia he and his friends were looking to fund the right organization with the right cases. They were capable of helping out in a significant way. They were all businessmen, mostly international high tech, but all were passionate about climate change and doing what they could to put the brakes on it. He said all the right things, but it sounded too good to be true. She remembered something her mother told her when she was in high school: *If a guy promises you things you're sure he can't deliver, run away.* She'd never called him, but he had called her to "touch base" twice since Banff.

Cynthia knew she'd never been great at figuring out men, or women for that matter. Still, her antennae were quivering. Something about this guy: maybe he was *too* polite. He didn't *offer* as much as *suggest*. She just didn't know. Against her better judgment, she picked up her cell phone and clicked on his number.

After barely one ring, he said, "Cynthia." His voice crackled as if from a distance, but he sounded happy. "I'm so glad we've stayed in touch since we met in Banff. How are the Advocates? Are you still fighting the good fight?"

"We are, Vlad. We're plugging along." Cynthia decided to dispense with the pleasantries. "I think I finally have the case your organization can fund." Cynthia outlined the case to him. She swiveled back and forth in her chair while she talked about the case against Yukon and DEP. Her marathoner's legs were tightly crossed, her right foot curling around her left calf.

"This sounds excellent. This is exactly the kind of case we've been waiting for. Anything you can do to slow down or stop the permitting process in Pennsylvania would be excellent. I think, however, perhaps you are not giving yourself enough credit. I'd like to see your organization be much more vigorous and out front. I like that you want to go after the permitting process and the violations of these scoundrels at Yukon, but what about the pipelines? At least five are proposed to run across the length of the state. There are compressor stations. As you know, some of these are in people's backyards. Think of the racket, the air pollution. Then you have the LNG facilities proposed for the Ports of Philadelphia, Baltimore. That will destroy the ecosystem of the Delaware and Chesapeake." Vlad spoke like an evangelist. An evangelist with a Russian accent.

"Well, we certainly oppose all of those, but . . . baby steps. Our budget for the Bradford County case is $400,000, about half of our current annual budget. We'd need almost all of that to be able to handle the one case. You're talking about a significantly larger expenditure of time and resources. We have a small staff. I'd have to hire another half dozen lawyers and some citizen activists to make a dent in the kinds of activities you're talking about."

By now, Cynthia's head was resting in her hand, her eyes were closed, and she was stroking her eyebrows with her fingertips. Some of her fine blonde hair hung in her face. She wasn't above exaggerating the cost, since she thought it was likely that Vlad would low-ball her if he came up with any money at all.

"How much?" The accented voice said over the phone. "How much would it cost to undertake this effort? All of it, not just your one new case."

Cynthia was certain Vlad was just pulling her chain. Leading her on. She almost wished he'd invited her to St. Barts to discuss this, so she'd know he was a fraud and could hang up on the bastard. Nevertheless, she wanted to appease this man who seemed to want to do what he could to slow down and stop the industry, this madness. She hoped if she asked for more than the $250,000 Winnie had suggested, he'd either laugh at her or maybe, just maybe, give her something approaching the budget they really needed to fight this case. Now he was asking to fund the whole organization. Big time.

"I don't know. Off the top of my head, I suppose we could do the entire effort you've described on a bare-bones budget of maybe five million a year, give or take. I'm just guessing, though."

"Five million dollars? That's less than half a million a month." Vlad's voice was loud, and Cynthia thought she detected a laugh in his voice.

Neither spoke for a moment.

Finally, in a small voice, Cynthia said, "We can probably do it for less; I'd need to figure out a budget, but—"

"Bare bones doesn't make any sense." Vlad talked over her. "I want to do this the right way. How about thirteen million? I'll get you thirteen million dollars." The man paused, then before she could respond said, "A million in seed money to get you up and running, then a million a month. The first two million will come in the next week. You'll have the checks overnighted or wired in the next several days. That will get you started. Then I'll send you one million dollars a month for the next eleven months. The money will come from at least ten different people, all good people, my friends and business associates, all with the same goal, but not from any single source." He waited for a response.

Cynthia looked at her phone and shook her head. "Vlad, I want to be sure I understood what you said. Did you say you're going to contribute thirteen million dollars? To the Advocates?"

"Yes, *this* year. My name will not be on any of the checks. The checks will all come from my friends and close business associates. Sometime in the next ten months we'll reevaluate and discuss our contributions for next year."

"I'm not sure we're up to this. We've been a small organization for so long."

"I trust you to do the right thing. Don't worry. I'll be behind the scenes pushing things along. Success is assured."

"I'm . . . at a loss. I can't believe what you're saying. Who are these people, your friends? I mean, their generosity is unbelievable. I need to, *want* to, thank them."

Vlad laughed. "They are people who think like us. They want to stop this filthy industry before it becomes too embedded in the economy to be stopped. These are people of substantial financial means, some high-tech, some who have family wealth and who want to do the right thing."

Rarely did tears come to Cynthia's eyes. She fought them back. "I'm overwhelmed. I want to get out a news release and have a thank-you reception for you and your friends' incredible generosity. I don't know what to say."

"That's another thing. Don't say anything. I don't want a press release, and I don't want anything public. Just hire the staff and move into the office space you need. Whatever filings you are required to do with the authorities, you should do them. I don't want you answering any questions from the press or acknowledging this gift. Say what you must and no more. Just make it seem like business as usual."

"But Vlad, people will notice. I mean, we're a small organization with a limited budget and a handful of employees. If this really happens, we'll move out of a very small office into a much larger facility and hire ten, maybe a dozen, new people. Everyone will notice. How do I keep this quiet? What do I say to my board?"

"Listen, I'm a very private man. Tell only the people you absolutely need to tell. You went for the brass ring, and you grabbed it. I understand you may have to file certain disclosures with the government, and that's fine. Of course, you'll do that. To the extent you do not have to make a big deal about this, don't. The important thing is that you stop this nasty business. Are we clear?"

"Yes. Of course. What can I do to thank you?" She had to ask this question, and her heart stopped beating while she waited for the strings. The awkward solicitation. The date. The weekend on a yacht. How terrible would that be? Really? What would she, *could* she, do? What *wouldn't* she do? There had to be strings attached. Strings. She steeled herself. If she said no, would the money disappear? She held her breath, bit her lip, and clamped her eyes closed.

"Win, or at least slow the bastards down." Vladimir spoke evenly. Charmingly. Believably.

She hung up and sat at her desk for a full minute, tears streaming down her face. As she composed herself, she looked at the spreadsheet with its puny budget and deficit blinking on her laptop screen. She realized it was entirely irrelevant. The next spreadsheet would have ten times, fifteen times, as much money in it. Three times as many employees. An additional office location, Pittsburgh or Williamsport, maybe both. She closed the lid of her laptop.

Cynthia dabbed at her face with a Kleenex, then walked into Winnie's office, not trying to hide the red eyes, tears, and streaked mascara, and said, "You're not going to believe this."

12

Reunions

Mike was scrolling through dozens of emails in his inbox when he came across one from his boss, Roger Alden:

> Mike – I have a new case for you. This involves alleged contamination of a private water well caused by gas drilling up in Bradford County. It's possible that the well was contaminated before drilling began, but our geologist does not believe drilling contaminated the well. I need you to jump on this as soon as you can. See me right away.
> --R

Oh crap, Mike thought. He was overloaded as it was and didn't need more work. He picked up a legal pad and pen and walked to Roger's office. Roger was on the phone but waved him in.

When Roger hung up, he made some notes on his laptop, and Mike said, "We're getting cases from Bradford County, now? That's way outside of our region."

Roger shrugged and pushed a pile of papers sitting on the corner of his desk toward him. It was like a poker player pushing all of his chips into the middle of a game of cards. "It's Kate Gerard," he mentioned the name of the new Chief Counsel, "she wants us to be cross-trained and handle matters we don't normally get. That way, we can step into any case at a moment's notice if another region is understaffed. Since there's no Marcellus Shale or drilling in our region, we've started handling some drilling cases."

"Yeah, but I'm already overwhelmed with cases in *our* region—all of those waste, mining, water, and civil penalties cases you've assigned to me. If I get this case, I'll have to learn a whole new area of the law, oil and gas. I'm already working sixty hours a week. Plus, I'll have to work with a new inspector, someone I've never met before. Some kid right out of school or some old geezer hanging on until retirement. That will require a lot of time just to get to know the guy."

Roger looked at him, then conspicuously glanced at his watch. "Think of it as a big pay cut to reward you for all of your recent success."

Mike smiled and hoisted the pile of papers. Even though much of the work was now done via email and most reports were electronic, he was amazed at how much paper still floated around the office.

He returned to his office and dumped the new pile next to four other piles of cases on his desk. Then he scrolled through his emails and smiled when he saw one from Melissa Shelton. He recalled the young woman, a geology trainee, maybe twenty-five years old, brown hair, blue eyes, curvy, a bit *zaftig* his father would have said, pretty face, whom he'd met at a departmental training session last year. She was sweet and fun, and he was attracted to her. From her response, it seemed as though she was attracted to him too.

They huddled in a corner of the bar and talked late into the night after the others had retired. She was in a relationship at the time, so it went no further than a serious flirtation, including many lingering touches on each other's arms and friendly hugs. He recalled her saying something about a jealous boyfriend. Nevertheless, there was a long, unusually intimate farewell hug, warm and full of promise, at the end of the session.

He scrolled to the bottom of her email. Her signature block said she now was a licensed professional geologist in the Eastern Oil and Gas District. He scrolled back to the top.

Hey Mike, looks like we'll be working on this together. I received a call from Ms. Bruno-Campbell about a month ago to investigate a water well complaint in Bradford County. The woman said drilling and fracking had contaminated her water well. Yukon Oil and Gas has a drill pad about a mile away. The main drilling and activity occurred earlier this year, with no complaints.

The family now says their water has been contaminated by the drilling. I went out there and personally took the samples and investigated the complaint. Some of the parameters came back high, and methane was over the limit. Unfortunately, there was no pre-drilling testing, and in that part of Bradford County, a lot of wells have very high methane that comes from near the surface, i.e., not from fracking. The other really high parameters were E. coli and fecal coliform, but that is from cows and septic systems, not fracking. Also, I found there was no connection between the drilling and the water well. Everything else I found was either naturally occurring or background levels.

I sent a standard form letter to the Campbells advising the well was contaminated but most likely from natural causes. Ms. B-C called me a couple of days later, and let's just say she used language I prefer not to repeat in an email. One of the things she said was she was going to hire a lawyer and file an appeal from our decision.

I assumed one of our lawyers up here in Williamsport would handle any appeal, but I later learned someone out of Harrisburg would be taking the case. I asked around and found out you got the short straw. LOL. Looks like we're finally going to have to work together. ;-) LMK if you want to get together up here to look at the site or if you want to go over any background info. – Missy

Mike thought for a moment and then replied:

Missy – you heard right. All of the lawyers in OCC are being cross-trained. Even though we don't have any Marcellus Shale down here, the Chief Counsel wants us to be able to handle drilling cases anywhere in the Comm. I still have not received any notice of appeal. I'll let you know if a trip to Bradford County is warranted. If this becomes a real appeal, I'll want to tour the site.

I think I owe you lunch, anyway! Congrats on becoming a licensed PG. Mike

Missy replied almost immediately:

Hey Mike, Thanks for the PG thing; that was a lot of hard work. Now that I passed the test, I think you owe me dinner! LOL. :-) Missy

Missy- is there any chance any contamination is coming from a source on Yukon's pad other than the drilling? Maybe a spill on the pad???
Dinner it is. Next time I'm up your way

Mike- always possible. They never reported any spills, but that is always possible. Also, Yukon also has a freshwater impoundment next to the pad. It was designed and supposedly used for prep water for completions and holds >5 million gallons. It was dug out, no blasting, so I doubt it's causing any problems. Also, if it leaked, then only fresh water would leak out. When you come up here, I'll show it to you. :)
I was kidding about dinner. You really don't owe me. Missy

A moment later, Mike replied.

Are you sure it was only used for fresh water?
Also, Ms. Shelton, the pleasure of your company is requested. This is a formal invitation to take you out to dinner to celebrate your PG license. ;) Mike

That's what they tell me. Invitation accepted. Missy

Mike smiled then continued scrolling through his emails, deleting and triaging them as quickly as he could. As he scrolled through his emails, a new one popped up at the top. He opened the email from Roger.

Mike – here's the appeal we discussed this morning. I see the citizens have the Pennsylvania Advocates for the Environment representing them. They have not been involved in many (any?) drilling cases previously. I guess they are late jumping on the bandwagon. Also, their lawyer is Winnie Hedges. She was a lawyer here many years ago and left us to fight the good fight with the Advocates. We can talk about her later. I'm attaching the notice of appeal. --R

Mike clicked on the PDF attachment:

BEFORE THE
COMMONWEALTH OF PENNSYLVANIA
ENVIRONMENTAL HEARING BOARD

JARED CORNELIUS CAMPBELL	:
and	:
	:
TERESA BRUNO-CAMPBELL,	:
H/W,	
	:
APPELLANTS,	

v.	:	EHB Docket No.
	:	_____
COMMONWEALTH OF PENNSYLVANIA,	:	
	:	
DEPARTMENT OF ENVIRONMENTAL PROTECTION, APPELLEE,	:	
	:	
	:	
and	:	
	:	
	:	
YUKON OIL AND GAS CO., PERMITTEE.	:	
	:	

NOTICE OF APPEAL

NOW COME the Appellants, Jared Cornelius Campbell and Teresa Bruno-Campbell, husband and wife, by their attorneys, Pennsylvania's Advocates for the Environment and Winifred Hedges, Esq., and file the below Notice of Appeal, as follows.

SUMMARY OF NOTICE OF APPEAL. Appellants own an historic residence in Washington Township, Bradford County. Appellants' ancestor, Cornelius C. Campbell, was one of the original settlers in Washington Township in the early 19th Century. Appellants leased the natural gas drilling rights to their 700-acre farm (the "Property") to Yukon Oil and Gas Company, Permittee ("Yukon"). Late last year, Yukon drilled three horizontal natural gas wells. In addition, Yukon constructed an impoundment on the Property to hold fresh water. Several months ago, Appellants suspected their drinking water well was contaminated by Yukon's activities. Appellants contracted with Core Services to test their well water, and contamination was found. Appellants believe and therefore aver that as a result of Yukon's hydraulic fracturing ("fracking") and other related completion activities Yukon and/

or its contractors contaminated the Appellants' drinking water well.

A complaint was filed with DEP. DEP investigated the Appellants' well. In a letter sent to Appellants by the Department, the Department through its representative, Melissa Shelton, P.G., stated that Yukon's activities did not contaminate the Campbells' water well. Appellants vigorously dispute the Department's determination and at the trial of this case will prove otherwise. Since the Department's determination is a final action, this appeal follows.

***

Mike quickly read through the rest of the appeal and printed a copy. He had never litigated any cases against the Advocates or their general counsel, Winnie Hedges. He had met her on a number of occasions, seen her lecture at legal education programs, and was impressed with her knowledge and ability. She was brighter than most lawyers and had attended Vassar College and Columbia University Law School. If ever there was a lawyer who could make a point by lowering her already soft, confident voice, it was Winnie. She would be a formidable opponent.

Tall and refined, Winnie dressed like she had walked out of a Talbots catalog, or maybe the women's section of Brooks Brothers. She was a WASP through and through. With her aristocratic good looks and blonde hair, Mike's father, may he rest in peace, would have called her "a real *shikse*." This would not have been in the purely pejorative context of "don't you dare bring home a *shikse*"—something Mike had heard more than once—but in the non-ironic, mildly pejorative, purely descriptive sense. Mike didn't know, but he expected her husband likely was named Bart or Prescott. He suspected they owned a golden retriever named Fenway and had two kids, named Ainsley and Chip.

With Winnie Hedges on the other side, the case would be challenging. He heard that Winnie was scrupulously ethical and would come straight at him. There would be no knife in the back.

When the knives were drawn, she would fillet him from the front.

Mike wondered whether Yukon would be represented. It wasn't mandatory for the permittee to be represented in a case such as this. Many companies, even large companies like Yukon, would take the position that this was purely a battle between DEP and the neighbor. He always found that risky and unwise, though, since the worst that would happen to the department was its determination would be overturned. Like all other lawyers, DEP lawyers hated to lose cases. If they did lose, DEP lawyers would say it was "no big deal." In a case like this, the permittee, on the other hand, could be required to conduct an expensive cleanup and provide water. Mike didn't have to wonder very long.

A new email popped up on his monitor, this one from Jacob Berliner, his nemesis in the U.S. Dynamics case and the well-known environmental litigator at FU. Of course, no one at Finkel & Updike simply referred to the firm as FU. They wallowed in it.

Mike recalled Berliner was a graduate of Harvard College and Harvard Law School, where he served as an editor of the Law Review. He Googled around a bit and saw that Berliner had argued a handful of prominent environmental cases before the U.S. Supreme Court and dozens of cases before the federal appeals courts and federal district courts. The man was legendary.

Mike, who was just a few years separated from his Penn State and Vermont Law School degrees, wondered if he should feel inadequate. At the same time, he recalled that U.S. Dynamics ended up paying a huge penalty—$995,000. He was responsible for that achievement. It would have been larger except the governor, through his general counsel and then through Kate Gerard, told him to take the settlement so the defense contractor could avoid the ignominy of paying a full one-million-dollar fine. Whenever Mike talked about the penalty, however, he always referred to it as a "million-dollar civil penalty." He felt his success spoke volumes about his skills as a litigator.

Mike, it looks as though we're going to be in another case together. I represent Yukon Oil and Gas, and we will be handling the appeal filed by PAE. I've attached our entry of appearance form to the EHB. I'm sure that you will vigorously represent PaDEP which has made the correct decision by refusing to require my client to provide water. I expect that we will be in the case to back you up. You will be dealing largely with my senior associate Darius Moore who will be taking the lead in this case. Can we arrange a call for tomorrow? Let me know what time works for you. Looking forward to working with you again.
Best,
--Jake Berliner

Mike focused on two words:

Darius Moore.

Again.

Lovely.

Mike wasn't sure if he would rather oppose him, as he did in the U.S. Dynamics case, or be on the same side. At least if he opposed him, he knew how to deal with him. Mike sat back in his smelly old judge's chair and stared at the ceiling.

His thoughts drifted to law school in Vermont. He'd dated a woman in his first year of law school, a law student from Boston named Abby Roth. Nice girl. Sweet. Sexy. Their relationship was red hot at first, then fizzled after three months. A week later, she was with Darius Moore. Mike suspected something was going on between Darius and Abby well before the official breakup. For reasons he never fully understood, he was willing to forgive Abby, but he never forgave Darius.

About a year after graduation, Mike saw in the alumni newsletter that the two of them had married.

By then, Mike wasn't jealous of his former classmate; he was happy to be doing exactly what he always wanted to do. He was long over his relationship with Abby. He did wonder, however, how he and Darius would interact now that they were on the same side of a case. Mike tried to bring his A game to every case. He hoped his A game would be enough.

Mike thought back on his cases in his four years with DEP. In those with more than two lawyers, there always seemed to be at least one goofball among the counsel, someone who was out of step, bottom shelf, or didn't see the whole picture. As he thought about Winnie, Berliner, and Darius Moore, Mike wondered if he was the joker in this deck.

13

"Recon patrols provide timely and accurate information on the enemy and terrain and confirm the leader's plan before it is executed." U.S. Army Ranger Handbook

The man walked about a mile through the woods and crept up on the objective. He'd been well trained in the military, and he knew how to do this as stealthily as possible. He intended to stay out of sight of anyone who might be occupying the structure or passing by. When he could see the roof through the woods and just over the hill, he established his observation post, piling a few rocks on top of one another in a short arc so he wouldn't be visible from below. Mud covered his face, reducing any reflection and the possibility of standing out in the woods.

He lay down on his poncho and slowly lifted his head until he could see the entire objective. He placed a branch in front of him for additional cover and made sure he could see through the leaves, further minimizing what little there was to see of him from below.

He watched the house, two-story, brick. It had a distinctive mark carved into the chimney, CCC-1814. A BMW SUV was parked on Campbelltown Road. In front of the house was an address sign that read *1000 Campbelltown Road*. Another smaller sign below it read *Campbell Manor*. He observed a white male, roughly six to eight years old, on a bicycle in front of the house.

A patrol must not let the enemy know that it is in the objective area.

He flattened himself onto the old green poncho. He checked his watch. It was 0910 hours. He waited. He was good at waiting.

The late spring earth was full of smells, mostly pleasant, but some foul. He liked the aroma of the vegetation, the ferns, bloodroot, Solomon seal, but he despised the smell of rotting wood. It made him think of caskets, and caskets made him think of why he was here.

Hatred.

Hatred. Pure and simple. A basic human emotion. Raw.

He turned that over in his mind. It was like a glowing ember—a different appearance from each angle, but the same thing no matter how you looked at it.

Every five minutes, he pushed his head up over the rocks and surveilled through the leaves to the house. After twenty minutes, the 6-YO-WM laid down his bicycle and went inside. The bike was on the ground near the front door. At 0950, the front door to the house burst open, and two WFs, one an adult and the other a small female about eight to ten years old, and the aforementioned 6-YO-WM bolted from the house. He could hear the adult WF yelling commands at the young WM and WF. The car started, and he could hear Bruno Mars, *Just the Way You Are*, blaring loudly. The vehicle pulled away. It was 0952. He patiently waited another ten minutes.

At 1002, he made his way down the hillside, careful not to disturb the underbrush on the hillside across from the house. At the bottom of the hill, he looked back up, memorizing his return route through the ferns.

The only thing he carried was a package. Wrapped in brown paper. It was marked "Mrs. Paxton, 2000 Campbelltown Road, Campbelltown, PA." Inside was an empty box filled with newspaper. An excuse and decoy in case someone was home. *"Excuse me. Do you know where I can find Mrs. Paxton . . . ?"*

And a handgun. A Smith & Wesson. It was a 9mm and reasonably compact. Not his weapon of choice, but American and common. Concealed in the right-hand pocket of his windbreaker.

He approached the house and rang the doorbell. He kept his hand in his right pocket. Just in case.

No answer.

He waited a full minute, then rang again.

Nothing.

Quiet.

He walked around the house to the back.

On a walk-by several days earlier, he had not seen any evidence of a dog but kept his eyes open, and in his other pocket kept a baggie with some morsels of poisoned meat, just in case.

The grounds were well-maintained. Gazebo in the backyard. Fire pit. Fancy gas barbeque range on the patio. Weber. Stainless steel.

Nice.

Another bicycle. Many balls—soccer, baseball, softball—in the wet grass. Two baseball gloves sat on a fancy patio table. The rear entrance was a sliding glass door. It looked fairly solid, but could easily be breached with a rock or brick. Or a bullet. He could pick the lock in about two minutes, if needed. He made a mental note. He set the package on the patio table and continued searching the ground.

Finally, he found the large, round metal lid. About one meter wide, rusty. Its dark red paint had oxidized long ago. Just off the patio, slightly buried in the weeds.

The water well.

The objective.

Slowly he turned around and observed the surroundings. The house was in a shallow valley. It was surrounded by fields, woods, and small hills. Campbelltown Road. *Pretty.* He saw no one. Heard no vehicles. In the distance, he heard some cows mooing.

He checked and saw a hasp on the well cover, but there was no lock on it. That made his life easier, no need for a bolt cutter on his next visit. *Good.* He found a rusty metal handle on the lid and pulled. The lid moved with great groaning and screeching from the rusty hinges. He pulled it open and found the prop hidden in the weeds next to the well.

He pulled a small flashlight from his pants pocket and shined it into the hole in the ground. The well was constructed with brick, at least for the first four or five meters until he could not see down any further into the darkness. The bricks were covered with dark-green moss. It looked hand-dug. He had no idea how deep it was, but probably shallow. Fifteen to twenty meters, no more. The smell was dank. Musty. Rock and water. Plumbing and an electrical line for the pump ran up and out of the top of the well, then into the house.

He looked around and found a pebble. Huddled over the well, he dropped the stone into the hole. A moment later he heard the splash. The water probably was no more than seven or eight meters from the surface.

Good.

He knew Pennsylvania was the only state in the United States without well construction standards. He guessed the well was not brick-lined to depth. Thus, it held a relatively small volume of water. That would make his job easier.

Good.

He was still on his hands and knees inspecting the well when he heard a vehicle on Campbelltown Road. He looked up and saw the BMW flying back toward the house. Fast. *Shit.* He closed the well. He stayed low and tossed some leaves on the lid.

The car door opened even before it was fully parked. The WF, the child, left the door open. Music poured out of the car. An Adele song. *Chasing Pavements.* He hated Adele.

The WF child ran to the front door, and he heard her open it with the key.

Avoid detection by the enemy.

He hid behind a nearby bush. Low. Crouching on the ground. He pulled the Smith & Wesson from his pocket and chambered a round. Five seconds later, the sliding glass door opened. The WF ran out, coming directly toward him.

He raised the gun and aimed at the girl through the bushes. Part of him said just to aim for her leg or arm, but his training told him otherwise. Torso. Or head.

The girl ran to the edge of the patio.

Feet from him. Less than two meters.

Her eyes swept across the yard.

She looked directly at the bush, the one he was hiding behind.

She wore jeans.

Sneakers.

A powder blue T-shirt that read, *Campbelltown Pioneers Softball.*

His right arm rested on his knee. He aimed at her torso. The "o" in Campbelltown.

A bullseye over her heart.

Safety off.

Finger tightened on the trigger.

Controlled his breathing.

Ready.

Then she turned away.

The girl hurried to the table and picked up the baseball gloves. Then she saw the decoy package and picked it up. The girl read the label.

Crap.

He leveled the S & W again and prepared to shoot the girl in the back. He took a deep breath and began slowly to let it out.

Suddenly, the WF in the BMW leaned on the horn. She allowed it to blast for a long five seconds. The noise pierced the pastoral surroundings.

The girl looked up. "Found 'em!" She shouted and tossed the package onto the table.

Clutching the baseball gloves, the girl ran back into the house, slammed the sliding door and threw the latch. Thirty seconds later, she was back in the car. He could hear the adult WF yelling at the girl before the car door slammed. The BMW pulled away, made a fast K-turn, accelerated up Campbelltown Road, and was out of sight.

His breathing had become rapid. He took a minute to control

it. Safety back on. S&W back in his pocket. Then he made sure his recon efforts could not be detected. He rearranged the leaves on the well lid until it looked untouched—no excess debris on the patio. There was no sign he'd been there.

He started back toward the woods, the rally point, walking fast. He'd gotten to the road when he remembered something.

The package.

Crap.

He jogged back to the patio, scooped it up, and headed back across Campbelltown Road and into the woods.

The recon element returns undetected to the Objective Rally Point.

Mission accomplished.

14

Old Friends

Mike sipped his coffee and spread out the documents Missy had sent to him. He had more documents on a split screen on his monitor. His call with Berliner and Darius Moore was set to begin in fifteen minutes. He expected this would be a get-up-to-speed kind of call. Nothing more. The phone rang. He glanced at the caller ID. It said only *Washington, DC.*

"Jacobs."

"Hey Mike, this is Darius Moore at Finkel Updike in D.C. How are you doing?"

"Fine." Mike thought for a moment about his former classmate and then his former girlfriend Abby. "How's everything in D.C.? Abby?"

"Great. Actually, we live in Virginia, and I work in D.C. Abby and I have been married for four years now. We have two kids I adore but barely see, a Porsche Cayenne to drive around the rugrats, a cabin on the bay in St. Michaels, and partnership track. That kind of thing. How about you?"

"Oh, still saving the world from your clients, still single, driving a beat-up old Jeep Cherokee these days, no entanglements. I can say, though, I'm having a good time."

Darius Moore laughed. "I can't say I'm surprised."

Mike hesitated, then asked, "What's Abby up to these days? Is she well?"

"Yes, super, actually. She worked for DOJ for a little over two years and took a break when we had our first kid. Now she's home with them, probably for another year or two, unless we decide to have some more. She knew I'd be talking with you today and asked me to say hello, so hello from Abby."

Mike thought briefly about the curly-haired woman from Boston he met on the first day of law school. She wore jeans and some kind of peasant top, a pretty face. He was . . . *smitten* came to mind. She was sweet and smart and kind. For the next two months, their lives were a steady stream of law school classes, study, sex, repeat, not necessarily in that order. Then the relationship fell apart. In a matter of weeks, she ended it, and one week after that, she was with Darius Moore. Mike had a special spot in his heart for Abby and, for reasons he couldn't explain, he was never angry with her.

Darius Moore was another story. He actually hated the guy through most of law school. Every time he saw him with her. He never thought of himself as jealous, but he was. Also, he suspected that everyone in his class knew that Abby had dumped Mike for Darius Moore. This annoyed and embarrassed him.

Darius Moore was a legal genius. Arrogant and haughty, for sure, but mostly obnoxious. Mike hoped Darius had changed, but during the trial they fought a few months earlier, Mike could see that he hadn't. Maybe he was even worse. He shook his head.

"Well, I'm sure there will be an opportunity for a beer, and we can catch up then," Darius Moore said. "I guess you saw I'm in this case, the Yukon fracking case. Jake Berliner is the partner in charge, but for the most part, I'll be taking the lead."

"FU lets *associates* take the lead? I'm shocked." Mike laughed. He just couldn't help himself.

"*Senior* associate, thank you very much. I'm just a year or two away from a partnership. Anyway, I wanted to reach out to you prior to our call with Jake. Have you thought about discovery?"

"Yeah, I was thinking relatively minimal discovery, interrogatories to the Campbells, expert interrogatories, depositions of Mr. and Mrs. Campbell, that's about it. The burden is on them, and my geologist will be a solid witness. My whole team is good."

"What about their experts? Have you even *thought* about taking depositions of their experts?" Darius Moore asked.

There. There he was. The Darius Moore he despised.

Supercilious asshole.

The same shmuck he knew and hated in law school.

"Yes and no. I guess you may not recall, but the board's rules do not allow us to take the depositions of experts without an agreement between the parties. I see no reason to allow a deposition of my experts, so that will preclude deposition of the Campbells' experts."

"Well gee, Mike, your plan seems a little sloppy. I've taken depositions of experts all around the country—California, Colorado, New York, Texas. I don't know how you can do a case like this without expert deps."

"We can discuss that. There's no rush. We're going to have at least six months to conduct discovery. Anything else?"

"Interrogatories. Are you planning on filing any, or is that something else you avoid in Pennsylvania?"

"Very funny." *Asshole.* "Yes, I have a fairly standard set of interrogatories. I'll adapt them to this case, add what I need to customize them for this appeal. Also, I have a standard set of expert interrogatories, the board has seen them before, so I know they're not going to sustain any objection to them. We generally exchange expert reports a few weeks before the trial. I can send my reports down to you before I send them to the appellants' counsel so you can have a preview. Also, later this week, I'll send you my standard set of EHB interrogatories. Feel free to borrow from them."

"No need. I have plenty of interrogatories in the can here. I'll draft mine on my own."

"Just keep in mind, the board gets annoyed if you submit too many questions. We don't have a specific limitation on the number of interrogatories, but if you ask too many questions, you definitely will incur the wrath of the judge," Mike said.

"Okay, so how many?"

"The federal district court here limits you to twenty-five interrogatories, and the board follows that as a rule of thumb. I'd keep it under thirty."

"Thirty? Really? Okay."

"That includes subparts."

"What about your client?" Darius Moore asked. "Can we have access to your records? I mean, we're on the same side and all."

"Same side? Right. Departmental policy would require you to do a file review like anyone else, or file a request for production of documents. I don't see any reason to be that formal, so I'm happy to make our non-privileged documents available to you. We can avoid the formalities."

"Uh-huh. And depositions?"

"Depositions? You don't want to take depositions of my clients, do you? I mean, if you want to meet my clients and interview them, I can make them available. Why tip your hand to the other side in a deposition?"

"Well, we have to get everyone on the record, you know? We don't want any surprises at the trial, no one changing their story."

"Actually, I don't know. My clients will speak truthfully with you when we meet. They're not going to change any stories. Getting them on the record only helps the Campbells. Honestly, I can't think of any cases when the permittee's and department's interests were aligned and where the permittee deposed the department's witnesses. What you're suggesting is unnecessarily aggressive. Let me put it this way: It's a bad idea."

"Um-hmm."

"Seriously. I'm happy to make my clients available for a meeting, no court reporter, no lawyers from the Campbells," Mike said. "We do this all the time. That's much safer."

"Safer? Is that how you play your cases?"

"When I'm expecting to win? Yes."

A reminder popped up on Mike's monitor. "Looks like we have to dial into the call. If Mr. Berliner is there, I can just hang on, and you can go get him. Whatever works."

Darius Moore laughed. "Actually, he's in Abu Dhabi. I think they're twelve hours ahead of us."

"Okay, unless you're also in Abu Dhabi, it looks like we have to dial in."

"I haven't been there in three months, so let's sign off and dial back in."

"Well, I look forward to working with you again," Mike said, gritting his teeth.

"Of course," Darius Moore replied.

15

Boys Will be Boys

They ended the call, and Mike made a quick pit stop to the men's room. He came back and dialed in a minute late. He could hear Darius Moore and Berliner, laughing.

"Good morning, this is Mike Jacobs."

"Mike, Jake Berliner here. I guess Darius told you I'm meeting with some clients here in the Gulf States."

"Darius was his usual careful self and only told me you're out of the country." Mike threw Darius a bone since his erstwhile adversary had, in fact, told him, even bragged, about Abu Dhabi. He didn't pause to wonder why he did that for him. He just did it.

"Well then, let's get right down to business. I have several more calls to make yet, and it's already after 11 p.m. local time. What are your thoughts about this case?"

"Sure. I plan to defend the department's determination. Our geologist says there's no connection between the drilling and the Campbells' water well, and we'll defend that decision. Also, if the Campbells try to attack the integrity of the department's actions, I'll certainly challenge that."

"So far, that sounds reasonable," Berliner said.

"From our perspective, it's a fairly straightforward case," said Mike. "For witnesses, I plan to call my geologist, the oil and gas inspector, and one expert witness. I want to keep my case sharp and to the point. If I can do it, I'll have my witnesses on and off the stand in one day. Keep in mind, the burden of proof is on the Campbells."

"I hear you," Berliner said, "and we largely agree. You know, we've handled literally dozens of water contamination cases like this around the country for Yukon and other energy companies. We've developed a very successful game plan, and I'd like to stick with it. Darius, why don't you tell your fellow Vermonter what we'd like to do."

"Yeah, Mike. We want to take extensive discovery. I want to show that the Campbells were drinking crappy well water long before there was any drilling. I plan to take depositions of both Mr. and Mrs. Campbell, maybe their kids if the court—board—will allow it, and any others who might use their water. Also, some neighbors and friends, since they would know that the water in the area has been crappy for a long time."

"Well, that will be time-consuming and expensive for all of us."

"I hope so," said Darius Moore. "The Campbells should know this is a blood sport."

"A blood sport," Mike repeated.

"Yeah. Also, as you *probably* know, the board's rules do not allow depositions of experts, unless all sides agree, but we don't see how you can have a case like this without expert depositions. We'll try to get an agreement so we can take the depositions of the Campbells' experts."

Mike seethed. He had just reminded Darius Moore of this not twenty minutes ago. Now he regretted covering for him for his lapse about his partner's whereabouts. He rubbed his eyes. "Actually, we do this kind of thing all the time. I mean, we go into many cases with no depositions of experts, and we're quite successful using their expert report for cross-examination."

"Okay, that seems a little sloppy. When we talked earlier, you said you'd allow us to interview your witnesses. We appreciate that. I'd like you to consider whether we can take their depositions too."

"Like I said, I don't see any advantage in doing that. Frankly, whatever small advantage it is you think you're going to gain, you're going to lose something because the Campbells will learn more about our case. Maybe something they might not have learned otherwise. If you *really* want to piss me off, you can send me a notice to take my clients' depositions."

"Yeah, nothing personal, Mike, but aren't the Campbells going to take the depositions of your clients anyway? Has that even occurred to you?" Darius Moore said.

"Of course, it's occurred to me, Darius. You may be surprised to learn that I even thought this through. We don't know how much money they have, and they may decide against taking extensive deps. Also, even if they take deps, they may not take deps of all of my clients or could ask the wrong questions. Why help them out? Frankly, you've come up with exactly the wrong idea."

"Boys, boys. Litigators will be litigators." Berliner laughed like a father separating two rambunctious five-year-olds engaged in a fistfight. "Let's all take a deep breath and think this through. There's no need to rush. I'll be back in the states in two days. How about if Darius and I come up to Harrisburg and meet with you, Mike? We can discuss the case, opposing counsel, and all that stuff. We'll take you out to a nice dinner afterward."

"Well, Jake, I'm happy to meet. The dinner part is out of the question, though. The governor wouldn't appreciate it if lawyers for a big oil and gas company took one of his lawyers out to dinner."

Berliner laughed heartily. "That's funny. He didn't seem to mind when I took him to The Palm when he was in D.C. last month. I get it, though. We can find something more on your budget when we break bread."

"One final thing," said Mike. "My geologist and I have been wondering if there was ever a leak from the on-site freshwater impoundment. If there was, that may have had an impact on groundwater. Also, was it always used for fresh water? Was it ever used for produced water?"

Neither Berliner nor Darius Moore responded. After a long moment, Berliner said, "I've never heard anything about any leaks. Darius?"

"I know nothing about this."

When the call was over, Mike sat at his desk chewing on the peanut butter and jelly sandwich he'd made for his lunch. This case was quickly becoming a huge pain in the ass, and it had barely begun. It was bad enough when you ended up fighting with opposing counsel, but he was fighting with the lawyers who supposedly were on his side.

Less than half an hour after the call ended, an email popped up. It was from Darius Moore. Mike clicked on it and saw he was serving the department and the Campbells with interrogatories, a request for a site visit of the Campbell home, and deposition notices of the department's geologist, inspector, district oil and gas manager, and regional director. He clicked open the interrogatories and flipped to the last page. There were ninety-nine interrogatories, *not* including subparts. He had also attached copies of his discovery for the Campbells. This included 150 interrogatories each, deposition notices for the Campbells and their children, and document requests.

Mike knew from experience that it must have taken a couple of days to craft all of these discovery requests. Mike had no doubts Darius Moore had these in hand when he and Mike had their conversations less than an hour earlier.

Mike shook his head. *Perfect. Sonofabitch. Asshole.*

16

We must always take sides. (Elie Wiesel)

A day later, Mike looked at an email inviting a call, then dialed the number displayed on the screen. Two rings later, a woman answered. "Hello, this is Winnie Hedges."

"This is Mike Jacobs. I hope you remember me."

"Of course. The last time I saw you was at that concert at the Forum. You were with a young woman, pretty; I think her name was Nicky. The two of you were a cute couple. Are you still together?"

Mike paused. A flood of memories washed over him. "You have a great memory. Nicky and I have always just been friends. She lives in Philly now. With her wife. You were with your husband, Bart . . . Prescott . . ."

"John."

"Right," Mike said, feeling foolish.

"Well, it's good to catch up, Mike, but I wanted to talk. I see you're representing the department in the Campbell appeal. I wanted to see if we could cut through some of the discovery BS and save our clients some time and money."

"Did you happen to see the email from Yukon's counsel at Finkel & Updike?" Mike said.

"FU?" Mike could hear the smile in her voice.

"Exactly."

"Yes. I got a lovely missive from our colleagues at FU. I think both of my clients and their children received 150 interrogatories *each* and have been scheduled for a week of depositions in some dungeon on K Street in D.C. Also, everyone in Washington Township has been subpoenaed."

"If it makes you feel any better, my clients received almost as many interrogatories, and everyone up to the governor has been noticed for a deposition. The secretary's furious, and I have to get out a motion for a protective order. I hope you don't think I had anything to do with Yukon's eagerness for this case."

"I know you well enough, Mike. You have a good reputation. I also know the department and Yukon are on the same side in this case. I filed the appeal, and Yukon can have anyone they want representing them, even, or especially, FU."

"So, are you planning on doing anything about Yukon's discovery?" Mike asked.

"You know I can't share that with you. After all, you do represent the evil Department of *Economic* Protection that refused to protect my clients' water supply. Plus, you'll probably call Darius and Jacob at FU right after this call and tell them whatever I tell you. But don't be surprised if you see a motion for a protective order and objections in the next day or two."

"Actually, I'd be surprised if you didn't file for a protective order. Between you and me, our friends at FU went a little overboard."

"My geologist has gone over both your geologist's letter as well as the underlying data," Winnie said. "We think the department was just flat wrong in refusing to protect the Campbells' water supply. I'd like to see the department correct its mistake and issue a new letter in which you'll require Yukon to provide water to my clients. Also, my geologist says there's a direct connection between Yukon's Marcellus well and my clients' water well. The presence of methane proves Yukon is contaminating the aquifer, and I hope the department can stop it."

"I'll see if there's anything we can do for your clients. I doubt it since we've already taken a pretty firm position, and now we're locked in litigation. Also, FU. I would've been surprised if you hadn't asked, though."

"You mean the law firm representing Yukon, I assume."

"Exactly," Mike said, laughing.

There was a pause in the conversation. Finally, Winnie said, "Mike, I also wanted to give you a heads-up. I have nothing to do with the political or activist side of things at the Advocates. I'm the *advocate* at Pennsylvania Advocates for the Environment. All I focus on is the legal side of things."

"Okay, now you're scaring me," Mike laughed. "Are you going to send a letter to the governor asking that I be fired? If he does fire me, I'll be sending you a resume. I heard you guys got a grant or something and recently expanded. A lot."

They both laughed. Her laughter was low and breathy, the kind of sexy laugh that Mike imagined hearing from Marilyn Monroe or Scarlett Johansson. He tried to picture Winnie and Googled until he found her photo on LinkedIn. She was fifteen years older than he was. In the picture, she looked perfectly proper and professional, a dress with a modest neckline, a blazer, and her blonde hair pulled back in a ponytail. Still, she had just the slightest hint of a Mona Lisa smile.

"Nothing that drastic yet," Winnie said, still laughing. "I understand there may be a protest on Monday afternoon in front of the DEP office building on Market Street. A busload of people from Bradford County and their friends."

"Will this include papier-mâché heads? Are you inviting any Antifa or Guy Fawkes types?" Mike asked.

"Well, the ones I've heard about will be a bunch of moms and dads and children from Bradford County. Grandmas and grandpas. Handmade signs and probably some bottles of contaminated drinking water they will offer you DEP folks the opportunity to drink. That kind of thing."

"This will be when? I'm sure the secretary will want to have some cookies and lemonade ready for them."

"Monday at noon. That way all of your buddies at DEP will see them and can think about what these folks are enduring when they go out to lunch. Also, they'll be sure to make the evening news. Like I said, I have nothing to do with this, but I didn't want you to be blindsided."

"I never had any doubts. FYI, I'll have to pass this news up the chain of command. I'm sure the Capitol Police will want to know. I don't know anything about permits, but be sure to have your people check into that."

"We already got them, but thanks."

"So did I hear right?" Mike said. "Did the Advocates just have a major expansion?"

"Yes. Some grants and gifts came in all at once, and we decided it was time to expand."

"A new office?"

"Offices. We moved to a better place on State Street facing the Capitol, and new, small, offices in Pittsburgh and Williamsport. Nothing extravagant."

"More lawyers?"

"We're working on that."

When the call was over, Mike strolled into Roger's office. Roger was on the phone and he pointed to his guest chair. Mike had been friends with Roger since he began at DEP. Roger was twenty-five years older than Mike and a mentor par excellence. He took a seat and scrolled through emails on his phone while Roger finished up.

As soon as Roger hung up, Mike said, "Hey Roger. You know that lovely fracking case you gave me? The one with the sweet guys from FU who supposedly are on our side? I just spoke with Winnie Hedges—who is not on our side—and she told me there will be a protest by the appellants and their anti-fracker friends on Monday in front of the DEP building. She wanted to give us a heads-up."

"Winnie told you there would be a protest? I'm not surprised. She's a straight shooter. You know she's on the legal side over at the Advocates. I'm sure she'd have nothing to do with any protest. She's a great lawyer . . . very sharp . . . a lovely woman . . . sweet girl . . ."

Roger's voice trailed off for a moment, and Mike noticed the faraway look in his eyes and the hesitation in his voice. Mike thought, *Winnie would have been a new lawyer, about twenty-five years old when she started at DEP. Roger would have been in his early thirties and a seasoned veteran in the office. Both were still single back then. I wonder . . .*

Winnie was a Bryn Mawr girl, Episcopalian, Baldwin School, Vassar, old family money, a second home in Bar Harbor. Roger was from the tough side of Norristown, not afraid to mix it up then or now, Jewish, a public-school kid whose father owned a furniture store. Roger and Winnie were really different kinds of people, but who knows? Maybe a *When Harry Met Sally* kind of thing, without the comedy. Maybe a tragedy.

Did the two of them have a thing? It was possible. Maybe more than that. This would have been a good ten or fifteen years before Mike arrived in the office. He made a mental note to dig around with Sandy, his secretary, who would have been around back then and knew all the dirt on everyone in the office.

"Roger?" Mike said softly. "So . . ."

"Send me an email with the details, and I'll forward it to the chief counsel and the Capitol Police. I'm assuming this is going to be a peaceful assembly? At least as far as Winnie knows?"

"That's what she said. Moms and dads, children, effigies of me burning in hell, that kind of thing."

"Got it. The usual." Roger smiled at him. "Hey, look, bud, can you close that?" Roger pointed at the door.

Mike smiled. "Are you going to fire me?"

Roger shook his head. "This is just a heads-up. You know that it's budget season at the Capitol?"

"Oh yes. When the legislators stay up late a few nights a year and then brag to their constituents about how hard they work? Do they still have those old Army cots they roll out in the gym so the TV news can report how tough it is to be a state senator, even though they all have fancy apartments right across Third Street?"

"Seriously, Mike, Kate had me in her office the other day." He was referring to the new chief counsel. "She's received word from the governor's general counsel that she's going to have to cut five positions statewide, five lawyers, if the budget goes south. She doesn't want to do it and she's pushing back, but I've heard they told her to make a list. Honestly, she's looking to cull the weakest ones in the pack. Underperformers. Chronic lazy asses.

Lawyers who have lost important cases, especially ones that will embarrass the governor."

"And you're sharing this because . . ."

"Well, you're not an underperformer or lazy. But all of these cases in the Marcellus have a lot of media attention. They end up on social media, TV, and newspapers, and people are interested. When we go all the way to a trial, the governor is expecting positive results."

Mike and Roger looked at each other for several seconds. Finally, Mike said, "I get it. I have to win, or I may end up on Kate's list. Trust me; I want to win. This case isn't going to be helped by our friends at FU. It's clear they have testosterone poisoning and will charge into the cannon fire even if that's entirely the wrong thing to do. I just hope they don't screw this up for us. For *me*."

"Me too." Roger was no longer smiling.

17

Unless required by the mission, the unit avoids enemy contact. The leader's plan must address actions on chance contact at each phase of the patrol mission. U.S. Army Ranger Handbook

The man observed the WF with her two young children from the observation post in the woods overlooking the house. They entered the BMW and drove away at 0955 hours. He'd learned from his previous experience, and this time he waited a full half-hour after the car drove off. He saw no movement during that time and finally decided it was safe to approach without coming into contact with any hostiles. He'd watched the objective for days and knew the WF would not return with the children until sometime after 1300 hours. They'd all be carrying cups from Starbucks.

He picked up the two plastic containers he'd brought with him. One was bright yellow, *Prestone Concentrate Antifreeze/ Coolant*. Ethylene glycol. He'd rejected the more popular *Prestone 50/50 Prediluted Antifreeze/Coolant* since it was, well, diluted. Why lug around a bottle that was half water? The jug was the familiar yellow and black color, one gallon, and weighed about ten pounds. The cost was $10.87.

The other container was liquid bleach. He could have bought the Clorox, but it was all the same stuff. Sodium hypochlorite. The jug looked like a Clorox container, not that it mattered, and was 121 fluid ounces, not quite a gallon but close enough. This also weighed about ten pounds. The cost was $2.67.

A few days earlier, he'd gone into the 24-hour Walmart late at night when he knew he could get in and out quickly. He wore his hat down low and wore his dark green windbreaker and sunglasses. He knew there were cameras but figured the surgical mission could be done fast enough. He kept his head down the whole time to avoid detection and any direct eye contact.

The only thing that surprised him at the Walmart was the large number of men shopping at 0300 hours. Texas, Okie, Arkie accents. Then it occurred to him: These were workers coming off shift at the drill rigs. Maybe he knew some of them. He got out and away from the parking lot as fast as he could. His total cost, with tax, was $14.35. That was the out-of-pocket cost to do what he planned to do. Less than a steak dinner at the local Outback Steakhouse. He paid cash.

He hefted the two jugs and was glad the surprising weight was evenly balanced in his hands as he slipped down the steep trail from the observation post. After he crossed Campbelltown Road, as before, he looked back to make sure he hadn't created a disturbance in the lush green foliage on the hillside at the edge of the woods.

He stashed the jugs on the side of the road under a bush so he could conduct a quick recon of the backyard. This check would take no more than two minutes since he already knew the layout and wasn't planning to open the well cover until he was ready to execute the final action. Just a quick surveillance to make sure there were no surprises.

He rechecked his shoulder holster. The Smith & Wesson 9mm was where it should be, under the green windbreaker. He wore a shoulder rig since he knew his hands would be holding the jugs. If he needed the gun, he didn't want to risk fumbling with the containers to pull it out from his pocket or belt. From years of practice, he knew he could draw the gun and fire it in under two seconds. At close range, he wouldn't even have to worry about aiming. Just point and shoot.

He approached the house carefully. It was quiet. Only one car was ever parked in front of the house during the several times he'd surveilled it. Other than the WF, he hadn't seen any adults, and he assumed that she was single or her partner wasn't around during the week. He crept up to the sliding glass door in the back and looked in. Dark. No one was home.

Good.

He looked around the yard. An assortment of balls and sports equipment was scattered on the lawn and patio but nothing seemed out of place. He turned and looked for the cover to the well. It was as before. Undisturbed.

Good.

He bent over to make sure it was still unlocked. It was.

Check. All set.

Then something hit his back. Not hard, but enough to make him clench his balls and anus. He froze. The hair on his neck stood at attention, and his senses went on high alert. He held his breath so he could hear what was behind him. He began to plan his next move. All of this occurred in a fraction of a second.

"Hey, mister."

The voice. High-pitched. A woman? A child?

He stood slowly, raising his left hand into the air, his right reached for the gun in his shoulder holster.

"Okay. I'm going to stand up and turn around slowly. Take it easy, lady." He kept his breath even.

He turned but didn't see anyone. He put his hand on the grip and eased off the safety.

"You a cop, mister?"

He scanned the patio and the yard beyond. Then he saw him, partially hidden behind the shrubs, the 6-YO-WM, his hand in a baseball glove. He wore a dark blue New York Yankees T-shirt, jeans, and sneakers. The kid had longish hair and a trusting smile.

Crap. A problem.

"Why do you think I'm a cop?" He lowered his left hand and slipped the gun from the holster. He tried to hide it under the windbreaker.

"'Cause you have a gun. I saw it when you leaned over."

He hesitated to answer.

"You want to play catch?" the kid said.

"What . . . what are you doing home? I thought you had softball practice today."

"Tee-ball. I play tee-ball. My sister plays softball. Anyway, I want to quit. I like soccer."

"Then who was it I saw getting into your . . . mom's car?"

"Isabella, she's my sister, and her friend. Her friend's name is Emma. She slept over. My sister's a brat. That's what Mom calls her sometimes. Emma's nice though. They were up real late. That's okay because they made hot chocolate and gave me some so I'd be quiet. I told my mom I had a stomachache this morning, and she let me stay home and play video games. I want to play *Fortnite* or *Call of Duty 4*, but my mom and dad won't let me. They make me play lame games for kids because I'm six years old, but some of them are good. I play *Super Mario* and *Rocket League*. Do you play video games? Which ones do you play? Do you have kids? You want to play catch? I threw the ball to you before. It rolled over there."

Crap, I should take care of the kid. Do it. Now.

He pulled the gun out of his windbreaker.

"*Cool.* You *are* a cop. I knew it. Can I see your gun? Mom says we can't get a gun, even though Dad wants one. I heard him talking with Mom. He wants a nine liter or something like that because we stay in the country in the summer. I think it's like the size of a bottle of Coke, you know, a liter, only nine of them or something. I don't really know what that means because we're not allowed to talk about it. Is your gun a nine liter? I know my dad has a shotgun in the house. It was Grampa's shotgun. He keeps it locked up in the closet. Mom says only *law enforcement* should have guns. She calls cops *law enforcement*. Are you law enforcement?"

He pointed the gun at the kid.

"My name is Lucas. My dad always says Lucas *Campbell*, but Mom says Lucas *Bruno*-Campbell. What's yours?"

He allowed his finger to rest on the trigger. A little more pressure, a twitch, and the problem would be gone.

"Do you have a badge? I'd like to see your badge. Is it like a sheriff's badge on video? Is it silver or gold? You seem nice. You're quiet. Is everyone in law enforcement quiet like you?"

The man eased up the pressure on the trigger.

"Look, kid . . ."

"Lucas. What's your name?"

He paused. "Mister . . . Smith."

"*Mister*? That's a funny name for law enforcement."

"Did I say mister? It's *Secret Agent* Smith."

Crap, crap, crap. What the hell am I doing talking to the kid? And what is this Secret Agent Smith *bullshit? Really? Take the shot. Take the shot . . .*

"Cool. That's cool." Lucas pointed to Smith's right hand.

"What?"

"Your tattoo. On your wrist. A red *A* with a knife going through it."

The man pulled down the sleeve of his windbreaker. "That's not a knife, it's a sword."

"My mom says I can't get a tattoo. Now or ever."

"Look, kid . . ."

"Lucas."

"Lucas. Look, I don't have time to talk with you right now . . ."

Take the shot, asshole. Shoot the little bastard . . .

"That's okay. My dad never has time to talk either. He works all the time. Sometimes I hear my mom cry after she thinks we're asleep. He only comes home on weekends. He works in the city, *New York* City. He comes home late on Friday and drinks wine with Mom, and then he's too tired to talk. He sleeps late on Saturday, and we have to be quiet or play outside. Once I went into my mom and dad's room really early on Saturday morning, and they weren't wearing any pajamas or anything else. I told Isabella and she said they were *butt naked*. Isn't that funny? Mom told me not to talk about that with anyone, and now they lock their door when they go to sleep. I always wear pajamas to bed. Do you wear pajamas? I don't see my dad very much when we stay here in the country. You seem like a nice man . . ."

Oh Christ. What the hell?

"Secret Agent Smith" shook his head and eased the safety back on. Then he holstered the gun.

"Kid . . . Lucas. I need you to do me a favor. Go to the sliding glass door and stand there facing the house. Count to one-hundred-Mississippi. You know how to do that? Can you promise me you'll do it? It's really important. I mean, life-or-death important. It's like a special assignment from the FBI. Okay?"

"Cool! Hide and seek. Sure."

"Also, I need you to keep a secret. You can't tell your mom or dad I was here. Okay? That's really important too. Do you promise?"

"Will you come back? I like talking to you."

"Depends, Lucas. Depends on if you listen to me. Look, just do what I say and look at the door. Can you do it? Count to one-hundred-Mississippi. Don't look for me or tell anyone. Promise?"

"Okay, I promise." Lucas beamed a broad smile at him.

Lucas turned and covered his eyes with his hands, "One-Mississippi, two-Mississippi . . ."

"Secret Agent Smith" stood directly behind Lucas reconsidering what he'd just told him. Now there was a witness. *A witness.* The kid could describe him. Maybe not perfectly, but well enough. *White, male, short brown hair, tattoo . . .* He was a chatterbox, too. *No.* He had to prevent that. He put his hand back inside his windbreaker and withdrew the Smith & Wesson. He eased off the safety. Double tap to the back of the head. Top of the occipital bone. The 9mm round would take care of business. The kid—Lucas—wouldn't feel a thing. Pretty humane, really. It would be over in a split second . . . for Lucas. Wouldn't be the first time. *Those kids. The war. Afghanistan. "A war crime," the Colonel said. "Don't worry; we're sweeping this under the rug . . . Fog of war . . . Just following orders. Forget it ever happened."* A long time ago. Like it was five minutes ago. Of course, *he'd* have to live with this forever. He never forgot about it.

"Five Mississippi . . ."

He aimed, wanting to get the shot right.

For the kid's sake.

For Lucas.

He noticed his reflection in the glass door. He saw Lucas, cute kid really, not even four feet tall, covering his eyes with his little hands, counting, and a big man with a gun standing behind him, pointing the damn thing down at his head. One twitch away from ending the kid's life. Those kids. In the war. *Big man. Big asshole.* The image was hideous. Loathsome. Monstrous. It burned its way into his mind.

"Seven Mississippi . . ."

Crap.

He holstered the gun and took off as fast as his feet could carry him. He grabbed the containers at the side of the road and ran into the woods. He made it into the trees in less time than it would take Lucas to count to twenty-Mississippi.

Lucas had lied. He stopped counting at eleven-Mississippi and watched the man run into the woods.

18

Geology on a local scale is random and unpredictable.
(William Stone)

Anthony Fowler was on every "keep this guy happy" list at Yukon. A West Philly kid, he attended Overbrook High School, like Wilt Chamberlain and Will Smith. He obtained a bachelor's degree in geology from Penn State, with highest honors. He was recruited out of his Ph.D. program in geochemistry at the University of Texas at Austin. Anthony's original plan had been to get a Ph.D. and teach. Yukon made him the proverbial offer he couldn't refuse, and he detoured to corporate life and a salary with stock options and annual bonuses that were multiples of what a full professor could hope to make. It didn't hurt that he was one of a handful of African-American geologists. He was light-brown, tall, and powerfully built. He'd been a running back in high school but ignored several offers of college football scholarships to focus on his studies.

Anthony quickly moved up the ranks in a company that depended largely upon the capabilities of a small group of priests known as geologists. Yukon employed all kinds of geologists; the lowest-level ones sat in office trailers at drill pads behind ultra-high-speed, high-gig computers and navigated the drill bit through the narrow shale seams miles underground while the bit ventured out thousands of feet from the vertical borehole. At the top of the heap were the high priests, the petroleum geologists. They were the Indiana Joneses of the profession who could spend months at a time exploring for new unconventional formations and trying to determine the geographic extent of known formations.

Anthony was an environmental geologist, the company's most highly trusted troubleshooter. He was called upon as Yukon developed new facilities, when they drilled known formations and when they found environmental problems involving geologic issues. As a result, Anthony was constantly on the road and was a double-platinum member of United Airlines' Frequent Flyer club who couldn't recall the last time he'd traveled in coach. All he had to do was enter his membership number and the airline happily assigned him his preferred seat, 1A.

The closest he could fly to the Campbell pad was the Wilkes-Barre/Scranton airport in Avoca, Pennsylvania. The trip from Houston took eight hours, including a layover at Dulles. Then he had another two-hour drive to Sayre. As an experienced traveler, the trip was a mere distraction and presented nothing more than a different venue in which to work on his laptop.

Anthony had never been to the Campbell pad before, but when he arrived, it looked as familiar as his backyard in Hunter's Creek, outside of Houston. He had thoroughly studied the company's permitting maps, the Google Earth maps, aerial photographs, online maps conveniently provided by the Commonwealth of Pennsylvania, a series of LIDAR aerial photographs provided by Penn State, infrared photography, wetlands delineations, and other overlays and maps. In addition, Bones had emailed him dozens of photographs. Most importantly to Anthony, he had a complete set of historical paper USGS topographic and geologic maps for the areas in which Yukon had drilling operations. These he prized most of all.

Anthony planned to meet Norby Lafleur at the guard shack and was surprised to see Norby's office, a work trailer, right there at the entrance. As he waited for Norby, Anthony did his best to talk on his cell phone, despite the crappy connection, to another geologist back in Houston. He watched a guard in a gray uniform, a woman, walking the fence line. Both the fence and the guard were something he rarely encountered at a drill pad. After nearly an hour, he first heard, then saw, Norby's pickup crunching down the gravel drive.

"Hey there, Anthony," Norby said, shaking Anthony's hand. He was chewing on a long piece of straw. "How was the trip?"

"Same as always."

Anthony noticed that Norby was overly friendly, the way some racists are around Black people. It was his way of demonstrating that deep down he wasn't a racist. Anthony knew exactly what Norby was.

"How's that boy of yours doing? Caleb, right?" For some reason, Norby had taken an interest in Anthony's oldest son, although the geologist had three other kids.

"Right, right. He's great. He's already captain of the JV football team and straight A's."

"That boy's going places, I'm telling you. You tell him I'm getting him an LSU 2020 championship football, okay?" Norby smiled broadly and patted Anthony's shoulder. Some men are under the impression that taking an interest in some child, not their own, made up for their utter inability to raise their own kids.

"Well, look, let's get down to business," Anthony said. "Tell me what's going on with the impoundment."

Norby blinked. "I thought you were here to talk about our gas wells . . . But . . . the impoundment . . . not much. She's dry now. It was built and filled last winter. We put in five-point-two million gallons of fresh water and took out four-point-seven million gallons. We sucked 'er dry. Even accounting for any water that evaporated, you don't need to be a genius to figure out that something's going on."

"How long was the water in the pit?" Anthony asked.

"Less than a week, maybe five, six days."

"What was the weather like? Hot, cold? Damp, dry? Windy, still?"

Norby thought for a moment. "Cold, damp, and still. No chance we evaporated half a million gallons of water in that short a time."

"Who was your contractor? Maybe I've worked with them."

"Only if you got a new roof on your house in Philly." Norby didn't smile and shook his head. "Blade sent out a directive to all of us ops directors telling us to hire local talent for pit construction, and let's just say these guys didn't know their asses from a hole in the wall. On paper they looked okay, but in the field, they were complete screw-ups."

"Can I talk with the guy? Maybe find out some construction details. Is he still around?"

Norby glanced around. "I think this was his one and only. I wouldn't let him build another pit for us, and he disappeared. I heard from accounts payable a couple of months ago that his mail was returned as undeliverable. I have no idea where he went."

"It was used only for fresh water?"

Norby didn't look at Anthony. "Yeah, about that. Look, I've been schooled by our lawyers. Neither one of us is a lawyer, so this discussion isn't privileged or confidential."

A chill ran down Anthony's spine. He'd heard rumors around the company that Norby had ordered the freshwater pit be used for flowback. That was not only a violation of Yukon policy but a violation of the law. Now he knew for certain.

A minute later, they sat around the small card table in Norby's work trailer with a satellite phone between them. Jesse Ewing, an attorney-advisor in Yukon's general counsel's office in Houston, was on speakerphone. Jess was about Anthony's age and had worked for Yukon since she graduated from law school at the University of Texas. She was pretty in the Texas way. Like most women in the industry, she confided in Anthony how she'd faced her share of slights and innuendos, too many unnecessary hugs and kisses, but, fortunately, nothing particularly awful. She and Anthony enjoyed a friendship in and out of work, and when she wasn't trying to get Anthony and his wife to join her church, they made a point to double date with their spouses several times a year.

"Hey Jess, I'm up here at the Campbell pad in Bradford County, P-A- with Norby." Everyone knew Norby. "We're on speaker and using the sat phone from Norby's office."

"Man," *may-en,* "you get to go to all of the awesome places." Jesse was from Waxahachie, a distant suburb of Dallas, and had a strong Texas drawl, often turning one syllable into two. "Hi there, Norby."

"Hey, Miss Jesse."

"We need to run something by you," Anthony continued. "Is this conversation protected by attorney-client privilege?"

Jesse's voice became serious. "Uh-huh. You need me to close my door?"

"Yes."

They heard a door click shut.

"Go ahead, guys."

"Jesse, we have a little head-scratcher up here," Norby said. "We have this freshwater pit. It was built by some idiots from Philly. We didn't realize it at the time, but they did a lousy job, and it leaks some. Long story short, we were behind in our drilling schedule and under a lot of pressure to release the flowback. No choice."

"Uh-huh."

Norby ran his hand through his hair. "We had a logistical issue. Them frac tanks for the produced water got stuck behind a flooded-out bridge and couldn't get up here in time to hold the flowback. I needed a place to hold flowback water for only a few days. Just until the frac tanks arrived. As soon as they were up and running, we transferred the flowback water from the pit into the tanks. Not more than three days. We power washed the pit real good after that."

The sat phone crackled. Finally, Jesse spoke. "Am I hearing you right, Norby? You put the flowback into the freshwater pit?"

"Basically."

"Uh-hu'h. By any chance, was it designed to hold produced water?"

"Not exactly."

"Uh-huh. Did you tell PaDEP?"

"No, ma'am. It was the middle of the night. I sent Blade an email but didn't hear back until the next morning after the deed was done."

"How much flowback did you get in three days?" She asked.

Anthony knew that, over time, anywhere from twenty to ninety percent of the water used for completions returned to the surface. In the first three days, he estimated that as much as fifty percent of the water returned as flowback.

"Maybe a million gallons, maybe a little more than that," Norby said, looking in the direction of the pit.

Anthony did the math in his head. If a pit with five million gallons of water leaked a half-million gallons in five days, it could have leaked fifty to one hundred thousand gallons of flowback water in three days.

"Any signs of leakage?" Anthony asked.

"You mean other than the lawsuit?" Jesse replied. There was no humor in her voice.

Norby closed his eyes and shook his head. "No, ma'am. Nothing I've seen. Assuming it leaked, it's possible that the flowback never reached the spot in the pit that was leaking. It may not have leaked at all."

"You know, I was told by Darius at FU that PaDEP has been asking about the pit. Whether it leaked. Was it used to hold flowback?" Anthony said.

"Seriously? Who?"

"Someone named Mike Jacobs, a DEP lawyer."

"Jacobs," Norby said slowly. "Great."

There was another long pause as all three of them seemed to process the information they'd just learned.

"Norby, I shouldn't have to tell you this is *flarking* lousy news, both what happened *and* the timing." Jesse's voice had lost its usual lightness and was a low growl. "I mean, here we are in the middle of litigation with the neighbors and PaDEP over a potential leak from our gas well, and I'm *just finding out* the real problem may have been with produced water leaking from our *fresh*water pit. *Dagnabit.* I mean, do you see how bad this is for us? Three, four months ago, we could have gotten out in front of this. Made a few phone calls. Paid a small fine. Now, who knows? I'm going to have to deal with the *fucking* mess you've made."

Anthony sat back. He'd known Jesse for six years. She, along with ten thousand of her nearest and dearest friends, regularly attended the New Abundant Faith Church in Houston. The worst curses in her vocabulary were *flark* and *dadgummit*. Never, not once, had she ever used the word *fuck* in his presence. Until now.

He felt bad for Norby, but he knew this was a problem of his own making. He saw no reason to get in the middle of it.

Norby looked at his LSU football sitting in its stand on the table. "Miss Jesse, you just don't understand. We were under tremendous pressure to get the completions team out of the way so we could begin drilling the 2-H well. Everything that could have gone wrong did go wrong. As I see it, a lot of people made a mistake with this. We were out of alternatives."

"Yeah, but not to do something as stupid as putting flowback into a leaky freshwater pit. I mean, really."

The work trailer got warmer by the minute as the AC seemed to have no ability to remove the heat from the small space. Both Norby and Anthony were sweating. Anthony could hear the woosh on the line from Jesse's office and suspected it was equally steamy there, too.

"Well, guys, if that's it, I need to move on," Jesse finally said, her voice flat.

"This was confidential, right?" Norby asked.

"Yeah. I'll have to report this situation to Ben Bullock, though," Jess replied. "I have no idea what he'll do with it." Anthony recognized the name of Yukon's Deputy General Counsel, the company's number-two lawyer.

"You have to report it to Bullock?" Norby asked.

"Uh-huh. Sorry, Norby, I have no choice," Jesse said.

When the call was over, Norby and Anthony stood in the heat outside the trailer. Like most who worked in the upper echelons of Yukon, Norby never showed any sign of weakness. Until now.

"Hey, look, we have to talk after I'm done walking around the pad," Anthony said. "When can we get together?"

"Well, shoot, I'm leaving right now for a meeting in Susquehanna County out in the middle of nowhere. My afternoon is shot to hell. So's my evening. Tomorrow morning would be best."

"I was supposed to fly out of Scranton tomorrow morning. I can delay that. We need to talk, and I'd rather not send you any emails."

They made arrangements to meet at the Dunkin' Donuts in Sayre at 7 a.m. With any luck, Anthony would make the afternoon flight to Dulles and be home by 1 a.m.

"Say, how about if I drive you over to the impoundment?" Norby smiled weakly. "It's on the other side of the pad."

"Actually, I think I'm going to walk. I need to look at the pad and collect a few samples. Want to join me?"

Anthony hoped Norby would say no. This time, he didn't disappoint.

19

I walk slowly, but I never walk backward. (Abraham Lincoln)

"Well, I'm not in the mood for a walk," Norby said to Anthony. "You want one of my guys to go with you? Maybe the guard? I can get Bones over here in a couple of minutes."

"That's okay. I like to go at my own pace and, generally speaking, it's never the pace anyone else wants to go. What's the deal with the fence and guard, anyway? Not something I'm used to seeing at one of our sites."

"Nothing. Kids. .22's. I'm not taking any chances." Norby nodded in the direction of the field below the pad. "You got something for snakes? My guys have seen a few rattlers just off the pad."

Anthony held up his backpack and pointed to the red polycarbonate chaps dangling from a strap. "I'm all set."

"Okay, then. You got my number; call me if you need me."

Norby loaned Anthony a satellite phone, then the men shook hands, and Norby headed to his pickup. Anthony unhooked the chaps from his backpack and strapped them to his legs. Then he took his hard hat, bruised and covered with stickers from various companies, trade associations, and university gatherings, and fitted it to his head. He stepped away from the shade of the trailer into the ninety-degree heat, slipped around the chain-link fence, and started down the steep slope through the cattails that had emerged alongside the toe of the pad.

Anthony pulled the photocopied USGS topo map from his shirt pocket. The pristine original was safely back in Houston. He'd carefully sketched an outline of the pad and the impoundment on the map and then memorized it. He could do that. As he walked, he made notes on the map.

Anthony descended the steep slope, once part of a farm field, and the ground became mushy beneath his feet. He held out the map and oriented it to his location. A channel had been cut into the corner of the pad so the rainwater could flow from the pad's surface down to the field below. A pile of rocks, called a *level spreader,* had been placed on the side of the pad to prevent the runoff from eroding the pad. He was no biologist, but he knew sensitive ferns, cutgrass, and sedges—typical wetland plants—when he saw them. He had no idea how long it took for these plants to become established, but probably longer than the pad had been there.

He wasn't sure if the wet area in which he stood was a wetland created as a result of the construction of the pad, or if the construction guys had built the pad on top of a wetland. He didn't recall seeing any permits allowing an impact in or near an existing wetland. He knew that some of the construction guys had a *drill, baby, drill* mentality, figuring it was easier to beg for forgiveness than to ask for permission. They were wrong.

If the wetland formed as a result of the construction, Yukon would have an endless argument with the U.S. Army Corps of Engineers and DEP to convince them that no wetland was present prior to construction. If the construction crew built on top of an existing wetland, litigation and civil penalties eventually would follow. He wasn't about to open that hornet's nest, so he simply jotted "wet" on his map. *He* knew what that meant, but it was sufficiently vague to keep the lawyers happy.

Having stopped to examine the foundation of the pad, the hydrology, and the plants, he arrived at the impoundment nearly an hour after he'd left Norby.

The impoundment was in the wrong place. The plans showed it about one hundred feet to the west.

It was closer to the pad, sitting on top of an outcrop of shale.

You could build it there, but it would take a lot of extra blasting, bulldozing, and grading. Even then, it was possible the unblasted remains of the shale would poke through the liner.

Or you could just move the damn pit over a few feet to where it had been planned and avoid the shale altogether.

Holding the map in front of him, the geologist looked north. He envisioned a laser beam following the outcrop of the shale through the air and noted that on the map there was a house, located on Campbelltown Road, about 2,000 feet along the axis of the shale. The house appeared to be somewhat to the east of the shale ridge, probably built over a different rock formation. Continuing to sight along the map and his mental line, he observed a noticeable indentation on the ground, a stream channel which was unusually linear, nearly straight, meaning the stream followed some weakness in the underlying geology. There were also round dips in the terrain. Sinkholes. Not big ones. But he was pretty sure that's what they were.

The map said about one mile farther north, a half-mile past the house and along the same axis, was a reservoir. He reimagined the entire USGS map and recalled it was the Campbelltown town reservoir.

Anthony walked halfway around the impoundment, studying the ground. Now he was looking for evidence of other rock outcroppings. The next rock strata was called the Horseheads Limestone, and he hoped to find the interface, the place where the shale and limestone came together. He did see bits of native limestone scattered among the bits of shale. However, the area had been heavily excavated, so little remained of the evidence on the ground. Then he saw something that surprised him. He got on his hands and knees for a closer look.

A tooth.

"What the hell?" He said out loud.

A human incisor. Anthony had taken graduate courses in human anatomy and animal anatomy, as well as several courses in paleontology. He wasn't particularly interested in looking for dinosaurs, but since fossils were a part of any geological investigation, it was useful to know the basics. He had no doubt about it. There was no way to date the tooth in the field, but it was not fossilized. He dropped it into a baggie and shoved it into his backpack with the other samples and marked the location on his map.

Anthony looked around to see if there were any more teeth or bones. He'd found a lot of things in his geologic surveys, but this was the first tooth. After a few minutes of kicking the weeds looking for evidence or other parts of the human anatomy, he found none and continued on his survey.

An old blue lawn chair was in a small heap next to a flat area within a few dozen feet of the impoundment. He picked it up and was surprised to find it in decent condition. He carefully sat, directly over the ancient, low ridge of shale that poked through the pit lining. He was pleased it could hold his weight.

He opened the geologic map and oriented it along the axis of the ridge. The next rock unit, immediately adjacent to the shale, was the Horseheads Limestone. He did a quick Google search on his phone and learned it was described as "highly fractured, cavernous, particularly in its northern reaches. Known for Horseheads Caverns near Horseheads, New York."

He stood and turned, put his nose to the map, and traced a straight mental line along the shale ridge, imagining the location of the Horseheads Limestone. It went under the house and toward the township reservoir. The reservoir stood directly over the Horseheads Limestone.

"Crap," Anthony said out loud. The water in the reservoir, which Anthony recalled had been an old quarry, was fed by the stream and springs that followed the channel caused by the Horseheads Limestone. Any contaminated water in the impoundment could seep into the fractured limestone and flow directly underground to the reservoir. Owing to its cavernous nature, the limestone would be full of cracks and fractures, even caves. This explained the sinkholes. Assuming he was right, and given the right conditions, the water could travel through the formation unusually fast, from the impoundment to the reservoir in a matter of weeks or months. This was a millisecond in geologic time.

Even if the flowback water from the one incident was somehow hung up in caves in the limestone underground, adding hundreds of thousands of gallons of fresh water to it was sure to flush it out, and the contaminated flowback water would find its way into Campbelltown's water supply.

"Crap."

Anthony got out the sat phone and dialed a number from memory.

"This is Jesse."

"Hey, it's Anthony."

"Is Norby there? I want to apologize. I let my temper get the best of me. I *never* talk that way. Never, never."

"It's just me. Don't worry about it. I'm sure he's heard worse. I'm in the middle of the Campbell pad, down by the pit."

"And . . ."

"And it's bad. They deviated from the plans and built the pit right over a shale ridge. They probably wanted to get the pit a little closer to the pad. It looks like they knocked down the ridge and tried to flatten it, but you can see that the ridge pokes up, maybe three or four inches into the lining in places. Enough to puncture it."

"That's bad."

"Actually, it's worse," Anthony said. "There's this seam of limestone, called the Horseheads Limestone. It's adjacent to the shale. According to the USGS it's highly fractured and even cavernous. It runs right from our pit, straight under the Campbell residence and then right to the Campbelltown reservoir."

"What's the chance the flowback water is hung up in a cave somewhere and not going anywhere?"

"That's possible. If no one's complaining about their water, it's even probable. The problem is they're going to spud well number four soon. Knowing Norby, he'll have his water up here way in advance of the completion of the well. If he's got five million gallons of water sitting in the impoundment for more than a day or so, it's going to flush the flowback water down the valley toward that house and the reservoir."

Jesse waited for a few moments, then said, "PaDEP said our fracking didn't contaminate the Campbells' well. The Campbells appealed PaDEP's letter, saying our drilling and fracking contaminated their well."

"Technically, I think PaDEP is right," said Anthony. "I reviewed all of the documentation about this operation, and there's nothing wrong with the boreholes, cement, or the frack jobs. If there's a problem, it's this impoundment."

Neither spoke for several seconds.

"Okay, Anthony, what's your bottom line," Jesse said. "This means what?"

"Forget about any problem with the drilling or gas well. I think they're fine. It's like there's a leaky pipeline running directly from our pit to the Campbell house and on to the reservoir."

Jesse didn't respond right away, and Anthony wondered if he'd lost his sat phone connection.

"Jess?"

"Oh fuck."

20

Disobedience is the true foundation of liberty.
The obedient must be slaves. (Henry David Thoreau)

Mike's office was in DEP's new regional building in Harrisburg's suburbs, about seven miles from the main headquarters. The regional office had moved in the past year, so he drove to downtown Harrisburg and arrived a full half-hour before the rally was set to begin. He parked his car and strolled to the DEP building on Market Street. Two Capitol Police officers, in shirtsleeves, stood on the landing chatting with each other, appearing to enjoy the springtime weather. A Capitol Police cruiser was parked nearby on Market Street. Other than the usual early-lunch crowd, there was no unusual activity.

Mike considered going in and hanging out with some of his friends in the Chief Counsel's headquarters, but the day was so nice that he opted to jog across Market Street and sit on a bench at the bus stop. He had a perfect view and would be inconspicuous during the rally.

At about 11:35, a standard yellow school bus bearing the logo of the *North-Western Bradford County School District* stopped in front of the DEP building. Mike tried to imagine the three-hour bus ride and decided the protesters deserved some credit for making the trip like that.

The bus door opened, and people started filing out. They looked like typical people from the country or a college campus—jeans, flannel shirts, T-shirts, and work boots or running shoes, both the men and the women. There were a few kids, mostly under the age of five, and a number of older people, definitely senior citizens. Almost all of them carried handmade protest signs made on cardboard and construction paper—*No Fracking Way, Frack You DEP!, Don't Frack With USA*. They all seemed to like to associate *frack* with a similarly spelled expletive.

Several of the protesters headed up the short flight of stairs to the revolving door leading into the DEP building. Mike wondered why they were heading into the building, and then it occurred to him that the school bus probably didn't have a restroom. It looked as though the Capitol Police were chatting with them and being accommodating. So far, so good, the beginning of a friendly protest rally.

Two television vans arrived almost simultaneously, one from the ABC affiliate and the other from CBS. A well-groomed man in a necktie and slacks hopped out of the ABC van, and an attractive Black woman in a black skirt, heels, and a short-sleeve cotton blouse, slid out of the passenger seat of the CBS van until her heels touched the ground. The two reporters obviously knew each other as they briefly hugged and chatted.

While they talked, the ABC reporter tossed his suit coat into the van, even though the temperature was still in the 60s, unbuttoned the top button of his shirt, and pulled down his necktie about two inches. Then he rolled up his sleeves to just below his elbows—his man-of-the-people-look. The CBS reporter opened a compact and touched up her makeup. The school bus pulled away, and Mike figured the protesters probably wanted to be sure nothing blocked the cameras' view of the rally.

As he watched the preliminaries, Mike noticed the exit to the parking garage across the alley from the DEP building. A man stood in the shadows. The sun, almost directly overhead, provided a stark contrast, so it was nearly impossible to see him in the darkness of the garage. Another man, wearing a blue business suit, walked up to the man in the garage, shook his hand, and appeared to have a conversation with him.

"Hello, Mike." Mike shaded his eyes and saw Winnie Hedges standing over him. She was with two other women. Mike stood and extended his hand.

"Hi, Winnie. Are you here to watch the festivities?"

"I was about to ask you the same," she said in a soft voice. She wore a handsome Talbots-style dress, dark blue with white polka dots.

A city bus pulled up and discharged its passengers.

"Nah, just waiting for a bus," Mike said as he pointed at the bus.

They both smiled. Winnie put her hand on one of her companion's shoulders and said, "Cynthia, I'd like you to meet Mike Jacobs. He's the DEP lawyer in the Campbell appeal I told you about. Mike, Cyn is our Executive Director."

Cynthia wore a dark green woman's business suit. She had the build of a runner, and her blonde hair was pulled into a short ponytail. Mike guesstimated she was in her early forties, but she easily could have passed for early thirties. They shook hands.

"Nice to meet you, Mike, even if you are representing the forces of darkness." Cynthia smiled.

"You must be mistaking me for those lawyers at FU. I like to believe I'm one of the *good* guys."

"For the most part," Winnie said, winking. "Also, I'd like you to meet Ursula Goodperson, our Community Organizer. This is her show."

Ursula wore jeans and a bright green Pennsylvania's Advocates for the Environment T-shirt. She carried a bullhorn. Mike guessed she was about twenty-five, slender, almost a boy's build, with straight brown hair also pulled into a ponytail. Acne across her forehead. Black Converse sneakers. Her demeanor was serious; she never smiled. She eyed him warily as they shook hands.

"So, how's this going to play out?" Mike asked.

Ursula looked at her two colleagues. "I was here earlier and worked it out with the Capitol Police. The moms and dads and their kids march around in a circle, chant, I make a speech, we get on the local news, and go home. Then repeat. We need to keep this front and center until we stop this evil business."

"I hope you're not giving up any secret recipe," Mike said, smiling.

"No, I YouTubed it. How to run a peaceful protest march." She nearly smiled.

The city bus pulled away, and Mike watched as the man in the blue business suit walked around the corner and down the alley between the garage and the DEP building. The moms and dads slowly gathered in front on the sidewalk. One of the police officers had come down from the landing and motioned with his arms. It appeared as though he was advising them on where they could stand and march.

Ursula made eye contact with the other women then pointed to her skinny wrist where a watch should be. Cynthia and Winnie nodded.

"We're going across the street to join the marchers," Winnie said. A devilish smile spread across her attractive face. "Care to join us? It's a great way to meet women."

Mike smiled back at her. "Thanks. I think I'll watch from here. I wanted to see if you were going to burn me in effigy."

"Heavens, Mike. We're Pennsylvania's Advocates for the Environment, not rock throwers."

They shook hands, and the three women crossed the street. Both TV news crews had set up tripods not far from Mike, but the reporters and their cameramen had abandoned the tripods and crossed the street to get closer to the action. The cameramen lugged equipment on their arms and backs along with the cameras perched on their shoulders. The reporters carried cordless mics. Without hesitation, they approached the moms and dads and started interviewing them.

At one time, when Harrisburg was both a capital city and an industrial city, the Harrisburg Steam Heat Company had a whistle that blew precisely at noon to alert factory workers that it was time to put down their tools and pick up their lunch pails. Even though there was virtually no heavy industry left in the city, as a throwback to that earlier era, the steam company continued to mark the time. The whistle blew precisely at noon.

The protesters began marching in a tight-knit circle in front of the DEP building. Ursula, her emerald-green T-shirt sticking out in the crowd, gestured with her arms to get them to spread out. She hurried through the crowd prodding them like a sheepdog with her charges. It was clear the protesters were new to this and somewhat inhibited. It took her several minutes to get her people in proper position, with signs held high for the cameras, as they marched in front of the building. Ursula looked up at one of the officers who stood at the top of several steps leading to the entrance. He held up a thumb and appeared to smile. She waved back. About as friendly a protest rally as you could imagine.

At about 12:10, Ursula picked up the bullhorn and stood on a step leading to the DEP building. The protesters stopped circling and turned to watch her.

"My name is Ursula Goodperson from Pennsylvania's Advocates for the Environment and we're here today to send a message to the secretary of DEP and the governor. Fracking is destroying the pristine water in Pennsylvania, destroying the land, polluting the air, ruining the countryside we know and love, and destroying our towns. It is hurting our children. We have to stop fracking and have to stop these companies that are running roughshod over our government, land, and people. The oil and gas companies are trying to buy our government. It's shameful. This is a political issue, but not a Democratic or Republican issue. The people have to tell the politicians in Harrisburg and Washington that we no longer will tolerate the destruction of our homes, natural resources, and environment just to line the pockets of contemptible, uncaring, rich corporations."

She paused and the little crowd applauded politely. From the corner of his eye, Mike noticed first one and then about a dozen men, wearing blue work shirts and hard hats, file out of the garage. A couple of the men carried signs that looked professionally made—*Pro Union/Pro Drilling, Proud of America's Natural Gas, UNION!,* and *USA! USA!*

The counter-protesters aggressively crowded around the moms and dads, shouting *Drill, baby, drill.* Then, they took up a hearty *USA! USA! USA!* drowning out the Bradford County moms and dads, several of whom were locked in heated discussions with the drillers.

Outnumbered, the two cops fell back and took up positions near the doorway of the DEP building. In the distance, a police siren wailed, but it had to have been at least three or four blocks away.

Ursula tried to shout above the racket. Then she gave up and started to chant *One-two-three-four, no more fracking anymore!* The moms and dads took up the chant.

The groups tried to drown each other out. Several of the parents pulled their children away from the crowd. The male reporter and his cameraman retreated to safety across Market Street, but the female reporter plunged in, thrust a microphone at one of the counter-protesters, and started asking questions. Two more Capitol Police officers, in full riot gear, hurried out of the DEP building and tossed helmets and batons to the first two. Sirens converged from several directions.

By now, Mike was on the curb along with a small crowd of onlookers. The protest wasn't violent, but it had become loudly confrontational. He glanced at the man next to him. "Wow, this is turning into a shit-fest."

"Just you wait," said the man. Mike noticed a slight accent that he couldn't place. He locked eyes with Mike for a moment, and a smile spread across his wide lips.

Mike took a better look at the man. He was late forties, wearing a blue business suit with ice-blue eyes, sandy blond hair, and was at the peak of fitness. He was the same guy who had been at the garage a few minutes earlier. The man glanced at his phone. Mike thought he saw a tattoo on his wrist. The phone's clock clicked from 12:19 to 12:20. The man took one last look at Mike, and he smiled again.

About two dozen people in leather jackets, hoodies, motorcycle helmets, sunglasses, bandanas, and other improvised gear—all of it black—darted out of the shadows from the alley between the garage and the DEP building, chanting *Ho-ho-ho-ho, dirty fracking has to go!* They surrounded the startled union marchers and the two groups squared off, spilling into Market Street. Cars swerved around the crowd, horns blared and brakes squealed, stopping inches from scrambling human bodies. Ursula shouted helplessly into her bullhorn, inaudible in the chaos.

As if on cue, the black-clad protesters changed their chant to *Kill the drill!* One of them smashed a union marcher in the face with an object. Mike couldn't tell what it was, but the man went down hard, holding his bloodied head.

Police cars swarmed Market Street, the troopers in various gear, some only in uniforms, others in riot gear with automatic weapons. They jumped from their cars, organized behind their vehicles, and resolutely pushed toward the crowd in a flying wedge to separate the groups.

Some of the black-clad protesters turned on the officers, knocking one of them to the ground. Then the protesters started to move in separate directions. Most of the black-clad ones fell back to the alley between the garage and the DEP building where they fled, some being chased by police wielding batons and drawn weapons. The union workers retreated to the garage. The Bradford County group huddled near the corner of the DEP building, fear-stricken parents hugging their crying children and attempting to protect them from the violence.

Mike looked for Winnie and found her in her blue polka-dot Talbots dress and heels in front of the moms and dads, her arms spread protectively, shielding them. Even from a distance, Mike could see her defiant expression. He looked for the man who had talked to him. He had disappeared into the maelstrom.

Several of the black-clad protesters pushed their way between the moms and dads and the remaining union workers. They linked arms as if *they* were protecting the moms and dads. In the midst of the confusion, Mike saw a small boy, maybe five or six years old, separated from his parents, buffeted by the angry adults as he cried and staggered along the steps.

Without hesitating, Mike ran across Market Street, dodged the police, wove through small groups of scuffling protesters, and grabbed the boy. A fist swung toward Mike's head. He blocked it with his elbow as he shielded the boy with his hand and backed up toward the knot of moms and dads.

A foot hooked around Mike's ankle, and he tumbled to the pavement, still holding the child, protecting him from the impact. In a flash, a black-clad protestor reared back with a metal pipe. Mike kept his arms around the child, hands around the boy's head, and rolled onto his stomach, hunching his shoulders to receive the blow. None came.

When the shouting was over, a police officer helped Mike to his feet as one of the moms, shrieking and crying hysterically, grabbed her son from Mike's arms and receded into the crowd. Then he began to shiver. He took several deep breaths to calm himself.

"Sir, who are you? Which protest group are you a part of?" a Black woman asked.

It took Mike a full two seconds to realize that a microphone had been shoved in his face and he was being interviewed by the woman reporter and her cameraman.

"No one. Mike Jacobs. I'm not a protester, just a DEP lawyer who was on my lunch break."

"Well, you're a hero. You saved that little boy."

"I don't know about that. I just did what anyone would do."

***

That night, on *CBS Evening News*, the national broadcast, the lead story was, "What Would You Do?—Hero-Lawyer Saves Small Boy in Riot." The dramatic video caught Mike as he ran the gauntlet between the protestors and the police. It showed him as he scooped up the boy in the tumultuous protest and protected him with his body as he was pushed to the ground. Moments after the ordeal, Mike, his face bruised, blood trickling from his scalp and nose, looked directly into the camera and said, "I just did what anyone would do."

Almost as an afterthought, the reporter identified the boy as Lucas Bruno-Campbell.

21

Victory Comes in Many Forms

"What just happened?" Winnie Hedges asked the two other women.

Cynthia Voigt's elbows were propped on the conference room table, her head held in her hands. Her green blazer was sloppily draped on the back of her chair, her white tank top ripped and soiled from a bottle of putrid well water that had been tossed at her. Ursula Goodperson slumped in her chair, her T-shirt barely hung on her slim frame, one shoulder torn. She pulled obsessively at the damage to cover her bra that clung to her by a shredded strap.

"I'm so mad, stinking bastards," said Goodperson. "I had it all worked out—the Capitol Police, the networks, the people from Bradford County. This was going to be our moment. Our coming-out party. We were going to be the voice of reason among the ENGOs, the ones you could turn to when you wanted to reach the largest group of people who love Mother Earth. We were going to be all over the news. A positive message of support for our sisters and brothers who are getting fracked. Now we'll only be associated with a bunch of rioting assholes. Who were those people? The ones in black? They said they were there to protect us. From what? A bunch of labor union guys? What the hell?" Tears of rage streamed down her face, and she angrily wiped them away with the backs of her hands.

Winnie and Ursula looked at Cynthia. She shook her head. "This is awful, just awful. I don't know what happened. I never expected this. We have to regroup, regain the high ground. Before the rally, I talked with some of the people at the Sierra Club and the Riverkeeper. They wished me luck. They wished *us* luck. Actually, I think they were jealous. I was keeping us in the news. Relevant. A positive message. I just don't know what happened. We were totally blindsided."

"This is bullshit," said Goodperson. "We were set up. First, those so-called union guys came out of the garage, followed a few minutes later by those Antifa guys. This is bull. I'm the community organizer. I know people. I'm going to figure this out and then kick someone's ass."

Winnie and Cynthia said nothing. Finally, Goodperson got up and headed for the door.

"I think I have another T-shirt in a box in my office. This bra's a goner. I'm going to my apartment to take a shower and change. Do either of you guys want to get a beer later? Maybe pizza?"

Winnie shook her head, and Cynthia waved her hand in dismissal. Goodperson shrugged and left.

"What do we do now?" Cynthia said, her voice a blend of sadness and resignation.

"I'm going to do what I wanted to do from the beginning, litigate this case. I'm going to get a notice of deposition out tonight and request a site view, too. I'm going to start pushing hard in the appeal. This political stuff is all well and good, but I'm a litigator, and we'll beat them in court sooner than at protest marches."

"Did you see on *Harrisburg Capitol Watch* the governor is considering putting a moratorium on drilling?" Cynthia asked. "I mean, the story said it had nothing to do with the protest, but still . . . the timing. Maybe we did accomplish something."

"I wouldn't get too excited about that possibility," Winnie said. "Even though we don't have a formal severance tax, the state brings in tens of millions of dollars every year from the impact fee and other corporate taxes. Not only the state, but all those little municipalities getting hundreds of thousands of dollars a year each. It's a huge payoff, a legal bribe, free money, and all legal. They'd raise heck if that money went away. I don't see it happening."

"Then what are we doing?" asked Cynthia.

"We're doing what we have to do. Keep up the pressure. Give me the time to litigate this case."

Cynthia pursed her lips and nodded.

Winnie fought back tears of rage. "I'm heading home. You should too." She put her arms around Cynthia's shoulders and gave her a warm hug. Then she left and closed the door behind her. Cynthia took several deep breaths. Her cell phone rang. She didn't recognize the number.

"Hello?"

No response.

"Hello?"

"Cynthia, I trust you were not injured." It was Vladimir Zhirkov. He sounded chipper.

"Sorry, Vlad, you caught me at a bad time. I'm okay. Did you see the news?"

"Of course. I'm not quite ready to pop the champagne corks but maybe soon?"

"What?"

"Didn't you hear? Your governor is considering imposing a moratorium on drilling."

"Yes, but I think the chance of that happening is very small. The state is just raking in too much money to shut down drilling."

"Maybe yes, maybe no. If you put enough straw on the back of a serf, the addition of one more little piece will eventually make the poor serf fall to the ground. The action today was another piece of straw. Even if your governor does not put a moratorium on drilling, something like this will give the evil frackers pause. Do they really want to invest millions of dollars in a state where the governor could pull the plug on drilling at any moment? I mean, think about it. Perhaps instead of drilling more wells here or building another pipeline in Pennsylvania, they'll go elsewhere. Victory comes in many forms."

A thought crossed Cynthia's mind. "Vlad, did you have anything to do with the riot today?"

Vlad laughed. "What a silly question, Cynthia. You give me too much credit. I'm not a violent man. I do not believe in mayhem."

"But still . . ."

"Am I sorry people were injured? Of course. Do I think that this hurt the Advocates or our cause? Not at all. If you look at it in the overall scheme of things, it's not a bad outcome. You just keep doing what you're doing, and I'll keep doing what I am doing. Before you know it, victory will be ours."

"But—"

"Did I mention one of my colleagues, a man who made millions, *billions,* in high tech, wants to make a very substantial gift to the Advocates? He told me he would be sending you a check today in the amount of $250,000. Not too shabby, as you say."

"Vlad . . ."

"Don't worry, Cynthia. This is all on the up and up. Good things are happening, and your organization will be richly compensated."

Cynthia decided not to press her luck.

"Now, fill me in on the case," Vlad said. "These poor Campbells."

"It's a good case. Winnie's one of the best litigators, and if anyone can win, Winnie will do it. The main problem with their well is it is high in E. coli and fecal coliform."

"Fecal coliform and E. coli? Those are bacteria. What about actual fracking chemicals? Produced water, that kind of thing."

"Not so much. Our geologist says that high levels of bacteria can be caused by fracking—"

"And by cows relieving themselves near a water well and leaky septic systems." Vlad interrupted. "Not nearly as strong a case as having chemicals from fracking in the water."

"I'd like to say that they will hopefully show up, but of course, we don't want that in those people's well, do we?"

Vlad's phone crackled. "Of course not, Cynthia. Of course not."

After the call, Cynthia looked out the large window toward the Susquehanna River. Although she had washed her hands when she returned from the riot, she felt the need to wash them again.

22

Hail the Conquering Hero

Mike sat in his office trying to ignore most of his emails. Every other one started out, "Was that you on the news . . . ?" or "I saw you on YouTube . . ." He really didn't like being the center of attention and was hoping his fifteen minutes of fame would soon be over.

The phone rang. A 202 area code and a number that didn't register popped up on his caller ID.

"Mike Jacobs."

"The hero, Mike Jacobs?" It was Darius Moore, laughing.

"Yes, one and the same. You want an autographed picture?"

"No. Actually, Jake wants to know what you were doing at an anti-fracking rally. He needs to know if he has to call the governor and get you off this case."

"Seriously?"

"Maybe," said Darius Moore without a trace of humor.

"Go to hell, Darius. If you must know, I was across the street watching, *monitoring,* the rally. I wasn't *at* the rally. When I saw that kid, I just reacted like I'm sure you would have."

"Of course. You set the bar pretty high for all of us, brah."

"Sure, *brah.*"

"Now, about those depositions. What dates do you have that are open . . ."

Ten minutes later, Mike had finally gotten back to his work when there was a tap at the door, and Roger looked in.

"Do you have five minutes, or do I have to make an appointment with your publicist now that you're famous?"

"Ha ha, very funny," Mike said.

Roger didn't wait for an invitation but closed the door and sat in Mike's guest chair. "How are you feeling today? Your face looks a little bruised."

"I needed four stitches and have a wicked bump in the back of my head, but the doc said it's a good thing I have a hard skull. I ended up with a mild concussion, but all things considered, I'm pretty good."

"They have a video of the guy who pushed you and they grabbed the one who was about to slug you. The guy who pushed you was wearing a balaclava hat covering his entire face, and no one will give up his identity. The guy with the iron pipe actually was a girl and claims to be a political prisoner. This is a direct quote from her via the chief of the Capitol Police: 'You can put me in one of your black sites and waterboard me, pig, I ain't talking.' The judge was not amused and Ms. Anonymous is being held on $250,000 bond."

Mike made a face. "What the hell happened yesterday? I bumped into Winnie and two other women from the Advocates and they were talking about a *peaceful* demonstration. Basically, just enough chanting and sign-waving to get on the local news. Next thing you know, those union guys came out of the garage, and then the black bandannas showed up out of nowhere."

Roger shook his head. "A lot of information is public. The Advocates applied for a permit to demonstrate in front of the DEP building, and anyone can access that information."

"Yes, but what was the point of the violence? I guess the union guys wanted us to know they support drilling. I get that. As a group, they're big supporters. They were obnoxious, but not violent. The black bandanna guys, I mean, what the hell?"

"According to the chief, yesterday afternoon a new group called Frack You First!, with an exclamation point, posted on a new website that they had a successful action. They said their purpose was to protect the well-meaning but simple-minded moms and dads of Bradford County against the reactionaries who favored fracking. They also said they successfully protected them and countered the fascist drillers, lackeys, and phony so-called labor unionists."

"Nice. They insulted both their enemies and their allies. Okay, so how many did the police grab?"

"They only got the one girl from Frack You First! They also got two of the union guys. They released the union drillers, though, because there wasn't enough evidence to charge them."

"So basically, there was a violent protest on government property in which a group of moms and dads and children *and* a government lawyer were assaulted, and only one woman is being held responsible?"

"Actually, not a woman, she really *is* a girl," Roger said. "The one who assaulted you, who was getting ready to smash you with a pipe, appears to be about fifteen or sixteen years old. She'll probably go to juvenile court and get her record expunged when she turns eighteen."

"Awesome. I almost got beat up by a girl. Did they ever find the guy I saw, the one I told them about with the blue suit? I mean, it was weird, he looked at his phone, the time turned to 12:20, and he said, 'wait and see what happens next,' something like that. Next thing you know, the black bandannas were on the loose. He knew *exactly* when they were coming."

"Sorry bud, no one saw him, and he isn't on any video. Maybe you misunderstood him."

"That's possible, but I know I saw him talking with someone in the parking garage, and it probably was the union driller guys," Mike said. "Then I saw him going down the alley about fifteen minutes before the black bandanna clowns came screaming out of there. You know, I wonder why he'd be talking with *both* the union guys and the black bandanna guys. Maybe he was trying to start a riot? It's very odd if nothing else."

"You got me there."

"What do you think all of this means?" Mike asked.

"Don't know, but I did hear the governor is thinking about a moratorium on drilling permits."

"What? Because of the rally?"

"That, but mainly other pressure he's under," Roger replied. "The anti-drilling, anti-frackers are pretty powerful. There are a lot of people and money supporting them. A big part of the governor's political base is in the Philly area, and they think they get no benefit from fracking. It doesn't help that New York and Maryland have moratoriums."

"Yeah, but that was totally political. I'm no fan, but if you're going to ban fracking, at least do it for scientific reasons."

"The governors of New York and Maryland would say they *did* ban drilling for scientific reasons," Roger said, folding his arms.

"You know, I'd be more impressed with them if they only used non-fracked gas. They're treating Pennsylvania like some kind of Third World country."

Mike thought for a moment, "Has he done it? I didn't miss anything, did I?"

"No, it's just scuttlebutt from the Capitol. Probably just to get leverage on some bill he wants from the General Assembly."

"Okay, that's interesting. So, how's the kid? Lucas?" Mike asked.

"Other than being scared to death, he's in good shape. You know who the mom is, don't you?"

"I didn't at first, then it all clicked: Campbell. I think they're suing us, but I may have amnesia from my recent ordeal." Mike put his hands on his face and swiveled his head.

"Bingo. Actually, I've been on the phone with the missus this morning. She wants to meet with you to thank you if you ever go up to Bradford County."

"Jeez. Does Winnie know you talked? I mean, the Campbells are represented by counsel. Winnie."

"I told Ms. Bruno-Campbell I couldn't talk to her because of the attorney-client thing, and she let loose with a string of cuss words. If my mother had been around, she would've paddled her. It gave me an excuse to call Winnie though. She said as long as we didn't talk about the case she's fine with us talking about the riot."

"The *riot?* Is that what we're calling it now?"

"Pretty much," Roger said. "And you're the hero of the riot—our own Jean Valjean. So, Ms. Bruno-Campbell wants to show her appreciation. The secretary and his press secretary think it would be a splendid idea. Maybe all of this will appease some of the crazies. Are you okay with that?"

"Wait, the secretary? Crap. We finally get a new secretary who doesn't know my reputation and now this. The last thing I want to do is meet with the angry mama bear who sued us. You say the secretary wants me to do this?"

"Sorry, bud."

"Crap. I think I have a concussion coming on." Mike held his head for a moment while Roger stared at him. "All right then. If Winnie's okay with me meeting her, so am I. You know I'm heading up there tomorrow to visit the site with Missy Shelton, our geologist. I could hook up with Ms. Bruno-Campbell while I'm up there."

Roger shook his head. "Oy vey. Rachel, Missy, Teresa, all these attractive women you can *hook up* with." Roger made air quotes with his fingers.

"Come on, Roger. That's not what I meant. Besides, you have me all wrong. I've just been unlucky at true love. Besides, I've been seeing Rachel for a couple of months. There's nothing to worry about."

"I'm sure it'll go fine," Roger said. "Eat some spaghetti with the Bruno-Campbell family, drink a Coke, take a selfie with the kid, and come home."

Mike closed his eyes and shook his head.

23

Boys and girls in America have such a sad time together.
(Jack Kerouac)

Mike finished packing his Jeep. He'd sold his Prius a few months earlier because he needed a car that was more reliable in bad weather and could get around off-road. He loved the traction and reliability of the Jeep but missed the gas mileage of his old Toyota.

He played with Google Maps and entered the address of the café where he would meet Missy for coffee before they went out to the Campbell pad. As he was about to put his car into drive, he took one last look at his messages. He had a new text—

> Mike, I just wanted you to know, Jeremy at the office has an extra ticket to Book of Mormon at the Walnut Street Theater in Philly on Friday night. He invited me so I decided to tag along. I'm going to hang out with him in Philly next weekend. Have a good trip up north. I've had a great time with you but now I guess it's over. We had fun. I hope we see each other again sometime soon. Stay well. Bye. Rachel

Mike didn't need to squint to read between the lines. His relationship with Rachel wasn't built on much of a foundation. It was really just a friendship with occasional benefits. Deep down, he knew it was withering on the vine. Rachel had mentioned

Jeremy several times. He wondered if they'd have a formal break-up call or if this was it. A break-up text. Nice. A first for him. He exhaled and sent her a text.

Do you want to talk about this at all? I can talk now or later tonight.

It took a full minute for Rachel to respond.

Sorry. Really really busy. Maybe next week some time. Goodbye

Mike thought about it and concluded that neither he nor Rachel ever loved the other. Neither had ever uttered those words. He liked her. He'd been loyal to her, although he wondered if she'd been loyal to him. Assuming this was the end of their "casual" relationship, he would miss her company and hoped they might see each other from time to time. He knew this was unlikely and sighed. He put the car into drive and aimed it north.

About an hour later, Mike was driving on Interstate 81. He hit a number on his contacts. Two rings later, Missy answered.

"Hey Mike, are you on time?"

"Yes, I just wanted to confirm. I plan to be at the café by eleven. That's what Google says, anyway. Maybe a few minutes later if I hit any traffic."

"Great. We can get an early lunch, then head over to the Campbell pad in the afternoon. Where are you staying?"

"The Microtel in Sayre."

"Oh, that's new."

"And small rooms and cheap. Emphasis is on cheap. I hear there's a Hampton Inn and a Best Western in town too, but they don't take state vouchers."

"I'll make sure we end up in Sayre at the end of the day. I'll pick you up there, too, in the morning. Are you sure you can take care of yourself in the twelve hours we'll be apart?" She asked. There was a smile in her voice.

"About that. Are you free tonight? I really did want to treat you to dinner for getting your geologist's license."

"Is this a date or just a couple of colleagues having dinner?" She asked, laughing out loud.

"Okay, now you're making me feel all awkward. It is definitely one or the other," Mike replied.

"In that case, I'm free and would love to have dinner with you. Which one is it, though?"

Mike paused. "Let's see how dinner goes, and then we can answer that question."

As Mike hung up, it occurred to him that maybe it was a good thing he got a break-up text from Rachel.

Mike was passing Wilkes-Barre when his phone rang. He didn't recognize the number, a New York prefix. He clicked on it anyway.

"Mike? This is Teri, Teresa Bruno-Campbell. We met briefly on Monday after the rally. First, I wanted to check to see how you're doing?"

"Fine, I have four stitches, but they're under my hair in the back and you can't see them. How's Lucas doing?"

"Remarkably well. Little kids are pretty resilient. Do you have any children?"

"No, no kids."

"A wife? Are you working on it?" She asked. There was a laugh. More of a giggle.

"No, I'm single."

"Single?" She said a bit too brightly. "Gee, an attractive man like *you* is single?"

Mike's antennae were quivering. Why was this older, married woman digging? For a moment, he thought about telling her he was gay. "Well, I'm still waiting for the right girl to come along."

"Maybe you need a real woman, not a girl," she said, laughing. Her laughter was just a bit too high-pitched, giggly, and forced. Mike's antennae were beating him on the head.

"Okay . . . to what do I owe the pleasure?" He asked.

"I was talking to your boss, Roger, this morning, and I told him I wanted to do something nice to thank you after what you did for Lucas and our family. He told me you're on your way up here to Bradford County, and you'd be here for the next couple of days. So, I thought it would be nice if I made you a home-cooked meal. Would you like to join me for dinner tonight?"

"That's very nice, Ms. Bruno-Campbell—"

"Call me that again, and I'll smack you. It's Teri."

"Teri. I'd love to finally meet your husband and have a chance to talk with your kids in a more normal setting than the Capitol Police station."

"Well, Jared is in the city—New York—all week. He won't be home until Friday."

"And your kids . . .?"

She laughed heartily. "Well, we can have dinner either with or without."

"Definitely with. Like I said, I'd love to meet them in a normal setting."

"Of course. I was just kidding."

Mike explained he was having dinner with a DEP geologist that night, and they decided he would have dinner with Teresa and her kids at the Campbell house the following night.

Mike also decided that while it would be nice to have a home-cooked meal away from home, he would be sure to hit the road before the kids went to bed. The last thing he wanted was to be alone with this woman.

24

A System Designed by Geniuses to be Carried Out by Idiots, Part 2

Anthony Fowler, Yukon's geologist, sat in the twenty-sixth-floor conference room of the Yukon Oil and Gas Tower in Houston. His office, along with those of the other geologists, was located twenty floors below.

The conference table, made from rare Amazonian bloodwood, shined like Galveston Bay, complete with an oily sheen. The walls were adorned with original oil paintings of oil and gas rigs, derricks, and pumps, almost all composed with a setting sun to dramatically backlight the operations. A credenza held a huge stainless coffee urn and a tray the size of NRG Stadium loaded with delicious pastries, some of which had been ferried to the table on china plates, their final stop before being digested in the bellies of Yukon executives. A silver charger of cut luscious ripe fruit, large enough to feed all of the coastal plains of Texas, sat mostly untouched next to the pastries.

Professor Wilbur McCrory, Yukon's expert geology witness from Penn State, sat to Anthony's right. He was the only one wearing a tie, and it was a bow tie that went neatly with the bespoke three-piece suit that he filled. Anthony had read all of McCrory's books and articles on geology, studied with him when he was an undergraduate geology student, and had been the one who strongly recommended him to the company. He hoped his recommendation wouldn't come back to haunt him. McCrory had nearly finished his first pastry and was getting ready to indulge in a second, filled with sweetened ricotta cheese.

To Anthony's left was Jesse Ewing, his friend in the general counsel's office. Although she often wore pants to the office, today she wore a dark blue sleeveless dress. The dress fit trimly on her slender frame and set off her curly blonde hair. In front of her was a plate of sliced melon, a glass of water, and a legal pad.

Across from Jess was Darius Moore and Jake Berliner from FU. Anthony talked with Darius a couple of times a week, although the general counsel made it clear they were to limit their discussions since every hour of Darius Moore's time cost the company $1,200. A mere six minutes cost $120. A day of the thirty-year-old's time would cover most people's rent for a whole year. The legal bills were monitored carefully, and once a month, Anthony got an email from Jesse asking to be notified about any "telecon" that went on for more than eighteen minutes.

He'd met Darius Moore several times over the years at meetings, and a couple of months earlier Darius had invited Anthony and his wife, and Jesse and her husband, to watch the Houston Rodeo from a luxury box at NRG Stadium. After the rodeo, they watched Garth Brooks perform. By this point in his career, Anthony had been thoroughly wined, dined, and entertained by legions of lawyers and consultants seeking to curry favor with the rising star. His wife, however, who did not generally attend law firm marketing events, was duly impressed. After exchanging brief pleasantries with the group, Darius Moore fired up his laptop and reviewed emails without pause, banging out responses like a jazz pianist on a baby grand. His only food was a cup of black coffee, cooling quickly in the air-conditioned room.

Jake Berliner sat next to Darius Moore and wore a nice-looking dark-blue suit, no necktie. He wore owlish eyeglasses on his round face, a smattering of gray hair resting lightly on an otherwise bald head. Anthony had never met Berliner before in person, but he knew the man was the partner at FU who had the relationship with the big shots in the C-Suite. He was FU's 2,000-pound gorilla. This was the man Darius Moore worked for and worshipped. He wasn't quite sure why Berliner was there. He thought Darius was the only FU lawyer invited to the meeting.

Sleek white microphones dangled from white cords from the white ceiling and about a dozen white speakers were built into the ceiling and walls for audio and videoconferencing. An LG 120-inch video monitor hung from the wall, the Yukon logo glistening and revolving in the center of the screen. Norby Lafleur had been invited to attend by telephone from Bradford County, and he was holding as they waited for one more person to join them. Anthony had a good relationship with Norby, however, based on the grumbling he'd heard in the past day or so, he knew that the Director of Ops for Pennsylvania was skating on thin ice.

Norby called him a day earlier inveighing about his treatment; in particular, he was unhappy about not being invited in person to such an important meeting. Also, he was pissed that he alone seemed to be held responsible for using the freshwater pit for holding the flowback. He wanted to know why DEP's lawyer, Jacobs, was asking a lot of questions about him. He asked if Anthony had met Jacobs—he had not—and all Anthony could do was lend a sympathetic ear.

The space at the head of the table was empty. There was a little small talk, and most everyone checked emails on their smartphones and iPads while they waited and chewed on their pastries. The view, to the south through the glass wall, looked past other downtown office buildings, past Houston's sprawling development and the web of Interstate highways, and into the haze toward Galveston. The landscape was flat and brownish-green, and Anthony knew, if the sky were clear, you could see the Earth's curvature from this vantage point. It was an appropriate backdrop as the man they were waiting for was a son of Galveston.

Seven minutes late, at 9:07 Central Time, Blade Harris, carrying a small pad of paper and his iPhone, shoved open the door and flicked it shut behind him. It closed with a thud. He glanced around the room as he settled in. Around the office and behind his back, he was known by his alternate nickname, the *Houston Toad,* sometimes just Toad. Anthony assumed this had something to do with his appearance, bald with black speckles across his sunburned scalp, a wide face and wide body, somewhere around a size 54-short suit, and a perpetual scowl. Anthony had encountered real Houston toads on some of his hikes in the area, and he had to admit that Harris bore a striking resemblance to the amphibian. He had no idea why the man was called Blade, although that was more interesting than his given name, Blake.

"Let's get going," Blade said without any pleasantries. "Norby, you there, boy?" He asked in his Galveston twang.

They could hear clicking as though Norby was pushing off the mute button and then a moment later, "Yes, sir. Present."

Blade looked around the table until his eyes settled on Berliner. He made a face, then said, "Jake, I didn't realize you were coming. Who invited you?"

"Don't worry about it, Blade. I had other meetings this week in Houston, and I made time for your meeting. I have no doubt that Darius could handle it just fine but thought I'd come along to throw in my two cents."

"Does that mean you're going to be charging us $2,000 an hour or just two cents? Let me be a little more precise, I assume you're not charging us at all for this meeting, right? I'm not going to get a surprise from y'all when you email me your bill for FU's services next month, am I?" Blade narrowed his frog eyes.

"Sorry if I wasn't clear. Our relationship with Yukon is such that I'm here purely as a way of showing our appreciation and devotion to all of you. I'm not charging for my time, although I sure hope Darius is."

Everyone laughed except Blade.

"Well, considering what we pay y'all every month, y'all ought to show a *lot* of appreciation and devotion. More than just free tickets to see Garth Brooks."

Berliner nodded and pressed his lips together.

"And just so there are no surprises, I'm not gonna see a bill from y'all for that St. Regis Hotel, or first-class air, am I?" Blade asked, still not smiling.

"Actually, Blade, you won't see an invoice for the St. Regis, since we're staying at the Four Seasons. Like I said, the trip is on my dime."

Satisfied with the results of his cross-examination, Blade nodded. "Somebody fill me in."

This was the cue that Jesse was waiting for. She cleared her throat, and all eyes turned toward her. "Yes, sir. Two Decembers ago, we entered into a lease with Mr. and Mrs. Jared Campbell in Washington Township, Bradford County, P-A-. In November of last year, we began construction of a six-acre pad." Her voice was trembling, and she paused to take a slow sip of water.

"We wanted to begin drilling in February and needed a freshwater impoundment to hold water to frack the well. Our Pennsylvania operation hired a local outfit, called PITS, Inc., to construct the impoundment, and they began construction in late January. Apparently, they didn't have much experience and ran into trouble almost right away. When the pit was finally completed, there were problems. At some point, we realized the pit was leaking, big-time—"

"I'd like to add something," said the Cajun, cutting in over the speakers. "I wanted to hire TEX-OK from Amarillo or one of the other impoundment contractors we worked with in the past. All of the ops directors across the U.S. were ordered to hire local. We didn't have a whole lot of choice up here in P-A-. I felt like my hands were tied."

"I hear you," said Blade. "Didn't say nothing about hiring *incompetent* local contractors."

"Well, when Houston forces you to hire local and the one-and-only crew ends up being incompetent sumbitches, the blame for that shouldn't just fall on one person. Y'hear what I'm saying?"

No one spoke. Blade blinked his frog eyes. "We can discuss that later off-line."

Glances were exchanged around the room.

A moment later, Anthony's iPhone, which was silenced, lit up. It was a text massage from Norby:

He TOLD me to hire them!!!

Anthony glanced at his phone, double-checked that it was silenced, then placed it screen-down on the table.

Jesse continued. "Ultimately, we drilled three horizontal wells in February through April. They've been very productive, some of our most productive wells in P-A-, in fact. Drilling is set to begin on the next three wells later this month."

"So, what's the deal with these Campbells?" Blade asked.

"About a month ago, they decided their water well was contaminated, and the contamination came from our drilling," Jesse said.

"Need I ask? How was our drilling? Did it contaminate the water?" Blade asked.

"I'm confident that it did not," said Anthony, taking over. "I've examined all of the drilling records, the cementing records, and our production records, and I have every reason to believe our wells are performing to our construction standards."

"How about you, Norby? You also confident our wells aren't contaminating the aquifer?"

"I agree with Anthony," said the Cajun through the speakers. "Everything I've seen says the wells and the cement," like the others, he pronounced it *SEE-ment*, "are just fine. These wells are cased all the way down to the lateral, almost 6,000 feet, and we have no indication there's any contamination."

"Also, I've looked at the information provided by the state," Anthony said. "PaDEP's records do not indicate contamination from our Campbell well. I mean the Campbells' water well *is* contaminated, but not from us. They have a number of contaminants in their water that are nothing more than what you'd expect in the local farm water. They have a good dose of fecal coliform, E. coli, and other bacteria. I mean, the well is shallow, located next to a cow pasture, and not encased. What do you expect? This is typical of water in an agricultural area. No one seems to know how deep the well is, but it's probably picking up runoff from farming."

"How about methane?" Blade asked. "Do they have methane in their water?"

"They sure do," said Anthony. "So does everyone else with a water well in that part of Bradford County. The methane comes from naturally occurring shallow gas deposits. In that part of the county, there have been quite a few old-fashioned vertical wells drilled over the past century to no more than 2,000 feet, intercepting the pockets of shallow natural gas. No one's done the specialized testing to determine whether the methane in their well is shallow or deep, like from the Marcellus, but there have been several very credible recent studies showing the prevalence of shallow methane."

Blade looked at Professor McCrory. "Okay, professor, here's your chance. I understand that Anthony studied with you at Penn State. Was he a good student? Or do we have to send him back to school?" This was the first time Blade smiled that day.

"Actually, Anthony was one of my all-time best students. He's a natural. It's like he has X-ray eyes that see underground. That said, I've checked all of the same things he's checked, plus the extensive Penn State database, and my conclusion is the same. I'm happy to write a report. As soon as Mr. Moore gives me the go-ahead, I'll confirm these findings."

"Speaking of which," said Darius Moore, "we also have DEP's own report. Their geologist, Melissa Shelton, wrote a report saying none of your wells or your fracking impacted the Campbells' water well. I'll be happy to work with the professor to prepare an expert report for the trial."

Blade nodded. "So if it's all good, what the hell are we doing here?"

No one replied.

Blade looked in turn at each person in the room, waiting for a response.

Even Darius Moore looked up from his laptop to meet his gaze.

The only sound was the *whoosh* from the ventilation system.

25

What Are We Doing Here?

"Since no one wants to answer the question, let me rephrase it. If everything is goddamn rainbows and unicorns in P-A-, what the *fuck* are we doing here?" Blade asked.

Everyone in the room looked around, and their eyes finally settled on Jesse. Her hands trembled. She hid them in her lap and cleared her throat. "At some point, our Campbell Pit A was converted from freshwater to produced water. It seems to have happened after we fracked the 1-H well."

"Uh-huh," said Blade. "Norby, how large is that pit?"

Norby's voice crackled through the speakers. "Pit A is 265 feet by 305 feet and has an aerial extent of 80,825 square feet. It's approximately fifteen to sixteen feet deep, so it could hold approximately 5,242,300 gallons."

"Approximately?" asked Blade, smiling slightly for the second time that morning.

"Approximately."

"So, if an impoundment like that, full of fresh water, sprung a leak, the worst that would happen was we'd lose five million gallons of water, give or take," said Blade. "The aquifer would gain over five million gallons of fresh water, or the water would run off harmlessly into a nearby stream. Shit, there'd be some boys on the thirtieth floor who'd be pissed at losing over two-hundred-fifty-K worth of water, but the impact to the environment and neighbors would be slight." Blade ran a stubby finger across his bulbous lips. "So does somebody want to tell me how the fuck a pit designed to hold fresh water became a *flowback* water pit?"

The air conditioner, which ran continuously from March to November, supplied the only sound. *Whoosh.* The white noise drowned out the slight background hum that would otherwise sneak into the room. It also extinguished the sounds of gurgling stomachs and bowels.

"Norby, I'm talking to you, boy."

Again, there was clicking as Norby turned off the mute button. "Blade, let me give you a little history. The location of the pit was perfect in the sense of its location close to the pad. The geology didn't cooperate. The bedrock was a hard shale. In order to excavate to a sufficient depth, those Philly boys you wanted had to blast to loosen it up. Also, the pit was located just a few feet from the top of the groundwater and a few hundred feet above a Class A trout stream. Also, and we didn't learn this until much later, but when Pit A was constructed, very little local clay was available and none was used by the contractor under the linin'. The crushed rock and sand our specs required were unevenly spread in the base of the pit. In addition, them boys did a piss-poor job leveling the shale ridge that ran the width of the pit, leaving fairly large rocks poking up under the linin'. When the linin' material was laid on top of these rocks, the nubs were visible to anyone looking."

"And I'm assuming you approved this before it went into operation? Goddamn *nubs* and all?" Blade said.

Norby cleared his throat. "Yes, Bones took a long look at it. I did too, but the weather was against us, and we had almost no time before we went into operation. Those Philly boys were way behind schedule. I figured we'd go back in and fix it later when we had more time."

"Let's cut the shit. Did it *leak*? Did the bastard leak?" Blade asked.

The room was silent for a long ten seconds. Finally, Anthony said, "I wasn't there until a few weeks ago, of course, but according to my calculations, there was a substantial leak out of the pit. We probably lost 300,000 gallons of fresh water in the five or six days the fresh water was in the pit."

Again, the only sound for many seconds was the *whoosh* from the AC.

Finally, Blade looked at Anthony and asked, "What are the significant additional requirements for a pit holding flowback in P-A-?"

"I can answer that," said Norby.

"I want to hear this from Anthony," said Blade in a low voice.

Anthony nodded and said, "Additional protections would have been added if we intended to construct an impoundment to hold flowback. This would have included a double-liner system and monitoring probes placed in the subbase under the liner to detect leakage, layers of clay and sand, along with construction stone. It would have also included a network of monitoring wells surrounding the pit to detect the presence of contaminated water that leaked out of the pit. Basically, more liner, more subbase, and monitoring both inside the pit and below it. Pit A, of course, was a freshwater impoundment, so there was no need to add the monitoring we'd use for a pit holding flowback water. We did place one down-gradient monitoring well, but that's over by the drilling operation and probably doesn't intercept any contamination from the pit. When we placed the monitoring well, there was no reason to place it below a freshwater impoundment."

"Norby, why don't you tell us why this freshwater pit was used to hold flowback?" Blade demanded. "I don't want no bullshit."

"We were under intense pressure to begin fracking the 1-H well. Due to three or four winter storms that dumped a total of eight inches of rain and sleet that month, all of our construction had been delayed. Everything was a muddy mess. When we fracked the well, the frac tanks were on the Campbelltown Road not more than five miles from the pad. We didn't know that a bridge had washed out and our tanks were stuck on the wrong side of the crick. The road was so narrow and the mud so deep we couldn't turn around the frac tanks, so I had to order new ones, and the closest ones were in Tulsa. All of the fresh water that Pit A held had been used to frack the 1-H well. We needed to move forward to begin drilling the 2-H well, and Pit A was empty. Perfect. Problem solved. We planned to use the pit only until the frac tanks were installed, maybe two, three days. At that point, we didn't know the pit was a leaker. By the way, just so it's clear, I did send an email advising y'all that this was what we were going to do."

"Yes, I saw your email. We received it here at 2 a.m.," said Blade. "By the time I saw it at 5:30 a.m., the deed was done."

Again, the room was silent except for the *whoosh*.

Blade turned his froglike eyes to the professor. "Professor, you have anything you can say to enlighten us?"

The professor adjusted his bow-tie and said, "Groundwater is located a mere twenty feet below Pit A. Generally, groundwater moves very slowly. Contaminants, however, can virtually race through cracks and fissures in the rock, both the kind that exist naturally and the kind that are formed when blasting occurs. The blasting to construct the pit likely created cracks. Assuming for a moment that Pit A leaked, no one knows exactly when it began to do so. I'm assuming that, like similar operations, pipes, hoses, and other tools were used extensively by Yukon's workers in and around the pit. Any of these could have punctured the pit lining. Under ordinary circumstances, it's unlikely any contamination would quickly spread from the pit to the Campbell water well. If there were no fractures in the rock underground, it could be a matter of years, if ever.

"The Horseheads Limestone, which underlies the pit, provides a conduit for rapid movement of water, contaminated or not, from the pit to the Campbell residence and the nearby township reservoir. If the water is contaminated, and if it intersected the Horseheads Limestone, then it could reach the Campbell residence in a matter of months, maybe weeks. We could do dye testing to determine this, but that's what we know for now.

"One thing is helpful," continued the professor. "Based on DEP's own tests, the levels of contaminants we are seeing in the Campbell well do not indicate the presence of flowback in the Campbell well. I think it's very possible that if there is any completions fluid in the ground, it may be holed up in caves or fractures in the limestone. That's my opinion based on what we know."

The professor looked at each person in the room with the satisfied visage of a person who knows he is right.

"Do we think anyone at PaDEP knows about this?" Blade asked.

"Jacobs, Mike Jacobs, the DEP lawyer," said Darius Moore. "He asked me something about the pit the other day. Wanted to know if it had any issues. If Norby had said anything about the pit leaking." Darius Moore swallowed.

"*Who?* I've never heard that name," Blade said.

"Graduate of Vermont Law School. I knew him back in the day. Tree-hugger. Now he's an Assistant Counsel at PaDEP and their lawyer in the Campbell case. A lightweight."

There was clicking from the twelve speakers. "He mentioned me? Why does he keep mentioning me? Are you sure?" Norby asked.

"Yes, but he didn't seem to know anything. I think he was fishing."

Blade listened, then looked at Berliner. "Okay, Jake, we've been waiting for words of wisdom from the Oracle of K St. What are your thoughts?"

Berliner nodded, then tugged at his French cuffs and evened them. "The only thing that anyone knows is that at some point—allegedly—Pit A, which contained some thousands of gallons of *fresh* water, began to leak. Beyond that, we have no further direct information. PaDEP's letter correctly stated that Yukon's *drilling* operation was not the source of any contamination of the Campbell water well. The Campbells filed an appeal from *that* letter and that letter alone. This case is cabined by the four corners of PaDEP's letter, and the appeal has nothing to do with the pit. There is no direct evidence that the pit leaked or even *held* produced, flowback, or frack water, and that is entirely *irrelevant* to the case at bar. I see no reason for any of us to go beyond the language of PaDEP's letter and the appellants' appeal. Jacobs' questions are troubling since they could foreshadow some future

PaDEP investigation. For now, they don't matter in this case. The last thing we need to do is talk about the allegedly leaky pit before Pennsylvania's Environmental Hearing Board."

"In other words, no one says nothing about the pit. Right?" Blade said.

Berliner nodded, and Blade took the time to look at each one in the room. If someone did not respond out loud to his stare, he called their name. Each one eventually answered a short "yes."

"Norby, I'll call you later." Blade stood and pushed his chair back and walked out the door. He didn't bother to close it.

26

Let us always meet each other with a smile, for the smile is the beginning of love. (Mother Teresa)

Mike arrived at the Café, Ellie's Place, about ten minutes after eleven. The country-style restaurant was nearly empty. Missy sat at a booth, watching the door. She smiled brightly when Mike walked in.

Mike wondered: Should they shake hands? Hug? Maybe kiss cheeks? He extended his hand. She shook it but half-stood in the booth seat, and they hugged an awkward sideways hug.

"I thought you were going to stand me up." Missy had a great smile.

"Traffic. Slow going around Scranton. Sorry." Mike surveyed her face.

He sat, and they looked at each other. Missy had a resting face with a perpetual smile which made Mike smile back at her. This wasn't a first date, it was work, and Mike knew the difference. However, something about it had the feeling of a first date, a bit awkward but full of promise.

As they talked, Mike tried to focus the discussion on work, but one thing kept popping into his mind—

Missy sure is pretty.

The restaurant slowly filled to capacity, and Mike and Missy didn't leave the café until 12:30.

They talked about mutual acquaintances at DEP and that they had both been students at Penn State but missed each other by a few years. "Okay, mister, we probably ought to get down to business." Missy patted the top of Mike's hand. Then she stroked it.

"Is that why we're here?" Mike smiled and flipped his hand over so he could squeeze hers.

Missy squeezed back and kept her hand in his for several moments. "Okay then, on to business."

They spent the rest of their time at the restaurant discussing the Campbell case and Missy's letter to the Campbells.

"There's something I need to tell you." Missy looked at the table. Mike angled his head until he caught her eye.

"Okay. You're not going to tell me you got married since the last time we were together, are you?"

"Kind of the opposite. About six weeks ago, I told Richard we were over, through. He took it badly. I knew he would. He called me from his truck and begged me to change my mind. Then, around midnight, he called to tell me he wanted to come over again to talk. I told him no, but fifteen minutes later, he was banging on my door, yelling my name. I was scared to open it, and my neighbors' lights came on. Someone called the cops, and as soon as he saw the red and blue lights, he took off."

"Where do things stand now?"

"He still calls me every day. Sometimes I see his pickup sitting in front of my house with him in it. I think he's easing up, and I'm praying he's getting the idea that we're through. He was a jealous boyfriend; he could be mean and awful. I'm hoping he just goes away."

It was the one time she looked sad and weary. Mike couldn't read her well enough to say whether she looked that way because they had broken up or because Richard wouldn't leave her alone.

Mike was ready to back off, but Missy brought up the dinner he'd promised her, so they spent more than a few minutes discussing where they could eat among Sayre's limited options.

As they were about to get up, Mike blurted, "This is going to sound weird, so if you don't want to answer it, that's okay."

"All right. You have me nervous now." She smiled.

"Are you Jewish by any chance?"

She looked at him and half-closed her eyes, scrutinizing him. "Yes. Not particularly religious. Why?"

Mike tried to maintain an even expression. "No particular reason. Me too. We can discuss it later."

Missy turned her head a bit sideways and said, "Okay, mister. This had better be good."

Mike left a ten-dollar tip on a fifteen-dollar check, feeling sorry for the waitress because they'd monopolized the table for so long. As they left the restaurant, Mike noticed the wall behind the cash register. Instead of country-style knick-knacks, this one was covered with photographs of pickup trucks and drilling rigs emblazoned with a variety of logos from gas-drilling companies. Yukon was featured prominently in half of the photos.

After they dropped Mike's car in the nearly empty Microtel parking lot, Mike grabbed his briefcase, hard hat, fire-retardant coveralls, and hiking boots, then took the passenger seat in Missy's DEP Jeep.

"It's about a forty-five-minute drive to the Campbell pad," Missy said as she put the Jeep in gear. "There's really not a lot to see there since no drilling is going on, but we can look at the lay of the land, and you can see where the Campbell house is located."

Mike settled in for the drive.

"Yukon has a freshwater impoundment at the site," Missy said. "That's the one I was telling you about. I've heard rumors that maybe it was used for flowback water in February, but nothing definitive. I asked the inspector, and he knows nothing about it. I've seen no evidence of it being used for frack water, and the company line is that it was built and used only for fresh water. It's been empty since the last frack job they had in the neighborhood. We can take a look at that too."

"Good. I've been wondering about that since you told me the rumor when we first talked. I'd love to find evidence they used the pit illegally."

Mike thought about his last conversation with Darius Moore. He said he knew nothing about whether the pit had been used for flowback, and Mike wanted to believe him. Darius told him he would check with the operations guy, Norby Lafleur, and get back to him. Something didn't feel quite right, and he wondered what really went on at the site in the dead of winter.

"Did you get permission from Yukon for our site inspection?" Mike asked. "Part of me says we should tell them before we go onto their pad and part of me says we can show up whenever we want to."

"When a job is active, and I know that people will be on-site, I generally don't ask for permission; I just show up and check in at the guard shack. Since the Campbell pad is inactive, I thought it would be a good idea to give them a heads-up. They do have a small guard shack there, but it's empty most of the time. I called and told the Yukon guy you'd be joining me. That was okay, wasn't it?"

"Yes. Maybe I should've told their lawyer I was going to be on their drill pad. I mean, the department can do inspections even if there's litigation. Also, we're supposedly on the same side, so it shouldn't be a big deal. Any idea who they're going to send to the site?"

"Probably a low-level flunky, like a geologist." They looked at each other and laughed.

Mike watched Missy while they talked. She had shoulder-length light brown hair, sapphire-blue eyes, and a short, straight nose. She wasn't heavy, maybe *curvy,* Mike thought, in a very attractive way. His father would have used the word *zaftig*. Her face was tan, with a few freckles around her nose. It didn't look as though she was wearing any makeup. She wore a light blue, long-sleeved work shirt, unbuttoned, over a white T-shirt, tank top, or chemise. Maybe it was a teddy? Mike never could get the name of that female garment right. Whatever it was, it had a deep scoop neck showing off the top of her generous cleavage. Mike did his best not to stare. Of course, she wore jeans and work boots like any other self-respecting geologist. Mike's eyes were drawn to her.

"Where is the Campbell house?" Mike asked as the car sped past a herd of grazing cows.

"You mean the location of your dinner date with the hot, old married lady tomorrow night?" Missy asked, turning her head and flashing him a broad smile.

"No, my thank-you dinner for saving little Lucas from the crazed rioters."

"I've met Mrs. Campbell, I mean *Ms. Bruno-Campbell,* a few times. She's quite a number for an older woman. A real hottie. I can see why a woman her age would want to ply you with wine."

"Oh geez, Missy, you think she wants to *cougar* me?"

"Let's see . . . Her husband works in New York during the week, and she's bored. Nice hair. Good figure. I mean, you have to admit that she's hot—"

"And what, in her mid-forties? I'm not even thirty."

"I heard that forty is the new thirty," Missy said. She glanced at him and didn't bother suppressing a full-on smile.

"Well, other than the fact that she's married, what if I *did* like older women? I'm single, free to make my own decisions. Why not?"

She puffed out her lips and said, "Well, I'm only twenty-five. I guess that means I'm a good twenty years too young for you. If you like older women, I mean. Probably not hot enough, either."

Mike looked at her. "There literally is nothing I can say right now where I can't get into trouble. If I comment on your good looks? Trouble. If I say you're really hot? Trouble. If I say that, at your twenty-five to my twenty-nine, we'd be perfect together? Trouble. If I say, I have the hots for older women? Trouble. Younger women? Trouble. I'm just going to shut up before it's too late."

"You think I'm good-looking and hot?" Missy asked, glancing at him.

"See what I mean? I have a feeling I'll be hearing from HR tomorrow."

"Well, just to even things out, I mean only to confuse the HR people, and for no other reason, you *are* kind of cute." She drove a few hundred feet. "And you've established that we're both Jewish . . ."

"Now we're in trouble." Mike patted her shoulder with more of a rub than a pat, and they smiled at each other.

"Mike, I have something really serious to tell you," Missy said.

He shook his head. "Oh geez, I can't wait for this."

"We're here."

27

A good walk, spoiled (Mark Twain)

Missy slowed the Jeep next to a field of soybeans and came to a stop in front of a billboard-sized sign. Across the top was the logo of Yukon Oil and Gas Company. Underneath, it said *Campbell Pad,* followed by line after line of regulatory information.

"I hope the gate is open," Missy said as she turned onto the gravel access road.

"*Now* you're wondering about the gate?" Mike asked.

"This wouldn't be the first time I hopped a fence at a drill pad and walked a mile on an access road to get to a site. You got a problem with that, mister?"

Before he could respond, they drove through the wide-open gate.

Missy took the gravel road slowly through the woods. When they cleared a rise, the Campbell pad was spread out before them. The six-acre facility was on the side of a farm field with an earthen berm surrounding it. In the middle of the pad were three wellheads with their production trees, producing gas. The trees were steel fixtures sticking straight out of the ground, about the height of a man. The industry guys often referred to them as Christmas trees. These were not towering monsters like the derricks that preceded them. If you drove by a facility such as this, you could easily miss it.

The trees were hooked into a network of pipes that fed the natural gas to a nearby pipeline that came out of the ground on the opposite side of the pad. A handful of small structures and tanks were nearby. Water had ponded in some ruts and low-lying areas on the pad, but basically it was clear, almost like a black football field without grass. Surrounding it was a steep hill to the north and farm fields planted with greening soybeans. The whole area was enclosed by a chain-link fence topped with barbed wire.

Near the end of the access road were two modular buildings. One was small; the other was a full-sized trailer. Two white pickup trucks were parked next to them with Yukon logos on their doors.

"That's funny. The last time I was here, the big trailer wasn't here. I think that's Norby Lafleur's office." Missy pointed. "It used to be over at the Paxton pad."

Mike shrugged.

"Are you wearing fire retardant clothing?" Missy asked.

"No, I just have those FR coveralls I brought with me."

"Okay, put on your hard hat and safety glasses. With luck, they won't bother us and make you put on the coveralls. It's starting to get hot."

Mike hopped out of the Jeep, and Missy slid out of the driver's seat until her feet touched the ground. Mike followed her around the pickup trucks, avoiding the modular guard shack and office trailer. They walked toward the Christmas trees at the center of the pad. Ten seconds later, they heard a gruff southern voice call out.

"Hey! Y'all wanna sign in?"

Mike turned and saw a thin man, dark-tanned, average height, wearing jeans and a work shirt with the Yukon logo, an oil and gas-style hard hat, and safety glasses. Mike and Missy approached, and Missy held out her hand.

"Hey there, Bones. Good to see you again."

"Hey there to you too, Miss Missy," he smiled, gently gripping her hand. Friendly. "Y'all want to come inside? We have the AC cranked way up."

"Sure. This is Mike Jacobs, one of our lawyers from Harrisburg. I'm just showing him around. It's not an official inspection."

Bones nodded, quickly shook hands, then opened and held

the door for them as they entered the modular office. Inside, a fit man, fiftyish, crew-cut, was talking on a satellite phone. The man held up a finger with his free hand and then reached out and shook Missy's while he talked. A minute later, he ended his call and shoved the phone into his front pocket.

"Hey there, Missy," the man said with a distinctive southern twang. He smiled at her.

"Let me introduce you. Mike, this is Norby Lafleur. He heads up operations for Yukon in Pennsylvania, Ohio, and West Virginia. Norby, this is Mike Jacobs, one of DEP's lawyers from Harrisburg. He's working on the Campbell appeal."

The men shook hands.

"Jacobs," he said, and his eyes flicked upwards and to the left for just a moment. The smile evaporated from his face. "I've heard of you. Lawyer. You've been talking about me with our lawyer, Darius Moore, right? I wonder if I should have mine here too?" Norby asked.

Mike was taken aback.

"I don't recall talking about you in particular, Mr. Lafleur. We've talked about this operation. Your name may have come up."

"Is that a fact?"

"Feel free to call him," Mike said, "but we're on the same side in the Campbell appeal. Also, I'm here just to have a look at the site and get a look at the lay of the land. We're not doing any formal inspection or site view."

"Yeah, but Missy brought her knife; I wonder if I should have my gun with me," Norby said without a trace of humor.

"I'm not here to interact with you, really," Mike said. "I just need to see the site. I'm sure you know that Missy wrote the letter that said there was no geological connection between Yukon's drilling and the Campbells' water well. The Campbells filed an appeal from the Department's letter, and my goal is to support Missy's letter. If you want to call your lawyers, be my guest."

"Actually, I spoke with Mr. Moore yesterday. I told him Missy called, and y'all were planning a visit, and he said he was surprised. He said he'd like to speak with you, but tonight would be soon enough."

Mike and Missy signed the sign-in sheet. Mike glanced over the sheet and noticed a large number of visitors from many different companies had signed in over the previous week. He wondered if anything was going on.

"Do you really have to give us the safety lecture?" Missy asked.

"We always do." He smiled. "This here's the Campbell pad. Y'all need to wear fire retardant clothing, a hard hat, safety glasses, and steel-toed shoes while y'all are on the pad. If you don't have any of these, we'll provide them for you. Don't touch any of the equipment on the pad or go into any restricted areas. In the event of a fire or explosion, immediately exit the pad area. Do not attempt to put out the fire or approach the fire. Only trained professionals should put out any fire. Your safest egress is the access road. Our rally point will be the junction of the access road and Campbelltown Road. In the event of any emergency, please make every effort to meet up there. Any questions? If not, please sign this release."

Mike glanced at the short release, saw nothing offensive, and signed it, as did Missy.

The little group left the guard shack and began trekking across the pad. Norby took the lead with Bones at his side. Mike could see them engaged in a discussion. Norby did all the talking. Missy followed close behind them, and Mike intentionally dawdled so he could take his time observing the small details and take pictures with his phone. One thing he looked at was the six-foot high fence surrounding the pad. He'd been to other pads over the years, and none of them had fences.

Norby looked behind him. "Try to keep up with us if you can, Mr. Jacobs. I've never lost anyone on a tour and don't plan to start now."

"Sorry, just looking at the gear you have here. Very interesting."

"If you say so."

"What's the deal with the fence? I've been to other operations that didn't have a fence."

Norby stopped walking and turned around. "Kids, local kids. They're curious, and we've had a few to-dos. Not a big deal, but the fence helps to keep them back."

"What kind of *to-dos*?" Mike pressed.

Norby's face turned red. "Dirt bikes. A few potshots with .22's. Our system is designed to handle that. The fence keeps 'em off the pad."

Norby turned and continued walking. Mike looked around the open, hilly terrain, and the first house he saw was easily a half-mile and two hilltops away. He wondered, and not for the first time, how easy it would be for a determined terrorist, whether he was a fourteen-year-old kid on a dirt bike or ISIS, to sabotage a drill pad.

They reached the production trees a couple of minutes later. Norby turned around and held up his hands.

"That's as close as y'all can get. This here's the three well heads on the Campbell pad. We call these the Christmas trees. That's the 1-H, 2-H, and 3-H wells." He pointed. "Our goal is to drill seven more over the next few years for total of ten. These wells are particularly productive here, and we expect to be in production for a good many years. We connect directly over there to Yukon Midstream's pipeline. As you may have guessed, Yukon Midstream is owned and operated by Yukon Oil and Gas. Eventually, the Yukon Midstream pipeline hooks up with the America North Pipeline which provides sixteen percent of the natural gas for Philadelphia, New York, and parts in between."

"Do you control methane releases here?" Mike asked. "Some people criticize the industry for releasing too much methane at these pad sites."

"Mr. Jacobs, that's a little like asking a banker if they allow dollar bills to get blown out the door of the bank. It's the kind of a fool question I'd expect from someone uneducated, like a reporter. Of course, we do. That's our bread and butter. We make money on the natural gas, the methane that goes into the pipeline, not any that escapes into the air. You know those en-*vi*-ros think we don't give a crap about the environment. Look at this place. Clean as a whistle. Missy only called us yesterday to announce your little tour, so this is the way this place always looks. Clean. We require that. We take care of the wetlands and all of the bugs and bunnies here, too. Look at that."

Norby pointed to deer tracks in some mud on the pad.

"The deer can jump that fence and cross this pad and trust me, we have all kinds of critters that like it up here just fine. More birds, even seagulls, than you can shake a stick at."

"So you do control it?" Mike said, ignoring Norby's response. "You prevent any methane from escaping? Some people say that natural gas isn't all that efficient, that it contributes carbon to the atmosphere," Mike replied, not relenting.

Norby rolled his eyes and shook his head. "The EPA itself says America produces less airborne carbon today than ten years ago. Go on their website and look it up. They said this was directly a result of burning more natural gas. This well, the Campbell 2-H well, has already produced 139,000 Mcf of gas. That well alone has provided the Campbells with about $50,000 in royalties, and that's just one well. When we're done up here, they get back their property. We'll restore the pad, and you won't even know we were here. The gas results in less pollution than the alternatives, and it makes money, not just for my company, but also for the landowners and the townships that get your P-A-impact fee money."

Missy gave Mike a hard look. Mike ignored her.

"How deep is the vertical portion of your wells?" Mike asked.

"The Marcellus Shale is 5,900 feet below us, so over a mile. Also, one well has a horizontal lateral distance of about 10,000 feet, one is 12,000 feet, and the last is 14,000 feet," Norby replied.

"And the limiting factor on the distance of a lateral is?"

"Property rights and or geology. If you drew a giant circle around this spot, we're taking gas from a diameter of almost five miles. Think about that." He pointed to the ridges surrounding the Campbell pad. "You can't even see where our laterals end. Y'all might be surprised to know this, but not everyone wants us to take their gas. Also, in one instance, one of our competitors beat us to the lease, and they have the gas rights where ours quits. The Campbell 1-H well, this one," he said, pointing, "hits a fault about 10,000 feet over yonder. We couldn't get around that, so the lateral ends at the fault."

Missy had pulled out a USGS geological map with the laterals diagrammed on it. She grabbed Mike by the arm and pointed in the direction of the lateral. Norby and Bones also gathered around.

"Right here," she said pointing to the map.

"That's right, honey, the fault is 10,000 feet over there," Norby said. Looking at Mike, he added, "nearly two miles away. Way on the other side of that ridge." He pointed to a tall hill. The base of the hill was being farmed, but the top was wooded.

"Do you ever hear from any of the neighbors in the vicinity of the fault?" Missy asked. "I mean, if there's a place where there's a possibility of communication between the drilling and the surface, it would be at a fault in the rock units."

Norby glared at her for a moment and then recovered. He looked straight at her as he spoke. "No, no complaints. Our lateral terminates two hundred feet before it reaches the fault, so there's no chance of any communication. Plus, the gas would have to make its way over a mile to the surface. The chance of that happening is slim and none."

"How are you so sure of that?" she asked. "Your lateral is extending two miles from here, and if you're off by a hair on this map, you'd penetrate the fault."

"Geologists. We hire only the best geologists, honey. Most of our geologists here are local, Penn State, Lehigh, Pitt, so they have a good feel for the subsurface here in northern P-A-," Norby said with a smile.

As Missy rolled up her map, Mike said, "Any trouble with the cement," he pronounced it *se-MENT*, "when you were completing the wells?"

"Nope, none. The cement," *SEE-ment*, "went in just fine. It was a perfect cement job."

They continued walking around the perimeter of the pad, taking time for Norby to explain the water separator and the pipeline connection. When they reached the closest point to the impoundment, the four of them climbed to the top of the berm and looked down.

The impoundment was on the other side of the fence, about a hundred feet past an earthen berm Yukon built to control runoff. It was mostly dry, with puddles scattered across its expanse. The pit's black impervious liner was streaked with mud. Animal tracks abounded near the water. A gate in the fence was wide open.

"That's Pit A," Norby said, pointing. "It's empty now, but we can fill 'er up pretty quick the next time we're fracking here."

"So the impoundment is designed for just fresh water?" Mike asked.

"That's right. Typically, we over-design all of our impoundments, like this one. Whenever we do fracking nowadays, the flowback water goes into specially designed frac tanks we bring up here for that purpose. The fluid is hauled away for recycling or disposal."

"Do you ever put flowback water into the pit?" Mike asked.

Norby's face broke into a wide smile. *Forced*, Mike thought. "Of course not. That's a *fresh*water impoundment. All we ever put in there is fresh water, five million gallons of it at a time."

"Just *fresh* water?" Asked Mike.

"*Just* fresh water. Makeup water for completions," said Norby.

Mike thought for a second, then said, "You said this was Pit A. Where's the 'B' pit?"

"We planned on building a second impoundment and then decided against it. The name stuck."

Mike glanced at Missy, who had unrolled her USGS geologic map. She turned it to orient it to the impoundment.

"Am I reading this right, Norby? Was the impoundment built on top of a ridge of shale?" Missy held the map up and eyeballed it against the backdrop of the impoundment.

"You're right, honey," Norby said. He stood shoulder-to-shoulder with her and drew his finger across her map. "We encountered some shale, mostly pretty crumbly stuff, but our contractor was able to blast the harder parts successfully. We put layers of clay, construction stone, and sand on top of that to give us a smooth surface. The liner sits on top of all of that."

Mike pointed at the gate. "I see your security fence is open. That's not what you normally do, is it?"

Norby looked at Bones and said, "No. We're doing some maintenance on the impoundment. Routine stuff. Preventative. Our guys were down there earlier today and will be back later today, so they left the fence open."

Norby looked at his watch. "Hey folks, I'm running out of time, so how about if we head back and look at the wetland area below our pad that we had to avoid."

"If it's okay with you, I'd like to take a closer look at the impoundment," Mike said. Without waiting, he went through the fence and started scrambling down the back side of the berm, jogging and sliding down the steep slope. Missy followed close behind.

"We'll just be a couple of minutes," Missy shouted over her shoulder.

"I'd prefer if you didn't . . ." Norby said as Mike and Missy scrambled over the berm.

Mike ignored him and kept jogging.

28

I have found it a singular luxury to talk across the pond to a companion on the opposite side. (Henry David Thoreau)

After they'd made a little distance from Norby and Bones, Mike pulled Missy close as they walked and said quietly, "I got the feeling we were getting the bum's rush."

"Do ya think? You managed to touch a couple of Norby's sore spots. Something in me says this pond is another."

Mike smiled. "Maybe you can show me where that shale ridge was located?"

"Well, if they really blasted and leveled it, you may see some of the remaining ridge on either side of the impoundment, but it should be leveled flat through the pit where the ridge used to be."

They climbed the berm surrounding the pit and started walking around it. None of it was particularly impressive. It looked like a giant black swimming pool. Empty. Missy put her hand on Mike's arm and pointed to the area outside of the pit. She held onto his arm for several seconds.

"Wait a sec. You can see the remains of the little shale ridge over there. It's not all that impressive. Just a low ridge of shale, like Norby said. Probably more than a dozer could handle in spots, so you'd want to do a little blasting to get it out of the way. If you look on the opposite side of the impoundment, you can see where the ridge picks up." Missy pointed.

Mike squatted down on the berm directly over the ridge, looking back across the pit to where the ridge would have been.

"Look at that," Mike said, pointing toward the middle of the pit. "Do you see it? Those places where the floor of the impoundment is pushed up? Are those places where they never leveled the shale ridge?"

"It sure looks like it."

"What would that do to the liner?"

She put her pointer finger against her palm. "About the same as holding a knife blade against a balloon. You might get away with it for a little while, but eventually, kablam." She pulled her hands apart, imitating a balloon exploding.

Mike took out his phone and took pictures. He looked back toward the pad. Norby was standing on top of the pad berm, watching them. He appeared to be talking on his satellite phone.

"He's watching us." Mike said, pointing with his chin.

They continued walking around the perimeter of the impoundment. Mike pointed to a clearing outside of the impoundment. "Look at that. Looks like a campsite. Maybe when they were building the impoundment? Seems to have its own access road, too." Mike pointed to a trail through the dense woods.

"Yeah. Also its own dump," Missy pointed to an old blue lawn chair sitting upside down in the weeds. "That looks like a back way in here," she said, pointing past the clearing. "Maybe another time if we need to come back, we can sneak in when no one's watching us."

Mike raised his eyebrows. "You do that kind of thing?"

"Maybe. Is this attorney-client privileged?"

"Maybe."

"Then maybe I do, and maybe I don't." She smiled.

"You're too much," Mike said, laughing. "Fun. Funny."

They walked into the wooded area and looked back toward the pad. Norby and Bones were gone.

"Oh, I'm not all fun and games," she said, looking at her shoes. "This whole thing with Richard really has me unhappy. I'm so tired of dealing with him, his jealousy, his rages, the way he treated me. I really hope I'm done with him. I don't want to burden you with it; I mean, we barely know each other. Maybe someday we can talk about it."

Mike and Missy stood close. Very close. Mike put a hand on her arm and glanced around. Norby was gone. He wrapped his arms around her and hugged her tightly. She hugged him back, resting her head on his shoulder for several long seconds.

"What was that, mister?" She said as she held him. She lifted her head but didn't let go.

He released her. "You looked like you needed a hug. I hope I didn't offend you."

She smiled. "Don't apologize. I did need a hug. From you." She hugged him again, more tightly, making full-body contact. This was much more than a friendly hug. It was the kind of hug that could lead to things. They stood near the clearing like that for many seconds. Mike liked the way she felt in his arms. Her head was next to his, and it occurred to him that she had to be standing on her toes. That made him smile.

After they broke off, Missy slowly walked away and surveyed the campsite. Mike was close behind.

"That was a nice break," Missy said, smiling. "We've got to get back to work."

"You mean hug breaks aren't a part of the state employees union contract?" They laughed.

Mike kicked at some trash. He stopped when he found a rusty hibachi. "Look at this. Someone left their grill here."

Missy shoved something with her foot, a bright yellow object. "I think this is a chock like they use to hold truck wheels in place, so they don't roll away."

"Who leaves all this stuff at their campsite?" Mike wondered aloud. "It's like someone left in a hurry."

"So, was this here before the pit was dug? During? Or after?" Missy asked.

Mike walked to the end of the campsite to the narrow trail, weedy and overgrown. "Hey, look. I see a road down the hill. It branches off, and another trail goes up the hill. This might have been an old logging road. Maybe the back access for a farmer to his field."

Missy pulled out her map and showed Mike. "My map doesn't have any name for the little blacktop road down there, but it hooks up to Campbelltown Road about a half-mile from here. Like I said, a convenient backdoor."

Mike shrugged. "That's worth knowing."

They walked around the outside of the impoundment to a point where the terrain was lowest, and the berm was tallest. Missy stopped. She got down on her knees and put her face to the ground. Mike saw her do this and slowly approached. He got down on his knees and joined her.

"What is it? What do you see?" he asked.

"I'm not sure. It's dry, so there's no effluent coming out of the ground here, but I see residue staining a couple of rocks. It's like a dried-up spring. She sat up and surveyed the location, looking between the possible outfall and the pit. Then she took out her map and marked a spot with an X. She drew an arrow to it and wrote "*Poss. Spring?*" and "*Outfall?*"

"It's possible that when the pit's full, it leaks, and some of the water in the pit comes out here. Since the pit is empty, we can't see any water leaving the pit, but this is strange." She pried a rock out of the ground and sniffed it.

"Smell this." She held it next to his nose.

"Sort of minerally, sulfury, maybe chemical smell. Right?"

"Something like that." She took off her small backpack and placed the rock and a couple of others from the same spot into a plastic collection bag.

"You know, if only water was leaking out of the pit, I wouldn't expect to see any residue." She stood up and snapped several pictures with her phone. "To be determined."

The day had warmed up, and the temperature was close to eighty as they started back up the path to the impoundment. "Hang on a sec, will ya?" she asked.

Missy turned her back on Mike. As he watched, she stripped off her work shirt and tied the sleeves around her waist. When she turned back, she said, "It was getting way too hot in that shirt."

Mike glanced at her. Missy, like Mike, was damp with sweat. The scoop-neck white top was plastered to her frame, spaghetti straps and pink bra straps stretched to her nearly bare shoulders. Between the damp white fabric and her pink bra, little was left to the imagination. In a glance, he saw all of her ample breasts; a good amount of cleavage showed above the neckline of her clingy top. It took all of Mike's willpower to keep his eyes above her chest as they talked.

"Whew, that's better," she said as she tightened the sleeves around her waist.

Mike thought the same thing.

When they finished circling the pond, Mike reached the top of the berm just before Missy did. As she climbed for the top, he offered his hand and tugged her the rest of the way. They didn't let go. They laughed as they jogged down the inside of the berm. Mike squeezed her hand, and she squeezed back, holding on for several seconds as they walked.

Only one pickup truck remained at the trailer-office. Mike opened the door; Bones was inside, looking at his phone. The air conditioning slapped him in the face.

"Norby had to get back. Said he wanted you to call him later today. He asked me to wait so I could lock the gate behind you."

Missy entered a moment later, and the AC did what it often does to a woman's nipples. Bones ogled her from top to bottom.

Missy watched his eyes. "I guess we've all seen enough for one day," she said, crossing her arms over her breasts. "The impoundment, have you ever had any trouble with it holding water? I mean, it looks as though some of the shale ridge is poking up into the liner."

"No, never had a problem," Bones said. "That's Grade-A construction over there. Besides, it's just a freshwater impoundment. Even if we had a leak, we'd just be putting fresh water into the ground."

"What's below the impoundment?" Mike asked.

"I don't rightly know," Bones replied.

Missy spread the map on the small card table and leaned over. "Down-gradient here about a quarter-mile is Spruce Run."

She traced her finger down a ravine to the creek. "And if I'm not mistaken, over here is the Campbell residence."

Mike glanced at Bones and noticed that his eyes were fixated on Missy's breasts. He wanted to hit him in the face. Instead, he moved to block the man's view.

"You don't say," Bones said, finally looking at the map.

29

Common Courtesies

Missy and Mike pulled into the Microtel parking lot in Sayre at 6 p.m. Missy lived in Towanda, a good half hour south of Sayre.

"Do you want to head home and wash up?" Mike asked. "I mean, it was pretty hot out there. We could meet at the restaurant, or I could pick you up at your apartment."

"That's a lot of extra driving. A good geologist always carries around spare everything in a bag in her trunk. How about if I take a shower in your hotel room?"

"Okay," Mike said slowly. "I'll let you have my room so you can do that. I'll just wait in the lobby."

"I'm not going to make you sit in the lobby," she said, patting him on the shoulder. "You can watch TV or something. Just stay out of the bathroom." She turned and smiled. "We're grown-ups."

Mike thought about it for a moment. "No, I'll take my stuff upstairs and drop it. I think it'll be best if I wait for you in the lobby, then I'll come up and take my shower."

"Suit yourself." She shrugged.

Mike gathered up his suitcase, and the two of them approached the check-in desk. A young woman wearing a blue jacket with the hotel logo checked them in. "Here you go, Mr. Jacobs, two room keys. Also, here are vouchers for two breakfasts for tomorrow morning."

Mike was about to say something and then stopped. He glanced at Missy and they smiled at each other.

As they rode the elevator, Mike stood with his back against one of the walls looking at Missy. He was going to say something. Instead, he smiled at her, and she smiled back.

The room was small. It did boast a room-filling king-sized bed. A television was mounted on the opposite wall above a small desk. They squeezed into the room, and Mike shut the door. He looked at Missy and shook his head.

"What? You're not going to get all weird on me now, are you?" Missy said.

"No. You too, right?"

"Right."

They stood less than a foot apart and looked into one another's eyes. They said nothing. Everything in Mike wanted to reach out and hold her. Kiss her. Pick her up and make love to her on the king-sized bed. She stood close. She seemed to be waiting. Long moments passed.

Finally, Missy said, "Well, if it's okay with you, mister, I'm going to take my shower." Her voice was a whisper.

She turned and headed to the bathroom. Before she fully closed the door, she looked out and smiled. "See you later."

Mike unpacked his bag and put his clothes in the tiny nightstand by the bed. He heard her pee, and a couple of moments later, the shower was running. He stood near the door. Missy was singing in the shower. This made him smile. Then he grabbed one of the keys and went to the lobby with his laptop.

About ten minutes later, Mike was at a café table in the lobby, drinking a Yuengling Lager straight from the bottle and going over emails. He looked up. A man about his age stared at him from a nearby table. Mike looked around, then realized he was Richard Shelby, Missy's former boyfriend. Mike had met him briefly at the DEP meeting several months earlier in Williamsport.

Mike walked the few steps to the other man's table. "Richard, right?" Mike extended his hand.

Shelby glared at him, then took his hand. "Mike? Where's Missy?"

Shelby was several inches taller than Mike, with short blondish hair, and everything about him was hard. He had severe looks, a bony face, a muscular body, and Mike never saw him smile. At the DEP retreat, during the beer and wine gathering at the end of the first day, Shelby was the only "plus one" to make an appearance, and he made an impression. Not a good one. Shelby always had an arm around Missy or held her hand. He was very protective in a room full of friendly people, most of whom treated Missy like a sister. Mike couldn't imagine such a smart, sweet, pretty woman ever being with this man.

Shelby clamped Mike's hand until it hurt, then released his grip quickly.

"Uh, hello. She's upstairs, in my room, taking a shower."

Richard's expression was nothing short of murderous. "What?" The syllable was staccato, like a gunshot.

"Yeah, we got back from the field, and Missy said she wanted to take a shower before we went out to dinner. I lent her my room and came down here so she could have privacy. Total privacy."

For some reason, Mike felt incredibly guilty over the courtesy he'd extended to his friend.

"Key. Mike, can I borrow your key to get into your room?"

"I don't think Missy is expecting you." Mike looked at him warily.

"Key." Shelby held out his hand.

"No. She didn't say anything about you coming over. Besides, I thought you two were through."

Shelby looked at him and held out his hand. "I said *key.*"

Mike frowned. "This would be a good time for you to leave, Richard. We're done here." Mike turned slightly sideways and stood tall, his body clenched in anticipation of a sucker punch.

Shelby's nostrils flared. "Yeah. Right."

Shelby moved closer. Mike waited for the blow. Instead, Shelby did an abrupt about-face and strode out of the hotel. Mike watched him hurry into his pickup and drive away. He couldn't help but notice the gun rack which held a rifle of some sort. Mike was pretty sure this wasn't hunting season.

Mike went back to his laptop and waited in the lobby for a full half-hour for Missy. At first, he was curious about what was taking so long. Then he got bored. Then mad. He texted Missy.

Everything ok?

No response.

Mike looked for a house phone but couldn't find one. Finally, he went to the front desk and asked a tall man in a hotel blazer for the phone.

"Room 605? Sure. The phone is around the corner." He pointed to the hallway.

"Thanks," Mike said, and waved slightly.

He turned to find the phone when the clerk said, "Mr. Jacobs should be there now. He came in about fifteen minutes ago."

"What?"

"Yes. He said he lost his key. Happens all the time. I printed him a new one."

Mike jogged to the elevator and pushed the button several times. He started looking for the stairs when the elevator door slowly opened.

Missy and Richard exited quickly. Richard had a hand on her arm, guiding her.

Missy was in a blue-and-white cotton gingham top with unbuttoned sleeves and white jeans, flip-flops on her feet. Her hair was still wet and hung to her shoulders. She never looked at Mike but stared at the floor. Mike couldn't tell, but it appeared as though she had been crying and her face may have been bruised. Richard carried her bag.

"Hey Mike, thanks for the invite, but Missy's not feeling well," Richard said cheerfully and hurriedly. "I'm taking her to her apartment. Real nice seeing you again." Richard had his arm around Missy and pulled her along.

"Missy? Are you okay?" Mike asked as he followed them to the door.

The couple slowed.

"Yes," she whispered. "See you at work."

They were out the door, and Mike watched as Richard put Missy in her Jeep and waited until she drove off. Mike walked outside and watched. Richard turned and looked at Mike. His smirk was like that of a street fighter who had just given his opponent a severe beat down. He got into his truck and drove away.

When Mike got to his room, he was shocked to see his bed a mess. Someone had pulled it together, but just barely. A sodden towel was on the floor. The bathroom was still humid from Missy's shower, and some of her hair products were scattered on the sink.

He looked at the bed and with a quick motion tore off the bedspread. The sheets were damp.

"What the hell?" Mike said out loud. He was angry with himself for failing to protect Missy. Whatever happened in his room, he felt complicit.

He pulled out his phone and texted Missy.

Are you okay?

She didn't respond.

Missy?

No response.

Mike called her and after four rings, the call went to voice mail. "Hey Missy, it's Mike. Give me a call tonight, will you? Please? Any time, it doesn't matter how late. Okay?"

That night, angry with himself and concerned for Missy, he slept on top of the bedspread.

30

Paradise Paved

Cliff West, chief of the Washington Township Police Department, commanded a small and outgunned police force. The cheapskate township supervisors employed six officers, including the chief, four full-timers and two part-timers. They had to cover thirty-two square miles of farmland, mountains, and dozens of gas wells in Pennsylvania's Endless Mountains region. Fifteen hundred mostly underemployed full-time residents, and close to as many transient workers, sometimes more, populated the township. His department was barely large enough to handle their workload before all of the drilling and fracking. Once the drilling companies, the contractors, and their thousands of employees descended on the township, crime rose exponentially. Now they were in way over their heads.

The police department was too small to support a detective bureau. For all intents and purposes, Chief West was the only detective in the department. The other officers were busy patrolling, answering calls, breaking up bar fights, responding to overdoses, and dealing with irate hookers furious about johns refusing to pay for services rendered. They didn't have the time or skill for detective work. Chief West divided his time between ordinary administrative responsibilities, political responsibilities such as attending township public safety and township supervisors' meetings, training, coordination with the State Police and surrounding municipalities, and, to the extent he had time to do it, driving around the township in the patrol car with the word *Chief* prominently displayed on the front doors, so the residents didn't complain that all he did was sit in a fancy new office and talk on the phone. He was left with maybe fifteen minutes a day for detective work.

West had developed a triage system for detective work. If there was a murder or other crime requiring immediate attention, he'd handle it first. If a victim of a crime required some attention over and above something one of his officers could provide, that came next. At the very bottom of the list was looking for missing drillers and their RVs.

Four months had passed since Hector Torres had stopped into the office to file his missing person's report. The whole notion of a drilling contractor and RV being "missing" seemed preposterous to Chief West. Nevertheless, something about Torres's earnestness, maybe the fact that he was a veteran, a Marine nonetheless, caused this report to bother the chief at odd times of the day and night.

Things had quieted down, and he planned a whole afternoon to devote to detective work. In the morning, he called a cell number and smiled when Hector Torres walked into the station four hours later.

Torres buckled into the chief's Tahoe and said, "Hey, chief. This is a first for me."

The chief looked at him.

"Sitting up front in a cop car, I mean."

They shared a laugh.

As they drove through town, West apologized that the investigation had so few results four months after the report from Torres.

"Mr. Torres—"

"Hector, please."

"Hector, I'm still learning about this case. I'm hoping you can show me around the pad site and fill in details I know I'd miss."

They drove to Yukon's Campbell pad to look at the campsite identified by Torres, the last known location of Corsica and the RV. The chief drove about a hundred feet up Yukon's access road when he arrived at the locked gate. He asked Hector to check the lock. Torres jiggled it and held his thumbs down, making a face.

"I guess we can park here and hoof it," the chief said.

"Makes more sense if we go around back, anyway. That's where the campsite is." Torres directed the chief to the entrance of the steep, overgrown trail up to the campsite.

The chief had traded in his Chevrolet Caprice Police Pursuit car two years earlier in favor of a Chevy Tahoe SUV. This was another perk of the Impact Fee money. He loved the power of his old eight-cylinder rear-wheel-drive sedan but rarely got to exercise it fully. He figured, correctly, that an SUV would be much more versatile than the Caprice in a township with no Interstate highways.

Chief West slowly made his way up the narrow trail. Based on the broken vegetation, it looked as though another vehicle, like a small truck, had been through the area sometime in the past couple of months.

And at least one other vehicle.

Sometime not long ago.

The trail was steep and rugged. He wondered how anyone could manage it in an RV. He carefully navigated the ruts, tree limbs, and rocks, finally coming to a flat area a few dozen feet from the edge of an impoundment.

"Remember Hector, this is a potential crime scene," Chief West said as he got out of the SUV. "You walk behind me, preferably in my footsteps. Also, keep your eyes open for snakes. This area is full of them."

Chief West headed into the flat area, which resembled a campsite. It was rutted and there was a spot that looked like it could have been the resting place for an RV.

"That's where he was parked," said Torres. "There's the chock he put behind the tire to keep it from rolling down the hill."

"They're not too expensive, maybe ten or twenty bucks. Why would he leave that behind?"

Torres shook his head.

The chief pulled a camera from his shoulder bag and clicked off several shots. There was a blue folding lawn chair sitting upside down in a pile of weeds. He took a couple of pictures of that, too.

"That was his chair. He'd sit outside if it wasn't raining or snowing," said Torres. "The cold weather didn't seem to bother him."

"I think you can get them for ten or fifteen bucks at Walmart. Still, why would Corsica leave it behind?"

As they slowly made their way across the site, Torres called out to the chief, "Watch it!"

The chief jumped, thinking he was about to step on a rattlesnake. He narrowly missed stepping onto a rusty hibachi-type grill. It had charcoal residue, although the rain and snow had largely disintegrated the coals. It didn't look like it had been cleaned or used in some time, and it still had a slight aroma of charcoal, burnt meat, and festering bacteria.

"Didn't want you stepping onto his grill," said Torres.

The men climbed to the top of the berm and examined the expanse of black lining material that covered the pit. Torres explained the work they did and the challenges they faced. He pointed out the remains of the shale ridge.

"Those little peaks coming up through the lining, is that the shale?" Asked the chief.

"Yeah, and before you ask," said Torres, "we covered what we couldn't easily get out of the ground with extra clay and sand. They shouldn't be able to poke through the lining."

"You sure about that?"

"I hope."

The chief spent several minutes looking at the pit, especially the peaks of shale poking into the lining.

"So, chief, is this a crime scene?"

"Well, all we know is that Corsica's RV was up here in February. We don't know how many others have also used this as a campsite, parking area, or make-out area, before or since. I'm guessing the local teenagers might find this a convenient, out-of-the-way spot for some privacy. None of the stuff Corsica left behind is expensive, ten or twenty bucks a pop, but I wonder why he left it? I mean, even if the guy decided to head off for parts unknown, you'd think he'd take his stuff. Unfortunately, if a crime took place back in February, the site's just too degraded from the weather to be of any value to us. All we have is evidence of someone camping out. Nothing I've seen is evidence of a crime."

Even as he said this, Chief West didn't believe his own words.

31

Perhaps the truth depends on a walk around the lake.
(Wallace Stevens)

At 6 a.m., Mike ran four miles along what he assumed would be an empty country road. He was surprised by the volume of traffic as he crossed a stream and proceeded through farmland. Mike rounded a bend and was astonished to find in the middle of a cornfield a modern, four-story office building, the regional headquarters of a Colorado-based drilling company accompanied by a huge parking lot full of drilling equipment and pickup trucks. The frontage of the building and storage area was about a half-mile. He continued running until he came to a small woods where he turned around and returned to the hotel.

By 7:30 a.m., Mike was balancing a cardboard cup full of hot coffee (the label on the giant urn said *bold)*, a bowl of oatmeal, and an English muffin. His fire-retardant coveralls and boots were stuffed into his backpack and his hard hat dangled from a strap. He looked out on a lounge full of people, all eating free breakfast, and no empty tables. He made eye contact with a man, bald but with a full beard, wearing a Yukon Oil & Gas Company work shirt. He pointed at the empty seat at his small table.

"Thanks. I thought I was going to have to eat this standing up. My name's Mike." He held out his hand after he set his food on the table.

"Nice to meet you, pardner," said the man with an accent, maybe southern, maybe Texan. "I'm Cal. Saw you standing there looking a bit forlorn, and I'm not expecting anyone for breakfast."

"I guess you work for Yukon?" Mike asked as he spread strawberry preserves onto his muffin.

"Good guess," replied Cal pointing at the logo on his shirt. "I do site prep for them all over the country."

"I was just at a Yukon site yesterday. The Campbell pad," Mike said nonchalantly as he sipped on his coffee.

"Really? I'll be heading out there later this morning. I'm on second shift."

Mike angled his head. "That's funny. I was there yesterday and the site was completely empty. I mean Norby Lafleur and Bones were there, but nothing else was going on."

Cal laughed. "Well, that's because it all started this morning. The first shift was out there before sun-up. Normally the second shift would go on at 6 p.m., but since we're setting up I'm getting out there early. If I'm lucky, I'll be home, well, back *here,* in time for breakfast."

Mike thought about the long list of names he had seen on the sign-in sheet.

This guy works for Yukon. Why am I talking to him?

"So what exactly is going on at the Campbell pad? I mean, of course, I know there's going to be a lot of activity there. But what exactly is it you're doing today?"

What the hell am I doing? Mike asked himself. *I am crossing a huge red line. If Darius ever learned about this conversation, he'd tear my lungs out.*

Cal finished his bacon and licked his fingers. "We're moving in the drillin' rig. That'll be going up in a couple of days. I'm hoping to have 'er up and ready to roll in ten days, two weeks max. Then the drilling crew will spud the new well as soon as the rig is ready to go." He paused. "You know, pardner, start drillin' the well."

Mike thought fast. "Of course. Everyone knows what spudding a well is. I think that's the Campbell 4-H well. Right?"

"That's right. Wells one to three are in operation, and this will be the first of four new wells going in."

"Right, right." *Get out of here. Stop it. Stop it right now!*

"I'm hoping the drillin' will be done in less than two weeks after that for each well. So the total time from now until we frack the first new well is twenty-two days if all goes perfectly, maybe a month if we have any delays."

Mike nodded as he sipped his coffee and made a mental note.

"Hey pardner, what did you say you do for Yukon?" Cal asked as he sipped on his coffee.

Mike hesitated, thought hard, then said, "I'm a lawyer. I meet with people like Norby, Bones. You know, regulatory and permitting stuff. With DEP. What a pain in the ass they are." Mike laughed a knowing laugh.

Shit! What am I saying? It's all true, right? I'm with *DEP.*

"I hear you, brother," Cal said, picking up the laugh. "I'm going to go get another coffee."

Mike looked toward the door and saw Missy coming in. "Hey Cal, looks like my ride is here. Good luck out there."

Mike grabbed his backpack and picked up his trash. He tossed the refuse on the way to meet Missy at the door.

She was wearing a blue short-sleeved shirt and jeans. Her hair looked like she had pulled it back and not much more.

"Keep moving," he said quietly, touching his hand to her shoulder. "I may have stepped over a line, and I'm hoping that guy over there doesn't see me getting into a DEP Jeep."

"Hello to you too, Mike," Missy frowned at him.

"Also, we have to go back to the Campbell pad."

32

Avoid detection by the enemy. *A patrol must not let the enemy know that it is in the objective area. If contact is made, move to the release point. The recon element tries to break contact and return to the ORP, secure rucksacks, and quickly move out of the area. Once they have moved a safe distance away, the leader will inform higher HQ of the situation and take further instructions from them.* U.S. Army Ranger Handbook

The man finished dumping one gallon of bleach into the old well and screwed the cap back onto the empty white container. He took a look into the well, not unlike his habit of looking into the toilet when he was done, and could see nothing but darkness. Now, unlike before, in addition to the smell of the dank well and water, he could smell the bleach and antifreeze.

Carefully and quietly, he placed the steel cover back on top of the well and covered it with leaves and twigs, making sure it appeared untouched.

The operation took hours to plan and days for reconnaissance, but less than ten minutes to execute. *Typical.*

Done. Now get the hell out of Dodge.

He backed up, picked up the jugs, one yellow, the other white. They were empty now and weighed almost nothing. He was policing these out. He knew from his previous visits he could jog to the woods in about thirty seconds. He'd be back at the observation post in about a minute. Then, it would take him just a couple of minutes to gather whatever other stuff he'd brought with him and shove it into his backpack. In a total of under ten minutes, he would disappear into the woods and never return.

"Hi, Secret Agent Smith." The voice was small and close by.

Unbelievable. The kid was some kind of freakin' ghost.

The man slowly turned and looked toward the voice. The kid had popped up from behind a shrub maybe ten feet away. He was wearing shorts, a T-shirt with the Batman emblem, and sneakers. Typical kid. Cute. He held a soccer ball. He'd drawn something on his wrist with a pen. The red A. *Unbelievable. Crap.*

"Kid . . ."

"Lucas, remember?"

"Lucas. What the fu . . . *hell* are you doing here? I saw your mom drive away an hour ago. Don't you have soccer practice today or something like that?"

"I did, but I told my mom I was sick. She still had to take my sister and her friend to practice. Do you want to kick the ball around? I'm pretty good. Watch."

He kicked it about twenty feet toward a practice goal. It slowly rolled to a stop.

"Do you want to know why I told my mom I was sick?"

The man shook his head. "Not really." He looked around to see if they were alone. He patted his windbreaker. The Smith & Wesson was where it was supposed to be.

"I told her that because I was hoping you'd come back and we could play soccer or catch or something."

The man was confused. "You want to play catch? With me?"

"Yeah. Maybe we could play fort."

The man shook his head.

"You know, cowboys and Indians, cops and robbers. We could use *your* fort."

He shook his head again. "*My* fort?"

"Up there." Lucas pointed toward the observation post at the top of the hill.

"What are you talking about?" Beads of sweat formed on the man's forehead and upper lip.

"Yeah. After you were here last week, I went up the hill and found your fort. I could tell you were there because I found an old poncho on the ground and some other stuff. I've been hanging out at your fort pretending I'm hiding from the bad guys. We could play fort."

Unbelievable. A clusterfuck.

"When's your mom coming home?"

"She said around 11:30. Sometimes she goes to the Starbucks in town, and it's more like noon."

The man looked at his watch. It was 1050 hours. As he saw it, he had two choices: get rid of the kid permanently or get the hell away from him and never be seen again. Either way, the mission was compromised. Severely compromised. *Crap.* He hated the thought of killing the kid. He could do it if he had to, he'd done it before, but that shit never left you. Never.

"Do you remember when we met before how I told you I'd only come back if you promised not to tell anyone I was here? Do you remember that?"

"Yes," Lucas said slowly.

"Did you? Did you tell anyone? Your mom or dad? Maybe your sister? A friend?"

Lucas looked down and shook his head no.

The kid was lying. He should kill him now and be done with it.

"Lucas, this is really important. You cannot tell anyone I've been here. It's secret agent stuff. I mean it. Don't even think about doing that."

Lucas nodded vigorously. "I promise."

"Okay. I'll play soccer with you. Kick that ball to me."

Lucas happily scampered after the ball and kicked it to him. The ball rolled within a few feet of the man.

At one time, the man had been a star athlete. His best sport was soccer, and his teammates called him *the Big Leg*. One more time.

"Lucas. I'm going to kick the ball, and you get it and kick it back. Remember, no hands in soccer. Also, remember, don't tell anyone I was here. Okay?"

"Okay!" Lucas spread his legs and crouched a bit in front of the small practice goal. He was about twenty feet away.

The man glanced at the backyard and the adjacent field. He decided where to put the ball, backed up three steps and, as he approached, faked with his head that he was going left, then crushed the ball to the right into the next field. Lucas fell over going the wrong way, and the ball flew over him and the practice goal, hit the apex of its flight at about a hundred feet, and landed about two hundred feet away. Then it bounced another twenty-five feet across the neighboring soybean field and rolled. The total distance was close to 250 feet.

"Wow! That was some shot!"

"Go get it, Lucas. Kick it back here. All the way. No hands. Show me what you've got."

Lucas ran after the ball. As soon as he turned, the man picked up the empty jugs, took a quick last look at the well, and ran in the opposite direction. Over the front yard. Across Campbelltown Road. Up the side of the embankment. He stopped just before he entered the woods and looked back. Lucas was still chasing after the ball in the soybean field.

What the hell am I doing? I should go back and kill the kid. The witness.

He patted his windbreaker. The gun was still firmly in his shoulder holster.

I can do this. I should do this. Crap.

If I keep moving, the kid will never see me again.

He turned into the woods and made it to his observation post less than a minute later, where he policed the small amount of stuff he brought with him. He quickly shoved the poncho and other gear into his backpack. He was just about to leave when he saw what had been left for him next to a tree.

A small kid's backpack with Luke Skywalker's image on it.

Several Star Wars action figures.

Two unopened juice boxes.

Two small, sealed, kiddie-sized bags of chips.

Two power bars.

Resting on a flat rock behind a tree.

Two.

One for Lucas and one for . . .

Oh crap.

Angrily now, he kicked the rocks making up the observation post with a violent kick-boxing move. The rocks tumbled onto the ground. He took off in a dead run.

Away from the house.

Stupid. Weak. Imbecile.

I'm so screwed.

33

Lips that taste of tears, they say, are the best for kissing.
(Dorothy Parker)

Missy didn't question Mike's request that they return to the Campbell pad. She stared straight ahead and didn't speak. Mike surveyed her face and noticed her cheek looked bruised. No black eye, but a definite bruise.

"Do you want to talk?" Mike asked.

Missy said nothing.

"Missy," Mike laid a hand lightly on her shoulder.

She looked at him with moistened eyes.

"Not now," she said, almost imperceptibly. "Maybe later. I'm so sorry."

Mike waited a full ten minutes as they drove, then told her about his breakfast with Cal. The conversation was a monologue.

Finally, Missy composed herself and began talking as though nothing had occurred the night before. "Crap, no one told me they were going to spud the well. This is the first I'm hearing about it. I'll have to talk with the inspector, but it's possible he didn't get the notification until after we talked last week."

"I hope you don't think I'm being overly dramatic, but it seems really odd to me that just yesterday we spent a few hours in the field with Norby and Bones, and nobody even mentioned to us that all this activity was going to start within a matter of hours. I wonder if they plan to use the impoundment?"

"I suppose they could make up some sort of a song and dance about us not asking the right questions—something like that. I mean, they knew we'd find out. They have to give notice to the department. It's not like you can hide a whole drilling operation."

They drove for several miles along empty country roads. Mike speculated endlessly about why Norby didn't tell them Yukon was going to begin drilling new wells. Missy looked straight ahead, not responding. As they approached a small wooded PennDOT roadside rest area, Missy signaled, then pulled in. Mike looked at her and furrowed his eyebrows as she put the Jeep into park. The rest stop had space for about a half-dozen cars, two picnic tables, and two porta-potties. It was deserted.

"Is everything all right—"

"Just shut up for a sec, would you? Sometimes you talk too much." Missy took off her seatbelt, leaned over and put her arms around Mike and hugged him in a tight hug. A moment later, Mike could feel the tears running from her face to his. He held her and stroked her hair. They said nothing.

Missy cried a silent cry. Her shoulders bounced up and down, but she didn't make a sound. The hug lasted for a full five minutes. Missy pulled away and wiped the remaining tears with the backs of her hands. Mike kissed her forehead ever so lightly. Missy leaned in, and her lips found his. They kissed quietly and gently, deep, warm kisses. Mike's free hand roamed the side of her face and wandered lightly along her arm. He caressed the back of her head and stroked her hair. After several minutes she broke off and followed with small kisses around his face.

Still holding her, Mike backed off to arm's length and angled his head. "What's going on? What are we doing?"

"Can we *not* talk about this now?" She replied. "I'll explain. Just not now. I mean, here we are in a DEP Jeep, and this is totally unprofessional of me, crying and kissing you like that. Talk about HR problems. Is there an HR jail?"

Mike swiveled slightly, leaned into her, so she had to sit back in her seat, and kissed her on her face and then landed on her lips. They kissed passionately for many minutes while the Jeep idled at the rest stop.

"That's what I think of your unprofessionalism and HR issues," Mike said, caressing the side of her face. "I have no idea what's going on, but I'm here for you. Whatever I can do for you. Anything. Just say the word."

"When we met a couple of months ago," she said, "I felt some kind of spark, but you were very loyal to that girl you were seeing, and even though part of me would've loved it if you'd initiated something, I learned something admirable about you. I was happy when I saw we were going to be on this case together. I mean I *really* like you. I'm not saying this is going anywhere or even *has* to go anywhere. It's just feels so cool being with you."

"And Richard? He acts like he's still your boyfriend. . ."

"Was. I told you I broke that off a month ago. He won't accept it. Said he wanted to stay friends, but that's not exactly working."

"Because of me?"

"No. Maybe in a way. I'd been trying to break it off with him for at least six months. Meeting you reminded me there are kind, gentle men out there. Men who would treat me like I ought to be treated all the time. Richard can be so darn nice to me sometimes and other times—"

"Psychotic?"

"Basically," she said.

"You're a smart woman, Missy. You know you're in an abusive relationship with him, don't you?"

"I don't know. The good times were really good."

"And the bad times . . ." Mike took a free hand and examined her face.

"That too."

"He hits you?" He asked softly.

"Not really. He just slaps me sometimes."

"Missy, Missy . . ."

"I know, I know. I've been trying to get out of this, like I said. It's just harder than I imagined it would be." Missy took a deep breath. "My father. He did this to Mom. She never left him. I asked her why and she said, *love conquers all*. Do you believe that?"

"No," Mike said without hesitation. "There's something wrong about that. This is not the way a man should treat a woman."

"Richard was charming, kind, doting, all of that when we met. I loved the attention. Then something happened. I don't know. Part of me just wanted us to go back to the way it was, before he became mean. I know better. I think."

They stopped talking and just held each other. Mike gently stroked her hair.

Mike pulled back as though he was about to say something, then had second thoughts. Missy put her arms around him and hugged him tightly, as tightly as the front seat of the Jeep would allow. She planted her lips on his again, and they kissed more deeply than before.

Mike's eyes were closed, but a light caught his attention, and he slowly raised his lids. Blinking red and blue lights.

"Oh crap."

A police officer stood outside the Jeep, bent over looking in. Tapping on the glass with the end of a baton.

"Step out of the vehicle, please. License and registration."

Mike and Missy looked at each other.

"Oops," said Missy.

As Mike's foot hit the gravel, he looked down at his clothing. His shirt was partially pulled out and half unbuttoned. As he straightened himself out, he saw that Missy had the same problem. She reached inside her blouse and flipped her bra back into position. Her fingers worked to fasten her buttons as she put herself back together.

Missy handed the officer her license.

"Ms. Shelton, I guess you're not the owner of this state vehicle?" The officer had a name tag: *Chief West*. He handed her papers back to her.

"No, no. Look, officer—"

"Chief."

"Chief. This is terribly embarrassing. I'm a DEP geologist and we were on our way to look at a drilling site and I pulled over. One thing led to another and . . . things happened."

"I can see that." The chief suppressed a smile.

He walked to Mike. "License?"

Mike handed his license to the chief.

"Mr. Jacobs. Are you a DEP geologist, too?"

Mike started to speak, but nothing came out. He cleared his throat. "Actually, a DEP lawyer."

The chief pushed his lips together tightly. Mike thought they'd probably handed the chief a hilarious story that would supply him with endless beers from the boys at the local bar.

"A lawyer . . . Were you two on some kind of break? Is this what you DEP folks do between inspections?"

No one spoke. Finally, Mike said, "Are we in some kind of trouble offi—chief? I mean, I don't think we were doing anything illegal."

"Not yet. Do you want me to give you the standard speech I give the sixteen-year-old boys? About having a gang of big men come along to finish what you started way out here in the woods? I mean, *really* kids." He smiled at them. "I know hotel rooms are tight due to the drilling, but please, get a room."

Missy's face turned a bright red.

"So we're not in trouble?"

"Are you okay with this, ma'am? You were a willing participant in this . . . break? Nothing forced on you?" The chief asked.

"Yes, yes I'm okay. I started it and, really, I was hoping something like this might happen. I don't mean you, chief, I mean the kissing, and all we were doing was kissing and a little more maybe, but that was it, and Mike's so darned nice and it turns out he's a good kisser, a really good kisser, and . . ."

The chief waved his hands in the air. "Please, miss, no more details. I get the idea."

"Yes, I'm fine," Missy said, not meeting his eyes. "I'm nervous and babbling, but yes, I'm very happy in fact. Well, I was until about five minutes ago." Missy smiled.

The chief waited in his Chevy Tahoe SUV until Missy pulled out of the rest area.

Mike and Missy looked at each other and broke into peals of laughter as Missy carefully obeyed the speed limit. "Oh my God.

When I looked out the window and saw the chief, I nearly peed myself," Missy said.

"Yeah. It's been about fifteen years since the last time that happened to me. It's actually a funny story. Some time I'll have to tell you."

They both took deep breaths.

"Okay, mister, did you say the Campbell pad?" Missy asked as the laughter subsided. "I think we're going to be late." Missy drove the rest of the way, saying little and smiling a lot.

From time to time, Mike glanced at Missy. She looked at him, too. When their eyes met, they both laughed.

34

A half-truth is the most cowardly of lies.
(Mark Twain)

Missy's DEP Jeep fell into a line of pickups and tractor-trailers carrying heavy equipment along the Campbelltown Road. The going was slow—twenty miles per hour in places. Two or three times, Missy ventured into the oncoming lane to pass, but it was impossible on the narrow country road, and she always had to veer back into place.

"It's going to take us hours to get there at this rate," Mike said. "Once we get to the access road, it could take another hour just navigating the driveway with all of these trucks in front of us. I have a feeling we could be stuck in traffic all day."

"I have an idea," Missy said. "Hang on."

Missy sped up, entered the opposite traffic lane, then drove on the opposite shoulder at about sixty miles per hour. Mike white-knuckled the hand grip over the door. A pickup truck rounded the bend coming toward them, then honked loudly as it sped by. Without warning, Missy cut the wheel and turned onto a narrow, blacktopped farm lane. After about two hundred yards she plowed the Jeep into the underbrush. She wore a demented grin. The Jeep skidded to a stop in the dirt, and she shifted into first gear. The Jeep slowly climbed the embankment. Brush and overgrowth slapped the bumper as she drove up the narrow trace.

"Jesus, Missy, what the hell? Where are we?"

"The back door," Missy said, flicking her eyebrows up and down.

The Jeep continued climbing. Missy cut back and forth to avoid a large, exposed rock and then cut back again to avoid a tree limb that had fallen across the old trail. Branches spanked the windshield, and, more than once, Mike covered his face. After several minutes of climbing, Missy pulled into a flat opening.

"We're here," she announced with a smile.

Mike looked at her. "You crazy."

"I'll take that as a compliment." She still gripped the wheel.

She turned off the ignition and said, "It's a Jeep thing; you wouldn't understand." She laughed heartily.

Mike shook his head and grabbed his hard hat. "Do we have to go back the way we came?"

Missy jumped out and pointed past the front of the Jeep, "I don't think so. According to the map, the trail, or what there is of it, continues in a loop back to the road. Easy in, easy out." She laughed happily.

They walked around the campsite kicking at debris, then scrambled up the side of the impoundment. It was dry, even drier than the day before. The wet spots seemed to have evaporated. The sounds of trucks and workers from the nearby pad were loud and continuous. When they reached the point closest to the pad, they climbed the side of the berm, and Mike put his hand on Missy's shoulder before they crested the bank.

"Are we supposed to be here? I mean, ordinarily, you would go through the main access road and sign in at the guard shack, right?"

"Oh Mike, don't be such a baby. I'm a DEP geologist and you're a DEP lawyer. DEP is permitted to make inspections at any time, day or night. Certainly, we're allowed to be here when the operator is initiating operations. When we start walking on the pad, just act like you own the place. Let's stay out of their way, though, since there will be a lot of activity and workers all over the site. If anyone asks why we didn't sign in, just tell them we're on our way to do that."

"You do this much? You seem to have the routine down."

"I can also teach you how to walk out of a country biker bar with only a smile as your weapon when you're being hit on by a three hundred-pound motorcycle dude who's had one six-pack too many."

Mike shook his head.

They looked through the open fence gate at the top of the berm, and Mike couldn't believe the difference. There were dozens of trucks, pickups, semis, and everything in between, all loaded with gear. Also, at least fifty workers crawled all over the pad. Five modular buildings had been set up about a hundred feet from the wellheads. The derrick hadn't been raised yet, but a team of men were climbing all over it.

"I'm blown away," said Mike.

They went through the open gate and began walking the perimeter of the pad, keeping far away from the workers and equipment. At one point, they walked past several workers in yellow work shirts with *Adams Rigging* logos. Mike nodded tersely.

All of the workers wore work clothes with different logos and emblems. Mike didn't see anyone wearing the Yukon logo.

"Where are all the Yukon workers?" he asked.

"These guys are all contractors. That's the way the drilling industry works. None of the operators ever have more than two or three of their own employees on a pad at any time. They always hire contractors to do most of the work. That way, they never have to deal with laying off a lot of employees during slow times. They leave that up to the contractors."

"Nice. Great business plan if you can get away with it."

Mike wanted to take pictures of the operation, but felt that would be too obvious. The last thing he wanted was to draw attention to the two of them. They continued walking around the pad until they reached the modular office.

A woman wearing a grey security guard outfit and badge stood in the doorway. She was one of the few women Mike had seen on the pad that day, other than Missy.

"Hi, I'm Missy Shelton, and this is Mike Jacobs," Missy said authoritatively. "We're from DEP. Is Norby or Bones here?"

The guard looked her over and said, "DEP? Is that a trucking company?"

"No, the Department of Environmental Protection."

"Sorry, you missed them. They left about an hour ago and won't be back until later this afternoon."

"That's okay, we can catch them later."

"Mr. Mayfield is here though."

Missy looked at Mike and shrugged.

The guard said something to someone inside the office. A moment later a big man, bald, beard, wearing a Yukon-logo shirt and jeans came through the door, then looked from Missy to Mike. A big smile formed on his face, and he held out his hand. "Hey, there, pardner. I didn't expect to see you so soon."

Mike's guts clenched. Then, as nonchalantly as possible, he said, "Oh, hi, Cal, I didn't expect to see you here either. I'd like you to meet DEP's geologist, Missy Shelton."

35

It is better to offer no excuse than a bad one.
(George Washington)

While Cal and Missy stood outside the modular office chatting about the operation, Mike engaged in a tense conversation with Darius Moore on Cal's satellite phone.

"Explain to me again why it is that we're in litigation, and you're standing on my client's site, the locus of the litigation, without my permission?" Darius Moore asked. "I mean, shit, Mike, forget about asking my permission; you didn't even give me the courtesy of a text to tell me you were going up there. Then, on top of that, yesterday, you spent how many hours interviewing my client's operations director? This is litigation. In what world is that acceptable?" His voice was a low rumble.

"Yeah, about that, the department has the right to enter onto any permitted facility at any time to conduct an inspection. That's what we were doing. I never expected the operations director for all of Pennsylvania—"

"— and West Virginia and Ohio," added Darius Moore.

"Like I said, I never expected your operations director to be at the site. I thought they would send a laborer or somebody with the key to let us in at the gate. I didn't interview him. He gave us a tour of the facility, which was very nice of him, but we never talked about the case."

"Well, last night, he told me differently. He said you discussed drilling and fracking, including questions about whether there was any communication between the fracking and the surface. Also, he told me you asked Mr. Benson, Bones, about releases from the impoundment. Crap, Mike, you know better than that. You'd go insane if I had a conversation remotely like that with one of your clients without you being present."

"Look, it started out innocently enough as an informal inspection, and one thing led to the other. I never thought of it as an interview or unofficial discovery. Everything he said you could find on Yukon's website."

"Bullshit. This is bullshit. You're entitled to your opinion. Frankly, I think that was highly unethical, and I'm reserving my right to do something about that." Darius Moore stopped talking, and Mike held his breath. "One more thing, what the hell were you doing talking with the site prep manager, Calvin Mayfield, this morning? He told me you posed as a lawyer for Yukon and had a discussion with him about preparation of the site for drilling. What the hell, Mike? I know we rarely saw eye to eye at law school, you were always one of those soft-headed environmentalists, but I never thought of you as being unethical."

"I'm not unethical. I never told him I was one of Yukon's lawyers. I told him I was a *DEP* lawyer and that I did regulatory and permitting work. It was just two guys chatting over breakfast."

"That's not what he says. He was adamant he never would have talked with you about anything other than the weather if he'd known you were a DEP lawyer. Frankly, I believe him. I'm not inclined to give you the benefit of the doubt considering what happened yesterday."

"We'll just have to agree to disagree," Mike said.

"Actually, I don't want to agree to anything with you. I haven't even gotten to the part where you and that geologist lady were sneaking onto an active site and then snooping around. Tell me you were just looking for a secluded place for a little ass *au naturel*, and I'll feel better about it."

"What? What are you talking about?"

"Don't pretend to be so shocked. I have it on video, Mike. You and that geologist girl were hiding in the woods near the impoundment making out yesterday. I saw her strip down to her camisole. Really? I haven't even shared this with Jake Berliner. I don't want to give the guy a heart attack."

"What the hell are you talking about?" Mike said tentatively.

"Video. Dude, this is the twenty-first-fucking century. Yukon has high-res, low-light video cameras all over the place at all of their sites. This way, they don't have to have a guard at every site 24/7. All of the sites are monitored down in Houston at a central security facility. I've seen the video. You and that geologist girl making out. At least you didn't get on the ground and rut around, I hope."

Mike squeezed the bridge of his nose and took a deep breath. "You're making much ado about nothing, Darius. I hugged her, a friendly hug. I'd do that in front of you. Missy and I are close friends, and I didn't think you were spying on us, so I hugged her. You can call it whatever you want, but that's all it was."

"Something's going to happen, man. I'm not sure if I just report you to your chief counsel, to the governor's general counsel, to the judge, or to the disciplinary board, but something's going to happen. Honestly, dude, if it was one slip-up once, I'd probably look the other way. But this?"

"Don't threaten me, Darius."

"It's not a threat, dude. It's an announcement."

Mike took a deep breath, then said, "I'd like you to think about what you'll gain if you do this. First of all, there's a good explanation for everything we just discussed—the inspection, a misunderstanding about what I said at breakfast, heavy traffic getting to this place today so we used the back entrance, a friendly hug. Second, last I checked, we're on the same side in this case; we're not opponents. We're supposed to be working together. Finally, assuming you're successful and I get pulled from the case, it's not like you win and the case goes away. The Campbells and the Advocates will continue pursuing their appeal, and a new DEP lawyer will be assigned. Yes, you'll make my life miserable, but like I said, there's a good explanation for everything, and in the end, all you'll have done is piss off a bunch of people at DEP without advancing your client's goals at all."

Mike stopped talking and waited for Darius Moore.

After several seconds, Darius Moore said, "Let me think about this. I'm not keen about dealing with an unethical lawyer. *You.* At the same time, I'm concerned about the distraction this will cause in this case. If you represented the other side, I guarantee I'd go straight to your state's disciplinary board and let them sort it out. Crap, you're supposed to be on *my client's* side. I'm going to cool off a little and let you know tomorrow what I'm going to do."

Darius Moore clicked off. Mike walked fifty or so feet to reach Cal and handed him the sat phone.

"Well?" Cal asked.

"We're good to go," Mike replied, forcing a smile and steadying his voice.

"You need to see anything else, pardner? Any other info I can provide you with?" He smiled.

"I'm good." Mike looked at Missy.

"Just one question," Missy pointed in the general direction of the pit and asked, "The impoundment, is that for fresh water or flowback water or both?"

"Fresh water, ma'am. I was looking at the permit the other day myself, and it's a freshwater impoundment. That's all she was designed for. I'd never put flowback into the pit," Cal replied. He paused. "I'll send Tim with you to escort you back to your vehicle. Not worth taking any chances."

He called a laborer over and said, "Take these folks back to their Jeep near the impoundment." He looked at Tim. "No discussions about any operations here at the pad. Got that?"

"Yes, sir," said Tim.

Cal shook hands with Mike and Missy, and they started back around the perimeter. When they got to the berm, Mike said to Tim, "That's okay, we're just going to get into our Jeep down there. There's no need for you to follow us down. You can watch us from up here and save yourself the trouble."

"Fine by me," Tim replied. He looked over his shoulder and, with his back to the pad, violated every safety rule in the book and lit up a cigarette, shielding it in his hand.

"Just one thing," Mike said as he started down the berm. "What do you do here?"

"Just general labor. It's a paycheck."

Mike nodded. "I hear you. This pond, I've always wondered, is it for fresh water or flowback water?"

Tim puffed on his cigarette, then said, "Fresh water *and* flowback I guess. Them Philly guys who built it built us a freshwater pond. I mean we've used it for flowback water at least once that I know of, but generally it's a freshwater pit."

Mike glanced at Missy. "How's that? If it's a freshwater pit how do you use it for flowback?" Mike asked.

"Easy. Last winter, we reversed the pumps," Tim said, waving a hand back and forth. "Them frac tanks were running late coming up from Oklahoma or Texas or wherever, and the flowback had to go somewhere. It took about a half-dozen of us to pull it off in the middle of the night and it was wet and cold as hell, but we did it." Tim paused for a moment and sucked on his cigarette. "Am I allowed to tell you that?"

"Probably not. I wouldn't mention it to Cal or Norby if I were you. Don't worry; I won't tell them about the cigarette either."

36

The Single Worst Interview Ever in the History of Detective Work

After Hector Torres filed his complaint in February about his missing boss and RV, Chief West entered the information into the FBI's NCIC database. Also, based on Torres' statement, he developed a list of potential witnesses to interview, which he put into a file. The list of potential witnesses was short. It included all the employees of Chris Corsica's company. Since they'd headed back to Philadelphia or parts unknown within a day or so after Corsica had disappeared, West had no practical way of interviewing them. If, for some reason, he needed to interview them, then he had a plan to contact local police departments where they lived or worked and ask for help with interviews.

Two names did appear on Torres's statement of individuals who were potential local witnesses that West had a chance of interviewing. Norbert Lafleur, the director of operations for Yukon, and Quincy Benson, aka Bones, Lafleur's assistant.

Both men claimed to be incredibly busy and mobile. Both had laughed at West when he called and asked them to come into the station to be interviewed. Neither had the time or inclination to meet. West had driven to Yukon's field office on several occasions and never once saw either man. In his discussions with other Yukon employees at the work trailer, which served as an office, he was politely told that both men traveled incessantly and good luck trying to pin them down.

It was luck that brought West face-to-face with Norby. West was buying some chewing gum at the Speedway store in Campbelltown when he saw a man, about six feet tall, cropped haircut, military bearing, pull up in a white pickup truck with a Yukon logo and start pumping gas.

West approached him. "By any chance, are you Norbert Lafleur?"

The man leaned against the pickup as the pump clicked off the gallons. He took a long look at the chief. "Depends. Are you here to arrest me, officer?"

Southern accent. West couldn't place it. Deep South, plus an extra twang.

"It depends. First of all, it's chief. Second, are you Lafleur?"

"Sorry, chief, it may only be noon to you, but I've already put in a full eight hours today with another eight hours to go. I'm Lafleur, ev'body calls me Norby."

"You mind if I ask some questions about a man named Chris Corsica?"

Norby looked up at the clouds, then said, "Ask away. Not sure I can help you. We have hundreds of contractors working for us at any time. I think I remember him, but I'm not sure. If it's the guy I'm thinking about, he was a Philly boy, a contractor we hired to build an impoundment over at the Campbell pad. Did a crappy job, and we terminated his contract. Last time I saw him, he was working on the job, sealing together the pit linin'. I called him a few days later to deliver the bad news and never saw him again." Norby smiled.

"One of his men, a Hector Torres, reported him missing. Would you know anything about that?"

"Sorry, chief. Like I said, I deal with dozens of contractors and, over the years, thousands of their employees. There are days I can barely tell you who I am, let alone any of my contractors." Norby forced out a chuckle.

West was about to say something else when Norby said, "That guy, Corsica, went missing? When?"

"Right after the work was done. Probably the day after you delivered the bad news."

Norby shook his head. "I barely keep up with the contractors we have on the job. I don't have a clue about the ones who've moved on."

"You sure there isn't any detail you can help me with? It may seem trivial to you, but might mean something to the investigation. I'd personally appreciate the help. Anything at all you can recall about the guy?"

Norby looked up at the gathering clouds. "Army Ranger. I think he was the one. We connected on that. Both of us were Army a long time ago. Nice enough guy. That's really it."

West nodded. "So you wouldn't know anything at all about the whereabouts of Mr. Corsica or his RV?"

The pump clicked shut, and Norby repeatedly clicked the nozzle until some gasoline spilled down the fender. "Sorry, I really can't help you. Say, look, I'm done filling my tank. If you and I are done, do you mind if I take off? I'm heading over to Sullivan County now for a meetin', and I'm already runnin' late."

West decided to press his luck. "You know, sometimes when you start thinking about something, the details come back. It can take a few days. Maybe he said something about where he was going. Maybe something about a woman. Anything. How about if we set an appointment for next week and you can come into my office, and we can talk? It would help my investigation a lot. I'd appreciate it."

"Yeah, about that. I really don't have the time. I wish I could help you, but I can't do it."

West looked at the ground for a minute. When he looked up, his expression had changed. His eyes were on fire. The Mayberry friendliness had disappeared.

"Damnit, if you *wanted* to help me, you could come to the office for ten minutes and talk."

"Not sure I like your attitude, chief. Like I said, I don't recall *anything*." Norby opened the door and got in. The chief grabbed the door before he could shut it. Someone looking at the scene wouldn't be able to tell if he was going to close it for Norby or yank him out of the truck.

"Yeah, even as you're talking to me, you're recalling more and more. He was a contractor from Philly, he built Yukon an impoundment, you fired him, he was an Army Ranger. That's what I mean."

West held the door as Norby put the key in the ignition. He noticed an American flag decal on the door and pointed at it. "You consider yourself a patriot, Mr. Lafleur?"

Norby flinched. "What? Yeah, of course. Served my country. I'm a patriot."

"A patriot would come in and talk with the police chief when someone goes missing."

West handed Norby a business card which Norby pocketed without looking.

"You got a card?" West asked. Slowly, Norby reached into his breast pocket and handed him a business card.

West closed the pickup door as gently as the valet at a five-star hotel.

As Norby drove off, West thought to himself, *Hell's bells, that SOB knows something.*

***

Two days later, West was scrolling through the dozens of emails that had accumulated overnight. One was from a police department in Williston, North Dakota—

> Chief West-- We found the recreational vehicle you posted on the FBI's NCIC database. It was located in an isolated area of the city near the Missouri River. The RV had been abandoned and set on fire. The contents were all destroyed in the fire, and the RV pretty much melted to the ground except for the engine block and other heavy-duty parts. Forensics work was nearly impossible, but we did confirm that no human remains were in the RV. Forensics identified the VIN number you supplied off the engine block. I've attached photos of what's left of the RV to this email. We will hold the remains of the RV in our impound lot for thirty (30) days, then send it off to

the scrap yard. If you want it, please let us know how you would like to claim it and pay for its transportation. If I can be of assistance, please send me a reply email.
CPL John Wallace, Williston, N.D. PD

The chief looked at the email for several minutes. He had exactly zero dollars in his budget to transport what was left of Corsica's RV, and he had no forensics capability to further analyze it. Based on the email, it looked like forensics would get no additional information out of the scrap metal and melted plastic anyway.

An idea came to him. He pulled out Lafleur's card and dialed his cell phone number.

"Norby," the voice crackled.

"Mr. Lafleur, this is Chief West. Good news, we found the RV. Corsica's RV."

"What? You did?"

"Yeah, and amazingly it's in *great* condition. Hardly a scratch on it."

Long pause. "Really? You sure it's Corsica's?"

"Sure. I have a good friend at the PD where they found it. They identified it from the photos and the VIN number. They're going to ship it to us tomorrow, back of a flatbed truck kind of thing."

Another long pause. "Where, where did they find it?"

"That's the thing. It was in Williston, North Dakota. Any idea what it might have been doing in North Dakota?"

"Not a clue. Like I said, I ain't seen Corsica since the night I fired him."

"Night you fired him? Right. Anyway, why North Dakota? Any ideas?" West scribbled notes furiously.

"Shoot, that's where the Bakken Oil Play is found. Kind of like the Marcellus Shale, only mostly oil, not natural gas."

"So maybe Mr. Corsica headed out to North Dakota to build impoundments out there?" West asked.

"Don't have a clue. Then again, what you said makes perfect sense. Of course, he probably headed out there for work . . . You say they found his RV?"

"Yep. I'm looking at pictures of it now. 2001 Winnebago Brave. Not too bad shape considering its age."

"What'll happen with it when it gets here?"

"Oh, it's not coming here. It's going right to the State Police forensics lab in Harrisburg. Best forensics lab in the country. They'll do a complete forensics workup of the RV. They'll tear it apart like you see on TV. They can find hair, fingernails, blood, semen, you name it. The forensics will tell us a lot."

"Right."

"Okay, Mr. Lafleur. I just wanted to ease your mind about Corsica's RV. Thanks for all of your help." West hung up on Lafleur before he could reply.

Chief West sat back in his chair. *That SOB will be calling me before the day is out.*

37

With a kiss, let us set out for an unknown world.
(Alfred de Musset)

Missy drove slowly and carefully down the trail to exit the campsite. On Campbelltown Road, they drove past a long line of trucks waiting to get onto the Campbell pad. Neither Mike nor Missy said a word. Finally, she pulled into the same rest stop where they had kissed earlier that day. She turned off the ignition and hopped out of the Jeep. Mike followed her to the bench at the picnic table.

"What's going on?" she asked. "Suddenly, I see you doing things I just don't expect from you. I mean, this morning, I told you one of the reasons I liked you was you seemed very ethical in your relationships."

Mike reached out and took her hand. "Jeez, I don't know. Sometimes I get into litigation, and the gloves come off. Dr. Jekyll and Mr. Hyde. Maybe it's Darius Moore. He just gets under my skin. Maybe it's Abby, his wife, that whole thing."

Missy looked at him and angled her head.

"Long story from ages ago. I promise to tell you. Anyway, he's the smartest guy I know, so smug and sure of himself I just want to beat him at all costs. The ironic thing is I can't really beat him here since we're on the same side. I have no good excuses, but I'd never lie to you."

Missy held his hand with both of hers. "I'm not sure what this is, but Darius is on *our* side. The *Advocates* are on the other side. I really like you. I mean, I really, *really* like you. I don't want to see you get in trouble. Don't BS me. Can you work this out?"

"I think so. My boss, Roger, he'll support me. I think anyone looking at this objectively will see it the way I laid it out for Darius."

"What was the deal back there with Tim?" Missy asked. "Gosh, he admitted putting flowback water into the freshwater pit."

"At some point, we'll issue them an order and civil penalties, but I'm not sure what we do with that just yet. When do you get those test results back?"

"I dropped them at UPS this morning, overnight delivery. We probably won't receive the results for a couple of weeks, maybe longer, depending upon how backlogged the DEP lab is. This definitely helps. I'll call someone I know at the lab and ask them to test for a few more parameters."

"This study you did, the one that resulted in the letter to the Campbells, it focused on whether Yukon's gas wells communicated with groundwater at the Campbell property, right?"

"That's right," Missy said.

"Did you look at whether a leak of flowback water from the impoundment could reach the Campbell's water well?"

"No, I had no reason to look at that. At the time, we all thought it was just a freshwater pit. I was looking at communication from the deep rock units a mile underground to the surface, not surface to groundwater."

"So it's entirely possible that if there was contaminated water in the impoundment that leaked out, it could have gotten into the Campbell's drinking water?"

Missy rested a hand lightly on Mike's arm. "Not just possible, but I'm sure of it now. The question is when, not if."

They said nothing for several seconds. Then Mike moved his head closer to Missy's and she wrapped her arms around him. They looked at one another, no words, until Missy stood and took Mike's hand. She led him to a path into the woods, and they walked, hand in hand, a few dozen feet until the parking lot disappeared behind the trees. She turned, closed her eyes, and gently pushed her lips against Mile's. They held each other close, kissing and gently touching for long minutes.

"What was that whole thing?" Mike asked when they took a breath.

Missy giggled. "A kiss, silly. I didn't want to have to explain myself to that nosy police chief again if he happens to pull into the parking lot."

They both smiled.

Mike laid a finger on her face and looked at the bruise on her cheek.

"If Richard ever touches you again, I'll kill him."

"I think you might, but I can take care of myself."

"I'm sure you can," Mike said, looking into her moist blue eyes. "I wouldn't want anything to happen to you. I really care about you."

Mike backed away and pursed his lips to stop the words that he so badly wanted to say. It was too soon. He was shocked at how quickly he'd become attached to Missy. Shocked and happy. Maybe this would blossom into the relationship he'd wanted for years. He didn't know. Right now, he was on the crest of a wave. The best thing to do was ride it.

38

Great Expectations

Mike and Missy visited three other well pads that afternoon. At about 5 p.m., Missy drove into the parking lot of the Microtel and took a parking space far from the entrance and other cars. She hopped out and walked to the back of the Jeep. Mike left his things on the back seat and joined her.

"Hey, what's going on?" Mike asked.

"Shh, you talk too much," she replied.

She embraced him tightly, then stood on her toes, pressed her body fully against him, and kissed him deeply. Mike tenderly caressed her hair and kissed her as sweetly as he knew how.

When they were done, Mike held her in his arms and looked at her. "Okay, that was nice, but . . ."

"I wanted you to have my kiss on your mind as I drove away and you got ready for your date with Teresa." Missy continued to press her body against his. "I wanted you to know I'm hoping I can be more than your sad girl geologist friend."

"Don't worry about that," he said. "And, if I can remind you one more time, this isn't a date. It's a thank-you dinner with an old married lady and her kids. That's it."

"Uh-huh. Do I need to remind you that I've met her and she's hot? Her hubby lives in New York most of the time, and I'm guessing she has ulterior motives. I'll be sexist for a moment; call it woman's intuition. You're a very attractive man. If I were you, I'd be careful about drinking from any open glasses she serves you. Maybe you should only drink out of unopened soda cans and beer bottles."

Mike laughed and hugged her tightly. "Please be careful with Richard," Mike said. "If you're really done with him, you need to set boundaries. Maybe get a PFA—"

"PFA?"

"Protection-from-abuse order. I have a lawyer friend in Williamsport, Simone King, who can do that for you. I'm concerned for you. I really am."

Her mouth found his, and she kissed him again, long and soulful. "Why are you so darn nice?" She asked, her eyes sparkling with moisture.

They made arrangements to have breakfast at Ellie's Café before Mike headed back to Harrisburg, then they shared a long, lingering hug. Mike watched her Jeep until it disappeared in the traffic on Elmira Street.

39

Benjamin: Mrs. Robinson, you're trying to seduce me! Aren't you?
Mrs. Robinson: Well, no. I hadn't thought of it. I feel very flattered. ("The Graduate")

At close to 6:30 p.m., Mike parked his car behind a red BMW X6 SUV outside the house at 1000 Campbelltown Road. He had driven past the house with Missy and noticed the handsome exterior and beautiful garden. He approached the front door carrying a fifteen-dollar bottle of wine from the state store in Sayre. The door opened before he could knock. Teresa greeted him with a smile.

She was wearing a gauzy white off-the-shoulder gypsy top and tight-fitting designer jeans with multiple intentional rips across her thighs. Mike noticed her four-inch heels and bright red toenails. She held the door open.

"I'm so glad you could come. As we say back in the hood, *mi casa es su casa.*"

Mike had assumed she was Italian, not Latin. Not that it mattered, but now he wondered. He approached her and offered his hand, extending it as far in front of him as he could. She slithered around it, threw her arms around him, and gave him a warm hug. She smelled of some kind of cologne, tomato sauce, garlic, and cooked onions.

She didn't let go right away, but leaned back and said, "You're even cuter than I remembered."

"Uh, thanks," Mike stuttered. "You look great, too. Ms. Bruno-Campbell, I'm happy you invited me for dinner. It's so much better eating with a family than on my own."

She made a face. Mike thought she looked like she had bitten into a sour pickle. "If you call me that one more time, I may have to slap you." She laughed, although Mike thought she was probably serious. "It's Teresa, but you can call me Teri." Mike had let go of the hello hug several seconds earlier, but she hadn't. And it wasn't a social hug. Her hips were clamped tightly against his.

"Okay Teresa, Teri. I'll be more careful next time."

She finally let go but slid her hand down his arm to grab his hand. "Let me show you around the house. I've only recently finished decorating." He trailed behind, allowing her to lead him from room to room, ending up in the living room.

"This room was one of the original rooms when the house was built in 1814. I think Jared's great grand-whatever used this as a combination office, living room, dining room, and kitchen." She pointed to the large stone hearth. "I came close to tearing that monstrosity out, but the architect said it was structural, and the interior designer convinced me to keep it. I updated everything else."

Indeed, she had. The walls were painted a bright plum, and the carpet was a contemporary swirly design. The furniture was all deep and modern, Mike thought. *Uncomfortable.* The walls were adorned with paintings that were more paint splatter than landscape. The only thing he liked was the only thing she didn't touch: the fireplace.

"It's fun. Don't you think?" She asked.

"Wow, I really love what you've done with this place." It wasn't his house, so why not compliment her design skills?

The same music played from room to room throughout the house, no doubt coming from an Amazon Echo or Google Home device. It sounded like the kind of music you'd hear when getting a massage at a spa. Other than that, the place was quiet. Too quiet. Mike's antennae, which had been quivering since he got the invitation, stood erect.

"Where's Lucas? I'm looking forward to seeing the little guy again. Your daughter, too."

Teresa giggled. "Oh, they both wanted to have dinner with friends, instead of with the boring adults. Kids. Don't worry; the parents will be dropping them off at about 7:30. You'll have plenty of time to see them before bed. We'll have the house all to ourselves for a good hour or so." She rubbed his arm with her hand. "Can I get you a glass of wine? Maybe a cocktail?"

"Sure, wine would be great. In fact, let me help you."

He followed her into the kitchen. It was a modern marvel. It was countrified—Martha Stewart would approve—but was also ultra-modern. He doubted Teresa had actually designed it herself, but he had to admit it was an attractive and innovative room, like something out of a design magazine.

Teresa busied herself next to a small wine bar. Mike stood next to her and saw the bottle had already been opened; the cork was on the counter. Another bottle stood next to the first, unopened. She looked up at him and smiled. "It's a Cab, Shafer Hillside Select, 1997. Are you familiar with it?"

"Wow. I've read about it," Mike said, examining the bottle. "I may have seen a bottle behind the glass wall at the state store. It's a little pricey for me on a state salary. This is the closest I've ever come to it."

"I think you'll like it. We have nearly a case of this in our collection in the wine cellar. Jared focuses on Chianti, because he thinks that's what I should like since I'm Italian, but I prefer a good Cab. I have another bottle here for later if you really like it."

"Oh, I'm sure I will. I have a long drive back to the hotel, you know, so I think I'll limit myself to one or two glasses."

"Don't worry about that. We have plenty of beds. Heck, half of *my* room is empty."

Mike struggled to remain expressionless.

She took two expensive-looking goblets, poured generous glasses, and handed one to Mike. He found himself watching carefully the entire time she handled the wine. If she did slip something into it, it would have been in the bottle before he got there. If they were both knocked out from something, he hoped he would come to first. Then she held up her glass and touched his. "Thank you, Mike. My family and I thank you from the bottom of our hearts." She put the glass to her lips.

Mike sniffed the wine, then drank deeply. It had a delicious bouquet and was unbelievably good, dry, and complex. He had a second sip.

"Jared wasn't too happy about me taking the kids to the rally. The way it was described to me was it was just going to be some local people chanting and trying to get on TV. I never expected anything like what happened. You not only saved Lucas, you really saved our whole family."

"I hope all I did was what anyone would've done. I'm happy I helped Lucas, but I think anyone else would have done that, too."

"Actually, I don't believe that," she said, sniffing at her wine. "Those are nice words and that's what you're supposed to say. But I don't believe it. I think most people would've run away or hidden. It's very easy to *say* you'd take action when you're not confronted with a dangerous situation. Honestly, when I told you before you're a special man, I meant it."

Teresa set down her glass, leaned forward, put her hands around Mike's neck, and kissed him gently on the lips. A dry kiss. She held her hands behind his head and stroked the back of his neck. "That's for being a genuine hero," she said softly. "That and another special treat . . ."

"Uh, what would that be?" Mike asked carefully as he pulled away.

"My homemade pasta dish, of course, silly." Her hands slowly made their way from his neck across his cheeks until she tapped his nose with a manicured finger.

Other than the constant come on, incessant touching, and now the kiss on the lips from this older, married woman, Mike was surprised that he found her quite charming and forthright. Disarmingly so. She was actually funny, probably not intentionally, but really funny nonetheless. Also, she was honest and insightful. He liked that in people. Between Roger and Missy, he had gotten worked up about what she really wanted from him. Now he wanted to believe he was wrong. He hoped, perhaps, he was experiencing some of her ethnic ways with the hugging and kissing, plus a dose of raw emotions from a mother for saving her son. Still, in the back of his mind, he thought, *please not anything else, please.*

"Thank you. I feel as though I've already had my share of treats at your house." He held up the glass.

"Oh, there's more to come." Again, she giggled.

Teresa picked up her glass and walked to the Viking stove. A heavy covered skillet bubbled away. "This is my special tomato gravy with spicy Italian sausage imported from Staten Island, arugula, and parmesan. I started cooking it for you this morning."

She took a wooden spoon and stirred slowly, then held it at Mike's mouth. She cupped her free hand under his chin, resting her pinky on his face. "What do you think?"

Mike did not keep kosher. His mother had kept kosher, and his brother—the rabbi—of course, kept kosher. Over the years, Mike had been completely non-kosher, then started becoming more conscientious about it. He told friends he kept "kosher-lite." Rather than worry about two sets of plates or buying kosher meat, he only ate vegetarian, cheese, or fish in his apartment. Outside of his apartment, he would still eat some non-kosher chicken and, on rare occasions, beef. He never knowingly ate bacon, pork, or shellfish.

Never.

Not ever.

Except today.

"It tastes great," Mike said, accepting the spoon into his mouth and chewing on a chunk of sausage. "Spicy, but not overly so."

Teresa took a cloth napkin and gently dabbed his lips.

"You see? That's exactly what I tell Jared. He thinks my gravy, I might add it's my nonna's recipe, is too spicy. Our kids eat it; they love it. Jared's kind of a white-bread-and-mayonnaise guy. The kind you'd expect to find out here." She waved around the spoon. "You seem like a good rye-bread-and-spicy-pastrami guy. Maybe a big-juicy-knockwurst man. Are you a big-knockwurst man, Mike?"

They both chuckled. She picked up her glass and again grabbed Mike's hand. After showing him the rest of the house, they ended up in the living room. Mike noticed every chair had some object sitting on the seat. The only place to sit was the sofa. Teresa pointed to it, he sat, and she sat next to him, kicking off her shoes.

"So tell me, what does your husband do?" Mike asked.

Teresa rolled her eyes, then took a gulp of wine. "Ugh, private equity. He buys and sells businesses and travels all over. We hardly ever see him. We're lucky to get him on the weekends. It can be pretty lonely without a man around here during the week. He's never here, so I have to sleep in a cold empty bed. I'm a hot-blooded woman and miss having a warm man next to me, if you know what I mean."

Mike took a sip and nodded. "Well, it sounds like he's working very hard for the family. That's good."

Teresa made her sour-pickle face. "I don't know. Sure, the income is great, but not the loneliness, not for me or the kids. I mean, Lucas started with this thing about having an imaginary friend who's a secret agent. All he talks about is his friend Secret Agent Jones or Smith or something silly like that. He started using a sharpie on his wrist to write the letter A on it. He says the secret agent has a tattoo like that."

Synapses fired in Mike's brain. A tattoo with an A? He couldn't place it. "His imaginary friend is a grown man? Maybe you should have someone talk with him about that."

She waved her hands in the air. "Trust me, last week it was Batman, next week it'll be a flying cat. Someday you'll have kids and get it."

"Well, Jared works in private equity? That's pretty lucrative, isn't it?" Mike asked.

"I suppose. He makes a crap-load of money. We have a nice condo in the city—Manhattan—and this house we use during the summer. Honestly, I'd rather have a house on the beach in Jersey. If I'm going to have to spend a lot of time alone, I mean with the kids, I'd rather be at the shore."

Mike felt his stomach gurgle.

Teresa inched very close while they talked. Mike backed into the armrest until he could retreat no farther. Her bare foot, with the bright-red toenails, was hooked well over his leg. Teresa patted him on the thigh as they talked, as though she were emphasizing a point. Then she began to stroke it, first near his knee, then a bit higher each time. Mike was really uncomfortable.

Also, he was strangely turned on.

He looked at his watch. "I don't know about you, Teri, but I'm getting hungry. Your sauce smells *really* good right now. Maybe we should eat before the kids come home?"

"Sure, we could do that," she breathed. "Or . . ."

Teresa leaned in until her face was just a few inches from Mike's, and she closed her eyes. Her off-the-shoulders blouse gaped open as she leaned forward. Mike could easily see she wasn't wearing a bra. Her breasts nearly spilled out of her loose-fitting top. He pressed his head into the corner of the sofa as far as it would go, but it wasn't far enough. He could feel her breath, scented with tomato sauce, sausage, garlic, and wine, on his lips. Teresa's hand had inched its way to his upper thigh. Her eyes were closed, her mouth half-open, and she licked her lips as she slowly zeroed in on his.

Mike was shocked to realize he was aroused.

Excited.

She was an attractive woman, and she was coming on to him. Big time. If he wanted her, all he had to do was surrender.

This was very, very bad.

Get out. Get out.

Now!

"Dinner," Mike blurted out. "Definitely dinner. I'm starving, and your nonna's sauce smells awesome. Plus, it would be great to be done eating before Lucas and Emma—your kids—get here."

Mike lightly placed a hand on Teresa's bare shoulder, careful not to dislodge her gypsy top, and in one miraculous move he gently swiveled her, pushed her back, kissed her quickly on the forehead, slid off the sofa under her leg, which was now draped around his torso, and did all of this without spilling a drop of wine. He walked toward the kitchen without looking back.

A few moments later, he heard the click-click-click of her shoes on the hardwood. "You men, all of you, one-track minds. Not *my* track, mind you. What about my needs? What I want? All you think about is food. My fault is being such a good cook. An *excellent* cook. Learned at my nonna's elbow. That's not the only thing I'm good at." She dipped a wooden spoon into the skillet and sampled the sauce between her lips and tongue. "I'm good at other things, too, you know. Fun things. Things we could both enjoy . . ."

They were eating dinner when the children burst into the house. He glanced at the clock and noticed they were a good half-hour late. Mike didn't have to wonder if the delay was intentional.

40

Questions

At 7:30 a.m., Mike and Missy drank coffee together at Ellie's Café. The restaurant was full, a mix of locals and drillers. Mike sat, as he always did, with his back against the wall facing the door. He knew it was overly dramatic, but the inspectors had taught him it was better safe than sorry.

Mike talked about his evening with Teresa. He didn't spare any details—every hug, touch, and kiss— leaving out only that he had been oddly and unexpectedly turned on. Missy said to him, at least three times, "I told you so." The whole time they talked, Missy was beside herself with laughter. They agreed it was a good thing he'd never again have to be alone with the woman.

When they finally returned to business, Mike said, "So what do you make of this so-called freshwater pit that was used to hold produced water?"

"I'm astonished a company like Yukon would do that. First of all, the pit wasn't designed or built to hold frack water. Second, I checked with the inspector, and they never gave us notice they were going to use it for frack water. That's two significant violations right there. If the pit was leaking, well, that might explain the presence of some of the constituents in the Campbell water well. It may not have all been naturally occurring background levels."

They agreed Mike would talk about it with Darius Moore. He was almost certain Norby was behind all of this.

The waitress had served them three cups of coffee each, and they both declined a fourth. Mike glanced at his watch. "So when do you think we can see each other again? I really want to get to know you better."

"Me too," replied Missy, stroking the top of his hand with her forefinger. Mike smiled when he noticed she'd painted her nails blue. "I don't want to rush things," she said, "so I'm not sure how we handle this long-distance friendship. I mean, I could come down to Harrisburg sometime, or you could come up here for a date, but maybe that's too much too soon? I mean, it's a long trip. Kind of an overnighter and we're just getting to know each other."

"We have the case going on. Let's see if there's a way we can work in a date before our next meeting. That should be in the next couple of weeks. Is that too much?"

"No," replied Missy. "That should give us a little time to cool off and think about what we're doing here. It's not like we can't talk fairly often. Let's plan on it." She patted his hand.

"Do you want to cool off?" Mike asked with a smile.

"Not really." Missy grabbed his hand and squeezed it.

After breakfast, they stood next to Missy's Jeep and hugged goodbye.

"Do you have to go?" She said in a small voice.

"If I don't go soon, I'm not going to leave."

Missy said nothing for a moment, then stood on her toes and kissed him on the lips. "The real problem here is neither one of us wants to let go."

Missy moved her arms from Mike's back to his shoulders and gently pushed him away.

"You sure about that?" Mike said as he stepped back.

"No. If we stand here for another ten seconds, mister, I'm going to change my mind."

Mike leaned over and kissed her cheek.

"I'll see you as quickly as I can. I have a feeling we'll be talking soon. Remember what I said about Richard. I want you to promise you're going to call my lawyer friend in Williamsport about that PFA."

Mike watched Missy drive away and then sat in his Jeep and scrolled through the dozens of emails that had accumulated since the morning. He had one from Roger.

I need to see you the moment you get in. This is important.
Thanks.
Roger

"Crap," Mike said out loud.

Mike had adopted the tell-all, as-soon-as-possible approach with Roger whenever he'd done something that warranted a confession. Mike learned over the years it was better to preempt the bad news with his explanation than to have to explain it after Roger had heard it from someone else. Although both he and Roger were Jewish, Mike would sometimes start those conversations with, "Forgive me, father, for I have sinned." Generally, by the end of the talk, they were both laughing.

His curiosity ate at him, so while he sat in the lot, he dialed his assistant, Sandy. "So, I'm having loads of fun up here in Bradford County."

"That's what I hear," She replied. She'd lived in Harrisburg for nearly thirty years, but her voice was still laden with a Schuylkill County accent.

"Roger. Have you seen him this morning?"

"Yeah, he's been storming around here. Doesn't look happy. Keeps muttering to himself. You know he only mutters to himself when he's angry."

"That muttering. Would he happen to be muttering *my* name by any chance?"

"Would it be appropriate for me to tell ya that?"

"Of course. Not only are you my assistant, but one of my best friends."

"Then yes. You seem to be at the top of his list."

"Any idea . . ."

"No, he hasn't shared. I don't think he's lookin' to give ya' free tickets to Hersheypark. He asked me three times already when you'd be back from Sayre, and it's only 8:30. I think you'd better get back soon. He's pissed about something."

They ended the call, and Mike started the engine. He had no doubt Roger's terse email had to do with Yukon. He rehearsed his *mea culpa* speech all the way from Sayre to Harrisburg.

41

Unfinished Business

Teresa stormed through the house. Neither Lucas nor Isabella were ready to leave. They would be late for 10 a.m. soccer practice.

"I don't know why we're paying for sports and lessons for you kids. You both say you want to be on a team with the other kids, but neither one of you can be ready when it's time to go."

She looked into the family room. "Hey, Google. What time is it?"

"It's 9:50," replied the box.

No matter how riled up Teresa was, the Google voice, feminine and slightly Midwestern, was pleasant, calm, and authoritative. No emotion whatsoever. No matter how late the kids were running. Nothing seemed to irritate Ms. Google. Teresa hated the voice. *Bitch.*

"Kids, it will take fifteen minutes to get to practice." She found Isabella texting on her phone in the kitchen and gave her a light shove. "Move it."

Lucas was on the floor of the family room, attempting to tie his sneakers. "Just leave that for now, Lucas. I'll get it for you when we get to the field."

Teresa tugged open the front door. Sitting on the small stoop were four cartons of bottles. They were Walmart *Pure Spring Wal-Water* bottles. A brand she never drank. She looked up and down Campbelltown Road.

No cars.

No trucks.

Nothing out of the ordinary.

She stooped down. The bottles were the sixteen-ounce size. Twenty-four clear plastic bottles to a case. Ninety-six bottles in all. Twelve gallons. Shrink-wrapped in plastic. A piece of paper was stuck into an opening cut into the shrink wrap, jammed between two of the bottles. She pulled it out.

The letter was typed on plain copy paper:

Yukon Oil and Gas Corporation

Dear Homeowner:

We wanted you to have this water as our gift. We suggest you use this for your drinking and cooking water needs for the next week or so. We are doing work nearby and that may affect the taste and color of your well water. During this time, we suggest that you not drink your well water. Your well water should return to normal in about a week.

Sincerely,

Your friends at Yukon Oil and Gas Corporation

The letter was unsigned. She shoved the letter into her pocket, stepped around the cartons, and pushed the children to the car. As she drove to the practice, she wondered if the water had gotten worse in the past day or two. She didn't use it for drinking or cooking anyway, preferring expensive bottled Fiji Water for that, but now she was trying to remember if the well water had an unusual smell when she took her shower in the morning.

Strange.

The more she thought about it, though, the angrier she got.

Those bastards contaminated my well. They think they can buy me off with some crappy Walmart water? Sons of bitches!

She thought she would call that chubby DEP geologist girl later and find out what was going on. *No*, she thought. *I'll call my lawyers and let them figure it out.*

***

The man known to Lucas as Secret Agent Smith had abandoned the observation post and stood hidden in the woods behind a tree at the top of the hill overlooking the Campbell house. Waiting and watching. As the hour approached 0945, he knew the woman would leave the house soon. Through a spotting scope, he watched her as she examined the cases of water he had left. Watched as she read the letter he had written. Watched as she looked up and down Campbelltown Road.

By now, he was sure the ethylene glycol and sodium hypochlorite were fully mixed in the water well and probably at a concentration that might hurt someone. Like a little kid. The thought of Lucas drinking the water, laced with antifreeze and bleach, had bothered him enough that he made sure the family had sufficient drinking water until the crap flushed itself out of the well. The local library provided a handy terminal to write and print the letter. No more than several days, a week at most, and the water would be back to what it was before.

Now it was on them.

The kid would be okay.

He had a clear conscience.

Absolution.

He pushed the Afghan children out of his mind.

Finally.

42

Mea culpa, Mea Culpa, Mea Maxima Culpa

Mike tapped on the door, and Roger said, "Come in." Roger sat with his back to Mike, scrolling through the emails on his computer, which was on a credenza behind his desk. Roger slowly turned and pointed to the door. Mike closed it with a click.

"I know what this is all about and let me just say that all of the things you heard are exaggerations and distortions," Mike said. "I went out to the Campbell pad with the geologist, Missy Shelton, on a site inspection and expected some low-level flunky would be there to open the gate. I never expected that Yukon's operations director for all of Pennsylvania would be waiting for us. We had a discussion, yes, but it was really generic in nature. I mean, we talked about drilling and fracking and what it can and cannot do at the surface. We never talked about any impact or potential impact to the Campbell residence. Really, and I mean this, most of what we talked about you could find on the Yukon webpage or a dozen other places on the internet. Also, it was pure happenstance that I bumped into Cal, Yukon's site prep guy, at breakfast. I never told him I was a lawyer for Yukon, just the opposite. I specifically told him I was a lawyer for DEP. Darius thinks somehow or another, I conned the guy to get information out of him. That's just not true. I wanted to tell you my version of the story, and I planned to tell you today as soon as I got back from Bradford County. I never expected Darius or Berliner to call you about this . . ."

Roger had leaned forward and propped himself up on his elbows as he listened. The cuffs of his shirt were turned up to his elbows, and his hands were folded beneath his chin. His mane of white hair was in its usual mid-day disarray.

"What the hell are you talking about?" Roger asked.

Mike blinked.

"Yes, I did email you this morning about wanting to talk about something serious, but I have no idea what you're talking about. Whatever this is, it can wait."

"No one from FU called you to complain about me in the past day or so?"

"Not yet. But it sounds like I may be hearing from them soon."

Mike closed his eyes and shook his head. "Okay, yes, I was planning on discussing this with you. I think it's much ado about nothing, but it definitely can wait. Your email. What . . ."

"That woman, Bruno-Campbell, the one you wanted to have dinner with up in Bradford County? Tell me what happened." Roger said this in an even tone, his face expressionless.

Mike gritted his teeth. "Teresa? I never wanted to have dinner with her. *You* told me to have dinner with her. You said the secretary thought it would be good for PR since I'd saved her kid."

"Okay, so . . ."

"So, nothing. She and her family have a lovely house up there, in Campbelltown, named for her husband's family. We had a glass of wine and talked. Her kids didn't show up until after dinner, so I was more than a little uncomfortable being in her house for over an hour, just the two of us. I mean, we don't even know each other. We talked about her family and her husband's work. She told me she really hated Campbelltown, and the house was just a summer home for her family. Her husband's homestead. She made a huge point of telling me she would prefer having a house at the Jersey Shore. We never talked about her case. I promise. I told you I wouldn't talk about her case, and we never did. Is she saying I milked her for information about her case? Did Winnie call you?"

"No. I wish she had. Nothing as mundane as that," Roger said without smiling. "Winnie did not call me. Between you and me, I know you've had a few girlfriends since you came to work for the department, and you're some kind of a ladies' man. Let me put this delicately. Ms. Bruno-Campbell called me to tell me that you came on to her. She said she prepared a nice thank-you dinner and expected you'd behave like a gentleman. Instead, you were all over her. She claims she pushed you away multiple times, and you kissed her several times even though she didn't want it and told you to stop. She said you repeatedly suggested that the two of you head into the bedroom for *adult time,* whatever that is. She claims you didn't cool down until her kids came home for dinner."

Mike was stupefied. "This is a joke, right? You know none of this happened, or at least happened the way you're describing it."

"It's no joke, son." Mike knew as soon as Roger called him *son* how serious this was. He often called him *bud,* but he never called him *son,* except on the most serious occasions. "She sounded really upset when I spoke with her. I want to hear your version of the story."

Mike shook his head. "It's a lie. Everything she's told you is a lie. She's crazy. Some kind of crazy cougar lady. She's more than fifteen years older than me. I'm guessing she has a thing for younger men. I didn't even get in the front door, and she threw her arms around me. I mean on the front steps. Honestly, between her hugs and kisses, I hoped she was just grateful, or being Italian, or both. Let me tell you what really happened."

Roger didn't smile. He just looked at him.

Mike spent the next half hour going through the details of everything Teresa had said or done, every innuendo or direct suggestion, hug, kiss, touch, and attempted kiss. He noticed that Roger didn't take notes. When Mike was done, he took a deep breath and sat back in his chair.

Roger nodded. "Of course, there's no way to verify your version or hers. I don't have to tell you that the mood of the country and our governor is not to discredit the painful statement of a woman about a sexual assault."

"Christ, Roger, I didn't assault her," Mike said loudly. "*She* assaulted *me*. It's her word against mine. You've talked to her, what, twice? You've known me for the past four years. We've been in the goddamned trenches together. In a mine shaft together. I've been open with you about everything. The death of my mother, my relationships with women, Patty, Sherry, Nicky, everything. Honestly, I can't think of anything I've held back. I don't assault women. I've *never* done that. I *wouldn't* do that. I *ask* before I even hug a woman. I hope you'd take that into consideration."

"You admit that you kissed her?"

"I admit that *she* kissed *me*. I didn't invite it."

"What the hell were you thinking, son? I mean really. You never should've kissed her, a virtual stranger, alone, in her house."

"She kissed me! What the hell was I supposed to do? I didn't want to go there in the first place. You, the governor, the press secretary, you all made me go."

"We didn't make you kiss her . . ."

"I. Did. Not. Kiss. *Her*. She kissed *me*, dammit. She set this up. I was happy to see her boy, Lucas. Hoped I'd meet her husband. No one was home other than that crazy woman. She was trying to seduce me. You know me. I did the right thing. Damn you!"

Roger looked at him and held up his hands. "Mike, take a breath."

Mike seethed. Roger was his friend. His confidant. Like an older brother. If anyone knew him, it was Roger. What scared Mike was that others who did not know him would leap to the wrong conclusion.

Roger nodded slowly. "Of course. Something bothers me. She told me she was telling me this just for my information and, I'm quoting, *not to get you in trouble*. I think if she really felt this happened, she'd've done more than call just me. Assuming for a minute what she said was true, I'm not sure it rises to the level of sexual assault. Maybe it does, but hell, I'm no expert. It sounds more like a bumbling and inept first date. If she said no and you touched her or kissed her against her will, then that would be a battery, at least, and probably assault. She told me she *wasn't* going to call the chief counsel or the cops, and she just wanted to keep this between us, Teresa and me, for my information."

Roger exhaled and leaned forward again. "Even believing every word of her story, *as I should*, the question remains, why didn't she throw you out of the house the first time you tried to kiss her? Or the second time? She told me all of this happened before dinner. Son, if something like this happened to my wife, you can be sure Jill would've socked you in the jaw, pushed you out the door, and called the cops first and me second. You would not have made it to the pasta course, that's for sure."

Roger half-smiled at Mike.

"You have to believe me, Roger. She's a lonely woman in an unhappy marriage. She told me that several times. *She* was all over *me*. I was so worried about you, the secretary, and others who wanted me to have this thank-you dinner with her, I just figured I could joke and laugh my way out of it." Mike paused. "What are you going to do about this? Are you calling Kate?"

"Christ. About that. Our policy says I *should* call the chief counsel, or HR and let them deal with it." He scrubbed his face with his hand and squeezed his eyes together. "Frankly, I'm afraid they'd just chew you up and you'd be out of here within an hour. At the very least administrative leave for weeks or months until the inquisition is over. If I didn't know you as well as I do, that's what I'd do though. Let someone else deal with this. I'm taking a goddamn gigantic risk not calling them. But that's what I'm going to do."

Mike nodded and said, "Thank you, Roger. I mean it. What she's saying is bullshit. She knows it's her word against mine, and she's a liar."

Roger stared into Mike's eyes and said, "You'd better not be lying to me, son. I better not find out that Ms. B-C- was telling me the truth. Everything in me says she's making this up. If I'm wrong, heaven help you. You won't have to worry about the chief counsel or HR. I'll come after you myself."

"I swear. I don't know how to be more sincere," Mike said.

"The only question I have is *why*?" Roger asked. "Why would she do this? We may not be on the same side, but with Yukon and

FU in the case, it's not like she's getting some kind of advantage in litigation. Let's say you disappeared from the case; she has to know I'd just assign someone else. Any thoughts?"

"This has nothing to do with the case. Actually, I think she's angry at me for not taking her up on her offer to go with her to her bedroom. Her *many* offers. It's all about me at this point. She's angry at me and maybe embarrassed or resentful that she opened herself up and I turned her down. This is Teri, Ms. Bruno-Campbell, getting even with me for *not* going to bed with her. That's it."

"I'll check with Jill tonight. She has a much better sense of people than I do." Roger rubbed his hand across his chin and then nodded at Mike.

Mike got up to leave.

"Wait a minute, bud" Roger said. "This business with Yukon. Before I get a phone call today from yet another happy customer, what's the deal?"

Mike took a deep breath and sat down in the same chair. It was still warm.

43

Awesome

At exactly 9 a.m. Eastern, 8 a.m. Central, Anthony Fowler, who was in his office in Houston, dialed into FU's conference bridge number. The robotic voice told him one other person was on the line.

"This is Anthony."

"Hey Anthony, it's Jesse. I'm still at home; I should be in a little later."

"Okay. Is Darius on?"

"Darius? Darius? Earth to Darius. I guess not."

"Assuming we finish up at nine, be sure he doesn't charge us for a full hour," Anthony said.

"Yeah, don't worry about that. We have a program called *Probitatis* designed to keep him honest. I get a report from *Probitatis* the same day I get his bill. It's a Big Brother kind of thing. It compares my calendar, phone company call records, and our internal time records to his bill. If it sees something that looks suspicious, it sends me an email, and I can question the bill. Frankly, it scares me."

The speaker emitted a tone and the robotic voice said, "A new caller has joined."

"Sorry about that, guys. I was just finishing up a call with a client in the Emirates," said Darius Moore. "We ran a few minutes late. I read all of the emails, but I sense you didn't put everything into the email. Can somebody fill me in on what's really going on in Bradford County?"

"Sure," said Anthony. "I was out there last week, looked at the site, and I've gone through all of the documentation. I'm convinced our drilling and fracking had nothing to do with their water quality. A big part of their water problem is agricultural runoff and naturally-occurring methane found near the surface."

"Awesome," said Darius Moore. "You can start writing that up as our expert report. Be sure you don't make any versions of your report. I want you to overwrite every time you make a correction. You can send me the drafts marked attorney-client privileged, and I'll call you with my comments."

"It's not that simple," said Jesse. "Anthony, tell him what you found."

"Yeah, Darius, so when I was out there, I saw the freshwater impoundment, not too big, a little larger than a football field. Anyway, the contractor built it right on top of a shale ridge. I spoke to Norby, and he told me the contractor was supposed to avoid the ridge. In the end, the contractor blasted the ridge to level it. Unfortunately, he didn't level it perfectly, and you can see little peaks pushing up the lining of the pit. They're anywhere from three to six inches high."

"So, what? The shale punctured the lining?" Darius Moore asked.

"Probably. Get this: The impoundment contractor was a roofer who was trying to get into the natural gas business. Norby says he was, and I quote, a complete fuck-up."

"Awesome."

"As they say on TV, but wait, there's more. The little ridge is right next to a limestone formation called the Horseheads Limestone. That limestone is full of fractures, and it even has caverns when you get a little further north into New York State. I think it's possible there are small caves in the limestone in Bradford County. I'm pretty sure I saw some depressions on the surface, which probably are sinkholes caused by caves that have collapsed near the surface."

"Awesome. Where exactly does this limestone go?"

"In a straight line from the pit, downgradient, and right under the Campbell residence and right through the Campbelltown reservoir about a mile away."

"Awesome," said Darius Moore.

"Yeah, Darius," said Jesse. "There's one more thing. This is where it *really* gets awesome. The pit was permitted and constructed as a freshwater impoundment. It was built just to hold the makeup water for the completions. Unfortunately, it leaked about half a million gallons of fresh water in five days. Get this: Norby was in a big hurry and the frac tanks were running late after they completed drilling the first well. Let's just say it's unclear exactly what happened, but it looks like Norby made a unilateral decision to use the impoundment to hold the produced water until the frac tanks were ready to go. The flowback water probably was in the pit for no more than three days."

"How much flowback water did they have in the pit?" asked Darius Moore.

"Maybe one to two million gallons."

"Let me guess: You think it leaked," Darius Moore asked.

"Very likely. We'll never know but I'm estimating about fifty to one hundred thousand gallons of flowback water leaked out of the pit."

"Awesome. Did Norby have authorization from anyone to use the pit for produced water?"

"He says he called Blade Harris here in Houston and left a message. Blade says Norby called in the middle of the night when he wasn't here. By the time he listened to his messages in the morning, the pit was already being filled. He didn't call him back to stop him, though. It looks like we were in a hurry to get the well into production. The frac tanks were running about three days late, and this was the only way to move the process along without having the frac tanks in place. No one, not Norby, not Blade, stopped our guys from filling the pit until the frac tanks were in place. Once the frac tanks were set up, they pumped the produced water from the pit into them and power washed the pit."

No one said anything for a moment. Finally, Darius Moore said, "In other words, once the horses were way out of the barn, we closed the door."

"Pretty much," said Jesse.

"Did anyone happen to tell DEP about this when we used the freshwater pit for produced water?" Darius Moore asked.

"No," replied Jesse.

"Do we know what happened with the produced water that leaked out? Is it locked into the formation? Moving through it? Coming out somewhere?"

"It's possible we may be seeing the leading edge of the plume in the Campbells' water well," said Anthony. "It's really diluted once it gets there, but some of the constituents DEP found in the well water, like methane, are found in produced water. It's minute amounts, but it may be there. It could also be that we're seeing nothing more than natural contamination. As of now, the amounts are so low that it's hard to tell if it came from our pit."

"Awesome."

"I checked DEP's online water quality report for the Campbelltown reservoir. The water quality there was good as of three months ago. It's what you'd expect for a reservoir that gets water from springs in limestone. No significant contaminants."

"So if there's any produced water in the limestone formation, it hasn't reached the reservoir and may never reach the reservoir," said Darius Moore.

"That's possible," said Anthony. "It's also possible you have a slug of 100,000 gallons of contaminated water that hasn't yet made it to the reservoir. Some of it may have contaminated the Campbell's private water well. We haven't drilled any monitoring wells below the pit, so we don't know where the leading edge of the plume is at this point, if there's a plume at all. In this carbonate rock, it's possible the produced water is stuck in an underground cave or caves and isn't going anywhere. It's also possible that if you were to put, say, five million gallons of fresh water into the impoundment and hundreds of thousands of gallons of it leaked into the limestone that you'd push the contaminated water all the way to the reservoir."

"What's Norby have to say about all of this? I mean, a lot of fingers are pointed at him," said Darius Moore.

"He's really pissed," said Anthony. "He feels like he's been singled out to be the fall guy. He wanted to hire a tried-and-true pit construction outfit from Texas which we've used all around the county, but Blade told him to hire a local outfit and the pickin's were slim. He says he hired the best of the group in P-A- and feels like he's being screwed because the guy messed up. On top of that, he says Houston pushed him to complete the 1-H well and start drilling the new 2-H well, even though the frac tanks weren't in place. He had to wait for the frac tanks to show up and wanted to wait a couple of days to begin drilling the 2-H well, but you know Blade's mantra."

Darius Moore was silent for a moment. "Drill, baby, drill?"

"Yep."

"Anything else I should know?" Darius Moore asked.

"Just that he blames, of all people, the DEP lawyer, Mike Jacobs. He said this wasn't a big deal until he became involved, and now it's blown out of proportion."

"I'm no fan of Jacobs, but he doesn't have anything to do with this," said Darius Moore.

"I know, but it's better than any of *us* getting blamed."

"Let me see if I can summarize the legal issues," said Jesse. "The impoundment was improperly constructed, violating our DEP permit. It was designed for fresh water, but we put flowback water into it without getting DEP's permission. Another violation. It wasn't designed for flowback water and doesn't have the kind of lining you'd normally use for produced water or any of the monitoring wells DEP would require. Another violation. We had a leak of produced water from the impoundment into groundwater. That would be yet another violation. Our produced water from the impoundment may have contaminated the Campbells' water well. Another. There's a big slug of produced water hiding out in a cave somewhere between our impoundment and the reservoir. That's probably a violation. Finally, we're getting ready to fill the impoundment with fresh water, probably in the next two weeks, it will leak like a sieve and push the contaminated water all the way to the Campbell house and the reservoir. More violations. Did I get all of the issues?"

"You got the main ones," replied Darius Moore. "In addition to the contamination issues and violations of your permits, there's also the issue of giving notice to DEP. We have to notify DEP both for contamination and threats of contamination to waters of the Commonwealth."

"So . . . do we notify PaDEP now, since the contamination is still in the ground, even though it's been there since February?" Jesse asked. "What's your advice?"

For several seconds all they heard was static on the line. "Darius?"

"Just thinking it through. I'm trying to figure out if we can fix this. You do want it fixed, don't you?"

The line was silent for a moment. Finally, Jesse cleared her throat and said, "Yes. That's why we pay you the big bucks."

"Okay, the regs say you have to give notice *immediately*. Now it's been months, so the next question is whether it makes a difference if we give notice today or in two weeks . . ."

They were all silent for several seconds. Finally, Jesse spoke. "Can you research those issues and get back to me in writing this afternoon? We'll need your assessment of the law, next steps to comply with the law, and possible outcomes of any potential enforcement actions by DEP. I'd like to do a call no later than 3 p.m. Central."

"I have some things this morning and afternoon, but I'll move them around. I'll have to get a few of my associates cranking on this if we're going to have a chance of making your 3 p.m. deadline, so that *Probitatis* program of yours is going to see multiple lawyers here doing research at the same time on the same subject. I want to be sure that's okay. Honestly, it would be better if I had until 5 p.m. Is that okay, too?"

"Central? Then sure," replied Jesse. "You know, Norby wants to put a patch on the impoundment and begin filling it with fresh water in the next couple of weeks so he can start completions on the new wells as soon as the guys are done drilling."

"Wait a minute," said Anthony. "If he doesn't patch it right, he could push hundreds of thousands of gallons of water into the Horseheads Limestone, which would push the contaminated water all the way to the Campbell house and the township reservoir."

"Awesome."

***

As soon as he hung up, Anthony speed dialed Jesse's cell phone. She answered on the first ring.

"I was just about to call *you*," she said.

"So you know why I'm calling?"

"Let me guess: You and your wife finally want to come to my church on Sunday."

"Guess again."

"Hmm, maybe you want to know my legal opinion on whether we have to notify DEP about the possible ongoing contamination."

"You *are* smart for a lawyer. You know, Darius is one of the smartest lawyers I've ever worked with, but he takes pretty aggressive positions. Not exactly my style."

Anthony listened to the staticky hum of the telephone line for several seconds. "Jesse?"

"Yes, just taking a thought-break. Okay, I think we do have to notify DEP. Their Clean Streams Law regulates both pollution and the *potential* for pollution. But making that notification is way above my pay grade. Yours too. Let's wait for the opinion from Darius, but in the meantime, I suggest we verbally report it up each of our chains of command."

"And if they don't do that? Make the report, I mean."

"We've done our jobs. We've told our supervisors. Whatever you do, don't send your boss any emails. That'll look like you're covering your butt. I'll send you one in about an hour to cover both of our butts. I can do that without being too obvious. No cc's either. Got it?"

Exactly one hour later, Anthony received an email from Jesse:

ATTORNEY-CLIENT COMMUNICATION
PRIVILEGED AND CONFIDENTIAL

Anthony— As we discussed, we have both reported the Pennsylvania matter to our superiors. Like I said earlier today, please wait for legal advice from our counsel at Finkel & Updike and directions on next steps, if any, from your supervisor. Call me if you have any questions.

Jesse Ewing, Esquire
Attorney-Advisor, Yukon Oil and Gas Co.

44

All-nighter

Teresa stood by the kitchen door listening intently. Except for its usual creaks and the sound of the air whooshing through the vents, the house was quiet. She'd checked on Lucas an hour earlier. He was asleep. When she last looked in on Isabella, her daughter appeared to be asleep, but may have been faking it. In any event, they'd both been quiet for nearly an hour. Her housework was done, so she took her laptop and plugged it in next to the kitchen table.

When they fixed up the old house, one thing Jared had insisted on was an excellent high-speed internet connection. It took an instant to connect to Google Chrome. Teresa spent several seconds staring at the screen. She could shop for a sexy chemise or teddy in a few keystrokes, but she wasn't quite sure how to search for what she wanted right now. It took her several tries.

Fracking

This search revealed fourteen million results. Way too many.

Fracking chemicals

This search turned up fewer results, 1.6 million, but some were so technical they were over her head, and others were completely useless rants. She had attended the College of Staten Island—from time to time she had to remind Jared's snotty Ivy League friends it was part of the City University of New York system—like Baruch and Hunter Colleges—and she had obtained a liberal arts degree. While she'd taken basic science and computer courses, she was anything but a science or computer whiz. Much of the technical materials baffled her.

Anti-fracking

This search revealed information more in line with what she was beginning to learn and believe. Unfortunately, there were literally hundreds of blogs and posts that didn't appear to come from any kind of scientific perspective. Many were awful stories told by people who said their lives were ruined by fracking and fracking chemicals. They talked about their contaminated water wells, animals dying, and children harmed. Most were personal stories and didn't seem to be based on anything scientific. She was surprised by how many vegan websites had anti-fracking information. Teresa was no scientist, but she wanted something based on hard information. Something the frackers couldn't easily dispute.

Frustrated, she texted Caitlin hoping her friend could set her on the right path:

When we talked the other day, you said there were some university studies on fracking you felt were trustworthy. Can you remind me which are the "good" universities?

Almost immediately, she received a text in response. She glanced at the time on her iPhone. It was after midnight.

Like I said, there are quite a few scientists I like especially independent scientists who are researching fracking. Probably the two most prestigious universities, the ones I trust most, are Duke and Cornell. They haven't written as much as others, but they are high-class colleges. I think you can trust the studies coming from them. Good luck!!! :-)

Teresa knew she couldn't simply search for Duke or Cornell. She thought about it for several minutes and then finally composed her search.

Duke university and Cornell university and fracking reports or studies

Bingo. Pay dirt. Here were studies written by researchers at two of the most prestigious universities in America. These were not Caitlin's independent scientists or anonymous researchers at insignificant, no-name colleges but big-name professors at top-notch schools. The first story to pop up was *Water Use has Risen 770% Since Fracking Began*. Next was *Exposure to Fracking Chemicals and Wastewater Spurs Fat Cells*. After that was one from Yale University, *Fracking Outpaces Science on its Impact*.

She was able to follow some of the information in the studies but found it quite helpful that there were news articles and commentaries written *about* the studies. Many of the articles were critiques written by the frackers or their enablers and, after reading a paragraph or two, she skipped those.

All of this seemed interesting but not altogether relevant to her until she found a study called *Increased Stray Gas Abundance in a Subset of Drinking Water Wells Near Marcellus Shale Gas Extraction*. She struggled through it and grew increasingly alarmed. It said the amount of methane found in drinking water wells near Marcellus wells was unhealthy. It was written by Duke researchers and published in the *Proceedings of the National Academy of Sciences, NAS*. She really had no idea what the NAS was, but it sounded important, and she was fairly certain that not just anyone could publish there. This had to be big. She highlighted the parts she felt were important and printed out the NAS report.

Teresa's head was spinning. Studies from serious universities, not little colleges in Podunk, were turning out peer-reviewed papers showing fracking chemicals were finding their way into water wells. In particular, methane was being found at very high levels, so high in some places that the government said it reached unhealthy levels. One study showed there were metabolic changes taking place in mice as a result of exposure to fracking chemicals. Others showed the fracking chemicals were toxic and should never be ingested.

Teresa read about Dimock, in Susquehanna County, a mere twenty-five miles from where she sat. She read how their water wells were contaminated from drilling. The people who were affected said their water, their lives, were ruined. She had no doubts. Stories about other towns, like Dish in Texas, where the water wells were contaminated with fracking chemicals, also appeared on her screen. What concerned her the most was that the drilling companies either completely tied up the government agencies in litigation or the agencies were in bed with the drillers. Teresa's heart raced as she read the accounts.

Teresa's DEP water report, indicating the level of methane in her water, was somewhere in a pile of papers in Jared's home office. She was pretty sure the level was high, but she didn't recall exactly how high. She shuddered at the thought.

Teresa remembered talking with DEP's geologist as well as her lawyers, all of whom told her that in her part of Bradford County it wasn't unusual to find some naturally occurring methane in water wells. Some of it originated near the surface, while other methane originated deep in the ground in the fracking wells. Specialized testing could tell which was which. She couldn't recall whether the report from DEP or the report she'd received from her lawyers told her from where her well's methane originated.

She found a reference to a book, *Amity and Prosperity,* about families impacted by fracking in Western Pennsylvania and downloaded it onto her Kindle. The book had won the Pulitzer Prize. *The* Pulitzer Prize. She read it for two solid hours. As she read, she grew scared and angry.

In her forty-two years, Teresa had never been an activist about anything. Now a loud voice in her head shouted at her. The bastards at Yukon were destroying her water, the air. Even though the Campbell family always used bottled water for drinking, some studies showed that inhaling the contaminated water, like when you took a shower, was worse than drinking it. Also, using the water for washing dishes left a residue of chemicals on your dishes, pots, and pans. Her kids were eating and drinking the stuff. They were all breathing this crap.

Teresa got angrier as she read the online articles. *How can they do this? These asshole bastards are fucking up my water . . .* my *water! They are messing with me and my family, shit-eating, assholes!*

She thought about Caitlin and her other Bradford County friends.

She texted Caitlin:

You up?

About thirty seconds later she received a response:

I am now

Can I call you? About fracking? I have some serious questions

Give me three minutes to pee and wash my face and I'll call your cell. I'll talk to you anytime about this

Teresa sat back in her chair and stretched. She was shocked when she looked out the window and saw the first glow of morning light. Her phone told her it was after 5 a.m. The only time she'd ever pulled an all-nighter was the crazy night when she attended her friend Angelina's bachelorette party in Vegas.

Until now.

45

There's No Explaining Some People's Actions.

The day after Chief West's call with Lafleur, he received a call from Bones Benson, and they made an appointment to meet at the station the next day. At precisely 10 a.m., a thin man in work clothes and a scraggly beard presented himself at the police department. Mildred, the department's ancient secretary/receptionist, met him at the counter.

"I'm here to see Chief West. I wanted to see if I could kinda like help him out."

Mildred eyeballed him suspiciously. "Your name, sir?"

"Quincy Benson. My friends call me Bones."

"Quincy 'Bones' Benson? Huh? Wait here, Mr. Benson."

Mildred shuffled back to Chief West's office. Her bedroom slippers scraped on the new vinyl floor.

***

"I'm Chief West." They shook hands. "Come around here and join me in our conference room. You want coffee? Water?"

"Nah, I'm all coffee'd out. I'm good."

The conference room had no windows, just a large mirror that took up much of one wall. The furniture was old, gunmetal colored, uncomfortable. With the door shut, the only noise was the sound of the air blowing through a vent. As they settled in, West pulled out a pad and scanned Benson's appearance. He resembled every other Southerner or Texan he'd met doing work in Bradford County. Nothing unusual or special about this one, except that he was thin. No obvious tattoos, scars, or amputations.

"So, Mr. Benson, I was hoping you could answer some questions."

"Bones, just call me Bones. I heard you had some questions about a contractor we laid off about four months ago. I wanted to see if I could, you know, help out."

"I stopped by your office at the drill site two or three times and left cards in the door for you. Also, I called the number one of your men gave me, said it was your cell phone, but I guess you never got my messages. It would have been a help if you'd returned my messages. I did talk with Norby the other day, so I guess I finally got through."

Bones shrugged and smiled weakly.

"What do you know about this Chris Corsica? I guess you heard we found his RV in North Dakota."

"I barely remember the guy. Norby's the boss, and he has me running around and dealing with contractors, truckers, employees, you name it, all over the Northern Tier. We've probably had three or four impoundment contractors over the years here in P-A-, and I can't even begin to tell you how many other contractors."

West jotted down on his pad, *Says he barely remembers CC.*

"I'm sorry to hear that, Bones. I was hoping you'd be able to help the investigation. But if you know nothing, then you know nothing." West pushed back his chair and began to stand up.

"I do remember one thing." Bones remained seated. "Norby and I went to deliver the bad news, and we met Corsica at his RV. We were very apologetic and felt bad for the guy. Here he'd invested all this money going into the impoundment contracting business. Did you know he was a roofer back in Philly? Anyway, we sat around his RV and shot the breeze for fifteen or twenty minutes. He offered us coffee in a mug, and I was happy to get it. Uh, Norby had one too. The night was cold and wet. In any event, I suggested to him that the Bakken Play was going strong out in North Dakota. I told him if I was him, I'd pull up stakes and head out there. A man could make a mint building impoundments in North Dakota."

Benson says he and NL met with CC in his RV to tell him he was fired. Had coffee in a mug. Benson suggested that CC head out to N. Dak.

"Really? It sounds like you had quite a visit with Mr. Corsica."

"Well, we weren't buddies or anything, but I felt for the guy. Norby, too. Starting a new business and all. A regular workingman. A vet, too. Army Ranger. I just wanted to help the guy out. We both did."

BB and NL wanted to help CC. Vet- Army Ranger. Felt sorry for him.

"How did you leave it? Was he angry? Cordial? I mean, if it was me, I wouldn't be too happy about the situation. You tell me."

"Cordial, I'd say. He wasn't happy, of course, but he seemed to get it. He had a bottle of Jack Daniels which he offered us, and he pulled out a couple of clean glasses. We all had a mouthful or so of Jack, wished him good luck, shook hands, and that was the last I saw of him."

Cordial meeting in RV. Fired CC then CC offered and they drank Jack D. Everything was friendly.

"So you sat in his RV, probably touching the table, chair, maybe the door. You also touched and drank from a coffee mug and glass: you and Mr. Lafleur. Your DNA would be all over the RV. Right?" West asked.

"Hunh, I never thought of it that way. Police thinking. What do you know?"

"Did you ever hear from Corsica again?"

"No, like I said, we're not buddies."

Never heard from CC again.

"So even though you fired him, and suggested he travel maybe two-thousand miles from home for work, you parted on good terms?"

"Yep. Real good terms. It was nothing personal, just business. Corsica was a real businessman, and he got it. That was about it."

Ended on "real good terms." "Just business."

West stopped writing. For fifteen seconds, he stared at Bones who looked at the floor.

The table.

The ceiling.

Anywhere but at the chief.

Oldest trick in the cop handbook.

Finally, Bones said, "Now that you mention it, I don't know where I heard this, but I think one of my men may have said something about hearing from Corsica a month or two after he left P-A-. I don't remember who it was, but he said something about him getting a job building impoundments for some outfit in North Dakota. Something like that."

One of Yukon men said he heard from CC that he got a job building imps. in N. Dak.

"Do you remember who told you that?"

"Nah, sorry, it was just in passing. I'll put my mind to it, but I doubt I'll come up with the name."

No clue who told him this. Benson making this up as he goes along.

West pushed a button under the table twice, and two seconds later, Mildred walked into the room.

"Cliff, you have a call."

"Can you tell whoever it is I'll call back?"

"Says it's urgent. Police business."

She smiled and left the door open as she shuffled out.

"Bones, do you mind waiting a minute or two. I'm sure this will be quick. You sure you don't want a cup of coffee?"

"Nah, thanks." Bones shrugged.

West left and pulled the door shut, making sure it locked. The second oldest trick in the cop handbook. He nodded at Mildred, who smiled broadly. Then he got two cups of black coffee and walked to the hallway behind his office to watch Benson through the two-way mirror. He handed a cup to Hector Torres.

"What do you think, Hector?"

Torres looked through the mirror at Bones, who sat impassively at the table. "He's a liar. That Bones is a lying bastard. He's even worse than Norby. Throws his weight around, what there is of it. Chris hated his guts, and there's no way he sat around drinking coffee and whiskey with the guy. Especially if they'd just fired him."

At first, Bones sat quietly. Then he looked at his phone and realized that he had no reception. He looked around. After several minutes, he got up and tried the door. It was locked. He sat again. Then he got up and walked around the table. He looked at the two-way mirror, inches from the chief and Torres, who were invisible through the glass. He went back to the door and tried it again. It was still locked. He knocked on it quietly.

"That guy made us put the pit over that friggin' shale ridge," Hector spoke through gritted teeth. "Not where the plans showed it. Said it had to be closer to the pad. Set us back several days. No talk at all about extra pay for the extra work. No way he would have done that without Norby's approval. I never heard a nice word from him about anything. What a jerk."

"What about this business of Chris going out to North Dakota?"

"That's pure BS. We rented a big dozer, a D-8. That was $14,000, cash, upfront, for a two-week rental. Chris never would have abandoned that. Also, we had a crew of four guys, me included, up here. No way he would've just pulled up stakes and left town without at least telling us. Something happened to Chris. Bones and Norby know what it was. I'm sure they were involved in whatever happened to him."

The chief thought for a moment. "I'm going to apologize in advance for something I'm about to do. Just don't get mad at me. I think you'll see why I have to do it in a minute."

Torres furrowed his eyebrows but said nothing. The chief patted him quickly on the shoulder.

The chief put down his coffee and re-entered the room.

"Hey chief, your door was locked. Kinda' got me spooked." Bones began to stand.

"Sorry, Bones. The latch is a little tricky. You should have knocked. Mildred would have been happy to let you out. Look, it's a good thing you're still here. You can clear something up for me. That was the State Police, the forensics guys. They found a lot of blood all over the floor, steering wheel. Corsica's. Old blood, too. At least four months old. What do you know about this?"

Dramatically, the chief turned his legal pad to a blank sheet. "I expect you to tell me the truth."

He looked at Bones, his hand ready to write.

Bones said nothing. He looked away from the chief and, after a full five seconds, said quietly. "I think he cut himself. On a piece of metal getting into the RV, sticking out of the side of the door. Bad cut. Took a few minutes to stop the bleeding. I think that's what it was, but it was months ago, and I'm not sure."

Admits Corsica's blood in RV. Says he cut himself on piece of metal sticking out door. All made up.

West waited, but Benson said nothing further.

"One more thing. Do you know at all Corsica's assistant . . ." he glanced through his notes like he didn't recall the name at first, then said, "A little spic guy named Torres, Hector?"

"Yeah . . ." Bones smiled weakly at him.

"I haven't been able to locate the guy, but I think he's probably gone back to roofing in Philly. How'd you get along with him?"

"Good enough."

"Based on my investigation, he seems like a shifty little Mexican guy, if you ask me." The chief winked at Bones.

Bones nodded and smiled. "My feelings exactly. I never trusted the greaseball."

"Well, do you think he could've done something? You know, to Corsica?"

"Now that you mention it, yeah. *Yeah*, I bet he had something to do with this. They were always arguing, fighting, that kind of thing. I wouldn't be surprised. You find him, and I think you'll see that wetback had something to do with this."

"Do you think he could be MS-13? Something like that?"

Bones looked up to the ceiling. "Now that you mention it, yeah. If anything violent happened to Corsica, I bet it was Torres. That Corsica was okay, but that little greaseball, he's trouble."

The chief watched Bones carefully as he spoke, then said, "Okay Bones, this has been very helpful." He and Benson stood.

"Whatever you do, Mr. Benson, don't talk with anyone about this, okay? That's standard operating procedure."

Bones nodded.

West walked the man to the door of the station. Just before he left, West said, "Don't you think it's funny that Corsica headed out to North Dakota and left behind his equipment and team of men? Just like that. I mean, it seems really odd to me."

"You got me there, chief. You know, and I'm trying to be helpful here, maybe it was that spic, Torres, who took the RV to North Dakota. There's no explaining some people's actions."

West watched Benson cross the street and get into his white pickup truck with the Yukon logo. He went back to the conference room, knocked on the mirrored window, and indicated that Torres should join him. Then he picked up his pad and jotted down:

Admits to Corsica's blood in the RV. "No explaining some people's actions."

46

If you don't want to slip up tomorrow, speak the truth today.
(Bruce Lee)

Chief West returned in the afternoon from a meeting on the other side of the township. Mildred had left him four pink-slip telephone messages. One was from a township supervisor ("Call him back immediately"), one was from Corny Campbell, currently a resident at the Shady Acres Home and Rehab Center, ("Says his son stole his property and he's been kidnapped and wants you to come and rescue him"), one from his wife (no message), and one from Norby Lafleur, ("Call him when you're free"). West dialed Lafleur first.

"I was hoping you'd call me," West said. "I have some interesting news."

"Okay," Lafleur said slowly.

"The PSP forensics lab in Harrisburg got back to me today. You'll never guess what they found."

Lafleur was quiet.

"You want to guess?" West asked.

"Yeah, I imagine you found some of Chris's blood on the floor. From the piece of metal stickin' out of the door."

Bastard got that from Bones.

"Well, Norby, you're half-right. There was blood, but not from the door. They checked that thoroughly all afternoon. No jagged metal and no blood on the door. A lot of blood on the floor, though. No, I'm not asking about that. What else do you think they found? It's even more confusing."

Norby said nothing for several seconds. "Maybe they found my DNA in Corsica's RV."

The chief glanced at the receiver in disbelief. "Exactly, Mr. Lafleur. Like I told you a week ago, the lab picks up everything—hair, fingernails, blood, even DNA from your lips on a glass. It's amazing what the lab can do today. Of course, they found Corsica's DNA everywhere. So where do you suppose they found *your* DNA?"

Again, there was a pause. "I don't have a clue. Bones probably told you we had a real nice conversation with Chris, Chris Corsica. I'd forgotten all about that. We were sad we had to let his company go, but he understood. We had coffee, even a little whiskey. It's not like I touched everything in his RV but, well shoot, the table, the chair, the door, coffee mug, bottle of Jack."

"And?" West waited. This was the third oldest trick in the cop handbook.

"Oh, shit, yeah. The glass, the damn whiskey glass. It was broken. The light wasn't great in the RV and crap, I didn't see that the glass was broken. I guess I cut my thumb. I'm guessing the lab found some blood residue. My blood."

"That's exactly right, Mr. Lafleur. We found all of those things with your DNA. And we did find some blood residue containing your DNA and, of course, Mr. Corsica's blood residue with his DNA. We were wondering how that happened. I'm glad you explained it to me, though. It makes perfect sense."

"It does? Well, of course. We were all laughing about the glass. I think Bones may have even cut his finger on it, too, when we were cleaning it up."

"Actually no. The only blood residue we found in the RV was yours and Mr. Corsica's. Just the two of you. Most likely from the broken glass. I mean, what else could have caused the blood residue and your DNA to be inside the RV?"

"You got me. I'm pretty sure Bones cut his finger, too, cleanin' up. Cut it bad and bled all over the place."

"If he did, he didn't leave a trace of blood DNA behind. Just yours. And Mr. Corsica's, of course."

"Maybe your forensics team will turn up Bones's blood yet."

"I doubt it. They're done with the forensics of Corsica's RV. Now, Mr. Lafleur, this is purely a formality. I don't know whether they do this in Louisiana, but here in Pennsylvania in order to close the investigation, I'll need your statement. It's pretty informal, no court reporter, just a tape recorder. Can you come down here to the station, let's say tomorrow morning at 10 a.m.? We'll just go over the same exact stuff we've talked about, and then that'll be that."

Lafleur did not respond immediately. "Do I need a lawyer?"

"Absolutely not, but if it makes you more comfortable, you can bring one, of course. In my experience, only guilty people bring a lawyer. All they do is slow things down. If you want, I can recommend a few criminal lawyers here in Bradford County, but that's your call."

Norby hesitated, then said, "Well, shoot no. If this is going to close out the investigation, let's git 'er done. I can see how a lawyer would muck things up."

"There you go. I hope to have you out of here in ten minutes, fifteen max. I know you're a busy man and what you're doing really helps us. We appreciate it."

After the call, West pulled out his Sony IC Recorder. It was the size of a small matchbox. He plugged it into his laptop to fully charge it. After he got Lafleur's statement, he would plug it into his laptop and run it through the Dragon program to convert the questions and answers into text. Even though West was an old-fashioned, small-town cop, he could appreciate modern technology.

He knew he was getting closer to the truth.

47

Trains Passing Each Other Moving in Opposite Directions

Mike stared at the monitor. The email from Winnie was sent to him, Darius Moore, and Berliner. It was simple enough:

> Counsel: Attached please find a notice of deposition and request for a site view. I would like to schedule the deposition in Williamsport and do these events back-to-back to save all of us travel time. I've arbitrarily selected July 1-2, as the dates for these events. Let me know if it is absolutely impossible for you to attend on these dates. I do not want to put off these two important discovery events, so please try to arrange your calendars. Thank you.
> Winnifred Hedges, Esq.
> General Counsel
> Pennsylvania's Advocates for the Environment

Mike scanned the deposition notice. It was for Missy. The request for the site view was for the Campbell Pad. He had less than two weeks to prepare Missy for her deposition. This was more than do-able as she was already quite familiar with the site and her report, of course. He decided the right thing to do would be to call Darius Moore and invite him to meet with Missy prior to the deposition.

He was still thinking about calling Darius Moore when his phone rang. The caller ID simply indicated *Washington DC.*

"Jacobs."

"I see your buddy at the Advocates didn't waste any time getting out a deposition notice," said Darius Moore. "Pretty coincidental you saw her the other day and suddenly there's a deposition notice, don't you think?"

"Are you referring to the riot? Do you think Winnie and I stood around drinking coffee and talking about the discovery in this case while the men in black were throwing bottles and rocks? Cut me a break."

"I'm not cutting you any breaks. You don't get any breaks. This is my case, and I'm not going to let any government lawyer screw it up for me."

"Excuse me, am I talking to Darius Moore, or am I talking to a fucking lunatic? You need to chill out, Darius. We're on the same side in this case, remember?"

"Are we? Are we? Then you need to act like it. Honestly, I don't know if I can trust you."

"Are you threatening me? What are you going to do about that? Are you going to run to Jake and have him call his buddy, the governor? Try to get me pulled from this case? Bigger men than you have tried to do that to me over the years. I suggest you settle down and we discuss next steps, just like a couple of colleagues who are on the same side."

Mike heard Darius exhale. "What do you have in mind?" Darius Moore asked almost sweetly.

"I see Winnie has set the deposition for Williamsport. That makes sense since she also wants to do a site view. The Campbell pad is a lot closer to Williamsport than Harrisburg. Also, Missy Shelton, our geologist, works out of the Williamsport office. If you're available, I can set up a meeting with Missy for the day before the site visit, and you can meet with her. Ask her whatever you want about the case, so long as it's not protected by attorney-client privilege."

"I'll have to check my schedule. Do they have any decent hotels up there?"

"They don't have the Plaza or Four Seasons, but they have a couple of the low-end Marriott and Hilton hotels, Courtyard, Hampton, that kind of thing. I'm sure you can find something."

"Okay, then, I want to schedule a full day, eight hours, with Shelton. I agree not to ask her anything genuinely protected by attorney-client privilege, but everything else is on the table. Got it?" Darius Moore said.

Mike looked at his receiver and said, "You can talk with her about anything having to do with *this* case, as long as it's not privileged. I'm not going to allow you to have unfettered access to my witness. As far as time is concerned, she's a busy person. Her territory covers all of the oil and gas counties in the Northeastern part of Pennsylvania. The deposition and site view will take two days out of her schedule as it is. I'll give you two or three hours if you really need it. Honestly, I don't know why you'd need more."

"I guess that's the difference between a D.C. law firm and a state agency," said Darius Moore. "Obviously, we're a lot more thorough."

Mike winced. "One more thing. We talked about this before. I hope you're not planning on asking questions to her in the deposition. All you'll do is give Winnie and the Advocates ammunition to use against us. Every deposition I've ever taken has resulted in unexpected testimony coming out. Also, at times it results in a lot less than I expected. Every question you'd ask could open the door for Winnie. I'm pretty confident she's going to cover all the ground she needs to cover, but you never know when you might ask a question that opens up a whole new area she hasn't considered."

"That's my prerogative, of course, but I hear you. I'll do whatever is in the best interest of my client."

"Honestly, I don't understand the tension between you and me. Don't let that get in the way of our clients' interests."

"That's pretty condescending, Mike. I get it; you work for a state agency whose mission is to protect the environment. I knew you as one of the tree huggers at Vermont, but I always thought you were a pretty rational guy. My client does what it has to do in an environmentally safe manner, producing clean-burning natural gas. We abide by the law. You issued a permit, and Shelton issued a report supporting us. I'll leave it at this: If I do decide it's in the best interest of my client to take Shelton's dep, I'll give you a heads up. That's it."

"Nice speech, Darius. Save it for the next meeting of the Shale Gas Association. I have a client, and my client's interests temporarily intersect with yours. I still don't get the animosity. Whatever screwed-up problem you have with me, don't let it get in the way of our clients' interests."

"Back at you, Mike."

When they were done, Mike hung up, got onto the floor, and cranked out thirty-two push-ups until he could barely push himself to a sitting position. Then, as he stood and swatted the dust from his hands, he looked out the window at the semis moving in opposite directions on the Interstate highway, not far from his office. From this distance, it looked as though the Macks were going to crash into each other until, at the last moment, they passed each other on adjacent lanes.

48

Where to Begin?

The DEP receptionist, a friendly middle-aged woman, plump, with black, curly-permed hair, directed Mike to an internal conference room on the first floor of DEP's Williamsport office. The room was standard government issue. Faded eight-by-ten photographs in plastic frames depicting Pennsylvania state parks were strategically placed, one for each wall. Narrow tables were pushed together to form a square, metal and blue-cloth chairs, and a projection screen and whiteboard at the front of the room. The well-used whiteboard had the faded remnant of the last several scribbles demonstrating that either the board itself or the eraser was worn out. A *Kilroy was Here* stick drawing was the only thing clearly discernible in the lower corner of the whiteboard.

Mike scrolled through his emails while he waited for Missy. His plan was to meet with her on Monday to prepare her for both the deposition and the meeting with Darius Moore. He hoped to have dinner with her, get her through the meeting with Darius on Tuesday, attend the site view on Wednesday, and then the deposition on Thursday. Busy. That, at least, was the plan.

At 9:55 a.m., Missy came into the room carrying a pile of papers and folders. Mike couldn't help but notice that her breasts rested on top of the large stack that she carried. He stood as she entered the room, and she smiled broadly at him. As soon as she set down the papers, she put her arms around him and the two hugged warmly for several long moments, finishing with a quick kiss.

"I missed you," she breathed into his ear.

"Me too." Mike pulled his head away from their hug and had to restrain himself from kissing her more passionately. Instead, he moved to kiss her on the cheek. She intercepted and kissed him deeply.

"Any word from Richard?" He asked as they pulled apart.

"All the time. He calls, I tell him it's over and he should stop calling me. Then he begs forgiveness. I hang up, and he calls back. Sometimes this can go on for hours."

They sat next to each other at the table. Mike took her hand.

"Did you call my lawyer friend about a PFA?"

"Not yet." Mike made a face. "I keep hoping he's going to stop acting like a child, and we can just break up like normal adults."

"I don't know, Missy. He's already been violent with you. You never told me what happened in my hotel room, but was it . . .?"

"Rape? I don't know. I don't think so. Maybe. I didn't want to have sex with him, and he surprised me when I was in the shower. He asked me a lot of questions about you and wanted to know if we were sleeping together. I told him, honestly, we're just friends. He moved me toward the bed even before I'd dried off and begged me to do it one last time. I didn't want to, but he ripped the towel off me and pushed me onto the bed. He was on top of me a moment later, and I realized his pants were down. He held me down with his arm, but I didn't really fight or scream. I guess I hoped if I did it with him, that would be it. When we were done, I told him, *reminded* him that was it. He got furious and slapped me."

"Yeah, the bed was still damp when I got upstairs—"

Missy covered her eyes with her hand, "Oh. I'm so sorry about that. What was I thinking? I just wanted him to go."

"Look, I don't do criminal or domestic law, but if that wasn't rape, it was damn close. He pressured you, forced you, really, so that's probably something. Maybe domestic abuse. Then again, you said yes. I just don't know. The slap was assault, battery definitely. You could go to the police on that alone. At the very least, you need to see a lawyer."

"I keep hoping this will be it. I don't want to do anything to hurt Richard; he's been a part of my life for years now. I just want him to go away."

"I have a feeling Richard's not going to go away quietly. We know he's violent. There's no telling where that will end. You really need to talk with my lawyer friend. Please. She deals with this crap all the time. You don't have to go as far as getting a PFA, maybe some kind of restraining order, but you need to know your rights, talk with someone who actually knows the law in this area. She's a really good lady and a good lawyer. If you want, I can call her and let her know you're going to call. Maybe I can get you a friends-and-family discount."

Missy smiled, and neither talked for several seconds.

Mike squeezed her hand and let it go. "We need to get to work." He looked at the stacks of paper. "Ugh, where do we begin?"

With confident authority, Missy organized the papers and files into six piles in under thirty seconds. She picked up a file and said, "Right here."

49

Snippy

Mike spent hours drilling Missy on possible questions Winnie might ask. Both of them were a bit punchy as they began the third hour of Mike's intense questioning and tutoring.

"Remember, the primary rule is you have to answer every question honestly," Mike said.

"Okay, no fibbing, like Mike does." Missy smiled.

"Be very careful when answering questions."

"Is that like being honest?"

"Just answer the question you're asked," he said.

"You don't want me talking about my cute lawyer, too?"

"Missy, listen really hard to the question Winnie asks you. If she asks a question and I don't object, be sure to give her as short an answer as possible. Answer the question, but no more. Got it?"

"Yes, sir." She narrowed her eyes.

"That reminds me, don't be snippy. Don't ever let her get to you. The worst thing that could happen is if she manages to get under your skin and you lash out somehow and say something you really don't want to say."

"You know, *you* get snippy sometimes." She smiled and patted his hand.

"You're making this very difficult, you know."

"See? Snippy."

Mike rubbed his forehead. "That reminds me. Try not to show any emotion."

"Got it. Try to act more like Mike Jacobs."

Mike smiled. This wasn't easy. They were both mentally tired from a full morning of preparation.

"Also, listen for a moment after she asks you a question to see if I make an objection. I probably won't make any. In a deposition, there really are only two legitimate objections. One is called the form of the question. That would be where Winnie asks you two questions that are built into one, like, *When did you stop beating your wife?* The other is if she asks you a question which calls for a privileged communication. Let's say, for example, she asks you about the meeting we're having today. That's a privileged communication, and I'll object. Got that?"

Missy said nothing.

"What's the matter?" Mike asked.

"I was practicing waiting for an objection."

Mike burst out into laughter. "You're too much. We are *not* supposed to be having a good time right now. This is supposed to be serious. Are you even listening to my instructions?"

"Yes."

"Yes?"

"I'm not sure how I answer the question, *yes*. Maybe *I* should object. Form of the question, counselor." She giggled and threw her arms around him. "I *really* like you, do you know that?"

He put his arm around her and hugged her shoulder to shoulder, then gently pushed her away.

"The same goes for our meeting with Darius Moore tomorrow. It's not going to be a deposition, but treat it the same way. He'll be asking you questions and trying to have a conversation with you. I suspect he'll have an expert with him, too. I'm sure they'll want to know all about the study you've done and your letter to the Campbells. We're not going to act in a hostile way, but we don't have to trust them either. Smile a lot. That should be easy for you, but I don't trust him for a minute. I really don't know what his angle is. He's been irate with me, and that makes no sense. It might just be his nature. I just don't know. So let's be very careful."

"Yes, sir, Mike."

"I'm really serious about this; he concerns me."

Missy pushed her way in front of Mike, pushing Mike's chair back. She wore a broad smile

"What, what are you doing?"

"I need a break from all of this, counsellor."

She put her arms around his neck and started kissing Mike's face. A few seconds later, their lips were locked together in a long, luxuriant kiss.

This is so wrong . . . so unprofessional . . . so good.

Mike stroked her face and turned his head to get a better angle . . .

Cough. Cough, cough.

They opened their eyes. The receptionist stood in the doorway.

"Uh Missy, I tried to call, but the phone was busy."

They straightened themselves. Mike looked at the phone. A stack of files had toppled over during their kissing and knocked the receiver off the hook.

"Oh, I'm so sorry, Sally," Missy said, squeezing her eyes together. "This is terribly unprofessional of me. What? What's going on?"

"Someone's here. On the other side of the security door. For you. Your friend," she made air quotes with her fingers, "Mr. Shelby. Says he needs to see you. Loud and obnoxious as usual. Says it's important."

Missy turned to Mike, "Stay here."

She got up and headed for the door, straightening her blouse as she walked.

"Wait a minute, what's he doing coming to your office?" Mike said. "I think you need to put your foot down and tell him to stay the hell away from you."

"I can deal with this."

Mike watched her walk down the hall and felt like a jerk sitting there while she dealt with her ex. Sally hadn't moved from her spot near the door. Her arms were folded, and she glared at Mike.

"Missy is one of the nicest girls I know. Don't you dare hurt that girl. Do you understand me?"

Mike nodded. "Don't worry. I think we're all on the same side here. You keep looking out for her too, okay?"

He got up and followed her to the reception area. When Mike got there, Missy and Richard were on the other side of the glass reception door. He knew from experience that the door unlocked electronically. Sally stood behind her desk with the phone in her hand.

Mike could see Richard waving his hands wildly and Missy standing with her back to the door, her hands planted on her hips. Mike waited for a few moments then went through the door.

"What's he doing here?" Richard said loudly.

"I work here. What are *you* doing here?" Mike asked.

"This is personal, just between Missy and me. Buzz off," Richard said.

"I'm not going anywhere until you leave. Missy and I are getting ready for a deposition, and you're interrupting us."

"Is that what you call it?" He said approaching Mike and moving within six inches of his face. Then he bumped Mike with his chest.

"Back off, dude," Mike said in a low voice. "Get any closer, and I'll put my fist in your face. In fact, just get the hell out of here."

Richard took a step back and Mike watched his shoulders, arms, and hands for any sign of movement. Instead, he saw Richard's lips move. He couldn't quite make out what he was saying as he was mouthing words.

"What did you say?" Mike turned his body sideways in a defensive posture in case Richard tried to hit him. He clenched his guts, getting ready for a sucker punch.

"You're screwing her, you bastard. That's it, right? You're screwing my woman."

"Get out of here," Missy said. "I'm not with you anymore, and it's none of your damn business who I'm seeing. Leave me alone."

Richard backed up, squinted his eyes, and nodded. "I wasn't sure before; now I know."

He turned and went to the outer door, tugged it open, then turned around and looked directly at Missy. "No one screws around behind my back."

"Richard, for one last time, we're *through*. Over. Done. Finished. Get it? Leave me the hell alone."

Richard turned on his heels and began to walk away. Then he turned back and shouted at Mike, "I'm going to kill you, you Jew-bastard. You're a dead man."

They watched as he hurried across the street and into his pickup. The tires screeched as he pulled onto William Street and blew through the light onto Third Street. Mike could plainly see the gunrack in the back of the cab. It held two rifles. Mike had no idea what kind, but he was sure they were the kind that shot bullets.

"What do you think? Call the cops?" Missy asked.

"Crap. I don't know. Can we call my friend now and make an appointment to see her about that PFA?"

Sally buzzed them back through the electronic door. She was still at her desk with her hand on the phone.

"I was ready to call security. I heard every word through the monitor if you need a witness," she said.

"Thanks, Sally. It's all over," Missy said, patting the woman on the hand.

Sally shook her head. "Trust me, honey. When they're bad like that, it's never over."

50

Sleep after toil . . . does greatly please. (Edmund Spenser)

Mike and Missy found a small Italian place down a side street in Williamsport. It was close to 10 p.m. when they finished drinking their coffee. The conversation slowed, and neither seemed to know what to say next. They both played with their wine glasses.

"I don't want this to sound like a corny come-on," Mike said, "but I have a big hotel room. It has a bed and a sofa, and you're welcome to stay with me. I'm concerned that if you go back to your apartment, Richard will do something stupid, and I don't want to take the chance he could hurt you."

"I bet you say that all the girls," Missy said, reaching for his hand. "I have a pretty long drive to get back to my apartment anyway, and it *is* getting kind of late. Plus, I reloaded my bag with my change of clothes after last week so it *would* be the most practical thing to do."

"Practical? I bet you say that to all the guys," Mike said, smiling. "I'm serious, though. This is not a lame way of getting you into my hotel room. I'm really concerned. I wouldn't want anything to happen to you. You need to decide what you're going to do about *tomorrow* night and all the nights after that. It's not going to be enough simply to tell Richard to get lost."

"Let me deal with that when we meet with your lawyer friend on Friday." She squeezed his hand tightly.

Mike's room wasn't a suite, but it was roomy. Hotels in Williamsport gave you a lot of space. It had a king-sized bed, sofa, good-sized desk and chairs. Somehow, he could use his state voucher to stay in the hotel, so he knew the room couldn't be too expensive, even at normal rack rates.

They went up the elevator together, standing close. An older man was on the elevator with them, and he glanced at them a couple of times. The corners of his mouth rose in a slight smile, but he got off a floor below. Missy looked at Mike and smiled.

As soon as the doors closed, Missy said, "Awkward."

Missy carried a small bag that more closely resembled a large pocketbook than a suitcase or overnight bag. Although Missy had a change of clothes and a toilet kit, she giggled when she told Mike she didn't have anything to sleep in. Mike lent her a dress shirt. When she came out of the bathroom, holding her clothes and bra, the shirt came down to above her knees. Mike noticed she'd left the top three buttons unbuttoned, showing off a good bit of cleavage, and he thought she looked sexy in his shirt. She posed for a moment, and they both laughed. Mike had changed into his green Vermont Law School T-shirt and loose-fitting gym shorts for bed.

"I'll take the sofa; you take the bed," Mike said.

"That's not fair. It's your room. You take the bed," Missy replied, standing near him. She took his hand. "If you want, we can *both* take the bed, and I'll trust you to stay on your side."

Mike thought back on an earlier occasion with his best friend, Nicky Kane, and their months' long arrangement when they shared a bed and nothing more than conversation. He did not want to go down that road again. He took the spare pillow and blanket from the closet and set up camp on the sofa. Then he went to the bed, leaned over, kissed Missy on the forehead, lay down on the sofa, and turned out the light.

A few seconds after darkness enveloped the room, Missy asked lightly, "So, are you dating anyone now by any chance?"

"No, I told you I'm single. I'm not dating anyone either. I was seeing a woman until a few weeks ago, but it was very casual, and it started fizzling out months ago until it finally just ended. By text message, if you can believe it."

"Good, I mean, thanks for telling me that." She paused. "Have you ever been married?"

"No. How about you?"

"No. Richard asked me about a dozen times, but I never agreed to it. Thank God for that. Ever engaged?"

"No. You?"

"Yes," she said. "A long story and a long time ago. I promise to tell you sometime." Another long pause.

"How did Richard happen?" Mike said.

Missy hesitated a long time before answering. "I actually saw someone, a counselor, about this. I guess I have self-esteem issues. That's the basic thing."

"What? Really? You seem to be a pretty confident woman."

"Really? I think it has to do with when I was younger, a teenager. I was pretty chunky all the way through college. I weighed a lot more than I do now. It takes work to keep my weight down. I try to exercise every day."

"You look great."

"Oh, Mike. That's why I . . . like you. Anyway, I wanted to be with a guy, and let's just say, I was with a lot of guys."

"*With*?"

"*With* a lot. Try not to exercise your imagination too much, please. Too many. In the end, I never got any guy. I was the slutty girl in college who slept with all the guys but never ended up with anyone."

"I find that really hard to believe."

The sound of the shower loudly dripping reached them and tapped out ten seconds.

"*Anyway.* Then Richard came along. He was so nice. Protective. I felt as though I finally had a long-term relationship that wasn't just based on one-nighters. Then he became protective and ultimately jealous. I never had that, and at first, I didn't mind. I actually liked it."

"You *liked* it?"

"I liked the attention. I liked the fact he was with me for more than one night. No guy had ever been jealous or protective.

"Then he just became crazy. Overly protective. Jealous of everyone. Demanding all of my time. Suspicious whenever I hung out with anyone, man or woman. Mean. Awful. Ultimately, he became scary. I started suggesting we have a break a year ago, but he just held on more tightly. A couple of months ago, I told him we were over, and he flew into a rage. I feel like an idiot."

"You're not an idiot."

"Do you say that to all the girls?"

Mike lay on the sofa in the darkness, thinking.

"You said a couple of weeks ago that you're Jewish," Mike said. "Shelton doesn't sound like a Jewish name. Another story?"

"My dad changed his name from Schechter to Shelton. When I asked him why, he said he did it for work. Neither of my parents are religious, maybe non-religious or anti-religious. My grandparents, all from Romania and Moldova, were pretty observant. We weren't."

"Hmm," Mike said aloud. "I'm glad to hear that."

"You're glad my parents are non-religious?"

"No. That you're Jewish."

"That's more than a casual observation, isn't it, mister?" She said quietly.

"Probably."

"Okay, your turn," Missy said. "I know both of your parents are dead. What can you tell me about them?"

Mike didn't answer for a long time, then said, "I promise to tell you everything you want to know, but we have a busy couple of days, and we could be up all night talking. I'd love to do that sometime, really. We'll have this conversation as much as you want. Just not right now. Okay?"

"Okay, only if you promise we can continue this soon. All night long sounds like a plan."

"Promise. Good night, Missy."

"Good night, Mike. I really," she paused. "I really *like* you."

"I really like you too, sweetheart."

Suddenly, there was an explosive pounding on the door. "Hey, you asshole, LET ME IN," said a male voice.

Mike sat up, grabbed a nearby room phone, and was about to call the front desk when he realized the banging was on a door across the hall. He could hear the door open.

"Duane, you mo' fo', it's about time you got here," said a second male voice from across the hall.

"Hey buddy, I brought beers," said Duane.

"Chips and salsa too, I hope," said the second voice.

He heard laughter until the door slammed closed.

Missy had bolted across the room and was on her knees next to the sofa. She held Mike tightly, her head buried in his chest. She trembled. Mike could feel her heart pounding. He stroked her hair. After the hallway was quiet for several minutes, she tenderly kissed his face, searching for his mouth in the darkness until he moved so that their mouths connected. He loved her soft lips and the way she kissed him, slowly, her tongue languidly twirling with his in rhythm together. She placed her free hand on Mike's chest and gently stroked it. After many minutes, she backed a few inches away and took a deep breath.

"That scared the crap out of me," she whispered. "I'm sorry if I acted like a baby."

"Scared me too, hon. Don't worry about it. You're with me. Go back to sleep."

She took a deep breath and placed her mouth near his ear. Almost imperceptibly, she whispered, "Would you like to join me over there?"

In the dim light, he saw her point to the bed.

Mike hugged her tightly and sighed. "Very much. I really want to. More than you can imagine. It's already way after one, though, and I have a feeling if I joined you over there we wouldn't be doing much sleeping. That would be really awesome, but I need to be sharp the next couple of days and so do you. I'm going to hate myself for saying this, but let's wait. I'll take you out on a proper date when neither of us has anything special to do the next day, and let's see what happens. Sometime soon. I promise."

Mike instantly regretting turning her down. He put his hand behind her head and caressed her hair and she moved her face close to his. They kissed again, a long soulful kiss. Mike knew he was doing the right thing. *Dammit.* Finally, she returned to the bed but not before she let her hand drift from his face to his belly, which she gently stroked.

Mike lay on the sofa, listening to Missy breathe. After several minutes, her breathing became rhythmic and full of sleep.

***

About ten minutes after Mike fell asleep, a shadow appeared at the foot of the hotel room door. It lingered for thirty seconds. The knob jiggled ever so slightly, but the door was double locked. Finally, the shadow moved away. Had Mike been awake, he would have heard the stairway door open and close. Footsteps echoed in the concrete stairway.

51

Fancy Meeting You Here

At exactly 7:30 a.m., the elevator doors opened and Mike and Missy walked right into Darius Moore. He wore a sweaty University of Pennsylvania T-shirt, shorts, and running shoes, with a white hotel towel draped around his neck. He looked up from his iPhone and then back and forth from Mike to Missy. He smiled broadly at Mike.

"Darius, I thought you'd find a nicer hotel," Mike said, shaking his damp hand.

"There weren't too many choices, so I'm staying here."

"I'd like you to meet Missy Shelton, DEP's geologist."

Darius smiled as he shook her hand. "DEP's geologist? Nice meeting you."

"We have a lot of stuff to do over the next couple of days, and I wanted to get an early start."

"An early start. Is that what you call it, Bro?" Darius Moore asked with a wink.

"I guess we'll see you at DEP's office at 10 a.m.?" Mike asked.

"Looking forward to it." He was still grinning.

Mike and Missy watched Darius Moore as he boarded the elevator. He grinned at Mike until the doors closed.

Missy waited until the elevator doors were fully closed before she looked at Mike and said, "Busted."

"For all he knows, we were meeting in a conference room upstairs before we came down for breakfast."

"Or, and stick with me on this, it's complicated: He saw you and me getting off the hotel elevator at 7:30 in the morning and assumed we hooked up."

Mike closed his eyes and shook his head. They found a table, and Mike laid his briefcase on a seat to claim it. As they poured coffee at the breakfast bar, Mike noticed Missy looking at a man eating breakfast and reading *USA Today*.

"Do you see that guy over there?" She pointed with her chin. "That's Professor McCrory, the head of the geology department at Penn State."

"Are you sure?"

"I took two classes with him when I was getting my bachelor's degree and had a seminar with him when I got my master's."

Missy approached the professor and lightly tapped his shoulder. "Professor McCrory?"

He looked up from his paper. "Ms. Shelton. How very nice to see you again." He shook her hand warmly with both of his as he rose to his feet.

"This is Mike Jacobs, a DEP lawyer. He's also a Penn State grad, bachelor's in physical geography."

The men shook hands. "You must have known my good friend Professor Pierce Lewis."

"Of course, my faculty advisor."

"Then you must sit with me. We have a fair bit of catching up to do before our meeting at ten o'clock."

Mike looked at Missy. "I'd love to do that, professor, but your lawyer, Darius Moore, has made it clear to me he does not want me talking with any of his potential witnesses unless he's present or has given me permission."

"But all we'll do is talk about Penn State and our mutual friends, maybe Penn State football," the professor said, shaking his head.

"I apologize, but I had this conversation with Darius just a few days ago about someone else, even if it's just a social visit. He made it very clear."

"Well, it seems more than a bit silly, and I don't get it. Rules are rules, I suppose. You really should've stuck with geography," he said, smiling. "By the way, Ms. Shelton, I read your study on the Campbell well, and it's first-rate. I'd give it a solid A. We can discuss what you did and did not take into consideration later this morning."

At that moment, Mike looked up and saw Darius Moore approaching them, walking quickly. He was still wearing his sweaty running clothes, his eyes ablaze.

"I was just coming down to grab a cup of coffee, and look what I've found here. Mike, you just can't help yourself, can you?"

"What?" Mike said. "What are you talking about?"

"I'd think by now you'd know to stay the hell away from my witnesses unless I give you permission to talk with them. You did not have permission to talk with my expert witness."

Mike, Missy, and Professor McCrory all stared at Darius Moore.

"Wow, Darius, just wow. The professor was Missy's teacher at Penn State. We were just saying hello."

"Yes, Mr. Moore," said the professor. "In fact, I invited them to join me for breakfast, but they declined and said they weren't permitted to do so. Silly rule if you ask me."

Darius Moore locked eyes with Mike. "This is what happens when you can't trust someone."

Mike looked at the others and bit down on his lips. "Don't worry, Darius. No one is trying to pull a fast one. You need to get a grip."

They all watched as an attendant maneuvered a fresh coffee urn into position.

"Well, nice to see you again, professor," said Missy, taking Mike by the arm to drag him away.

"You too, Ms. Shelton. Nice meeting you, Mr. Jacobs. And like I said, nice work on that study."

Mike thought he detected a wink from the professor. He definitely noticed Darius Moore's eyes widen. They moved across the room to their table while Darius leaned over and talked rapidly in the professor's ear.

"Your buddy's a piece of work," Missy said quietly. "Is he always that friendly?"

"Only when he's in a good mood."

They sat at their table after getting coffee. "I can't believe Yukon got the head of the geology department as their expert," Missy said. "He's one of the top geologists in the United States."

"I'm not surprised. That's exactly what I would've done if I were Darius. The only problem with college professors, though, is they tend to teach a bit too much." Mike affected a British accent, "Harumph, well, my dear lad, yes, I do see your point. Brilliant. I hadn't considered that before I wrote my own report, but you may be right. So I need to reassess my entire opinion." He resumed his normal voice. "That kind of stuff totally messes with your case, and I've seen it happen. If Darius can keep him under control, though, it will be hard for Winnie to beat the head of Penn State's geology department."

"I do think it's ridiculous we can't sit and have a nice breakfast with him. An old professor is more than an old friend. I'd love to catch up." Missy shook her head.

"Actually, I do see Darius's point. Stuff just comes out when you have a conversation with your opponent. I mean, if anyone says anything negative about your report, the first thing I'm going to ask the good professor is whether he'd give your report a solid A."

"You wouldn't do that. Would you?"

Mike didn't reply. Instead, he hid his face in his coffee cup and took a long sip.

52

This Is Not a Deposition

Mike glanced at the clock. The meeting had stretched on for almost two hours. The conference room, the same one Mike and Missy had used the day before, was capable of holding twenty people. Today it felt cramped. Darius Moore, Professor McCrory, and Norby Lafleur sat opposite Mike and Missy. It didn't help that the air-conditioning barely worked, and the temperature in the room had risen to nearly eighty degrees. Darius had removed his jacket. Mike wore slacks and a short-sleeve shirt, but he felt clammy. Professor McCrory kept his jacket on. Missy wore a reddish-violet cap-sleeved T-shirt and somehow managed to smile through most of Darius Moore's questioning.

McCrory had a neat stack of papers in front of him that he hadn't touched. Darius Moore only had a single yellow pad and a BIC pen. Mike and Missy were surrounded by messy stacks of papers. Norby had nothing. He said little and scowled at Mike and Missy when he wasn't texting on his phone.

"So did you or did you not take into consideration the shale ridge that ran from the Campbell pad to the Campbell residence?" Darius Moore asked.

"Like I told you before, yes, I took it into consideration," Missy said. She glanced at Mike and pursed her lips.

"Exactly how did you take it into consideration?"

Mike's eyes bored holes into Darius Moore.

"As I already said, the mere presence of the shale ridge did not have any impact on my decision. The ridge acted like a barrier to lateral movement of groundwater and other subterranean water. In other words, water on one side of the ridge would move along the ridge reasonably faster in geologic time and only very slowly laterally through the ridge. Water could still move through it, but at such a slow rate, it hardly mattered."

"What do you mean, it hardly mattered? This case is all about whether any contamination came from my client's drilling operation and somehow contaminated the Campbells' water well."

Mike was about to say something when Professor McCrory spoke up. "Mr. Moore, anyone with the slightest degree of knowledge of hydrogeology knows that water moves through certain rock formations quickly and through others slowly. It's all relative. I think it's clear to all of us that water moves through this shale slowly compared to the other rocks found in this area. By slowly, I mean *thousands of years*, not days or weeks, but *years*. Does that help you, Mr. Moore?"

Darius Moore gave Professor McCrory a withering look which the professor seemed to ignore, but he added a thin smile. "Of course. But I want to hear it from Ms. Shelton."

"And you have, at least three times," Mike said. "What the hell, Darius? I thought this was going to be a friendly meeting, but it's sounding more and more like a deposition to me."

"Don't get me wrong, Mike, some of what I'm doing is testing Ms. Shelton to help prepare her for her deposition."

"I'm eternally grateful to you for you trying to do my job for me. But I've already taken care of that, thank you. Can we move on?"

Professor McCrory cleared his throat. "Ms. Shelton, did you take note of the Horseheads Limestone?"

"Yes, I did, Professor. It crops out at Horseheads, New York, and has been described by the USGS as being highly fractured. Also, it's described as cavernous in its northern reaches, in the vicinity of the town of Horseheads. Neither the USGS nor the Pennsylvania Geologic Survey calls it cavernous in Pennsylvania, but that remains a possibility. The limestone is adjacent to the shale, and the two of them run in a nearly straight line together from the vicinity of the Campbell pad, under the Campbell residence, and beyond. There's a reservoir, the Campbelltown Reservoir, about a half-mile below the Campbell residence, and the limestone seems to run in a straight line directly beneath the reservoir, too. They're unusually linear." She looked at Darius Moore. "That means they run in a straight line."

Mike had to stifle his expression, but he wished he could give Missy a high five.

"How did that figure into your geologic evaluation? By the way, did I tell you that you wrote a very fine report?" The professor said, smiling at his former student.

"You did, at breakfast, thank you." Missy returned his smile.

Darius Moore looked at Mike, angled his head, and furrowed his eyebrows.

"Of course. I noted the limestone as well as the other surrounding rock units," she continued. "My report was limited to the effect of drilling the borehole and hydraulic fracturing on the Campbells' water supply. I focused primarily on the borehole, which is located to the west of the shale and limestone. The borehole does not intersect the shale or the limestone."

She looked at Darius Moore. "It's like a seven-layer cake sitting on its side, Darius. The borehole goes through one of the layers of the cake, but the shale and the Horsehead limestone are entirely different layers of the cake." She smiled sweetly.

"Anyway, I evaluated the rock horizons through which the borehole traveled and took into consideration the steel casing running to the end of the vertical shaft that has been cemented into place by Yukon. The cement runs the entire length of the casing, over one mile. The presence of the limestone, or the shale ridge for that matter, did not have an impact on any potential contamination from the drilling. The shale acts as a barrier to lateral movement. I took note of it anyway." She looked at Darius Moore and added, "That means water on one side of the shale likely will not move through the shale except at a *very* slow rate, like, thousands of years."

The professor was about to reply when Darius Moore held up a finger and whispered in his ear. The professor nodded and sat back in his chair.

"I'm not a geologist, Ms. Shelton," said Darius Moore. "I didn't even stay in a Holiday Inn last night." That brought smiles around the table. Then he turned to Mike, "Right, Mike?" He looked back at Missy. "I just wanted to be clear that your evaluation focused solely on the borehole and the geologic rock units through which the borehole was drilled and not anything else."

"That's right. My assignment was really limited. I was asked to look at the potential effect of *drilling* on the Campbells' water well. I looked at the location of the borehole, the geological logs provided by Yukon's geologists, relevant scientific literature, the location of the borehole and laterals, and hydraulic fracturing vis-à-vis the Campbell residence, and made my determination regarding whether drilling had an impact on the Campbells' water well. I saw nothing indicating drilling or hydraulic fracturing had any impact on the water well."

"What about the contamination in their water?" Darius Moore asked.

"All background," she said. Professor McCrory nodded slowly as she spoke. Norby nodded vigorously.

"No one's water is pure H_2O unless you drink distilled water. All water has some trace amounts of minerals. Even bottled water. Maybe I should say, *especially* bottled water, for taste. It all depends on the rocks through which the water travels. If you have a well, it will also depend on whether you have animals or farming or even a septic tank nearby. The Campbells have a lot of E. coli and fecal coliform in their water, but that's due to the location and depth of the well. It's pretty common in agricultural areas with old, hand-dug wells. The methane, too, is naturally occurring. There's a lot of naturally occurring methane near the surface in that part of Bradford County, and I believe that's the methane the Campbells have in their water. Do you agree with me, professor?"

"Yes, that's exactly right," he said, his fingers laced across his ample stomach. "How do you explain the results of the lab the

Campbells hired, Core Services?" He asked. "They found a fair amount of contamination in the early spring, much more than the DEP lab."

"A fabrication. We've received a few other test results from them, and, as best as we can tell, they're all made up. The contact number is disconnected, and the attorney general is investigating. It's a pity, but some people will take advantage of other people who are in a tight spot, and that's what we believe happened there."

Mike glanced at his watch and looked at the side of Missy's face. She was going strong, but he knew the questioning would take a toll on her.

"Why don't we take a bio-break, maybe a lunch break," Mike said, looking at Darius Moore. "I know I could use one. We can continue in ten minutes if you want to skip lunch."

"Well, class, I know I could sure use one," said the professor. He stood up and made for the door.

Mike and Missy also stood. Norby and Darius Moore didn't move. Darius asked, "Hey Mike, can you stick around for a minute or so?"

"Sure." Mike looked at Missy and said, "I'll catch up with you in the break room in two minutes."

"I think Missy is pretty solid," Darius Moore said after she left the room. "She seems to know her stuff and if she can deal with tough questioning from me, she'll be able to deal with questions from Hedges." He paused for a moment. "Have you, has the *department,* looked at the possibility of contamination coming from anywhere else on the Campbell pad? I was just wondering."

Mike thought about the question. Darius never asked a question without a purpose. Everything he said was deliberate.

"Well, certainly there could have been operational problems. You know, the proverbial forklift which inadvertently backs over the fifty-five-gallon drum of liquid death. But it looks as though Yukon's pad is pretty well contained. Yukon didn't have any operational issues. Well, not any your client reported to the department anyway. I know the inspector took a good look at that, and Missy looked at that too. Unless you know something we don't know about your operations, it seems as though drilling and fracking, as well as day-to-day operations on the pad, did not present any problems."

"I can tell you we had no, and I mean *zero,* operational problems," said Norby, speaking up for the first time. "That pad was run textbook perfect."

"Did you look at anything else in the vicinity of the pad?" Darius Moore asked.

"You mean the impoundment?"

Darius nodded once.

"We've looked at that too," said Mike. "If the impoundment leaked and it held more than water, that could be a problem. Of course, the impoundment was used just for fresh water. Right, Norby?"

Mike and Darius looked at Norby. "That's a freshwater pit. That's all it held," Norby replied.

"It was never used for produced water?" Mike asked.

Norby glared at him. "Never means never."

"Did you find evidence of leakage?"

"There was an odd discoloration of some rocks just below the berm of the pit. Missy said it looked almost as though a spring flowed out of the ground and over the rocks, but it was dry. The pit was dry, so no water was flowing. There's no way to tell if water was infiltrating out of the pit and coming out of the ground where those rocks are located or anywhere else. She sent the rocks to the lab for analysis, but we still haven't gotten back the results. Missy said it was possible that if the impoundment leaked, then the leak could find its way into the limestone and eventually to the Campbell well. If it did leak, the limestone may have been a channel to carry contaminants in a direct line to the Campbell residence."

Mike paused. Norby vigorously shook his head. "No way," he said in his Cajun drawl.

"So rumors that the pit was used to hold flowback for several days are what, just rumors? Can you confirm for me that the impoundment didn't leak? That it wasn't ever used for flowback water?"

Darius Moore held up his hand to stop Norby, but the Cajun ignored him.

"Those rumors are bullshit. That pit was never used for flowback," Norby said. "It was and is a freshwater pit. We put our flowback in frac tanks. I can show you the invoices. That's it. Case closed."

Mike stared at him.

"You know, I'm getting sick and tired of all of this speculation that the pit was used for flowback," Norby said, slapping his hand on the table. "Y'all have no basis for saying otherwise, and it pisses me off to hear this fake news."

Darius Moore put his hand on Norby's shoulder. "Of course, whether or not the impoundment ever leaked is irrelevant to the case being litigated. I mean, the Campbells filed an appeal from Missy's letter dealing with whether drilling and fracking affected their well. The case has nothing to do with the impoundment."

"I know that," Mike said sharply. "If the impoundment leaked and somehow contamination got to the Campbells' well, that would be a separate enforcement matter, subject to substantial civil penalties and orders. The department reserves all rights. You understand that?"

Darius Moore glared at him. Norby got up and stalked out of the room, leaving the door open.

"Yeah, about that. Let me double-check and get back to you," Darius said quietly.

Mike eyed him suspiciously. "Maybe you could get back to me sooner rather than later on this. If there were problems, it would be in your client's interest to get out in front of it, make a disclosure before we find something ourselves."

Darius Moore locked eyes with Mike and spoke evenly. "Like I said, I'll have to get back to you."

53

Methinks the Lady Dost Protest too Much

The meeting ended an hour later, and Mike declined the opportunity of a late lunch with Darius Moore, the professor, and Norby. While he would've enjoyed talking with Professor McCrory, the constant bickering with Darius was tedious, and Norby just gave him the creeps. He made an excuse, and he and Missy got sandwiches from a nearby deli which they ate in the conference room.

They spent the afternoon finishing preparations for the deposition, which would take place in two days after the site view. Technically, under Pennsylvania's discovery rules, the Campbells were permitted to conduct a variety of activities during the site view: inspecting and measuring, surveying, photographing, testing, and sampling the property. Winnie and Darius had agreed the Campbells' attorneys and expert could come onto the property twice, once for a general inspection, and another time if they wanted to do other sampling or surveying. There wasn't a lot for the department to do to prepare for the site visit. He knew Winnie probably would show up with her expert, someone whom she had not yet disclosed, and most of the burden would be on Darius Moore and Yukon.

"The smartest thing Darius could do would be to have as few people as possible on-site during the site view," Mike said as he chewed his sandwich.

"But who's actually going to be there?" Missy asked.

"You and me, Darius, Professor McCrory, Winnie and her expert. Probably Norby and maybe Bones to lead us around. It's always possible Darius or Winnie will bring some others, but I doubt it. Most lawyers use the site view as an opportunity for some free and mostly unfettered discussions with the opposition. We try to get away with that because a site view is pretty casual. In my opinion, lawyers allow their clients to be off-guard and say entirely too much. Most lawyers want to limit the number of participants to avoid having one of them say something they shouldn't say."

"So, essentially, you want me to smile but not say anything?" Missy asked. "Are you telling me to look pretty and keep my mouth shut?" She scowled at him.

"Geez, Missy, I didn't say that. It's really important you not say something inadvertently and accidentally tip our cards. It's kind of like the deposition. Listen closely to the questions, carefully answer the question you've been asked, and no more. Also, because I'm sure I'll be pulled in several directions, don't get too far away from me. Stay close—"

"How close would you like me to be, Mike?" She leaned over and bumped his shoulder.

Mike rubbed his forehead. "Really close. Not hold-my-hand close, but . . . you know what I mean."

Missy giggled. She leaned over again and threw her arm around his shoulders. "You're funny when you're serious."

"There's one more thing. The rules don't apply when *we're* asking the questions. I'm sure I'll be doing my best to see if the Campbells' expert is aware of anything we haven't yet found. It looks as though you and the professor are already on the same page. Let's see what we can learn."

Mike was quiet for a few seconds as he stared at his notes. Finally, he said, "I think we've seen and heard all we need to know about the drilling and fracking. When we were out at the site a couple of weeks ago, that laborer—"

"Tim—"

"Right. Tim said they used the pit to hold flowback water. He said they reversed the pumps when the frac tanks were running late. That's plausible, even likely. I'm wondering though. We've heard nothing official on this. Sometimes people at the bottom of the totem pole really don't know what's going on, they just think they do."

"Yeah, and sometimes they know a lot more than the people at the top."

Mike nodded. "What do you think?"

"I'm really confident in my evaluation, and it helps that Professor McCrory agrees with me. The impoundment looks okay, except for those little peaks where the remains of the shale ridge are located, and that feature that looks like a seep below it. I thought Darius was a bit too concerned that we keep the case focused solely on the subject of the drilling and fracking and nothing else. I mean, if there weren't any problems elsewhere, why would he care? That potential seep wouldn't amount to much, but we'd need to do a lot more testing to determine for sure whether the pit leaked."

"You know what they say, methinks the lady protests too much, something like that," Mike said. "He knows I would do everything in my power to limit the testimony to the subject of the appeal. I mean, we have no interest in allowing the Advocates to rummage around in our underwear drawer."

She smiled at him.

"By the way, what's the status of the test results?" He asked. "I thought we'd have them by now."

"Me too. I've been calling every day. They keep telling me they're really busy and just one more day. I'm hoping later today or tomorrow at the latest. That will tell us a lot."

At about 4 p.m., Missy headed back to her apartment in Towanda to pick up some clothes. She and Mike decided it would be best for her to keep away from her apartment as much as possible until she had a chance to talk with Mike's lawyer friend. It occurred to Mike it would have been reasonable for him to suggest she stay with a *female* friend in Williamsport, but he didn't, and neither did Missy.

Mike looked forward to having dinner with her and talking and cuddling with her through the night. He wasn't sure how much longer he'd be able to put up with the middle-school-style kissing and hugging arrangement but wondered if their relationship—whatever it was—would turn into something more. He eagerly wanted that to happen.

54

Vlad, the Impaler

Cynthia Voigt sat behind her new desk, occasionally looking up to watch the brilliant sunset behind the distant indigo slopes of Blue Mountain, across the river north and west of Harrisburg. The early summer sun reflected brightly off the Susquehanna River. She never tired of the view. She wore white pants, a blue jacket trimmed with white piping, a white-and-blue top, and blue-and-green flowered scarf. She'd been cold all day in the air-conditioned office and never removed her jacket. Still, something didn't feel quite right, like how she sometimes felt before she got sick. Nothing specific. She couldn't put her finger on it. She had felt this way since she received the first hundred-thousand-dollar check from one of Vlad's "friends." The gnawing in her stomach grew as the large checks rolled into the old office like railroad cars, one after another.

Cynthia expected that when the Advocates jumped from being a $75,000-per-month operation to a million-dollar-per-month operation, her workload would increase accordingly. Still, she never anticipated the amount of work it would actually take.

The move to the new office had been aggravating since hardly any class-A office space was available. Unexpectedly, the move happened quickly, with little time for preparation or comparison with lower-priced alternatives. A sublet for an office opened up, and even though the new place was pricey, at least the landlord threw in the furniture left by the previous tenant, a Pittsburgh-based law firm that had closed shop in Harrisburg. As an incentive to sign the lease and move in immediately, the new landlord paid off the remaining few months of cheap rent at the old place and paid to move the Advocates into the new spot. Her head was still spinning from the move.

Cynthia was working sixteen-hour days. She spent a lot of energy finding the right people and restructuring the Advocates to accomplish its much larger mission. Also, she spent hours fending off the expected questions from other organizations, jealous of the remarkable transformation, and even from her members who questioned whether the organization would be sustainable and survive its growth.

Nevertheless, she finally felt the Advocates would be able to accomplish the goals she and Winnie had set out on that cocktail napkin so many years ago. Unfortunately, Vlad, the board, and her new employees all had their own agendas, and she spent a lot of time and energy managing expectations and driving everyone in the direction she and Winnie wanted the Advocates to go.

Cynthia looked at the spreadsheet on her laptop and sighed. She no longer had to worry about making ends meet. One of the things about the rapid expansion, however, was the need to provide deposits, mandatory advance rent, furniture purchases for the two new offices in Pittsburgh and Williamsport, salaries, significant public relations and advertising retainers, both to announce their new capabilities and become prominent in the public eye, and a hundred other expenses, which meant she had already spent the extra million-dollar seed money provided by Vlad's friends. The bank, however, had happily opened a half-million-dollar line of credit for the Advocates, and she was already $300,000 into it. That was all right, however, since she knew she would pay it down in under six months from the one-million-dollar monthly payments the Advocates received from Vlad's merry band of anti-fracking contributors.

She worried about a recent development. A friend had sent her a link to a "news" article on Facebook. It was published in an online newspaper called *The Harrisburg Trib*. To her knowledge, no such entity existed. She kept clicking on the article, trying to figure it out:

Advocates Call for Hearings on Fracking

Harrisburg, PA. An anti-fracking environmental organization, Pennsylvania's Advocates for the Environment, today called for a hearing in the General Assembly regarding why the Governor has not taken a stronger stand against hydraulic fracturing.

Cynthia Voigt, President of the Advocates said, "While we appreciate that the Governor has called for a moratorium, more must be done as quickly as possible. It's shameful what the Governor has done, allowing fracking to continue in Pennsylvania despite all of the scientific evidence. We call for hearings and an investigation."

A neighbor to the fracking in Susquehanna County, Pa., applauded the call for an investigation. "This should have happened years ago," said Peggy Jones whose well has been ruined by fracking. "It has been proven by a team of scientists at Cornell and Duke that my well has been affected by fracking . . ."

Cynthia had never heard of the *Harrisburg Trib,* had never been interviewed, and avoided criticizing this governor in the media. For the most part, he was a friend. She preferred to work with him and his energy advisors. She had no idea where the article came from or how they came to use her name.

Her cell phone began vibrating on her desk a moment before it rang. *Unknown Caller.* At first, she wasn't going to answer it, probably just a robocall, but then she thought better of it.

"Hello?"

"Cynthia, a pleasure to hear your voice. I hope I'm not taking you away from dinner or some of your well-deserved leisure time." It was Vlad.

She leaned back in her chair. "I'm still here at the office, Vlad. I probably won't get out of here for another hour."

"You need to develop some boundaries. It's never a good idea to spend all of your time in the office."

"Maybe when, or if, things calm down here, I can do that. I hope all is well with you."

In his customary style, Vlad dispensed with the pleasantries and launched into what was really on his mind. "My friends and I are very happy with what you've done with the Advocates since we made our investment. It's remarkable the change in policy you have achieved in such a short time. We're certain you will be able to continue all of your good work regardless of who is funding you."

Cynthia's guts clenched.

"Well, for now, we're so happy you and your friends are being so generous with us. We've made so many changes in the past month it's made my head spin. A new main office and two new satellite locations, just like you suggested. Plus, I've already hired six new people, three here, two in Pittsburgh, and one in Williamsport. I tried my best to steward the money you've given us, but everything's expensive. We're only just now starting to see the beginnings of change here in Pennsylvania."

"Yes, about that. Look, there's no other way I can say this. My friends and I have decided to go in a different direction. We appreciate everything you've done; we really do. The governor's call for a moratorium on drilling last week has really put the fear of God in the drillers, and already several of them have announced they're going to move their drilling operations to Colorado, Wyoming, and North Dakota. All much further from the Eastern markets. More expensive to transport which makes the gas less desirable. This is spectacular, more than we could've reasonably hoped for in a year's worth of effort. Actually, it's *everything* we hoped for. Who knew it would happen so soon? We will follow the bastards to those states and see if we can put the stake in the heart of the fracking industry there, too."

"Wait a minute, what do you mean you're moving in a different direction? We have a deal. I've spent more money than you gave me, expanding into a larger Harrisburg office and opening two other offices. We hired six new people, with four more on the way. I've signed leases and taken out a loan anticipating the million dollars a month that you promised."

"Promised? That's too strong a word, Cynthia. I believe I told you I *hoped* we'd be able to send you one million a month. There were no promises. Nothing in writing."

"You *did* promise. You said you'd reevaluate after eleven months, not after a month. You can't do this to me, to us."

"This is not a debate. I'm sorry. It's nothing personal. Like I said, we decided to go in another direction. A purely business decision."

Cynthia's brain raced. Withdrawing the promised payments wouldn't just set back the Advocates; it would destroy the organization. She'd never be able to pay back the gigantic line of credit. The cost of the leases alone would crush the Advocates. Everything she'd worked for. All of the goals. Done. *Finis.*

She took a deep breath, hating what was about to come out of her mouth. "Vlad, is there anything I can do? I mean, personally. To change your mind. I mean *anything*. You understand what I'm saying? I'd be happy to do that for you."

"Cynthia, Cynthia, Cynthia. You are a lovely woman, and my goal was not to make you prostitute yourself. This was merely a business decision."

"Vlad, you CANNOT DO THIS. We've only begun our efforts. This is a partnership, and you have very generously provided the money, and we have found the manpower. This is just a beginning, not an end. There is so much left to do, years of work. Please, I'm begging you. Don't do this to us."

"Cynthia, I am so sorry to see you degrade yourself. There is much more here than I could expect you to understand, issues that are much bigger than you and the Advocates. I'm sure you will carry on just fine. Now, it is time for us to part ways. Goodbye."

The line went dead. Cynthia took a deep breath, then hit callback. All she heard was an annoying buzz. She put her phone down and staggered to her feet. All of the offices were quiet, and the only light in the hallway was from Winnie's office. She steadied herself on the door jamb and gazed at her beautiful longtime friend—the woman she secretly loved from a distance for all these years.

Winnie was bent over some papers on her desk preparing for Thursday's deposition of the DEP witness. She was so pretty in her sleeveless blue dress. It was elegant and sophisticated like Winnie. After several moments Winnie looked up and smiled. It melted Cynthia's heart. It always did. With tears and mascara already escaping down her face, Cynthia said nothing. She hurried to Winnie, threw her arms around her, and sobbed.

55

In Sync

Teresa and Caitlin were at Teresa's kitchen table, nearly every inch of which was covered with papers. Teresa typed on her laptop. She had printed out many of the Duke and Cornell studies she'd been reading, as well as other reports she felt were important. The table also contained two large piles of papers Caitlin had brought with her.

Caitlin's daughter Emma was in the den with Isabella and Lucas. The dinner dishes and residue of Teresa's spaghetti and meatballs soaked in the sink. The aroma of Teresa's sauce lingered in the air.

Teresa wore jeans, the kind without rips, and a dark blue T-shirt that read, *Staten Island, USA*. Caitlin also wore jeans and a blousy, ancient T-shirt that said *NSYNC*. Caitlin hovered just behind Teresa, leaning on her friend's chair back as she typed.

"I think if we schedule the rally for a Friday night, we'll get more people," Teresa said. "Jared will be home, and maybe other dads will come in from the city. Also, most people aren't going to work on Saturday, so they may be more willing to come out on a Friday night to our meeting."

Caitlin shook her head. "Honestly, I don't think most of the dads who live here travel out of town during the week. Your husband's the exception. We need to schedule this when it's not going to conflict with some show on TV or a local baseball game. We really ought to make sure we can get the fire hall and double-check the local baseball and soccer schedules to make sure we aren't conflicting."

"I'm new at this. I'll follow your lead. Let's leave the date open and just type in the text."

An hour later, when they were done working, they had the basics of the flyer:

MOMS AGAINST FRACKING

ORGANIZATIONAL MEETING

DATE: July ____
TIME: 7:00 p.m.
PLACE: Campbelltown Volunteer Fire Company No. 1

Campbelltown residents!

Come and join us as we learn the TRUTH regarding fracking and how it is DESTROYING our community.

We will hear from Ursula Goodperson, a Community Organizer from Pennsylvania's Advocates for the Environment from Harrisburg, PA.

Our goal is to establish a local organization to oppose fracking and support all of those hurt by it.

Don't miss this important event.
All are invited.

"Do you think this says enough, maybe too much?" Caitlin asked. "I mean, there are a lot of us in town who are either against fracking or just want more information. The people who are against it will be there. I know them, and I'll call all of them to make sure they come. I really want to get the fence-sitters. I'm just not sure who to call."

"I think there are a lot of people we can call," Teresa said. "We can start with the ballet-lesson-moms and the soccer-

and-softball parents. The point is they have to know how this is messing with our water and air. It's screwing up our land. We own seven hundred acres, and I bet it's ruined the value of our property. I mean, who would want to buy land that's been screwed over by fracking? These assholes have made some of the neighbors rich, but at what cost? Most people are getting very little, almost nothing from their so-called royalties from those bastards."

Every time Teresa let loose with a word that her nonna wouldn't have used, Caitlin flinched or laughed.

"I'm so glad you're able to get the Advocates involved," said Caitlin. "That makes it look so much more impressive than if it was just a bunch of us moms. Don't get me wrong, there's nothing wrong with moms, but it just looks better with someone from Harrisburg coming here to talk to us."

"There's so much to do," Teresa said. "Do you want to speak? You could run the meeting."

"No way," said Caitlin. "I'm a behind-the-scenes kind of girl. Trust me, I've educated myself quite a bit, but I totally freeze up in front of a crowd. I can't. Public speaking scares me to death."

"I guess that leaves me. We need to get some of the other moms involved, but I'll speak at the meeting."

"Do you need to ask Jared?"

Teresa narrowed her eyes and twisted her face. "No, he does not control me."

Caitlin paused for a moment, considering her friend's response. "Sorry, don't get me wrong. There are all kinds of relationships. Some wives are independent, like you. Others, not so much. There is one thing we have to discuss . . ."

Caitlin hesitated.

". . . You know if you're going to take the stage, the mic, whatever, it would be really awesome if you didn't use the F-word and some of those other words you seem to use . . . a lot."

Teresa scowled, then let loose with a belly laugh. "Do you know I went to parochial school for twelve years in Staten Island? When I feel like it, I can speak like a perfect, proper lady, my dear. A proper fucking lady."

They both laughed, and Teresa side-hugged Caitlin.

"One more thing," Caitlin said. "Do you think we need security? I mean, the town's overrun by people who work for the fracking industry. Some are locals, but I'll bet there are thousands working for the frackers from out of town. It's possible some will show up and try to take over our meeting or carry on, or, you know, protest *us*."

Teresa nodded as she thought. "It *is* a small town and, obviously, I'm not from around here. Everyone local seems to know everyone else who grew up here. Someone from here who knows the police chief ought to talk with him about security. Do you happen to know him?"

Caitlin paused, her faced reddened for a moment, then she laughed, "Know him? I've known him since high school. He was my first husband. And I've had several other firsts with Cliff, pretty much all of them, if you get what I mean." She winked at Teresa.

They found that hilarious and laughed and hugged until they nearly fell over.

56

Bliss

Mike took Missy to his favorite restaurant in Williamsport, the Old Town Hotel. From the outside, it looked like nothing more than a corner bar which, in fact, it seemed to be. As you stepped inside, a big horseshoe-shaped oak bar, dark and ancient, filled the space. Workingmen, lawyers from the courthouse, and locals sat with their shots and beer. Other than the huge bar itself, it was nothing special.

When you passed through the curtains at the back, however, you walked into an elegant dining room with linen tablecloths that would have qualified as a great restaurant in any major city. Mike did a quick surveillance to make sure neither Darius Moore nor the professor were there, then he and Missy had a magnificent dinner and split a bottle of red wine. They tried not to talk business and ended up laughing. They laughed a *lot*. Mike paid the tab. It was a proper date.

They strolled back to their hotel, just a couple of blocks away, holding hands and enjoying the early summer air. Mike thought about all of the Daniel Silva novels he had read and, channeling his best Gabriel Allon imitation, stopped and looked back from time to time to make sure they weren't being followed. While he did see people on the streets, he really didn't have a clue if any were tailing them. When Mike and Missy got to the hotel, they walked briskly through the lobby and entered the elevator, with no sign of Darius Moore or the professor. Mike double-locked the hotel room door after hanging the *Do Not Disturb* sign on the outside knob.

"It's only a little after nine, what do you want to do now?" Missy asked. She always seemed to be smiling at him.

"You want to talk? We have plenty of time. Let's talk now," Mike said.

"Let's get ready for bed first." Missy smiled coyly at him. "I want to take a shower and then we can relax."

"We can talk on the sofa if that's okay," Mike said, pointing.

"Or the bed. We can sit and talk there too. It'll be more comfy." She hugged him, and they kissed deeply while they stood, until Missy broke it off. Missy took her bag and went into the bathroom.

Mike waited until he heard the shower door open and close. Then he unbolted the door and looked left and right down the hall. No one. The hallway was quiet. He double-bolted the door again and changed into his sleepwear—gym shorts and T-shirt. It occurred to him he was wearing his old green Vermont Law School T-shirt, the same one his friend Nicky used to wear to bed when they were together. Something about that made him feel awkward.

The shower stopped, and a couple of minutes later, Missy came out wearing Mike's dress shirt from the night before. The top three buttons were unbuttoned, and Mike tried not to stare at the fullness of her breasts.

"I thought you'd bring some pajamas, you know, or a nightgown or something."

"I decided I really liked wearing your shirt. It makes me feel good having it on." Missy rubbed her hand on the sleeve. "I'm glad you don't use starch." She pulled the cover down, climbed under the sheets, and patted the empty side of the bed.

"I thought . . ." Mike stammered.

"No, you *suggested*, and this is where *I* want to talk."

As Mike got into the bed on the other side, Missy turned out her light, leaving only the pale, yellow light over the sofa to brighten the room. Mike turned on his side and propped his head on his hand. Missy scooched next to him, her bare legs rubbing against his. She rubbed the top of his foot with her sole and trailed her fingers across his arm. "It's 9:30. How long do you want to talk?"

"You were the one with all the questions last night. I told you I'd talk as long as you wanted. We can talk for hours if you want. Generally, I don't fall asleep until about midnight."

Missy moved her hand from Mike's arm and slid it under his T-shirt, then very gently stroked his chest. "What if I'm done talking for tonight? Then what would you want to do?"

"I suppose we can watch TV. Maybe go to sleep early. I mean, we do have a couple of busy days ahead of us," Mike said.

She moved her face to within two inches of Mike's ear. "You're not being very imaginative, mister. Let's see, we had a great date, we have a couple of hours to kill before we need to fall asleep, we can sleep relatively late tomorrow morning, we're lying in bed together . . . Unless I'm mistaken, we both seem happy to be here."

Missy rolled her body fully against Mike's and ran her hand down his torso to his shorts, stroking him gently through the thin cotton fabric. "You seem *very* happy to be here, mister," she whispered.

Their mouths locked in a deep kiss. Mike put his hand on Missy's shoulder, and the shirt fell away, exposing her bare breasts in the dim light. He was surprised—and not—that she had somehow unbuttoned the shirt without him noticing. He ran his fingertips across Missy's warm arm, feeling the goosebumps form, then stroked slowly down her chest until he lightly cupped a firm, round breast. Missy gasped slightly and arched her back, pressing herself tightly against his palm. She pushed his head down until his mouth found the curve of a breast. He kissed and sucked, first gently, then more assertively. She caressed his ears and hair, breathing in short, rapid gasps as his tongue explored her swollen nipples.

Then, ever so lightly, she pressed the top of his head. Only a suggestion. Mike happily complied and placed a thumb on the front of her pelvis and the rest of his hand on her silky-smooth bare ass and rolled her onto her back as he kissed her body. She shivered and sighed each time his lips touched her as he kissed his way down her belly.

A word came to Mike: *bliss*. He hoped he knew the difference between love and lust and wondered if this was love. His feelings for her seemed deeper and more profound than mere desire. He cared for her. If it was love, it was the first time in a long time that he really knew it. He was so happy to be here with her.

Without warning, the room rocked violently at the pounding on the door. Mike and Missy were shaken from their erotic reverie, and, for a moment, he wondered if the hammering was from across the hall. It wasn't. Each knock was like an explosion.

He tripped out of the bed, forgetting that his shorts were around his ankles, and pulled on his T-shirt as he ran to the door.

"Call the front desk. Now!" He ordered. Missy was already on the phone.

Instinctively, he knew to stand to the side of the door. "Who is it? What do you want?"

"Open the goddamn door, you bastard. Open it!"

The voice was an unrecognizable screech. Animalistic. Desperate. "Missy! Don't, *please* don't. I'm sorry, baby. I'm begging you."

The voice clicked in Mike's brain. "Richard, get the hell out of here; I'm calling the cops!"

"I'm going to kill you, you bastard. I'm going to put a bullet between your fuckin' eyes."

The door shook violently from the pounding until, suddenly, it stopped.

Missy was huddled in Mike's arms. He held her tightly. They looked at each other and Mike held up his palms. Without warning, a klaxon erupted in the hall. The sound rose and fell from a low rumbling to a high pitch. Then a computerized voice came over a loudspeaker.

"The fire alarm has been activated. Immediately leave your rooms and head for the stairways. Do *not* take the elevators. Leave your belongings behind. The fire department has been called . . ." The warning repeated itself.

"What do we do? What do we do?" She shouted over the alarm. She was naked except for the shirt, which she held in a ball.

"Put on some clothes and your shoes." Mike shed his gym shorts and quickly pulled on his underwear, jeans, and running shoes. "Stay behind me. We're going to stay in the room until the fire department comes. I'm pretty sure Richard pulled a false alarm to get us out of the room. He'll be waiting for us outside. I don't know what he's planning to do, but he wants to get us out of the room."

"How can you be sure?"

"I'm not. But he has no way to bust down the door, so I'm guessing he pulled the alarm to smoke us out. If it's a real fire, the firefighters will get us out."

"I'm scared."

"I'm angry," he replied.

57

We Need a Body

Chief West glanced at his passenger, Hector Torres, who watched the woods roll by his window. West cleared his throat.

"Sorry, Hector. That was unproductive. We had to wait all day until after that trial was over to see the district attorney and, after all that, nada."

"He said he needed a body," Torres said, looking at him. "He said the hardest case to prove is murder, and it's even harder to prove when there's no body."

"In my opinion, District Attorney Gerlach is a lazy pussy. We have your sworn statement talking about the hatred between Corsica and Norby. They destroyed Corsica's business and hated his guts for screwing up the job. Then we have Norby and Bones admitting to blood all over the camper and giving contradictory fabricated statements regarding when they fired Corsica and when they last saw him."

The Chief rolled down his window and spat out his chewing gum. "When we finally got them into the station to give their sworn statements, suddenly their statements are identical. I tested those bastards, and they even used the same words. Practice makes perfect. Corsica did what he was ordered to do by Lafleur and Benson, and they threw him under the bus. He was screwed by those drilling bastards, and all of a sudden, he decides to host a nice little going-away party, coffee, Jack Daniels. What the hey, I'm surprised Corsica didn't serve tea sandwiches. Norby admits there was blood on the floor of the camper, Corsica's, his, and also Benson's since they were all so enthusiastic about cleaning up a broken glass. Blood. What's that tell you?"

"Unfortunately, Chief, it looks like Norby and Bones are sticking with their story. No one is around to contradict them. Plus, there's no camper. I mean, nothing where you could find actual blood on the floor. Corsica's RV melted in a fire in North Dakota. Even if there was residue, it was destroyed in the fire."

"Yeah, but what's important is Norby and Benson admitted to leaving blood in the camper. Either they did the murder there or they did the murder outside the camper and went back in, literally with blood on their hands."

West had been driving at exactly the speed limit, with a line of cars and pickups following him on the narrow country road, and now he was stuck behind a slow-moving utility vehicle carrying drilling equipment. He waited for a straightaway, then signaled and stomped on the gas. He loved the power of the eight cylinders as they cranked out full blast and shot him around the truck. As he pulled back into the lane, traveling ninety miles an hour, he glanced at his watch. It was 8 p.m.

"These boys never stop," West said.

"Yeah, they go twenty-four-seven."

"Fuck 'em. Even though we got a shiny new station, the county was better off before all of those bastards came to town. So few of our kids got drilling jobs and now it's too expensive to rent an apartment or buy a house. The town has been overrun by people who don't give a damn about this place or our way of life."

They were silent for a moment as they cruised closer to Campbelltown, then Torres said, "So how did the camper get out to North Dakota?"

"Maybe Norby hired someone to drive it out there, which would be pretty stupid, all things considered. I mean you'd have another witness; only an idiot would do that. Lafleur's a lot of things, but he's not stupid. I'm guessing they drove the camper to a place where someone could easily rip it off, left the keys in the ignition, and let it sit for a few days. Eventually, someone took it. These oil and gas boys travel all over the country. The camper ended up in North Dakota, but it could've easily ended up in Texas, Oklahoma, Colorado, wherever the hell they're drilling."

"And the fire?"

"I'll bet it was just dumb luck so far as Norby was concerned. Maybe somebody vandalized it. Maybe some asshole was using it as a mobile meth lab out there in North Dakota, and the thing caught on fire. We'll never know."

"Do you think there's any chance Corsica is alive?"

Without hesitating, West said, "None. I mean, the guy's been completely off the grid since he was fired. Granted, he didn't have a wife to go home to, but he did have family and, unless he's completely screwed up in the head, he would've tried to make contact with them. Also, the guy would've tried to use his credit cards by now. Even if Norby took his wallet and phone, he would've reached out to his bank for new credit cards. No one can go off the grid completely like in the movies."

"I know a few guys, survivalists, ex-Marines, they want to live off the land and such," Torres said. "You know, getting ready for the next coronavirus, Armageddon, or when the feds come for their guns. No reliance on technology, cell phones, you name it."

The chief looked at Torres and laughed. "I'll bet they head out into the woods in June, not February. Also, I'll bet they have a nice cozy hunting camp somewhere full of canned and freeze-dried food. Probably an arsenal and a few thousand rounds, fishing tackle. I've known guys like that, too, and by November, they're all back home sitting next to a warm fire, complaining about big government and living off food stamps and Social Security. No one heads into the woods in February with just the clothes on his back. Also, keep in mind, it's not like Corsica planned to go full Ted Kaczynski and was able to stock up and prepare for his life in the woods."

"So, where is he? His body, I mean."

"If you recall, winter took forever to get here. The ground was cold and wet but not frozen back in early February. You don't leave a body lying on the ground, otherwise the animals will have at him, and that will attract attention. I'm guessing a shallow grave somewhere. Probably pretty close to the campsite, although I suppose they could've driven him deep into the woods and dumped him. Those guys knew their drilling sites like the backs of their hands, but they're not from around here. If I had to guess, I'd say it was somewhere on one of those drilling sites."

"The DA says you can't bring any charges against them until you have a body. Yukon has about fifty sites in Bradford County alone, and the county's too large to search the whole thing. How do you find the body?"

The chief signaled as he prepared to turn into the police station. He pulled into the parking space marked *Chief of Police* and looked at Torres. "We smoke the bastards out."

That night, Chief West slept fitfully. A warm front had moved through Bradford County bringing rain and heat, and, at 3 a.m., it was still in the mid-seventies. Living in one of the coldest parts of the state, West didn't own an air conditioner. The fan in the bedroom window did little except stir the muggy air. His wife's back was to him; a strap on her thin nightgown had slipped off her shoulder, and she snored lightly. While he slept—half-slept, really—his brain tried to answer the unanswered questions of Corsica's disappearance. He rolled onto his back, fully awake, and listened to the early morning rain and chatter among some early-rising birds outside his window. Then he pulled himself up to a half-sitting position and turned on the reading light next to the bed.

He knew where Corsica was buried.

58

Smoking Gun

The morning was one of those tropical summer mornings after a nighttime rain, when the air is full of steam, and everything glistens for a short, magical time before the sun burns it off. It promised to be the kind of summer day best spent dozing by the pool, not trudging across a torrid drill pad. The air at the Campbell pad was heavy with an odd mixture of diesel from the equipment and pollen and manure from the nearby farms.

It was a few minutes before 10 a.m., and most of the litigants and their counsel and experts stood near Norby's mobile office. Mike and Missy held cups of coffee they'd picked up at the Speedway store. Mike wished it were stronger and he had more of it. Darius Moore stood away from the group, talking on his cell phone. Professor McCrory and Anthony Fowler chatted with the Campbells' geologist, Ruby Sunshine. Bill Benedict, the former industry insider and engineer for the Campbells, stood alone, hands in his pockets, looking glum. Winnie talked with Teresa a good twenty feet away from the group. Teresa wore jeans and a black T-shirt with the slogan *MOMS AGAINST FRACKING* printed in bold pink letters. They were all waiting for Norby and Bones.

Standing apart from the group, between them and the farm field, was a lone guard, the same woman in the gray uniform who had greeted Mike and Missy a few days earlier. Today she wore a sidearm. She occasionally looked at the group, but mostly she watched the farmland and the tree line.

A white pickup with a Yukon logo topped the rise on the access road, followed by a second white pickup, kicking up mud and dust which settled on the nearby trees. Norby and Bones, wearing identical Yukon coveralls, got out of their trucks and snugged on their hard hats. They walked to Darius Moore, who shoved his cell phone into his jeans pocket and spoke with them for several minutes.

"Okay, people," Darius Moore said. "Listen up. This is a busy drilling site." Yukon had arranged to have all of the workers off the pad during the site visit, so no work actually was taking place. "As you know, drilling has been finished on the number four well, and the company is getting ready to begin completion of the well tomorrow. A convoy of water trucks is waiting for us to get off the site before they start bringing water to the impoundment. According to the agreement we have between Yukon and the Campbells, Yukon is allowing the Campbells, their counsel, and experts onto the site for a general review of the site. You may take pictures. Sampling and other testing will be done at a later time. Please listen to Mr. Lafleur, who will give you further safety instructions."

All eyes turned to Norby. His face was puffy, and he looked rumpled. His eyes were bloodshot.

"Welcome ev'body, ev*ery*body." Norby's voice was unusually thick. "Y'all are at a ver' busy facility, 'cept no one's here. How's that for ya?" He chuckled.

Darius Moore started walking toward him.

"This here's yer safety talk. Bones is gonna take over."

Norby backed away and drank deeply from a water bottle. Darius Moore approached him, but Norby turned his back and walked away.

Mike looked at Missy and shrugged.

"Welcome, everyone. This is the official safety talk, and we'd appreciate it if y'all'd listen to this more intently than you do to the one you get in an airplane."

There was a small amount of laughter.

As Bones began, Mike leaned over to Winnie. "What's up with Norby?"

"Don't know. Maybe he has the flu?"

"Or he's drunk."

Winnie shrugged.

"Have you ever been on a drill site before?"

"Just a couple, years ago when I was a lawyer with the department," she said quietly, watching Bones. "That was before unconventional drilling, so those operations were much smaller back then. Nothing quite like this."

Winnie wore well-used hiking boots and Lee jeans, not the kind with rips, but the kind that looked genuinely broken in. Her nod to femininity was a pink golf shirt with a rounded collar and a tiny gold cross hanging from a thin gold chain. A wisp of golden hair had escaped her ponytail and hung over an eye. She was an attractive woman no matter what she wore. Her handsome looks were a deception for foolish men—and women—who looked no further than her appearance. Mike was sure she was ready to filet anyone straight to the bone, and today and tomorrow would be as good as any to show off her swordsmanship.

Unexpectedly, she took Mike by the arm and pulled him away from the group. When they were out of hearing range, she said, "Mike, there's something we need to discuss."

Mike nodded.

"Something strange has been going on with the Campbells' water. The other day, Yukon dropped off four cases of spring water at Teresa and Jared's house. They delivered a total of twelve gallons. There was a note, it said due to work going on in the area, the Campbells' well would have a bad taste and smell. They should drink the bottled water instead."

"Darius never mentioned it to me." Mike furrowed his eyebrows.

"Teresa called me up and told me about it. She said the well water did have an unusual smell and taste. I sent the lab up and had them test it at the well and the kitchen tap. We paid a pretty penny to get overnight results, and I got them yesterday as I was leaving the office."

"And . . ."

"When they tested the water a couple of weeks ago, they found E. coli, fecal coliform, and other bacteria present. Arguably from the drilling, but more likely just the usual contamination you'd find in a shallow water well sitting next to a farm."

"Okay . . ."

"Now they've found ethylene glycol and sodium hypochlorite. You know what that is?"

"Antifreeze and bleach. They're both used in the completion fluid. If that's the case, then it means that serious and real components of frack fluid are now in the Campbells' water well. Sounds like you found the smoking gun." Mike smiled at her and raised his eyebrows. "What other chemicals did they find? I mean, there are like sixty or seventy components of fracking fluid."

Winnie moved her head close enough that Mike could smell the slight wisp of cologne she wore. "That's the thing. The bacteria are gone. Ruby thinks the bleach killed them. The only things they found were bleach and antifreeze. Also, methane, similar to what they found before when they tested."

Mike shrugged. "Maybe it's the leading edge of the plume of crap entering their well from Yukon's drilling."

Winnie looked around then put her mouth almost against Mike's head. Her breath tickled his ear as she talked and was strangely sensual. "There *is* a crapload of antifreeze and bleach. Way more than you'd find in a load of frack fluid. Our consultants say if this was completion fluid residue that traveled underground from the gas well or pit and then mixed in the Campbells' well, you'd expect to find it in levels like parts per million or even billion. The lab found parts per *thousand*, not parts per *million*. That's a concentration thousands of times stronger than you'd expect. It's like the well is full of *pure* bleach and antifreeze."

Mike stepped back and looked at her. "Like someone was spiking the well. Is that what you're saying?"

She leaned in again. "Well, if that happened, it wasn't my clients' doing. Teresa would never do anything like that, and Jared is never around and frankly doesn't seem to care. I can't imagine they'd poison their own well."

"Then who?" Mike backed up again, and Winnie made a face and shook her head.

"You said Yukon dropped off a load of bottled water? Along with a letter? That sure makes it sound like they knew about this. If they didn't know about it, why would they drop off the water?"

She handed him the letter, and Mike scanned it.

"Is this a copy? Can I have it?"

She nodded.

He took out his phone and snapped a picture of the letter. "We call that a redneck pdf," he said smiling.

Mike walked to Darius Moore. "What's the deal with Norby?"

Darius shrugged.

"What about the armed guard? I never saw that before at a drilling site."

Darius shrugged again and said, "Nothing. Better safe than sorry. That kind of thing."

"Also, Winnie wanted me to express thanks from the Campbells for the bottled water."

"What?"

"Yeah, the bottled water Yukon dropped off because your guys fouled the well so bad with fracking chemicals that no one can drink from it."

"What the hell are you smoking, Mike? Yukon didn't drop off any water."

Mike handed him the letter, which he quickly read.

"This is bullshit. It's not on Yukon letterhead. Also, it says Yukon Oil and Gas *Corporation*. The official corporate name is Yukon Oil & Gas *Company*. No one at the company would make that mistake. This is phony, made up . . . Can I keep this?"

Mike smiled at him. "My pleasure."

"And what's the deal with the water?" Asked Darius.

"Four cases of bottled water. According to Yukon's letter, that's a gift to the Campbells since your guys poisoned their well."

"Fuck you, Mike. You know that didn't happen."

"I do know that Winnie had the well water tested two days ago and its full of frack fluid—ethylene glycol and sodium hypochlorite. She got the results yesterday."

Darius Moore looked at him. "Antifreeze and bleach. How do I know the Campbells didn't dump that shit into their well and cook this whole thing up?"

"I guess you'll have to ask them. By the way, you might relay to Yukon's management that they should start thinking about a good settlement offer. At this point, my operating assumption is the completion fluid came from your gas wells or your goddamn pit. Seriously, the department is thinking about shutting down this whole operation. It's leaking like a sieve. We're thinking about drawing a ten-mile radius around this well and closing down all of your operations within the circle. Also, tell the boys in Houston to start thinking about a civil penalty settlement in the seven-figure range, plus a cleanup."

Darius Moore narrowed his eyes and stared at Mike for a moment, then angrily turned away.

Mike smiled. As he stormed off, Mike glanced at Teresa and was a little surprised she was looking at him. He nodded, but she didn't respond. Then he realized she wasn't just looking at him, she was *staring* at him. If he looked away and then looked back several seconds later, she was still staring at him. He decided to make it a contest. After several unblinking seconds, she approached.

"I've been thinking about you lately," Teresa said.

Mike had no idea where this conversation was going, and he held his tongue.

"I mean, you told me you became an environmental lawyer to fight the environmental bad guys. You told me you wanted to help clean up the environment. Yet here you are working with Yukon." She waved her hand in the direction of the pad.

"I don't think we should be having this conversation," said Mike. "Your lawyer is right over there, and before we talk about this case or cleaning up the environment or Yukon, I need to get your lawyer's permission."

"I don't need anybody's permission to talk to you. I just find it incredibly hypocritical that you're working for the frackers. You should be working for the citizens, the environment, not them.

Yet here you are working alongside them." She pointed at some of the Yukon personnel.

"Teresa, we can't have this conversation. But I will tell you this: I'm doing my job. We made a decision and issued a letter. You filed an appeal. I'm not working for the frackers. I'm representing the department because you filed your appeal. That has nothing to do with my personal views on the environment."

"Oh really? It has everything to do with your personal views. You should be working for us, protecting the environment, not the frackers." Teresa's voice became louder, and Mike noticed several of the others in the group turning their heads to watch.

Mike searched around for Winnie and finally made eye contact. When he did, he waved her over.

"These frackers, these bastards, look what they've done to my family. Did they think they could fuck up my well and buy me off with some bottles of Walmart water? I mean, who do these goddamn frackers think we are?"

"Winnie," Mike said to the lawyer as she approached. "Teresa came over here and started a conversation with me about . . . I'm not sure what it's about."

"Teri, let's go over here and talk," Winnie said quietly.

As Winnie tugged at Teresa's sleeve to pull her away, Teresa turned her head and caught Mike's eye. "You should be ashamed of yourself."

Missy made eye contact with Mike. He made a face and held his palms up.

All of the experts stood together, whispering. While yesterday the professor had sported a navy three-piece suit, today he was in worn Red Wing work shoes, heavy-duty Carhartt flame-retardant work pants, and a long-sleeved work shirt. His outfit was festooned with pockets and tools. The other experts wore FR jeans and, surprisingly, long-sleeved shirts in the hot sun. It occurred to Mike that these were people who were experienced at working under these conditions.

Bones had finished the safety discussion. As they started walking the site with the group, Mike leaned over to Missy and said, "How are you doing?"

"I'm exhausted. That was a wild night. After the cops and firefighters were finally done with us at three, it was hard to fall asleep. I feel like I was awake all night." She leaned close to Mike and brushed the back of her hand against the back of his, and said, "Not exactly the kind of exciting night I'd been hoping for."

Mike smiled. "Me too. I'm sorry I agreed to schedule the deposition for the day after the site view. It made sense at the time, but now, not so much. I want to be sure you get a good night's rest tonight, so you're as fresh as possible for the deposition tomorrow. Since Richard is still on the loose, I think we're going to change hotels when we get back to town."

"Seriously?"

Mike nodded.

"Sounds like a plan," she said and smiled.

Mike put his mouth close to Missy's ear. "Do you know anything about bleach and antifreeze in completion fluid?"

"Sure. They're commonly used. They're both components of fracking fluid."

"Winnie's lab found them in the Campbells' well." He smiled.

"Really? I'm surprised. There's no connection between the drilling and the well. When did it appear? How much?"

"Yesterday or a day or two before that. In the parts per thousand."

Missy's eyes widened, and she shook her head. "I want to get Yukon as badly as anyone else, but there's been no fracking for months. They won't be fracking again here for a few days. Also, there's been no water in the pit since the winter. There's no connection from Yukon's gas well and the Campbells' drinking water well. If there was a connection, I'd expect to see levels in the parts per million. Not parts per thousand. I want to see the lab results and go over the geology again. Maybe I can sneak in a discussion with Professor McCrory."

Mike looked at her and nodded.

"Something's not right," she said. "This is too perfect. It feels like a set-up."

59

A Good Walk, Spoiled, Part 2

"Don't forget your job today," Mike said to Missy. "I've got one too."

Missy nodded, then drifted over to Ruby Sunshine and began a quiet conversation. Mike circled around the group in the direction of Bill Benedict.

They walked in ones and twos along the perimeter of the pad. Bones pointed out various components of the drilling operation while Norby lagged behind.

Technically, questions and answers were not a part of the site view. The lawyers and their consultants were permitted to view the site and nothing more. In keeping with the informality of the event and the reality of what lawyers do at such things, however, Winnie had asked several seemingly innocuous questions in response to comments made by Bones.

"We finished drilling the Campbell 4-H well two days ago and pulled the drill rig," Bones said, pointing in the direction of the wellhead.

"When did you say you'd begin completions, Mr. Benson?" She asked.

"It's Bones, Ms. Hedges. Like I said, we have a convoy of water trucks ready to go in Sayre. We have to do some routine maintenance on the impoundment, and once that's done, we'll begin filling 'er up. When we get five million gallons of water in the pit, we'll be ready to get started."

"That new lateral you're going to frack that you were talking about, how long did you say it was?" She asked.

"Twelve thousand linear feet," he replied, looking toward Darius Moore.

"In which direction?" she asked, surveying the horizon.

Bones oriented himself and pointed with a chopping motion. "Due north, ma'am, away from the Campbell residence, in case you're wondering."

She was about to ask another question when Darius Moore, who had been watching her intently, said, "Ms. Hedges, Winnie, I'd appreciate it if you didn't engage in any off-record questioning of my clients."

Winnie laughed a gentle mocking laugh and patted him on the shoulder.

After about an hour of touring the site, they arrived at the far side of the pad. Mike was sweaty and thirsty and was glad he brought an extra bottle of water. This was the only place where workers were present. Three men, all wearing bright blue coveralls and hard hats, watched from the backs of pickup trucks on the side of the pad. The logo on the trucks and their coveralls said *TEX-OK Water Services.*

Bones climbed to the top of the berm, and most of the group followed. "Down there is our freshwater impoundment." He pointed. Another five workers in blue coveralls lounged in the campsite area among a small dozer and a tiny front-end loader.

"It makes more sense for us to hold the water in the impoundment and use it for completions than it does to pump it out of individual trucks," he continued. "In addition, we have frac tanks lined up around the site to hold the flowback water. All of the water that comes back out of the borehole goes into them frac tanks. While spills are rare, if one should happen, it'll happen on our pad, which is lined and fully contained. We have a maintenance crew to make sure none of the produced water leaves the pad. It's impossible for the water to get into the ground."

Winnie looked at Darius Moore. "Darius, if it's okay with you, may I ask a question about construction of the impoundment?"

"The impoundment has nothing to do with this case."

"I know that. It's really just a matter of curiosity."

"I'll allow it, but that's it."

"Bones, what are the different layers in the construction of the impoundment? I'm just curious."

"Sure, ma'am. There's a layer of clay on the bottom, then a layer of construction stone, then a layer of sand on top of that. Then we have two layers of a heavy poly liner material. Each layer of the liner is sealed. Basically, they're glued and heat-sealed together. Keep in mind the impoundment is only used for fresh water. If we'd been constructing this to hold the produced water, there would be additional layers and other protections built in, such as monitoring wells."

"Thanks. I appreciate the information."

Mike raised his hand. "Darius, do you mind if I ask a question. Just a quickie."

Darius Moore shook his head no, then said, "Crap, Mike. Really? Okay, but that's it."

"Sorry, Bones, who are these guys?" Mike said, pointing at the workers in blue coveralls.

"I think I told y'all we had routine maintenance to do on the impoundment. It's like everything else on this pad. We do preventative maintenance all the time, especially when something's been out of action for a while. The impoundment hasn't been used since March, so before we refill it, we're going to do a little cleanup."

Mike nodded, then leaned over and whispered into Missy's ear. "If all they're doing is preventative maintenance, why do they have a bulldozer and front-end loader? Seems like a lot of unnecessary equipment to me."

Missy shrugged.

Bones jogged down off the berm and began to return in the direction of the office when Winnie raised a hand. "I'd like to take a look at the berm while we're here."

"I don't think so," Darius Moore replied. "We're here because of allegations of leakage from the well. There's no need to look at the impoundment."

"I wasn't talking about the impoundment's berm. I was talking about the berm off the pad. If the borehole or pad are leaking, then that most certainly is part of our appeal. While we're down there, I wouldn't mind taking a look at the impoundment, but that's not the reason I want to go down there."

Darius Moore shook his head and pursed his lips. "Okay, okay. It's very steep. Also, I was told the guys have seen snakes, rattlesnakes, in the area. It may not be the best idea for everyone to go down there. We're not taking responsibility if anyone falls and cracks open their head or gets bit by a snake."

Winnie didn't respond but immediately started inching down the side of the berm. Professor McCrory was right behind her and grabbed her hand. A moment later, Sunshine and Benedict also gripped hands, and the four of them headed down the side of the berm, linked together like some kind of square dance. Mike couldn't help but laugh and quickly pulled out his iPhone and snapped a picture. Winnie looked at him when she heard the click.

"It's for my scrapbook," Mike said. They both smiled.

Eventually, everyone was down at the bottom of the berm. The professor, Anthony, Missy, Sunshine, and Benedict all took a profoundly serious look at the base of the berm, with all but the professor on their knees. Professor McCrory pointed at various features on the side of the berm and lectured the group. By the time Darius Moore reached him to tell him to shut the hell up, he was done teaching.

Meanwhile, Winnie had walked through the open gate and climbed up the nearby berm of the impoundment to look down into it. She held Teresa's hand and pulled her up. Several of the others began walking around the impoundment.

Darius Moore stood near Mike and quietly said, "Christ, this has become a dumpster fire."

"Honestly, the more you make a big deal of it, the more you make it a big deal. Seriously, just go with it. Pretend it's nothing."

"It's not your fucking client. Maybe someday when you have real paying clients, you'll know what I mean." He stalked off in the direction of Bones.

60

I am going to open your graves and bring you up from them.
(Ezekiel 37:12)

The group had scattered across the area between the pad and the impoundment. In twos and threes, they had wandered to several locations for a closer look. Bones jogged back and forth like a sheepdog and held out his hands to gently encourage the group back to the pad. The guard kept herself between the group and the tree line.

Behind the pit, a car quickly and noisily came up the farm trail through the woods and onto the old campsite. When it cleared the woods, the Washington Township police SUV driven by Chief West pulled in next to the group. The chief and Hector Torres jumped out, and the chief surveyed the small crowd.

"Norby. I need to talk to him. Now." The chief looked at the members of the group.

Norby was gone.

Everyone looked around as if Norby was standing behind someone.

"What's going on?" asked Darius Moore.

"I need to talk with Norby and Bones. Immediately. Is Norby here?" The chief asked.

"He was."

"Bones, you too," the chief said.

Bones started to walk toward the chief, as did everyone else.

"What's this all about, chief?" Bones asked.

"Yeah, chief, my name is Darius Moore, and I'm the attorney for Yukon. You can consider me Mr. Benson's and Mr. Lafleur's attorney." He produced a business card which the chief shoved into his pocket without a glance.

"Well, counsellor, we have reason to believe your clients, Lafleur and Benson, killed a man named Chris Corsica and left his body in a shallow grave back in February. We're not sure of all of the details, but it was related to the construction of this impoundment and Mr. Corsica's failure to satisfy all of the design requirements, which resulted in a leak. We believe Norby and or Bones became enraged and killed Corsica, then buried his body nearby. I'm happy to arrest them right now unless I hear a good alibi or see evidence to the contrary. I think I know where his body is buried." The chief indicated with his chin toward the impoundment.

"What? What the hell?" said Darius. "Give me a minute to talk to my client."

Darius Moore and Bones whispered in each other's ears for at least five minutes. "You're saying Mr. Lafleur or Mr. Benson killed a man named Corsica and buried him right here? In the pit? Do you have any physical evidence of the so-called murder? Anything tangible, bloodied clothing, fingerprints, DNA, a confession, anything?"

The chief hesitated. "We're about to get that. It's right there." The chief pointed at the ridges poking up into the impoundment lining.

"So, the answer is no," said Darius Moore sharply. "If you want to go digging around on my client's property, you're going to need a search warrant."

"Darius," said Mike, "if you make him go and get a search warrant, he'll bring back a team of State Police guys and forensics people to open up the pit. That'll take days. You can be sure they'll do a whole forensics analysis of the pit from one end to the other. That'll hold up completion of the well by, what, a week? Maybe more. That's if they find nothing. If they do find a body, that could hold things up for several weeks. If Norby and Bones killed somebody, that's not on Yukon; it's on them. Why not let them take a look under the lining? They could be out of here in an hour."

Darius Moore gave Mike a menacing look. "I'm not letting any goddamn sheriff rip up the lining of the pit."

Mike shook his head, then looked at the chief. "Chief, you may remember me. We met last week. I'm Mike Jacobs, assistant counsel to DEP. That group of men over there, in the blue coveralls, they have all the equipment and are ready to do maintenance of this pit. They could probably pull up the lining and look at it in under twenty minutes. Here's my suggestion. If you find nothing, so be it, you go home, and this is over for now. If you find the body, then all bets are off. Would that be okay?"

Chief West nodded at Mike. "Sounds good to me. If I'm wrong, I'm wrong. No need to hold up Yukon's operations."

Darius Moore grabbed Mike by the arm and roughly pulled him several feet from the group. "What the fuck are you doing? This is none of your business. Stay out of it."

"It *is* my business. And if you dial back the testosterone for a minute, you'll agree with me. If Norby and Bones killed a guy and buried him under the lining, why would you or Yukon want to obstruct the investigation? If I were you, I'd throw them under the bus and not look like you're trying to protect them. You can do whatever you want, bro; that's on you."

Darius Moore rubbed his chin for several seconds and forced a smile. "Chief, give me a minute. This is way above my pay grade. I'm not saying no, just give me a minute to talk with one or two other people."

"Go ahead. In the meantime, we're going to cuff Benson and place him under protective custody."

He pulled the handcuffs out from his utility belt and handcuffed Benson, then handed him off to Torres.

"Does anyone know where Norby went?" the chief asked as he looked around.

No one responded.

"Crap. We'll deal with that later."

A very awkward and hot twenty minutes followed while Darius Moore walked away from the group and spoke, sometimes cursed, on his cell phone.

Finally, Darius Moore approached the chief. He held up his phone and read from the screen. "My client is Yukon Oil & Gas Company. You've alleged a crime that, if it happened, was conducted by Mr. Lafleur and or Mr. Benson without permission or knowledge of Yukon. While they may be employees of Yukon, their alleged actions certainly were not permitted or sanctioned by the company, and the company does not want to do anything to obstruct law enforcement. Yukon is happy to reasonably coordinate with you, and we'll make available to you our contractor to open up the seam in the impoundment. This is not a general waiver of my clients' Fourth Amendment rights. Also, this is not a fishing expedition, and if we don't find anything in a reasonable period of time, we're done. I'm not going to let you dig up the entire impoundment, just the seam where you think the body may be buried. We have important work we have to do and a convoy of water trucks waiting to fill up this impoundment. Do we have a deal?"

Arrangements were made, and the men in the blue coveralls entered the impoundment. The chief pointed to the area he wanted opened. A man with a device that looked like a giant box cutter went to the area where the peaks were the most prominent, about ten feet from the edge of the impoundment, and sliced through the liner. The entire group stood close to the impoundment, watching intently.

Thirty minutes later, the workers indicated they were ready to peel back the lining. The chief jumped onto the edge of the black liner and watched closely as the lining was stripped from the sand underneath. The workers peeled back one side, and then the other. It was like flaying the skin from a whale. It was apparent the rock ledge had been inartfully leveled. Jagged edges of sharp shale poked up several inches through the sand which, in turn, was saturated with water.

"Wait a minute," said Missy. "Can I get in there for a sec?"

Without waiting for an answer, she jumped into the pit, took a small trowel from her backpack, and dug in the sand. She plopped some into a plastic bag, sealed it, and said, "Thanks."

She walked back toward Mike and said, "That should have been dry. It's wet as anything."

With the chief standing next to them, the workers used shovels to scrape back the sand along the peaks of the ridge. With six of them digging, they were able to clear an area about fifteen feet long and six feet wide in ten minutes. Finally, the supervisor turned and looked at the chief.

"What we're finding here, chief, is saturated sand and some construction rock. Then, we go right to the ground surface. I'd expect to see more sand, a lot more construction stone, and clay. The area was not built to spec. One thing's for sure: We're not finding what you're looking for."

"I guess we're done here," said Darius Moore. "I want to conclude this operation so we can all get back to our business, and Yukon can do the maintenance on this impoundment they've been planning to do all day."

"Counselor, humor me for just a couple more minutes, and I'll get out of your hair," said the chief.

The chief looked at the flat area just inside the pit, where they all had been standing while the work took place, between the berm and the beginning of the shale ridge. It was about eight feet long and flat.

"Can you open this up right here? I was so fixated on the little peaks I didn't think to look right here where it's flat." He pointed to the area under his feet.

TEX-OK's foreman looked at Darius Moore, who said, "Go ahead. But this is it."

The team of workers took out their blades and went to work peeling back the lining. Almost immediately, the whole group saw a piece of black cloth, several feet long and buried in the sand.

The chief slid on blue latex gloves, then got down on his knees and tugged at the cloth. "This looks like a shroud. No, wait. It's a flag."

He tugged a little more, exposing a brass grommet. "Get out those brooms and sweep away the sand. The entire group leaned forward to watch. Torres gripped Benson's arm more tightly.

The cloth was almost entirely uncovered in under two minutes. On his hands and knees, wearing his latex gloves, the chief tugged at the cloth freeing it from the sand. He held it up: the U.S. Army's *Ranger* logo in gold on a black background.

"That's Chris's Army Ranger flag," Torres said loudly. "He flew it off of his RV. He was proud as hell of his service and never would've left it behind. We sure as hell didn't bury it under the impoundment."

The chief nodded. "The body's got to be right here. Someone, Norby and Benson, used this flag as a shroud."

Bones said nothing and stood still, stone-faced.

The chief spoke with the supervisor, and the men got out brooms and slowly started sweeping under where the flag had been. Ten minutes of sweeping later, all they found were rocks and sand and an empty Jack Daniels bottle. They widened the search area, well beyond where the flag had been, and found nothing.

"Hey chief, this has been going on long enough," Darius Moore said. "You have no evidence of a crime, no body parts, no nothing, and my client's operations are being held up. I have no idea why this flag or the bottle are here, but there could be a hundred reasons for that, having nothing to do with any crime. I think we're done."

"Hold on," said Mike. "What about the cameras, the high-res video cameras? You said the place was loaded with them."

"That's correct," said Darius. "But they were only installed in April, after a couple of acts of vandalism. The chief said the incident, if there was one, occurred in February."

"Wait a minute," said Anthony. "This didn't mean anything to me a couple of weeks ago, but when I was out here, I found something odd. Look what I found, on the ground right here below the berm."

Anthony pulled a plastic bag out of his backpack and held it up. Everyone gathered around.

"It's a human tooth, an incisor," said Professor McCrory.

"I agree," said Sunshine.

"No doubt about it," said Anthony.

"While none of the good geologists are dentists," interjected Darius Moore, "it does look like a tooth. We have no idea whose tooth. Again, there could be a hundred reasons why a random tooth would be found here."

Anthony handed the baggie to the chief.

"I can get this analyzed for DNA, but that'll take at least a week."

"Even if it's that guy's DNA, it doesn't mean he's dead, just that he lost a tooth." Darius talked loudly over the discussions going on around him. "We've got to get going and patch up this impoundment. My client has a lot at stake, and so far, this has been a gigantic waste of time."

The chief looked at the baggie and crumpled it in his hand. His shoulders drooped in defeat. "Hector, you can cut him loose."

He handed his key to Torres, who unlocked the handcuffs. Bones rubbed his wrists.

A loud crack from the hill above the pad shot through the valley, followed by a second. The guard collapsed, motionless. Bones was pitched to the ground like he'd suffered a body-blow, hollering in agony as he held his guts.

Mike sought Missy in the crowd. He found her, standing by Bones, just as she jerked into the air like a marionette and fell to the dirt, grabbing her arm, screaming in pain.

Two more shots sounded, this time coming from a point on the hill about two hundred feet south of the first ones. One whistled past Mike's head, and the second hit Torres in the arm. The chief also was hit in the arm. Torres pushed the chief to the ground and jumped on top of him.

As the group scattered for cover, Mike dove for Missy and shielded her with his body.

61

Adapt, Improvise, Overcome

The group of lawyers, consultants, lawmen, and workers had flattened onto the ground or fled. Bones, howling, writhed in agony at the edge of the pit. Mike covered Missy with his body, held her, and whispered in her ear. It appeared the guard, who was struck first, was dead before she hit the ground.

"Chief, the shooter has a clear range of fire. He took out the guard. You're the only one here who's armed. He probably wants to take you out too," Torres shouted.

"Okay, Hector, now get the heck off me."

Four more volleys plowed into the earth, inches from the two men.

"Got to protect my CO. I think . . . I think there's more than one shooter. I'm pretty sure that's two different rifles. Let's get you to cover. I can help you assault the ridge . . ."

Suddenly, a single shot rang out. Torres' body spasmed, and the air burst from his lungs.

"Torres, Torres! Hector . . ."

No response.

The chief placed his hand on Torres' neck and shook his head. Torres had taken a direct hit. His shirt was a sodden, bloody mess, a black entrance wound clearly visible.

Quickly and carefully, the chief picked up Torres, threw the man over his back in a fireman's carry, and ran to the woods, dropping him on the flattened campsite. The chief's body was covered with blood.

"Chief, are you okay?" asked Winnie.

He pulled off his blood-soaked shirt. Only a small amount of blood had soaked through to his T-shirt. "I think that's mostly Torres."

Winnie took the shirt and rubbed the blood from his arm. "You're right. I think you're okay. Looks like you have a flesh wound on your arm, but the blood was mostly his."

"He . . . saved my life . . " The chief looked at the Marine. "He took the bullet meant for me."

"Chief, chief," Winnie said, looking at the dazed man. "People are still out there . . ."

There was another volley of shots and screams. Bones was hit again, this time in the shoulder. Another bullet ricocheted close by. Then a second volley of shots, one coming close to Mike, ricocheted off the ground, and another pierced Sunshine's leg.

"We're sitting ducks," shouted the chief. "We've got to get everyone into the trees or behind the trucks. Everyone, MOVE, MOVE, MOVE!"

Some ran to the woods or behind the SUV; others were paralyzed by fear, frozen, easy targets. The dead and wounded, and the moaning from those who had been shot, made the clearing look like a battleground.

***

"Mike, I'm so scared. Do you think Richard . . .?"

"That's the only thing that makes sense. Can you move?"

"I don't know."

Mike looked toward the top of the hill, got onto his feet and lifted Missy in his arms. She draped both of her arms around his neck and held him tightly. He shuffled into the woods as quickly as he could. Two more shots rang out just behind him.

"It's got to be him. Richard. Oh God," Missy said, sobbing.

Mike stumbled through the underbrush as he carried Missy. He didn't stop until he set her down on the far side of the Chief's

SUV. Deep red blood ran down her arm like a river. He pulled off his belt and cinched it around her arm, above the wound. He pulled it tight and wrapped it around her arm several more times until the bleeding stopped.

Mike placed a finger on her chin and turned her head from the wound, so she looked into his eyes. "Until we get a real tourniquet, this will have to do. I remember something about releasing it every five or ten minutes or so and then tightening it back up. Don't move around too much, or you'll increase the bleeding."

Mike looked up in time to see Darius Moore carrying Bones over his back, running—lurching—until he got him to the woods where he collapsed. Bones was still alive.

The chief, who stood behind the raised tailgate of the SUV in his blood-stained T-shirt screamed orders at the State Police on his car radio, then unholstered his gun and jogged over to Bones. "Do you have any idea what the hell is going on?"

"Damned if I know." He spit blood from his mouth.

"Does this have anything to do with Corsica?" The chief yelled.

Bones hesitated to respond.

"Come on. Out with it. No more bullshit. No more lies. This makes a difference."

"I just don't know," Bones said slowly. "He's supposed to be dead. Norby killed him with that Maglite. It can't be him, shouldn't be him, but Norby's been convinced for months he wasn't dead when we buried him."

"Where, where's his body?"

"That's the thing. I ripped that Army flag off the side of his RV to cover him, respectful-like. Then Norby and me buried him under the linin'. Right where we looked." Bones indicated the pit with his chin. "We covered him with sand and then pushed the linin' on top of him. Figured it would be years, maybe decades, until anyone found him. Norby went back and looked for the body a couple of days after he killed him, and he was gone. Lately, things have been happening here, vandalism, potshots. Norby was convinced it was him shooting at the pad, vandalizing. I just don't know." Bones went into a fit, coughing up blood.

They looked up in time to see Darius making another run through the battlefield, this time with Sunshine in a fireman's carry. When he reached the SUV, he fell on the ground, managing to lay the geologist softly on the ground before his legs buckled.

Gasping, Darius said, "The guard is still out there, chief. I checked, but she's dead. Big hole in her chest. I think she was dead before she hit the ground. Also, I saw one of the maintenance workers was shot. He's too far away; there's no way I can get to him. Teresa's still out there . . ."

Darius got up and glanced toward the top of the hill.

"Wait!" shouted the chief.

Darius shook his head and ran back into the field. Two shots struck the ground just behind him. He ran in a zigzag until he got to Teresa. She stood in the field, shaking her fist toward the top of the hill.

"You goddamn frackers. You fucked with the wrong woman. Do you think you can silence me? Make me go away? You've got another thing coming. I'm not going anywhere. You're going to have to deal with me forever, you sons of bitches. Go ahead, try and shoot me, I dare you, you bastards. I swear, if I get my hands on you, you stinking asshole, I'm going to rip your balls off with my fingernails. You're not going to shut me up—"

A pair of arms appeared around Teresa's waist, and a hand locked onto a wrist. She was lifted in the air for a moment, then Darius sacked her with a perfectly executed open-field tackle, knocking the air out of her. He lay on top of her for a millisecond, then threw her over his shoulder and ran at full speed toward the woods. Teresa cursed loudly even as she gasped for breath. Darius carried her, dodging bullets until they were safely in the woods and on the ground. Teresa struggled to a sitting position and put her arms around his neck. She held him tightly and, as the reality of the situation hit her, was overcome with tears.

The chief squatted next to Darius and put his hand on his shoulder. "Crap, I thought maybe this blood was from one of the others. You were shot in the shoulder, man. You've got to stop running around, son, or you'll bleed out."

The chief jogged back to his vehicle and unlocked the storage compartment in the back of the SUV. He pulled out a black M16, which he quickly loaded. And a tactical shotgun. He shoved six shells into its magazine and then laid down both guns inside the tailgate of the SUV. He grabbed a medical kit and ran it over to the injured.

"Does anyone have any kind of medical training?"

"I do," said Benedict. "Army infantry, Germany, like forty years ago, they taught us the basics. I'll do the best I can."

Another volley of two shots ricocheted harmlessly among the trees. Then two more shots in the direction of the workers huddled behind or under their trucks. Then yelling as another worker was hit.

"We're sitting ducks," said the chief. It'll take a half-hour for the State Police to get up here, and we can't wait that long. I'm going up there and try to put an end to this."

"Wait a minute, chief, you can't do it by yourself," said Mike. "I'll go with you."

"Do you have any military training? Law enforcement?" Asked the chief.

"None."

"Does anybody?"

"I do," said Professor McCrory. "Engineers. Vietnam."

Chief West looked over the rotund seventy-plus-year-old professor and said, "With all due respect, sir, I think I'll need a younger guy. It's pretty rugged up there."

Mike placed his hand on the chief's arm and said, "Show me what to do with this shotgun. I've shot one before, and it's pretty much point-and-shoot. Right?"

"We don't really have much of a choice," said the chief. He showed him how to pump and shoot the shotgun. Then the two of them began to head up the old farm trail.

"Mike! Wait!" shouted Missy.

"Don't worry; I'll be back. I promise. I love you." He jogged to her and kissed her on the lips.

"I love you too," she said.

62

One of These Things Is not Like the Other

The chief began to lead Mike up the trail, then stopped and said, "Don't walk right behind me. Give me a good ten feet, otherwise we make too easy a target. Also, we're going to use hand signals and stay as quiet as possible. This means stop." He held up his fist. "I think the rest are self-explanatory."

"What do we do when we find Richard?" Mike asked.

"Richard? At this point, I'm expecting to see Corsica up there."

Mike made a face.

"So, whoever it is, what do we do?" Mike asked.

"Don't take any chances. This man is a stone-cold killer. Don't take any risks. Don't give him a chance to put a bullet in you. Do what you've got to do. Anything that happens up there is self-defense, so far as I'm concerned. *Anything*. Understand?"

Mike nodded.

"One more thing. You wait for my signal. I have experience dealing with crazies like this, and if I get a chance to bring him in, I will, but you wait in the woods covering me until I tell you to come forward. Okay?"

"Yes, sir."

The chief turned and walked cautiously along the old tractor lane. As the trail bent down the hillside toward the road, the chief started bushwhacking onto the disused path. His feet stirred the underbrush, causing it to rustle just loudly enough to be heard. Mike gave him some distance and then followed.

After ten minutes of a steep uphill climb, more shots rang out from about a hundred feet above them. The chief stooped and raised his fist. Mike also stooped down. They crawled on their elbows and knees through the underbrush.

Unexpectedly, the chief stopped and held up his fist. He stayed frozen. Mike had a hard time seeing beyond him through the brush. Suddenly, a large, wide snake, white spaces between brown patches, slid past the chief. It must have been six feet long. It slithered toward Mike. He pointed the shotgun at it, his finger on the trigger. He couldn't breathe. His heart pounded. Sweat streamed out of every pore in his body, his trigger finger twitching. It was all he could do to keep from peeing himself or shooting the damn thing.

The snake approached Mike, its tongue testing the air, its unblinking black eyes staring directly into Mike's. Mike rolled to the right as hard as he could against a log as the snake slithered into the woods just to his left. Sweat drenched his body. The chief watched over his shoulder, then smiled at Mike as the snake slithered by. He held up his thumb. Mike returned the gesture and was about to return to the trail when he smelled something bad.

Rotten.

Decayed.

The smell invaded his sinuses.

Permanently.

He looked at the log he'd been leaning against and realized it wasn't a log. It was blue. Filthy. Dirty jeans. Covered with maggots and worms. With a work boot at the end. Mike's eyes followed the object and saw, hidden in the brush, a belt and the bottom of a jacket. A soiled, cruddy windbreaker. Maybe blue or black, it was hard to say. And a hand. Or what was left of one. Just some bones and blackened sinew resting in the weeds at the end of a sleeve. Covered with maggots. The rest of the body was hidden in the undergrowth.

Mike gagged and rolled back into the trail. He had to swallow hard to keep the vomit from entering his mouth.

Mike was on his hands and knees in the weedy trail. He took several deep cleansing breaths and quietly called out, "Chief . . . chief."

After a moment, the chief turned his head and held up his fist. Mike waved furiously at him. After several seconds, the chief crawled back to Mike.

"What the hell, Mike? We're maybe one hundred feet from Corsica, and he's intent on killing us. If you have cold feet, just stay here, and I'll take care of this mess."

Mike shook his head and pointed at the body. The chief blinked and quickly looked back at Mike. Then he inched his way to the body and pushed away the brush. Mike could see a skull. Remnants of leathery, blackened flesh peeled away from the bone. The eyes were long gone, only dank cavities remained. The face, or what was left of it, was a sickening hive of insects. A ghoul. The stuff of nightmares. It was impossible to tell who it was.

The chief brushed some debris off the dead man's torso and something slithered out, away from him. The chief snapped his hand back and jumped. He looked again at Mike. His face was pale, white. He brushed the jacket several times, then held up the front flap. It bore a logo. *Corsica Roofing.* Then the chief pulled himself close to the skull and looked closely. After nearly a minute he backed away and laid next to Mike in the weeds. He was panting and took several deep breaths.

"It's wearing a Corsica Roofing windbreaker. Chris Corsica was wearing one the last time Torres saw him. Also, the skull is missing a tooth in front, and I'm pretty sure it's an incisor." He reached into his pocket and pulled out the baggie. "If I had to guess, I'd say it was this one. I'm no expert in forensics, but it's Corsica."

"What's he doing here?"

"This is a guess, but maybe he came to in the grave in the pit . . . can you imagine? . . . and managed to dig himself out.

Somehow, he crawled out of the pit and made his way up here. This is as far as he got before he expired. Poor bastard."

Mike nodded. Two more shots rang out, and Mike and the chief ducked into the weeds.

"Then who's up there trying to kill us?"

63

A Hard Day's Night

Mike and the chief kept their heads low in the weeds until the volley ended. Then the chief patted Mike's shoulder and continued elbow walking through the woods.

They moved quietly and deliberately. Mike could make out a figure through the brush, a man, in a small clearing up ahead. He carried a rifle and looked off to his left, away from them.

Again, they heard the report from another rifle, not more than a hundred feet to their right, farther up the hill. The man started moving in the direction of the other shooter. The chief waved Mike to him.

"Hector was right. There's two of them. Christ, it's Columbine. Nightmare scenario. Stay on your toes."

The chief and Mike squatted and then moved quickly through the woods to keep up with their target. Then they heard the unmistakable sound of a rifle being pumped.

"Hey you, you asshole. What are you doing?" A man shouted.

The voice was unmistakable.

Richard Shelby.

Two shots were fired in response to the question. One went wide in the direction of the chief and Mike. The other must have grazed Shelby.

"You bastard," said Shelby. "You shot Missy."

"Fuck you, asshole," said a second man, a slight accent. "I don't know any Missy. Anybody gets in my way I shoot them."

"You bastard. You're a dead—."

Shots rang out. Shelby flew backward landing on his back among the rocks. The shooter carefully approached him, rifle raised.

Mike watched through the underbrush.

"Who the hell are you?" Shelby said, gasping for air.

The man with the rifle pulled the trigger. He reloaded, then calmly pulled the trigger again. The shots rang out loudly, and Mike could see Shelby's body spasm on the ground.

The man spit on him. "You can call me Vladimir Zhirkov."

64

A Lucky Sonofabitch

Zhirkov reached into his pocket and pulled out another round. Just before he could load it into the sniper rifle, the chief jumped up and shouted, "PUT DOWN THE RIFLE. I'm Chief West, Washington Township Police Department. Let's end this."

The chief aimed his M16 directly at Zhirkov, his eye at the scope.

The Russian looked unconcerned. He said, "You all alone, chief? Sorry to say, but I'm pretty sure I saw the so-called guard go down twenty minutes ago. This is going to end badly."

"Yes, I'm alone, but it'll only end badly for you if you don't cooperate. Put your gun down and get on your knees."

"Or what, you'll kill me? A lot of people have died today. The guard, Lafleur."

"Norby's dead?"

"Prick thought he'd sneak up on me. I didn't even waste a bullet. Combat knife across the trachea. Very effective."

"What the hell? What's this all about?"

The chief slowly moved forward until he was out of the woods and in the clearing with Zhirkov. Shelby's lifeless body sprawled on the ground about ten feet away. Mike hid in the dense underbrush and didn't move, didn't breathe, anxiously awaiting the chief's signal as he'd been directed to do. Sweat poured from his body.

"I hate to say this, perhaps it sounds like a cliché, but it's just business."

"Business?"

"The vandalism, the bad water at the neighbor's house, now this."

"What? Why?" The chief kept his gun pointed at Zhirkov.

"Just speeding up the process." Zhirkov shook his head. "It can take such a long time for people to do what's right. Get over their economic self-interest, especially where some are making huge profits. It would happen eventually. Just not fast enough."

"What are you talking about? Were you working with him?" The chief pointed sharply with his M16, then trained it back on Zhirkov's chest.

"That asshole? I have no idea who he is. Just dumb luck. Seems as though I wasn't the only one with an agenda."

"Enough talk. Put that whatever gun down and kick it away from you. Then get on your knees. I'm taking you in."

"This fine gun? A compact sniper rifle, an SRS. Very effective. Very portable. A .308. Not as good as a Blaser or even my old Dragunov, but very effective in any event."

Zhirkov slowly put the rifle on the ground. He nudged it with his foot and then dropped to his knees.

Mike could see the tattoo on Zhirkov's hand through the brush. A red A with a sword through it. This was the same guy he'd seen in Harrisburg at the riot. He was stunned.

"Okay, chief, here comes the difficult part. The part where you have to cuff me."

"Not that difficult. You're going to cuff yourself." The chief reached into his utility belt and felt around.

"Crap, I gave the cuffs to Hector."

The chief took his eyes off Zhirkov for an instant as he glanced at his utility belt. In a flash, the man pulled a revolver from the back of his belt and shot the chief in the chest. He fell like a stone to the ground.

Zhirkov kept the gun extended and walked over to the chief who was curled up on his side. He pushed him hard with his boot and rolled him onto his back, bleeding but still alive.

"I forgot to tell you I carry this nifty Smith & Wesson. All-American. You never should've given me a chance, chief. Your best tactical move was to kill me the minute you got the jump on me."

"Don't move," Mike said. He stood up at the edge of the woods with his shotgun trained on Zhirkov. The man smiled at him.

"Michael Jacobs, I believe." The handgun was still pointed at the chief. "The hero of my little riot. We've never been properly introduced, but I've had my eyes on you."

"Drop the gun. I won't make the same mistake the chief did."

"You already did, my friend. Too much talk, Michael Jacobs." Zhirkov looked Mike over. "You look soft. I'll bet you never served your country. What are you, a hunter? No, wait a minute. A backpacker? Just a pussy backpacker." He laughed slowly.

"Put down the gun. I can shoot this faster than you can raise your weapon."

"You think so? What about that rattlesnake over there you just about stepped on?" He motioned with his chin. "You see you are facing an interesting tactical problem. Two threats. Both deadly. This is where proper military training would have helped. You want to deal with him first, or me?"

Mike didn't look. He didn't have to. Suddenly, the unmistakable sound of the snake's rattle. Close by. Maybe two feet away. Mike froze and exercised his peripheral vision. He could make out the snake coiled on a flat rock less than two feet to his right. Sweat poured down his back. His legs trembled.

"That's right, my friend, you really only have one move," Zhirkov said. "So do I."

In a flash Zhirkov raised his pistol and Mike pulled the trigger, blasting Zhirkov from five feet away, throwing him hard to the ground. Zhirkov managed to get off a shot, hitting Mike in the thigh, spinning him around with the force of the impact just as the rattlesnake struck.

And missed.

The snake slithered into the woods, and Mike dropped to the ground. As quickly as he could, considering the terrible burning in his leg, he pulled himself up and pointed the shotgun at his opponent.

Zhirkov lay on the ground with his eyes closed, blood seeping from his chest and mouth. Mike pumped the shotgun and trained it on him for ten seconds, waiting to see if he moved. Then he hobbled over to the chief, using the shotgun as a cane, hoping the chief might still be alive.

Mike ducked as another shot rang out, nearly hitting him. He looked back at Richard, who had pulled himself up and was leaning against a rock, covered in blood, his handgun aimed at Mike's head. Mike stared in disbelief. "*Seriously,* Richard?"

"That was pretty fuckin' dramatic, Mike. When they make the movie, the only thing left for you is to get the girl. Oh, wait a minute. That's *my* girl. I'm not going to let that happen."

"Richard, this is totally screwed up. Missy's down there at the bottom of the hill with a bullet in her from one of you—"

"Not me. That bastard you shot. Asshole shot Missy. *I* was aiming for *you.*" He coughed up blood and spit it to the ground.

"Look, I'm sure something can be worked out. Temporary insanity, PTSD. I don't know. Let's just take it down a notch and get out of here."

"What, so you can screw my woman? You think I'm gonna let you stick your dick in her again? Not gonna happen. Not a chance."

Shelby lowered the handgun and aimed it at Mike's groin, smiled broadly, and pulled the trigger. Mike clamped his eyes shut.

He heard the loud crack of a handgun. From *behind* him.

He opened his eyes. Richard was dead. A bullet directly between the eyes. Brain matter dripped down the rock he had leaned against. Mike turned and saw Chief West, up on one elbow, his handgun resting on the ground, smoke still rising from it. He hobbled over to the chief.

"Hang on, chief, I'm going to get you some help."

"You're a lucky sonofabitch," said the chief. He closed his eyes, breathed one deep breath, and died.

65

Even Snakes Are Afraid of Snakes.
(Steven Wright)

Mike shook uncontrollably. The world spun, the ground tilted beneath him. He was sure he was about to pass out. It took all of his willpower to keep himself upright. He felt a warm breeze and dead leaves fluttered around his feet. The only sound was the gentle swish, swish of nearby pines. A pleasant evergreen aroma reached his nostrils. He took deep breaths and did his best to settle himself.

Holding the shotgun, his finger on the trigger, he hobbled over to Richard and satisfied himself that he was dead. He had a dime-sized hole in his forehead from the chief's bullet, and blood and brain tissue were splattered against the rock behind him. Nevertheless, Mike kicked his handgun as far away as he could.

Next, he approached Zhirkov. Mike had no way of knowing what kind of shot the chief had loaded into the shotgun, but it was obvious that the Russian had taken a direct hit in the chest. Blood soaked through his clothing. Mike picked up his handgun and shoved it into his pocket. Then, aiming the shotgun at Zhirkov's torso, he kicked him in the side hard. He did not move. Mike watched his face waiting to see if, somehow, he was only playing dead, but he, too, had expired.

The burning pain in Mike's leg grew by the second. He reached into his pocket for his cell phone and pulled out what was left of the device. Zhirkov's bullet had traveled through the phone into his thigh. He wouldn't be calling 911.

Mike made his way to the chief and, with some effort, got down on his knees. The burning and aching in his wound were growing intolerable. He hoped the chief had somehow survived. He felt for a pulse in his neck, moving his fingers around, and detected none. Then he lifted his hand and felt for a pulse in his wrist. Nothing. Finally, he rested his head on the chief's bloodied chest and listened for a heartbeat. There was none. The chief had sustained a blast to his chest, and a pool of blood had spread around him.

Mike looked at the chief's utility belt and found his radio. He sat back in the dirt, keeping his bloody leg extended. He felt for his belt so he could apply a tourniquet to his leg and then remembered he had used it on Missy's arm. The three dead men all wore belts. He just needed to get one of those. First, he needed to call and get someone up here.

Mike looked at the radio. It was a Motorola, and he thought all he had do was push the button on the side and talk. He was about to do that.

"Put down the radio, Mike." A garbled Cajun-accented voice spoke to him from about twenty feet away in the woods.

Mike jumped.

He looked into the woods. Norby stood between two trees. Blood dripped from a wound across his neck and his coveralls were drenched with blood.

A bloody handkerchief was tied around his neck.

He pointed a handgun at Mike.

"Jesus Christ, Norby, you scared the shit out of me." Mike tried to ignore Norby's gun. "I'm going to use the chief's radio to call for help. These guys are dead, and that guy shot me in the leg. You look like you need help. We're going to need help to get out of here."

"We?" Norby said. He spat blood onto the ground.

Mike stared into the barrel of the gun, only a twitch away from being shot. Norby approached him through the woods. Surprisingly, Mike thought he heard crickets.

"Blade Harris, Yukon's VP of operations, *and* the VP of human resources are on their way up from Houston to see me this afternoon," Norby said as he approached. "You don't need to be a genius or a lawyer to figure out why. I gave those bastards twenty good years, and I'm getting canned for following their orders. Just a fall guy. They'll blame me when the lawsuits start flying."

"I'm sorry to hear that. I never talked to either of those people."

"Yeah, but you shot your mouth off to that goddamn black-ass know-it-all Moore. You cost me my job." Norby took a step onto a large flat rock at the edge of the woods about ten feet from Mike. He spat another glop of blood and mucus onto the ground.

"What are you talking about?" Mike asked.

"You blamed me for that goddamn pit. Anyone who'd listen, you were like, 'Norby put the flowback in the freshwater pit, Norby did it.' Shoot, man, I was just doing what I was told to do."

"I don't know what you're talking about. All I did was ask questions. I didn't tell anybody anything."

"Coward." With that, Norby aimed the gun and pulled the trigger.

The roar was deafening. The bullet careened off a rock not more than a foot from Mike and ricocheted into the woods. Mike fell to the ground.

Norby smiled a crooked smile. "How'd you like that? Scared you, huh?"

"Jesus, Norby, you could've killed me. Come on, put down the gun and let's get out of here. You need help. That's a nasty cut on your neck. I'm sure the situation's not nearly as bad as you think." Mike thought for a second. "I'll make up a story. Make you the hero. You killed the guys who attacked us. Let's get out of here first."

Norby coughed and spat more blood. "Wouldn't be the first time I kilt' somebody. Or thought I did anyway. That no good sumbitch Corsica. I laid into him like an RPG rocket with my Maglite. Twice. *Le connard* must've had the hardest skull of any man alive. Felt for the pulse and looked to see if he was breathing.

He looked good and dead too. Bones and me buried him under the pit linin."

"But you didn't kill him."

"I went down to the pit just before we filled it. There were footprints, muddy footprints all around the area where we buried him. I knew that bastard survived and got loose. When nothing happened for a few weeks, I figured either he crawled off somewhere and died or hightailed it out of Dodge. Then the vandalism started. I told Houston that it was probably local kids, dirt bikes, .22's, monkey-wrenchers, that kind of thing. It doesn't happen often, but it happens. They put up the fence, the cameras, and hired the guards. I think it was just that bastard's way of letting me know he was still alive and kicking. Waiting for me. Waiting to get even."

Mike didn't mention that he and the chief had found Corsica's body. He figured the longer they talked, the less likely Norby was to shoot him. He also hoped the State Police would make it up to the top of the hill at some point. He just had to keep him talking.

"Self-defense. I think you could argue self-defense. Nobody knows what happened that night. Tell them Corsica was mad at you because you fired him and went to hit you over the head with something. The Jack Daniels bottle. You defended yourself and hit him over the head with your flashlight. I think that'd work as a legal defense."

"Jew bastard lawyer. You and your kind think you're so goddamned smart. Maybe you've gotten all the breaks, have all the money, but I've had to work hard to get to where I am. Nobody's given me any breaks."

Norby stepped off the rock. Now he was less than ten feet away from Mike. The gun was pointed at his chest.

Mike was about to plead for his life, then he opened his mouth and was surprised at the words that came out. "Go to hell, you racist bigot. I've had to deal with racist, anti-Semite assholes like you my whole life. Pull the goddamned trigger while I'm lying on the ground, you goddamn Nazi-Klan coward. I'm going to die knowing the rest of your shitty life'll be spent in solitary in a supermax prison. Rotting away like the garbage you are. I'm sick and tired of your kind, you racist asshole. Go to hell."

Norby laughed, and blood gurgled out of his mouth in a froth. He raised the gun and, with a wobbly motion, aimed it at Mike's head. Suddenly, his arm twitched. Violently. His whole body contorted.

"What the hell?" Norby screamed.

Both men looked down at Norby's feet. He was surrounded by three, maybe five, rattlesnakes. The rock overhang on which he'd been standing had covered a rattlesnake den. When he put his foot on the ground in front of the opening, it was too much of a threat to the snakes, and the den attacked. These things happen in the woods.

Five more snakes, then ten, emerged from beneath the rock, striking and biting his legs and thighs. The sound of crickets morphed into the sound of dozens of snake rattles.

"Ow, oww! Get them off! Get them fuckers offa me."

Norby aimed the gun down and began shooting the snakes. One rattlesnake struck his hand and held on for several long seconds before Norby knocked it off with his other hand. Norby screamed and toppled over as his knees gave out, landing on a slithering bed, snakes striking him from beneath, winding through his shirt, up his pants legs, filling his body with venom.

Mike watched the attack, horrified. He lost count of the snakes. He had also lost track of them. He scabbed backward, then found the strength to regain his footing and backed away.

Norby's face was bright red and twisted in agony. He fired his gun until there were no more bullets, still pulling the trigger impotently until the venom paralyzed him. More and more snakes came out of the den, now biting him on his arms and face. Mike continued backing away. It looked as though there must have been twenty or thirty snakes crawling over the flat area where only moments before Mike had lain helplessly on the ground. Snakes crawled over the dead bodies.

Norby's screams became moans, and his moans became gurgles as his body twitched and flopped. If Mike survived, the scene would haunt his nightmares for years.

Mike was breathing hard. He knew he'd lost a fair amount of blood, and he hoped he'd make it down the hill with enough left to survive. As much as he wanted to turn and run, he was too worried about the snakes and, holding the gun that had been in his pocket, backed down the hill, stumbling on rocks and tree roots.

Then, something grabbed him from behind. It nearly smothered him.

He let out a howl and flailed his arms until they were pinned to his sides.

The gun was pulled from his hand.

He was in the arms of a State Police SWAT officer.

As he was hurried away, the last things Mike saw at the top of the hill were Norby covered with snakes. The chief, dead. Richard, dead. Vlad Zhirkov was gone.

66

Two Months Later

Mike propped his feet on the rail and leaned back on the porch swing. He tipped the beer, a Shipyard Export, and he sipped a bit from the bottle. The sun was setting over Acadia National Park and Somes Sound, in Maine, and he was at peace.

Two hands, blue-painted fingernails, extended around his neck from behind him. Missy hugged him, then kissed his ear. Mike reached behind him and ran his hand across her cheek. She came around to the front of the swing and stood before him, her hands still around his neck. She wore a white bikini top and a sheer cover-up skirt around her waist, her skin a deep brown which contrasted sensually with her white bikini. She was barefoot.

The scar on her arm had lightened considerably. Fortunately, the shot went right through her without hitting a bone. Through and through, the docs had said. Still, there was plenty of pain, and she spent most of the summer running back and forth to physical therapy in Bar Harbor. They both did.

Missy reclined on the swing and rested her head in Mike's lap, dangling her feet over the end. He draped his arm across her breasts, relaxing his hand on her shoulder. She turned her head and looked at his leg. She stroked the area around the scar on his thigh.

"How's that feeling today, babe?" Missy touched the area around it very gently.

"All things considered, pretty good. I'm glad I'm done with PT, but a little bummed I'll never be able to run a four-minute mile again."

"Again?"

"I never told you about that, did I?"

She lifted her head, and he responded by kissing her on the lips.

"I'm sad our summer vacation is almost over," she said. "This has been an awesome place to recover from all that stuff back in Pennsylvania."

"Well, we both had to use all of our sick and vacation days and just about all of our savings. I'm pretty happy whoever rented this Airbnb canceled, and we got a discount. It'll be hard to start back at work next week."

"What about me? I'm not just starting work; I'm moving from Williamsport to the Harrisburg office. At least when you go back to school, you'll know everybody. I'll be the new girl in class."

"You'll do fine, hon; they'll love you. You know, this summer has been a kind of a dream for both of us. When we officially move in together next week, that'll be more like reality—"

"And a dream," she said, smiling up at him.

Mike rocked back and forth in the swing for a few seconds, then said, "I spoke with Roger this afternoon. He told me Bones cut a deal and pleaded guilty on the accessory to murder charge. He'll be sentenced in another couple of months. Probably go away for five or ten years."

"What about Vlad? The mystery man?"

"I'm not sure the State Police entirely believed he existed. They thought I was in shock or something. It wasn't until their forensics people found the unknown blood and the spent .308 cartridges that they took me seriously. I'm the only one who ever saw him—and lived."

"That tattoo on his wrist? The A with the sword?"

"At first they thought it was a Russian gang thing, then some ex-military police guy showed me the emblem for Alpha Group, the Russian version of the Navy SEALS. That was his tattoo. His unit. Guy could have killed me with his pinky."

"Any word on him?"

"He's gone. In the wind, as they say."

Neither one spoke for several minutes.

"What about our case?"

"It's over. The Campbells withdrew their appeal. Yukon agreed to fix their impoundment. They agreed to put in a new fully-cased water well at the Campbell house, monitor the reservoir, and, get this, admit they had contaminated the aquifer."

"What? They did that?"

"It was either that or pay hundreds of thousands of dollars in damages. Roger told me he'd heard through the grapevine they offered half a million dollars to settle the case, but Teresa said all she wanted was for her well to be drilled deeper and cased and for them to admit they contaminated the water. She really wanted their admission on the record. The language was a little weaselly, but they admitted they did it." Mike paused for a moment, thinking. "Teresa." He shook his head.

"What about all of Yukon's violations? There must've been dozens."

"Roger did the consent order and agreement with Darius. In addition to fixing everything, they're paying a one-million-dollar civil penalty. Not the biggest civil penalty we've ever gotten, but still pretty big."

"How is Darius? Any word on his recovery?"

"I talked with him late this afternoon while you were napping. He went back to work after one week and was complaining it was taking him a while to get back into tennis, but he was determined to do it. You know, he was unbelievably brave. I'll never forget him running across that field carrying those people. I don't always see eye-to-eye with him, but he's basically a decent guy."

"Maybe he just wanted to rescue more people than you did?"

"You've become such a cynic." Mike broke into a wide grin. "Also, get this. He told me he'd been invited to Teresa's house. She says she really appreciated him saving her from the battlefield and wanted to make him a special thank-you dinner. He asked me if there was anything he should know before he took her up on her offer."

Missy had a devilish smile. "Really? What did you tell him?"

"I told him she likes expensive Cabernet Sauvignon, and Jared supposedly likes high-end Chianti Classico."

"And?"

"I told him Jared was in private equity in New York and sometimes didn't make it home for dinner."

"And?"

"He's a big boy. I'm sure he can handle himself." Mike laughed.

Missy laughed with him and put her arms around Mike's neck. He leaned over and they kissed. "I'm getting cold."

Mike put his hands under her and struggled to his feet. The pain in his thigh had largely subsided, but it was still there. Then he gently placed her on her feet and held her close as they watched the last bit of blood-orange sun slip behind the blue and purple pine trees on the other side of the sound. The last rays danced on the ripples of the water like a billion fireflies.

"You want me to get your fleece?" he asked.

"No. I think it's warmer under the covers. Why don't you join me, babe? There's something I'd like to show you." She smiled at him and gently ran her fingers down his chest, pausing at the top of his shorts.

Until two months earlier, Mike had rarely uttered the words "I love you" to anyone. Now, the words slipped past his lips freely. "I love you, Missy."

"I love you too, Mike."

THE END

Acknowledgments

This is a work of fiction. There is no place in Bradford County, Pennsylvania, called Campbelltown or Washington Township. There is no Yukon Oil & Gas Co., and it is not meant or intended to represent any drilling company. I've taken great liberties with the Pennsylvania State University, its buildings, programs, and course offerings. All of the characters are figments of my imagination. If you think you've found a hidden reference to a place, company, or person, you are mistaken—please refer to the first sentence.

There is an agency of the Commonwealth of Pennsylvania government called the Department of Environmental Protection, DEP (often called *PaDEP*, if you're not from Pennsylvania). I have taken great liberties and made up a *fictional* version of DEP. While I have modeled my version after the real DEP, it is, nevertheless, a fictional version. The people at DEP do a difficult job, sometimes under impossible circumstances. Generally, they are underappreciated. I admire them and the work they do.

I want to thank my friends and colleagues for their assistance with certain details, critique, and as beta-readers. They include Andy Bockis, Amy Bockis, Albert Davenport, Anniken Davenport, Laurie J. Edwards, Gregg Freeburn, Matt Haar, Christopher Markley, Joseph McNally, PG, Lisa McManus, Irwin Richman, Ph.D., Eva Siegel, Misty Simon, Judy Torres, and Louis Vittorio, PG. My apologies if I inadvertently left anyone out. Naturally, any mistakes found in this book are solely mine and should not be attributed to anyone else.

Thanks to my editor, Jason Liller, for helping to make this book readable. Thanks also to the folks at Headline Books, Inc., my publisher, particularly Cathy Teets, for all that they have done.

My children remain among my strongest supporters and cheerleaders. They have probably sold more of my books than I have. Thanks, Dina, Shira, David, Lev, and Aviv.

My Grandmother used to say, "the last is the best." Thanks to my wife, best friend, and woman-who-is-not-a-model-for-any-female-characters-in-any-of-my-novels, Gail. Her love, support, and tolerance for my writing are immeasurable.

Finally, in this day and age, a good online review is worth its weight in gold. If you are so inclined, I'd appreciate your commentary on Amazon, Goodreads, Barnes & Noble, or another online forum. Feel free to follow me on Facebook (Joel Burcat Author) or my website, JoelBurcat.com. Thank you for reading this book!

—JRB

Also by Joel Burcat

Fiction

Drink to Every Beast (Mike Jacobs, Book 1)
(Headline Books, Inc.)

Amid Rage (Mike Jacobs, Book 2)
(Headline Books, Inc.)

Non-Fiction

Pennsylvania Environmental Law and Practice
(Pennsylvania Bar Institute Press, Co-Editor)

The Law of Oil and Gas in Pennsylvania
(Pennsylvania Bar Institute Press, Co-Editor)